THE RELICANT CHRONICLES, BOOK 4

BONES AT REST

I0635554

AARON ROSENBERG

CRAZY 8 PRESS

Against her will, Seikoku drew the kogotano from her sleeve. It had been part of a writing set she had stolen once—she had sold the rest of the set but kept the blade, liking the way it fit in her hand, liking how light and sharp it was, and most of all liking the delicate blue butterflies enameled along the handle. Now she held it the way she had been taught once by a young man who had wanted to impress her, hand angled down, blade back against her forearm. With her other hand she removed her scarf and wrapped it around that limb, hoping it might provide some protection from a knife thrust.

"He's already long gone," she told the boy. "I don't know if you meant to rob him or kill him or both, but that's over and done. And I'm not some slow laborer, tired from a long day's work. I have a knife of my own, and I know how to use it. Keep at this and you'll only get hurt."

The boy hissed in reply and lunged in, quick as a snake. Seikoku blocked the blow with her knife and slapped the side of his head with her free hand, causing him to reel back and stumble, nearly falling but righting himself just in time. She'd hoped the pain would make him realize the untenability of his current endeavor, but it seemed to only enrage him. He snarled, eyes wide, lips drawn back, foam flecking the corners of his mouth, and charged her, more wild animal than small boy.

"Go home," she warned, careful to keep her distance even if from certain angles he looked small and weak and helpless. "There is nothing for you to gain here except more pain and humiliation."

But the face he turned to her was devoid of caution, devoid of shame, devoid of thought. It was fully feral, the eyes black pools, the mouth working as if already chewing her flesh, the nostrils flaring with each heaving breath. The boy pulled himself back to his feet, gripped his knife so tightly his fingers turned bone white, and screamed as he launched himself at her once more.

Crazy 8 Press is an imprint of Clockworks

© 2025 by Aaron Rosenberg

Design by Aaron Rosenberg
Cover art by Lilly Repine
ISBN: 978-1-892544-31-5

To Jenifer, Adara, and Arthur, who are everything I need

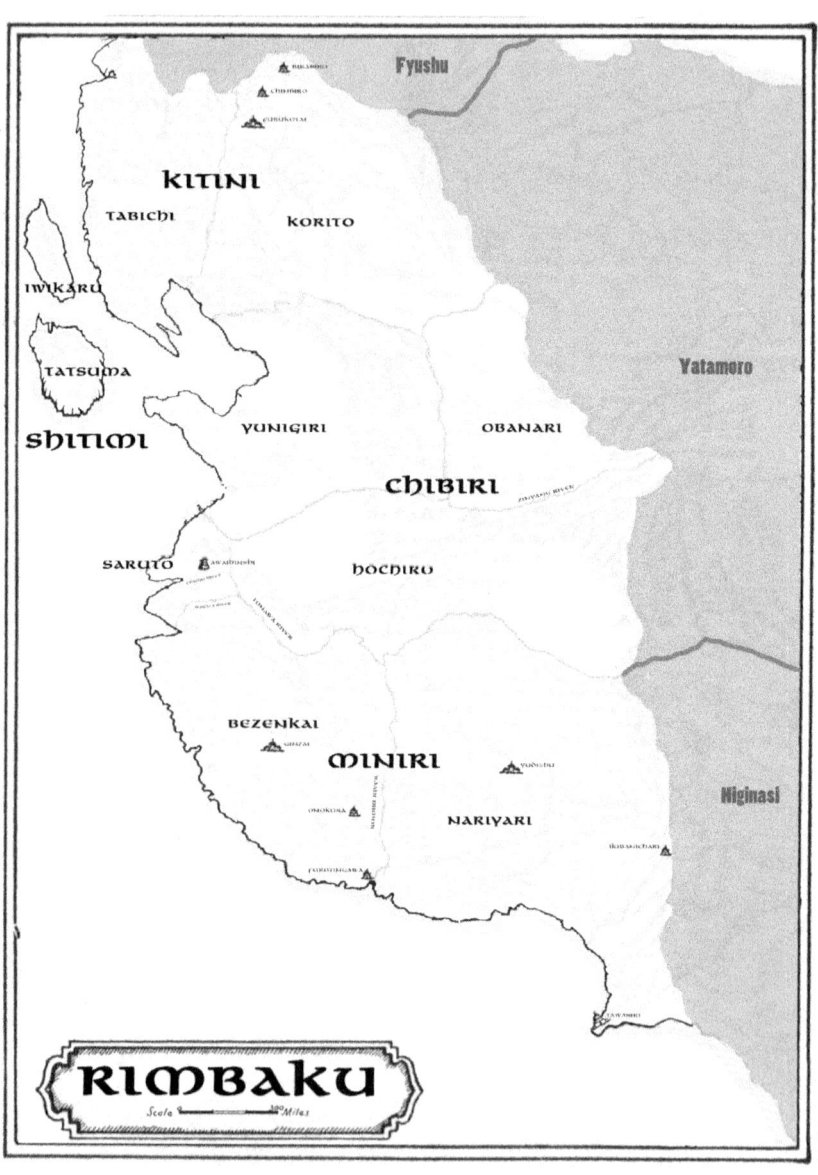

CAST OF CHARACTERS

Misataki Shizumi: Taikoro (Lord Commander) of the Honjofu, the empire's elite warriors

Hibikitsu: the young emperor of Rimbaku. Descended from the First Emperor, Taido Segei

Kagiri: A young man, older brother to Noniki. A Gensaiba ("legendary warrior") and one of the emperor's Rojiri (Imperial counselors). Nicknamed Giri.

Noniki: A young man, younger brother to Kagiri. A Rojiri and the first new Matekai (wizard) of Rimbaku. Nicknamed Niki.

Seikoku: A young woman and former thief

Maniko Kohori: Taikoro of the Honteno, Hibikitsu's household guard

Sunao Iensen: A noble, son of the late Rojiri Sunao Tadazi. House symbol is a black bear.

Heiayuki Futoba: A noblewoman, kin to the Ieyuki. House crest: a blue and green swallow.

Amani Denbi: Most senior of Hibikitsu's former Rojiri. House crest: silver star and crescent moon.

Watane Yatahei: A former Rojiri who was also Dogenkaishu, Lord Admiral of the navies. House crest: an emerald wave.

Orita Sadachi: Another former Rojiri. House crest: a bright blue hummingbird

Yoshino Nanami: Another former Rojiri. House crest: a yellow-and-black butterfly

Domo Haruta: Another former Rojiri. House crest: a red panda.

Etsuya Kenshin: Most belligerent of the former Rojiri, executed for treason. House crest: a thundercloud, in blue and gray.

Ieyuki Nagao: Another former Rojiri, held for treason. House crest: a golden swallow.

Chimehara: A young woman in Awaihinshi, a trader in House Chohu

Suda: A young girl from the gutters of Suranmui, adopted by Chimehara

Ruisoki: A boy whose parents were part of House Chohu

Kaemusei: The Silent Change, an inhuman being comprised of magic and hunger

Ibaru and Iraku: Two brothers, Untouched, who become the hands of the Silent Change

Chiyu Akaii: A chuisu in the aiashe (the Rimbakan army), stationed on the docks outside Awaihinshi

Yoshitaro: An aiashe on guard at the docks outside Awaihinshi

Kishin Narai: A wealthy merchant, leader of a cabal

Shizu Yokori: Narai's second in the cabal

Jiro Masute: Another member of the cabal

Eien Kawatai: Another member of the cabal, now deceased

Fujiko Oritano: Final member of the cabal

Jitu Kanai: A potter from Ginzai, one of Noniki's followers

Isoro: A young herbalist from Hochiro, one of Noniki's followers

Sanedi: A basketweaver, one of Noniki's followers

Sukame and Minawa: An old married couple, among Noniki's followers

Ratal: A fisherman, one of Noniki's followers

Amon: A netmender, one of Noniki's followers

Otokai: A horsetrader, one of Noniki's followers

Junko and Eiji: A couple who make clothes, among Noniki's followers

Kuma: A washer-woman from Shakomi, one of Noniki's followers

Obi Ren: A merchant whose house specializes in fish and fishing

Doiyu Soda: An imperial scribe in Aihiri

House Ayano: A merchant house specializing in weaving and textiles

Ayano Taketa: Head of House Ayano

Master Eijiri: A wealthy merchant and the head of house Chohu, a merchant house specializing in gems

Fuko Miyosi: A shosu (junior lieutenant) in the aiashe

Daishin Nishoji: A taisho (general) in the aiashe

Atsumi Izo: Another taisho in the aiashe

Masagi Matsu: Another taisho in the aiashe

Noboru Juniri: Another taisho in the aiashe

Ohiro: A gardener and caretaker, formerly for House Etsuya

Hajime: A dessert-maker with a shop in Bejinuri

Chiya: A little girl in Awaihinshi and a regular customer of Hajime's

Yuni: A cleaning lady in House Chohu

Ritaru: Another cleaning lady in House Chohu

Kaznori: A member of House Chohu

Madam Ponsoi: The senior housekeeper of House Chohu

Gou: A street urchin

Tokutomi: A guard stationed at the gates between Motohiri and Sakiriti

Akita: Another guard stationed at the gates between Motohiri and Sakiriti

Kazutai Katani: A shugodiri (minor noble) in Awaihinshi

Kazutai Takami: Katani's younger brother

Oguro: Proprietor of the Yue Judei ("Good Time") zaihaya

Yuki: A server at Yue Judei

Rilani: Empress of Fyushu

Yanitai Lai: Former Dogenriku (field marshal) of the Fyushan army. Killed in battle by Hibikitsu.

Nihiro Omeshi: Fyushan emissary to Rimbaku

Makono Takari: Fyushan dignitary, assistant to Nihiro Omeshi

Hu Yongian: Chief Ambassador from Yatamoro to Rimbaku

Shen Liang and Wei Bingwen: Ambassadors from Yatamoro to Rimbaku

Yakami Morinaga: Higinasan ambassador to Rimbaku

Yakami Tsuya: Ambassador Yakami's wife

Ogawa Kunetai: King of Higinasi

Ogawa Tsuni: Princess of Higinasi

Aganaka: An old ishtaya (tailor) with a shop in Bejinuri

Denaya: Aganaka's dead wife

Master Atunobu: A trader in House Chohu

Tanekate: Amani Denbi's major domo

Fume: Amani Denbi's guard commander

Ushi and Tane: Two of Amani Denbi's household guard

Yamana Muiada: A chef in Aihiri

Zhen Shu: A Yatamoran darakada and assassin, now deceased

Dai Yi: A Yataramarn darakada and assassin, Zhen Shu's partner

Diritan: A Honjofu

Nioko: Another Honjofu

Akino: A Honjofu, one of Shizumi's most trusted men

Geniji: Another Honjofu, Shizumi's self-appointed bodyguard when in the field

Dairamu: Another Honjofu

Isano: Another Honjofu

Norio Shinjuru: The Honjofu gunso, currently training new recruits

Manari: A Honteno

Wakiza Yukane: Karo of Atsani

Hasebe Towa: Karo of Bejinuri

Iwaki Matsu: A merchant in Awaihinshi

Itamon: A chuisu (lieutenant) in the Honteno

Reizei: The other chuisu of the Honteno

CHAPTER ONE

A s Misataki Shizumi watched, the young woman named Seikoku did a slow, graceful turn, admiring the beautifully painted screens that made up the walls, the polished wooden columns separating them, the gold-leaf pattern picked out in delicate detail across the ceiling panels that floated in a frame of dark-stained, polished yanokai, the brass scrollwork that shone at each corner and joint, and the panels that stood at intervals down either side of the long room, suspended from iematsu beams that were themselves surmounted by elegant gold rails connected to the high ceiling by more dark wood beams affixed there with yet more brass panels. "It's breathtaking," she agreed, her gaze slowly returning to the long, handsome wood table that took up the room's center and ran much of its length, dignified yet comfortable chairs lining it on either side. "But I still don't know why I'm here."

Beside her, Noniki laughed. Though not much taller than his companion, the young man exuded strength and warmth, his stocky build speaking to solidity and reassurance and his handsome features cast in the friendly smile Shizumi had begun to realize was his default expression. "Why shouldn't you be?" he asked, dropping into the chair at the table's front left corner and leaning back, already at home. "You helped save the empire, same as the rest of us."

The noise that emerged from the young woman's lips was as inelegant as the rest of her was lovely. "I didn't do anything. That was all you—and your brother." Her eyes flicked to the tall young man prowling the room like a great cat, his emerald armor gleaming even in the dim light of the few lanterns that had been lit thus far, his long face serious and his every motion powerful but controlled. Was that interest Shizumi saw? No, she decided. Not exactly. Or at least, not of a romantic nature. More curiosity mingled with uncertainty.

Ah, of course. She recalled what she had learned of the brothers thus far, how they had been separated, each believing the other dead, and had each made their way here to Awaihinshi, where they had been startled and delighted to be reunited. Seikoku had traveled with Noniki—and there was definite interest there, on both sides, if Shizumi's barracks-trained sense of such things had any accuracy—and thus had no doubt heard many stories about his brother. Yet meeting him in person would be new and unfamiliar territory for her, made even more so by his uncanny mastery of armed combat, which had evidently transformed him from the unassuming young man he had been into the fearsome warrior he was now. One could hardly fault her for being interested yet also trepidatious at their new acquaintance.

Any further musings were cut off by a single sharp rap on the door to the hall, followed by that same panel being slid open. Two figures entered, both tall and broad-shouldered—one garbed in the red armor of the Honteno, edged in gold to denote its wearer's rank, and the other dressed more comfortably in a beautiful silk kitoro with tsodami picked out in red thread and filled in with tiny flecks of ruby. The man wearing the robe was handsome, his face strong and clean-lined, his eyes sharp but not unkind—but his lips were compressed in a taut line that did not denote good humor as he groused, "Explain again why we're meeting here, and not in our perfectly good throne room."

"Because," the woman beside him answered in the easy manner of one accustomed to speaking her mind even to those of exalted rank, leading the way to the table as the guards outside closed the door again behind them, "that very same throne room is still being cleansed of blood and who knows what else." She nodded a hello at Shizumi, who returned the gesture, still trying to get used to the notion that she and Maniko Kohori, Taikoro of the emperor's own household guard, were now the same rank. "Besides which, this room is a lot easier to guard."

That was true enough—other than the secret passage they had found when investigating a recent murder, the only way in or out was the one door, and this room was also much smaller than the Rimbakan throne room, small enough to easily see the entire width and breadth at once. "Fine," the young man agreed, and allowed himself to be guided to a chair that had been placed at the head of the table. "Now then," Hibikitsu, Echo of Victory, emperor of all Rimbaku, declared, drawing his sheathed sword from his okube and laying it on the table before taking his seat and glancing at the men and women before him. "Shall we begin?"

Kagiri nodded and took the seat immediately to the emperor's right, directly across from his brother. Kohori had taken up a stance right behind Hibikitsu, clearly determined to protect him as usual despite being armed only with the ittei that was the sole weapon allowed to be carried in the emperor's presence. Shizumi moved to do the same at the far end, closest to the door, but was stopped by the young ruler's raised hand.

"Taikoro Misataki, please join us," he instructed, and obediently she settled herself beside Seikoku, who had folded into the chair next to Noniki with all the grace of a born dancer. "You too, Kohori," he added, and with only a small grumble the older woman took the chair opposite her.

"Much better!" Hibikitsu glanced around the table, and his face broke into a smile. "Now I believe I see the appeal! And to think, all these years I'd never even set foot in here!" Which made a certain degree of sense, as this was the Rojiri's council chamber and the royal advisors would have presented themselves before their emperor on his throne whenever he desired to speak with them. For him to have come here instead could be seen as an insult to him and his role as emperor, demeaning both the man and the title.

Fortunately, as Shizumi had quickly learned, Hibikitsu was not one to accept the old roles. Not anymore, anyway. Before he'd left for the border to personally deal with the Fyushan invasion attempt, he had always seemed aloof, distant, and alternately cold or enraged. His time away had changed him, however, and the emperor had returned as a friendly, engaging young man eager to hear new ideas and to explore new ways to restore his ailing realm.

Which was presumably why he turned now to his two new Rojiri, Kagiri and Noniki—having demoted the old advisors after they had objected to his new style of rule and dared oppose his authority—and asked, "So, tell me in earnest—how fares the capital?"

It was Noniki who spoke first. "Your Imperial Majesty," he answered, dipping his head in a bow after Hibikitsu gestured for him to remain seated. "Awaihinshi is injured, but still alive. The lower levels have taken the most damage, some of it extensive, but no single ring has been destroyed, and the gates are still intact and open." The fabulous layered city that was the nation's capital had been attacked by strange creatures of bone and magic, fantastical creations like several normal animals merged into one and imbued with sorcerous life. When Noniki, with Kagiri's and even Hibikitsu's help, had managed to do away with the strange being that had spawned those skeletal monstrosities they had all collapsed, their enchanted lives ended as quickly as they'd begun. Sadly, since they had primarily been airborne at the time, their demise had done as much damage as their earlier assaults, crushing homes and shops beneath their weight.

"We are working to clear away the damage, Your Majesty," Seikoku offered, and Shizumi was envious of the way the young woman spoke up so fearlessly, as if she were addressing some merchant or laborer rather than the empire's master. But then, Hibikitsu had such a disarming air about him, when he wished it, that she could hardly be blamed for being so at ease around him. "The people we brought with us," she continued, "were already looking for some way to serve you, some way to be useful. This was the perfect opportunity for them."

"And they have been very useful," Kohori agreed, for though her business was primarily confined here to the imperial compound of Aihiri, shining like an ivory beacon at the city's peak, she kept abreast of the city's business in general and had helped man its defenses during the attack. "Many of our laborers have chosen to concentrate on their own homes and those of their neighbors first, which is not unreasonable but means the other levels have lacked resources and manpower to effect repairs. Your friends are willing to go anywhere to help, and that has been a major boon."

Hibikitsu inclined his head toward Seikoku, and Noniki beside her. "Indeed, tell them we are in their debt," he stated. "I know they, and you, came here hoping for a new life. Please assure them that we will make certain they are able to obtain that." He frowned, though only briefly, following it with a small sigh. "There is so much to do!" he complained, not at the small assemblage so much as to them. "What else, besides repairs?"

Kohori cleared her throat and glanced around the room, taking in the empty chairs at the far end. "You will need more than two Rojiri, Your Majesty," she pointed out in that quiet, patient way of hers. Shizumi wondered if she would ever be able to capture that same air of wisdom and leadership. Maybe when she reached her fellow Taikoro's age? "It is a start," she continued, nodding at the brothers, "but only that. And," she added, raising a gray-shot eyebrow and shrugging to indicate this was not just her personal opinion, "perhaps you should select the next members from among your own nobility?" For despite their many talents and abilities, the brothers were in fact commoners. Indeed, other than the fine armor and sword Kagiri carried, and the sturdy clothes and walking staff Noniki bore, Shizumi was not sure the brothers had anything to their name.

Nor was she the only one pondering this question, for Hibikitsu was suddenly eyeing the pair closely, his head tilted slightly, one long-fingered hand stroking his chin. "Have either of you any accommodations yet?" he asked them. "For it occurs to me that the rank of Rojiri does not convey any direct recompense, it traditionally being occupied by those who already hold lands and titles and wealth and thus do not require anything additional."

Noniki laughed. "We've been staying down in Mazihini—is that right?" He'd directed the query to Seikoku, who nodded. "There's a granary down there that collapsed, had to be completely emptied out and cleared away, so we've been bedding down in that space." He shrugged. "It's been pleasant enough so far, and we're used to roughing it." He and Seikoku and their friends had crossed much of the empire to get here, if their stories were to be believed. And Shizumi did—something about the young man had convinced her that he spoke the truth.

Kagiri rubbed the back of his neck, appearing slightly embarrassed. "I arrived in the city with friends," he explained, "including several merchants who already hailed from here. I have been staying with them until I can find something of my own."

"That will not do," their emperor declared, tapping a finger on the table before him. "I cannot have my royal advisors, the two men closest to me, sleeping in ruins or imposing upon friends! We shall institute some sort of salary for the position of Rojiri, so that you will have funds to your name. As far as accommodations—" He glanced over at Kohori, and a gleam came to his eye. "As it so happens, there are several estates that have recently become vacant, and for which I shall need to find new owners." He raised one hand and ticked off fingers on it with the other. "Fujibuki, Sunao, Etsuya, Ieyuki—four in all." Then he pointed at Kagiri, Noniki, Kohori, and Shizumi herself. "And behold, two Rojiri and two Taikoro! Perfect!" He even grinned at Seikoku, who had the grace to blush. "I am sorry I do not have a fifth for you, madam."

Kohori was already shaking her head. "Your Majesty, I appreciate the generous and noble gesture," she began. "But I could never accept. My place is here in Aihiri, and I have no living kin, no family to tend to estates in my stead. Besides which"—she cleared her throat—"I am not certain all of those four are free to be awarded away."

"No?" Hibikitsu considered. "The Fujibuki are no more, with Haro gone," he stated after a moment's thought. "Though now that I think upon it their kin are the Umibuki, and there *is* a young man of that line—"

Shizumi raised her hand. "Your Majesty?" She cursed herself for daring to interrupt yet knew she could not stay silent.

"Yes?" Fortunately, he did not seem to take offense. "What is it, Taikoro Misataki?"

"If the young man in question is Umibuki Nihiro," she gathered her courage to say, "I regret to inform you that he is no more. He was slain by the same assassin who attempted to take your life."

Kohori was nodding. "She is correct, sire. I had just recruited him to the Honteno, and unfortunately it seems he and the assassin crossed paths—as cousins, Umibuki was in a position to potentially discover the charade, and so the assassin killed him." The older woman's face was lined with grief, and Shizumi knew she blamed herself for putting the young warrior in harm's way, but really wasn't it the assassin's fault and no one else's? Regardless, it did seem to indicate that the Fujibuki holdings no longer had any kin to claim them.

"We mourn his loss, as we do all those who died by that creature's hand," the emperor declared. "Do not blame yourself, Kohori—especially not when you and Shizumi ended the assassin's life, thus both saving me and avenging those he had murdered." He nodded. "So, that is one estate, then, that is available. And I know you would not gainsay me the right to award the Etsuya or Ieyuki lands to those I deem worthy?" The guard commander shook her head. It had been she who had stood against those two lords when they had rebelled and attempted to take the palace by force, Shizumi knew, defending the throne when the emperor had departed the city and left it in her capable hands. Etsuya had been executed for his treason, and while Ieyuki still languished in prison that was only because there had been no time since Hibikitsu's return to deal with the traitorous lord. "Then it must be Sunao you are cautioning against," the emperor continued. "Yes, you are correct—old Tadazi had many sons and he died nobly, another victim of that creature. His lands will go to his heir, with all due honors." He grinned at Noniki and Kagiri—and Shizumi. "Which leaves three, and three of you. One for each."

But Shizumi had had time to recover herself, and now she rose and bowed low. "You honor me, Your Majesty," she told him, "but I fear I cannot accept. I am a soldier, sir. I am *your* soldier. I will be out on campaign, facing your foes, and when I am not there I will be here, drilling my troops so that they might serve you better. I would have no time for estates, and neither need nor desire them." Kohori caught her eye and nodded, and the older woman's approval warmed Shizumi against the chill that prickled her skin at refusing a gift proffered by her ruler—who sat and regarded her with narrowed eyes.

For a moment, she stood frozen, trapped beneath that steely gaze. Then Hibikitsu slapped the table and laughed. "Ah, Shizumi!" he declared. "How did I manage so long with stuffed-up nobles like Fujibuki Haro when I could have had you at my side instead? Well said, and how can I take offense at such a display of loyalty?" She sank back onto her chair with a sigh of relief as the emperor turned to study his two Rojiri next. "And what of you two? Shall you also refuse?"

Kagiri opened his mouth to speak, already beginning to shake his head, but his younger brother cut him off. "I would be happy to accept, Your Majesty," Noniki declared, "and indeed, it will solve the problem of where to find homes for my friends as well." He smiled at his brother across the table. "And Kagiri and I can certainly share—we would be over at each other's homes all the time anyway!"

That seemed to win approval from both the emperor and his Gensaiba, who nodded thanks to his brother. And so that matter, at least, was settled.

Nor had Hibikitsu missed his guard commander's initial statement. "Yes, you are right, Kohori," he said now. "We will need additional Rojiri. At least two from the nobility, I think. And, since we have already two from less distinguished backgrounds, perhaps two from the merchants as well?" Everyone murmured agreement to this, for it seemed wise and balanced. "Very good. We will think on suitable candidates," he stated, "and urge each of you to do so as well." His gaze cut to the emerald warrior at his left. "You, good Kagiri, we now appoint as our Dogenriku, for surely your martial prowess makes you uniquely suited to the task."

There was little Kagiri could say to that other than to dip his head and intone, "I live to serve, Your Majesty. Thank you." For indeed, who could be better qualified to lead the nation's armies than the man who possessed all the knowledge and skill of the legendary Gensaiba matekan, the "wizards' blades," the great warriors who had protected the mages who had ruled this land before the Schism.

"You will need a Dogenkaishu," Kohori pointed out. This made sense, for the former head of the navies, Watane Yatahei, was one of those who had been stripped of his rank. "Perhaps one of the new noble-born Rojiri, once you find them, will be suited for such a role."

"Indeed." Hibikitsu surveyed those before him. "But I do not want only to think of nobles and titles," he declared. "If we are to rebuild not just our city but our nation, we must move forward. We must wean ourselves off the Relicant Way. We must learn to stand on our own feet once more, to take pride in our own work, develop our own skills! We must find a way!" They all nodded. For so many generations now, ever since the Schism, the people of Rimbaku had relied upon the Relicant Touch, that strange, mystical ability to absorb the talents and knowledge of the dead by consuming their bones. As a result, people never learned for themselves, never honed their own abilities—after all, why spend a decade learning to carve wood or cast pots or cook or farm or hunt or anything else when you could swallow a pinch of ground bone and gain those same skills in an instant? But the kingdom was languishing as a result, propped up on the bones of the past and never developing any new skills for the future. Hibikitsu was determined to change all that.

"We must find a way," he repeated now, rising to his feet, the rest of them scrambling to stand before him. "Think upon it. We shall reconvene tomorrow, and I hope to hear ideas on how we can at least begin what we all know will be a long and arduous road, but one we must travel if we hope to survive."

Everyone bowed and fell into a loose line behind the emperor as he collected his sword, restoring it at his side, and made his way to the door. "Shizumi," he called out, stopping just shy of the panel and glancing her way. "Ten minutes?"

She nodded, raising her clasped fist to her chest in salute, and watched as the guards opened the door and Hibikitsu strode through the opening, disappearing from view. But not for long, at least not for her. Because apparently her new rank of Taikoro had also come with a strange new task, though one to which she was well suited—

The Echo of Victory had decided that, in order to set an example for his people, he would not use aishone himself, avoiding the relic bones if at all possible. Which meant he now needed to learn how to fight without the aid of their magic.

And he had tasked Shizumi with training him.

As if reading her thoughts, Kagiri nudged her with his shoulder as he slipped past her. "Better you than me," he said, his solemn face creased in a smile, but the expression was too warm to be truly mocking and she laughed, acknowledging the truth to that statement.

Still, at least it meant she would get some exercise.

She just hoped the emperor would not be offended when she trounced him like a small dog worrying a ragdoll.

CHAPTER TWO

Maniko Kohori thought the emperor looked tired.

Heavy shadows ringed his eyes, and there were faint lines around his mouth that she had not noticed before. His hair was perfectly coiffed, of course, and his robes and jewelry immaculate, but that was as much a credit to his dressers as to any alertness on his part. Still, he had often had trouble sleeping since he had taken the throne several years before, and she personally considered that a good sign—better to have a ruler who was kept awake worrying that he might not be doing right by his people than one who slept well because he was not aware enough to have such a concern, or not compassionate enough to care. And so much had happened in the past few weeks, much of that in the days since his return, that it was small wonder he was not properly rested.

His eyes were clear and bright, at least, as he settled into the same chair at the head of the Rojiri's council table.

"Speak to me," he commanded, laying Kosshiki upon the tabletop as if the ancient sword were a symbol of his authority—which, in many ways, it was, for it had belonged to Hibikitsu's ultimate ancestor, Taido Segei, who had become the first Relicant Emperor. "Tell me of those you feel would do well as additions to your ranks."

That had mainly been directed at the two young men to either side of him, and Kohori noticed how they both shifted awkwardly in their chairs. After a moment the shorter, broader one, Noniki, spoke.

"There are a few among those who traveled here with me," he started, "who might—" But the emperor cut him off with a raised hand.

"I mean no insult to your friends," Hibikitsu stated, and his words were gentle but firm, "for I am sure they are decent folk, and honorable. But they are new to Awaihinshi, as you are yourself. To appoint one of them to the Rojiri could be taken as a slight to those who have lived here all their lives. Besides which, they would know nothing of the city's history, its politics, or its troubles."

That was a fair and valid reason, clearly put, and Kohori nodded to herself. She had always known that her emperor was intelligent, for she had watched him grow up and he had been alert and inquisitive as a child, interested in how things worked and what people felt and how to make the world better. Though the past few years had drained much of the warmth and cheer he had once displayed, it had not turned him cold nor cruel, and this was just further proof of that. For as emperor, he had no need to explain himself or his decisions to anyone, even his closest advisors.

Nor was Noniki offended, she saw. He nodded and looked slightly chagrined, but she took that more as his being embarrassed for not seeing that problem himself. "Of course, Your Majesty," he stated. "Unfortunately, I do not yet know anyone else here in the city." He glanced across the table, but his brother only shook his head. He, too, had arrived mere days ago.

Inevitably, then, the emperor's gaze slid past the brothers, past the equally recent Seikoku, to Kohori herself. "You have lived all your life in the city," Hibikitsu pointed out. "Do you have any recommendations for new Rojiri?"

Though she had known she might be called upon to offer ideas, Kohori still found herself surprised into momentary silence. Then she gathered herself and her knowledge. "There is Sunao Iensen," she suggested, wincing as her voice, accustomed to shouting orders, sounded harsh in such a sumptuous room. "He is Sunao Tadazi's son and heir."

The Echo of Victory frowned. "I know of Sunao Iensen," he admitted after a slight pause. "I will admit that, though I have never spoken with him beyond pleasantries, I have not conceived a favorable opinion. Proud like his father, with an air of entitlement about him, and no thoughts that I ever noticed beyond the latest trends in clothing and the finest food for his table." He flicked his wrist dismissively. "I will not completely refuse to consider appointing someone simply because their forebears held the post—that would be as unjust as continuing the tradition of letting them claim the role for that reason alone. But I do not believe he would be an asset to the Rojiri, or to my rule. Who else?"

Shizumi cleared her throat and Kohori shot her a stern look, along with a subtle shake of her head. But the younger woman raised her chin and when Hibikitsu waved for her to speak, she did so. "There is a noble named Heiayuki Futoba, Your Majesty," she began, but got no further.

"Heiayuki?" The emperor cut her off. "As in, kin to the Ieyuki, whose head, Ieyuki Nagao, even now languishes in my prison awaiting death for his act of treason?"

Shizumi dipped her head, her cheeks flushing, but stood her ground. "The same, Your Majesty. This is a kinswoman, only distantly related and returned to the city only yesterday, in part to comfort her family but also to seek what can be done to redress the wrong committed by her cousin."

Hibikitsu was still frowning but had not silenced her, so after an instant she continued.

"We were alerted to her arrival, Your Majesty," Shizumi explained, "because she immediately sent word requesting audience with you, that she might beg your forgiveness for herself and her family. Several of my Honjofu are familiar with the house and say she is spoken of very highly."

To his credit, the emperor was clearly giving the matter serious thought. "That does speak well of her," he conceded slowly. "And if I banished or executed everyone related to those who rose against me, there would scarcely be a noble left in the city. I will grant her audience and will consider what to do about her family—and her—once I have taken her measure myself. Anyone else?" Everyone shook their heads, and he sighed. "Very well. On to other matters."

Reaching into the collar of his kitoro, he drew out the small silken pouch almost every citizen of Rimbaku carried in similar form. Tossing it onto the table, he stared at the tiny bag as if it contained scorpions or spiders or some other deadly creature. "How," he asked, his eyes still on the pouch but his voice directed at those seated around him, "do we wean my people from the use of such a crutch as this? How do we convince them that aishone are holding them back, causing them to stagnate? How do we stop dwelling on the past so we can finally look to the future?"

For a second, no one replied. Then Seikoku laughed, her eyes sparkling. "You're the emperor," she pointed out, as casually as if she were not speaking to the ruler of all Rimbaku. "Why not just decree that they can't use them anymore? Make it illegal. Problem solved." There was something about the way she said that, the curve of her lips in a secretive smile, that made it sound as if it were some sort of joke only she understood. Not for the first time Kohori wondered about Seikoku and her story. She had met the lovely young woman down in the streets of Mazihini during the attack and had been impressed with her practicality and her ability to remain calm amidst the chaos. The past few days had confirmed that initial impression, yet she still knew nothing about who Seikoku was or what she had been before arriving in Awaihinshi. Not that she believed there was any danger there, but not knowing rankled her.

While she had been ruminating, Hibikitsu had been laughing. "Oh, yes," he replied, smirking at the young woman. "I could do that. And then the entire country would rise up in revolt. A fine help that would be! I'd get myself overthrown, perhaps killed, and they'd go right on using the cursed things!"

At his side, Noniki nodded. "It is deeply ingrained," he said. "We will have to wean them slowly and carefully. A little bit at a time. Like cleansing the body of some dangerous substance it has become accustomed to, even dependent upon."

"Perhaps you could somehow limit their use," Kagiri added. "Or increase their cost—people will be less likely to use the bones if they become too valuable to waste."

Hibikitsu nodded, tapping a finger against his jaw, but it was the younger brother he glanced toward. "Cleansing the body," he repeated, his eyes bright. "Yes, that might be just the thing." It was Kohori he now turned to as he continued, "I could declare a Saisaihyu."

She gasped, even as the others expressed confusion. "Your Majesty!" she blurted out, surprised past restraint or composure. "That's madness!"

"Is it? Perhaps not," he argued. "There is precedent. And it would fulfil my purpose." Seeing the puzzlement on everyone else's faces, he explained, "A Saisaihyu is an ancient rite, a nine-day period of purification and cleansing. During that time, you must avoid any outside influences and purge yourself of their touch so that you might restore yourself to balance."

Kagiri and Noniki were both smiling. "Outside influences including aishone," Noniki said eagerly. "That's brilliant!"

"And nine days—a good length," his brother chimed in. "Long enough for them to learn that they can survive without the bones, but short enough that it will not destroy anything. A trial run."

"Precisely." Hibikitsu was beaming. "It was originally set to that duration because it is longer than a single sihu, to demonstrate its importance. You agree, then?"

The brothers nodded, but Kohori frowned and rapped a fist on the table to get everyone's attention. "I do not," she stated. "Think about your safety, Your Majesty. How will we defend you from your enemies if my Honteno and Shizumi's Honjofu cannot call upon their aishone in combat? Unless you are willing to make an exception for your personal forces, that they may use aishone as needed to protect Aihiri and your person?"

She was sadly unsurprised when Hibikitsu shook his head. "No," he stated firmly. "That would defeat the entire purpose. The point is that everyone must purify themselves equally. No exceptions."

Kohori was not quite ready to surrender the point yet. "What if there is another attack, or another attempted coup?" she pointed out. "We will be powerless to protect you!" Which was not strictly true—even with aishone to grant actual skill, muscle memory still developed, so their warriors would retain some competency with sword and spear, particularly since most did not waste their precious relic bones on something as mundane as practice drills—but she knew all too well the difference between an expert warrior and a middling one, and it was often a deadly gap.

"But anyone attacking would be equally helpless," her emperor argued. "And it is only for nine days. I promise I will not venture beyond Aihiri during that time." He glanced at Shizumi, who shook her head, and then at Seikoku. "I have two in favor and two against," he told her. "What of you?"

"Me?" She shook her head. "I'm not a Rojiri or a Taikoro, Your Majesty. I'm only here as your guest, and while that's kind of you, I don't see how I should have a vote in all this." Which was fair, at least, and well said. But he did not let up on his gaze, and finally she sighed. "If you're asking me what I think?" She shrugged. "Why not, I suppose. It could certainly shake things up, and as Kagiri said, it's only nine days."

"Excellent!" Hibikitsu slapped both hands down on the table and pushed himself to his feet. "It is settled, then! I will have the decree drawn up at once. We will announce it tomorrow and begin the day after!" He was already headed for the door, sword in hand, and while Kohori hated his decision she was happy to see his enthusiasm and optimism restored.

She just hoped that same exuberance would not get him killed.

As they filed out, she fell in beside Shizumi. "This is certainly going to make matters...interesting," the younger warrior commented, keeping her voice soft so that it would not reach their emperor.

"Agreed." Kohori slowed her pace, letting the brothers and Seikoku get farther ahead, until they had exited and only she and Shizumi were left in the council chamber. Now at least she could return her voice to a normal volume as she turned to face her fellow Taikoro. "You know that, once they hear of it, his enemies will jump at this opportunity. He'll be at his most vulnerable—as will we." At least her own combat skill would not be diminished—like many women, she drew knowledge rather than physical talent, but she would still be forced to operate without the benefit of those accumulated generations' wisdom and strategy, the same as everyone else. Then, remembering who she was speaking to, Kohori dipped her head. "Most of us, at any rate."

The other woman nodded, politely acknowledging the revision and the reason behind it. During a Saisaihyu, her being Mukanichi would actually be an advantage—as she had never had the Relicant Touch, she had been forced to gain skill at fighting on her own, and thus it was her own talent and knowledge Shizumi relied upon, not anything drawn from any bones. "I am but one woman," she pointed out. "And my Honjofu will be as inept as your Honteno. Though at least we still have numbers."

Kohori could only wince at the truth of that. The Honteno had never been a large force, totaling thirty at their greatest. She had only had two dozen when the Rojiri had attempted their coup, and only half those had survived the days of attacks. The Honjofu had always been the larger force, close to two hundred in all, and still had most of those, which was why they had been aiding the Honteno in patrolling the grounds. Such a situation could not last forever, however.

But then Shizumi brightened. "Shinjuru is on his way here," she reminded Kohori. "With the recruits." Before his death, Fujibuki Haro had sent word to his other gunso, Norio Shinjuru, who had been in Iwikaru training their new recruits. He had ordered those recruits who were deemed ready to be brought back to Awaihinshi at once and had promised Kohori her pick among them to restore the Honteno's ranks. Though that had been a promise made by her predecessor—or, more precisely, by the assassin who had killed Haro and taken his place—it seemed Shizumi was still willing to honor that pledge.

Which made Kohori salute her counterpart now, fist to chest. "Thank you," she told the younger woman. "That will help immensely."

"Of course." Shizumi laughed, a short, sharp bark with more bitterness than glee. "Let us hope they arrive soon enough to do some good."

CHAPTER THREE

Amani Denbi, head of House Amani and formerly chief Rojiri to the Rimbakan Emperor, frowned. "Sit down, Yatahei," she urged, careful to keep her voice calm and placating rather than petulant. Inwardly, however, she sighed. Honestly, it was like dealing with children!

"I don't understand this," the most recent subject of her ire protested. He held in his hands a scroll, and waved it as he paced, the ink-stained parchment waving before him like a banner fluttering in a playful wind. "What does it mean? A Saisaihyu? What is he trying to say with this?"

"That should be obvious, even to you," Domo Harata declared over his teacup. "It is a time of purification. No outside influences. Including aishone." His eyes glittered over the rim of the cup, cold as an emerald in the snow, as always mismatched with what she had always considered the unfortunately chosen reddish brown of his house. "He wants to do away with the Relicant Touch."

"Foolishness," Orita Sadachi insisted, spraying crumbs from the pastries she had shoved into her mouth all across her bright blue robes as she spoke. "What will that accomplish? Without our aishone, who are we?"

"No one," Denbi agreed. "Which is exactly his point. The Echo of Victory"—she allowed a sneer to slip into her intonation, since they were alone—"wishes for his subjects to rise and fall on their own merits, not those of their ancestors." It was the same reasoning he had used for promoting that commoner, Misataki, to the head of the Honjofu—the promotion that had stunned her so much she had been unable to maintain her composure and had gone too far in lecturing the emperor on his mistake, resulting in her demotion and that of the other nobles seated here with her among her estate's rear gardens.

The thing of it was, in and of itself Denbi did not disagree with Hibikitsu's reasoning. The danger of their society was that people were not developing their own skills because they were too busy relying upon the skills the relic bones provided, and the bones were a limited resource. Once they ran out, what would become of the Relicant Empire? No one would know how to do anything for themselves and it would be too late to correct that error before the nations on their borders swooped in and tore them apart.

But there were limits to what should be allowed. That was her main issue with his ill-conceived approach. It was fine to expect your laborers and soldiers to actually master their craft for them-selves, so that they could continue to work and produce art and fight without the need of aishone. But to expect your nobles to do the same was sheer foolishness. They were nobles precisely because their ancestors had achieved great things, and so using aishone was just another way of manifesting that appreciation of their past. What was wrong with that? Wasn't it better to be guided by the wisdom of all your forebears than to rely solely upon your own wits and instincts?

And promoting someone above their station—that was a whole other issue, and a massive disruption of the very fabric of their society! What would their world come to if commoners could become nobles and nobles commoners? There would be no con-sistency, no respect for history and tradition, no proper stratifica-tion! It would be utter chaos!

So she had spoken her mind, doing her duty as Rojiri to advise her emperor on the error in his thinking, trying to help him cor-rect his actions before it was too late. And what had she gotten in return? Spite and insult and injury! Punishment and humiliation!

Well, if that was how the emperor repaid his counselors for their loyal service, she saw no reason to be loyal any longer!

Hence her calling this meeting. And now that she had plied her fellow nobles with tea and pastries and shared with them the imperial decree she had received this morning, it was time to discuss what to do next.

"Calling a Saisaihyu is indeed foolish," she stated, rising to her feet and smoothing her kitoro and kisoni, the one decorated with silver stars and the other embroidered with crescent moons, so that the two halves of her house emblem overlapped and formed a delicate interplay of shadow and light as she moved. "And it is just another indication that our emperor has lost his way. He was behaving erratically even before he departed the city—the fact that he would leave the safety of its walls and venture forth into the kingdom in person was clear proof of that!—but since his return he has been even more unpredictable, even more irrational. Even more unstable." She turned to face the others, knowing that her hair was perfectly contained in its taikamage, her posture perfectly erect, her face perfectly composed. Hours practicing in front of a mirror each day had allowed her to be sure her appearance was precisely as she wished it. "We owe it to ourselves and our people, to the kingdom as a whole, to remove him before he destroys us all."

Yatahei had paused his perambulations when she'd stood, and now he eyed her closely, the scroll hanging forgotten from one hand to pool on the ground by his feet, a ribbon of cream against the green and blue of his garb. "You are speaking of a coup," he stated bluntly. "Again. After the last one, I would have thought you'd had enough of such things."

It was true that the last attempt had not fared well, though ultimately Denbi herself had emerged from the conflict no worse off and perhaps slightly the better for it. She had lost a handful of her household guard but had eliminated two potential rivals within the Rojiri, especially that old blowhard Etsuya Kenshin, and had stood to gain favor with Hibikitsu for supposedly remaining loyal while her fellow counselors had turned on each other during his absence. Of course, that had all fallen by the wayside when she had dared oppose the emperor's plans, but none of that mattered now, and she waved it aside along with Yatahei's objections.

"What choice do we have?" she asked him instead. "If the

emperor is mad, is it not the Rojiri's duty to remove him from the throne, for the good of the empire?"

But, while not the brightest of men, Yatahei was also no pushover, nor was he a complete fool. "We are no longer Rojiri," he reminded her sharply. "We have lost that role—thanks to you."

The others—Harata and Sadachi and Yoshino Nanami—were all watching the exchange closely, and the air was thick with tension. Denbi attempted to defuse it with a smile. She had practiced that expression often, as well. "It would have happened soon enough anyway," she argued, "for how long could any of us stay silence in the face of such clear lunacy? You yourself might have been the next to give voice to your concerns, and to doom us all." She crossed the distance and laid a hand on his arm, the fine silk of his robe smooth and cool beneath her skin. "We cannot let that dissuade us from doing our duty."

They stood that way for a moment, eye to eye, and she could see the wavering behind her fellow noble's watery gaze. But then his eyes hardened, and he stepped back, deliberately breaking contact with her.

"No," he stated clearly, his voice firm. "I will not be party to such things. Not again. I am tired of it all—in truth, I am relieved to no longer be Rojiri, for it means I need not carry the weight of such decisions on my shoulders." The scroll fell from his hand to land with a soft thud in its own folds, a twisted pile of words and parchment. He bowed to her, then pivoted to dip his head to the other three as well. "I wish you all good fortune, and I will not speak of this conversation to anyone. But do not include me in any such discussions in future." And then he was gone, striding across the tiles of the garden, onto one of the paths that would lead him back to the estate's front gates and away toward his own lands.

Denbi watched him go, then turned to the others. "I am sorry our old friend lacks the stomach for such things, but perhaps it is better this way. It is no easy thing to stand up to your emperor, even when you know he is in the wrong. I hope I can still count upon the three of you to persist with me, for the good of the nation?"

She watched them closely as they mulled this question. From

Harata's smirk she could see he was not taken in by her rhetoric, but then he had always been a clever one, even if he was not willing to display that astuteness beyond the council chamber. Still, he nodded and hoisted his cup in salute. "For the empire," he said before taking a sip. "I will do what must be done, despite the risk." And for the reward, Denbi thought, but that was acceptable, and she acknowledged his pledge with a nod.

Sadachi was still considering. "I still do not understand how he thinks this will improve things," she muttered. "It will only confuse the commoners more." She was glaring when she glanced back up at Denbi, though that anger did not seem directed at her. "I am with you," the noble declared. "This is madness and it must be stopped."

That left Nanami, who had stayed silent throughout. Which was hardly unusual for her—even in council meetings she had rarely spoken, and when she did her voice was barely above a whisper. In truth the girl—for despite being a mother and grandmother Denbi could not help thinking of her fellow Rojiri as almost a child, with her slender figure and big eyes and long, silken hair still an unbroken black—had always been timid, but she could usually be counted upon to vote with the majority or at least those who were most vocal in their views. Thus, it was no great surprise when she bowed her head now, that raven-dark hair falling across the equally glossy black and brilliant yellow of her robes. "I will follow your lead, and trust in your wisdom and your dedication," Nanami said softly. 'What must we do?"

Denbi had to fight to keep the smile off her face as she rejoined her fellow conspirators around the low table, settling back down onto the cushions there despite the twinge in her back and legs from the motion. Ash and bone, she was getting old! But not too old to see clearly or to act decisively—as their emperor was about to learn.

"We must find a way to use this Saisaihyu to our advantage," she told the others, making her tone warm and inviting, a friend taking them into her confidence. "For nine days the Honjofu and the Honteno will be no better than children playing at soldiers. We will find a way to breach their defenses and claim Aihiri for our own, ousting the emperor and installing ourselves as the heads of the nation. We will rule wisely and well, as a united council."

With me at its head, she thought. But that was as needs be. There must always be one who led and others who followed. It was simply the way of things. And she would lead wisely and well, taking care of all those who came to her for protection and aid—

—and, too, taking care of those who dared to stand against her. Starting with the Echo of Victory, Hibikitsu himself.

CHAPTER FOUR

The boy glanced about him, taking in the apartment's details. Though not elaborate or ornate it was clean and functional, even handsome. "Adequate," was his only comment as he set on the floor the bakiro containing all his worldly possessions, which consisted of clothing, a few personal adornments, and a handful of notepads and scrolls, as well as his prized possession, a beautifully crafted suzeri kabo.

Skulking in the doorway that led from the sitting room back to the sleeping alcove, Suda scowled. "Adequate?" she repeated in that permanently roughened voice of hers. "Is that the best you can say?" In a blink she had crossed the room to get in his face, glaring at him with her large, dark eyes. "It's amazing!" And, as if to prove this fact, she twirled, arms wide, in a circle all around him.

The boy did not bother to match her scowl, his own wide face nearly devoid of expression, only the faintest curl visible to his broad lips. "If you say so," he replied in a bored tone that clearly dismissed her opinion as inconsequential.

Nor was Suda slow to notice the slight. Her spinning stopped at once, and she was back beside him, but this time with her knife in hand, the blade jutting above her thumb and forefinger and angled against her lower leg, ready to rise and strike in an instant.

But before she could deliver a killing blow a delicate hand landed on her shoulder, making the girl start slightly. The hand's mate settled on the boy's shoulder, though he gave no visible reaction to its presence. "Enough!" the word was clear and sharp, its tone brooking no disagreement, but the voice itself was lovely, sweet and rich and warm, a match for the intoxicatingly beautiful young woman it issued from.

"There will be no fighting here," Chimehara warned her two young charges. "We are one family now, the three of us. We work together toward a single goal—to further ourselves—and we defend each other against any who would stand in our way. You are free to disagree with each other, but if it ever comes to more than mere words I will be displeased and will act accordingly. Are we clear?"

Both children nodded, eyes downcast. "Yes, mistress," they intoned.

"Very good." She gave them both a quick squeeze to show that all was forgiven, then released them. "Ruisoki, we will put your things there," she indicated one side of the sitting room. "I own the apartment next door as well, and we will use that space for meals and lessons, while this will be for sleeping, bathing, and dressing. You and Suda will share this outer room. The sleeping alcove is mine. Understood?" He nodded. "Good. Now, set your bag down and come here." And, moving to the center of the room, she sank gracefully into a cross-legged position on the pillows arrayed there, adjusting her kitoro so that it did not snag or tear. "Both of you."

Suda grunted and dropped to the floor like a puppet whose strings had just been cut, and Chimehara resisted rolling her eyes. For someone with such speed and agility, the girl seemed almost to delight in moving awkwardly at times! Ruisoki joined them, taking his seat carefully. No grace there, but certainly precision, as she had noted about the boy before, though that had been in the way he had poisoned his own parents. Still, they were skills she could build upon.

First things first, however. "We live in interesting times," she told her charges, tugging a scroll from her sleeve and unrolling it so they could see the words scribed there. "This decree was issued just this morning, by the emperor himself. Can either of you tell me what it says?"

"No idea," Suda declared almost proudly, raising her narrow little chin in defiance. The girl was illiterate, something Chimehara knew would need to change, and quickly. It was one thing to not be able to read when you were scrounging off the streets in Suranmui, another when you were among civilized folk.

Ruisoki's eyes narrowed as he read. "What is a Saisaihyu?" he asked after a moment. "I have never heard of it."

"It is an ancient practice," she answered, pleased both at his reading skills and at his willingness to admit ignorance. There was no shame in that, provided you then worked to correct the gap in your knowledge—as she herself had done upon reading the decree, asking one of her colleagues she knew enjoyed history. "A nine-day period of purification, during which no aishone may be consumed."

The girl seemed uncaring—and why should she, when she had never been able to afford even the simplest relic bones before?—but the boy tilted his head, considering. "There will be a great deal of confusion," he stated matter of factly. "People will be unable to access the talents they rely upon."

"Yes, and thus it is the perfect opportunity for us," Chimehara agreed. "We do not require aishone, and so we will still have all our skills available to us, while others do not. We will take advantage of that."

"How?" Suda wanted to know, and for an instant the woman considered lying, but decided it was better to be honest with her students.

"I do not know yet," she admitted instead. "But I will think upon it, as will both of you."

Just then there was knock upon the apartment's outer door. Rising smoothly to her feet, Chimehara crossed the room. "Yes?" she called through the sturdy barrier.

"Mistress Chimehara," a voice replied from out in the hall. Young, male. "I bear a message from Master Eijiri. He wishes you to see him at once. There is an opportunity presented to House Chohu that he would like your involvement in."

"Thank you," she said. "Tell him I will be there directly." There was no way she could refuse, as Eijiri was the master of the merchant house which had taken her in. Besides which, she was intrigued. "You see?" she told the children who had risen silently to their feet and closed in behind her to better hear the exchange.

"Already, we find new opportunities. Now, Suda, I expect you to help Ruisoki get settled in while I am gone." And, ignoring the grimace from the one child and the smirk from the other, she turned away, humming under her breath as she went off to prepare herself for her meeting with Master Eijiri.

In Mazihini, a pair of young men stepped from an alleyway. They were clearly related, bearing the same short, slight build and pinched features, the same crop of untamed black hair, and the same dark eyes—eyes, that upon close inspection, contained a strange swirl as if of smoke and shadow trapped within. Both wore dusty rags, but the elder of the two carried a small pouch in his hand and hefted it with a smile.

"Now we can afford proper clothes," Ibaru told his brother. "Once we have those, we won't stand out so much."

"And food?" Iraku asked. He rubbed at his sunken belly, which growled in response. "I am starving!" He said the last with both pity and some degree of wonder, for during the months when they had been the servants and mouthpieces of the strange mystical entity known only as Kaemusei, the Silent Change, they had not needed any other form of sustenance. Their master was now gone, however, and much of its gifts had vanished, leaving the brothers penniless, aching, and hungry.

"Yes, and food," Ibaru agreed. He clapped his brother on the back, both of them marveling slightly at the ability to interact physically once more, for until recently their very touch would cause anything to crumble away and any flesh to wither and age. Though they regretted not being as powerful—or as impervious to harm, for what could hurt you when every blade disintegrated even as it brushed your skin?—they did enjoy being able to hold objects again. Like this pouch.

People were walking past, some eyeing the brothers warily, but most seemed engaged in some animated conversation. It appeared something had occurred, and the pair edged closer to hear. They listened in for several minutes, during which their confusion grew but so did their excitement.

"This is amazing!" Ibaru finally said. "A—whatever that's called—where no one uses aishone! Do you know what this means, brother?"

Iraku nodded. "We'll be the same as everyone else!" Because the brothers had been born Mukanichi, without the ability to absorb anything from aishone. That had made them outcasts, the lowest rung of society, mere beggars. They had eked out a meager existence doing whatever odd jobs were offered, usually tasks too disgusting or arduous for anyone else to contemplate and had often been beaten in the process by those who looked down upon them just because they had been born different. When the Silent Change had found them and chosen them, it had been a revelation, this idea of being wanted, of being valued.

Losing that had been devastating, and far worse than if they had never had it at all.

"Yes, we will be on equal footing with everyone else," Ibaru agreed. He fingered the edges of the corded leather tying the pouch shut. "And we will be able to secure a place for ourselves, and to contemplate our revenge." The waxed ends began to fray, the tough leather discoloring and cracking as if it had aged, before falling apart and leaving a small spray of dust to be carried off by the wind.

Not all of their master's gifts had left them, after all. As the pouch's previous owner had recently discovered when he had turned up his nose and walked by without offering them even a single small coin. He had paid the ultimate price for his arrogance.

And so would the man who had taken the Silent Change from them. The man named Noniki.

Elsewhere in the city, a large, sturdy woman in the uniform of the aiashe stepped out of the barracks just inside the outermost gates and adjusted her jingaso atop her head. A crescent-shaped scar puckered her left cheek and her pale eyes were sharp as she considered the streets before her, hefting her yanoi with the ease of long use.

"Ready, Akaii?" a fellow soldier asked, emerging just behind her, and she nodded, allowing a small grin to light her face.

"Ready, Yoshitaro. Let's go." Together with a handful of others, they set off toward the outer gate and the docks beyond, to take their shift at guard duty, Chiyu Akaii leading the way as befit a lieutenant.

But the woman's thoughts were far away as they marched. Indeed, the true Akaii had no more thoughts, for her body—blackened beyond recognition, eyes gouged out of their sockets—had been stuffed in among the rubble of a falling building just after the attack, to be written off as "an unknown resident, now deceased." The man who had murdered her and stolen her eyes had also taken on her identity, so thoroughly that the dead chuisu's comrades had never noticed the deception.

That could not last, however. The longer he posed as her among men and women who knew her well, the more likely he would slip up somewhere. His dark arts had given him not only the dead woman's semblance but her recent memories and most relied upon skills and knowledge, but that would not be enough if someone asked an in-depth question or referred to some deep secret or long-past shared event. He would have to find a new identity away from here, and soon.

And now there was this new information to digest. A Saisai-hyu! He had heard of such things, though only as ancient history. Yet the emperor was calling for one now! Fascinating—as were the opportunities such a time might present.

Still, he knew better than to be overconfident. Yes, the imperial guards would be weakened, off-balance, unable to access their ancestors' martial skills. But any decent commander would know this and do their best to compensate, shoring up their defenses and increasing their precautions. Plus, after his partner's recent failure, they would be even more on their guard against possible infiltration.

He would have to consider the situation very carefully. If there was a way to use this period to his advantage, he would certainly do so. But he would not rush in blindly, or gamble on too risky a chance. Better to wait and be sure before he struck, as he would only get a single chance.

For now, Akaii whistled a rough drinking song, the tune quickly picked up by her comrades, and laughed as she marched off to work.

CHAPTER FIVE

"Interesting," Kishin Narai murmured setting the scroll down upon the beautifully inlaid yanokai top of the small table. He glanced around him at the three people arrayed there, each as well attired as he, in clothes with little outward ornamentation but made from the finest materials and with the greatest skill, so that those of discernment would immediately notice the quality thereof and thus ascribe that same high value to the people who wore them. Such was the merchant's way, or at least merchants of their caliber. Quality over ostentation. Cleverness over brute force. Careful planning over emotional outbursts. Those qualities had led each of them here, to Motohori, where only the most powerful of the merchants might mingle with the lesser nobility.

And now there was this. A Saisaihyu. An event which had not occurred in a hundred years or more.

"Why would the emperor call for such a thing now?" Jiro Masute asked, flicking his long, beautiful hair back over his shoulder—though he was always careful now to flick it to the left, in order to conceal the ugly scar where that ear had been. "The city is still recovering from the recent attack."

"And thus is already off-balance," Shizu Yokori agreed, reaching out with a tiny silver fork and skewering a candied water chestnut from the bowl before her. She waved the delicacy before her as she spoke. "He could use that instability to right the city's course—or to tip it even further off-balance, if he chose."

"Perhaps," Fujiko Oritano offered, selecting a dumpling with her own fork and popping it into her mouth whole, raising a hand to cover her face as she spoke and chewed simultaneously, "it is one and the same for him. If you are afraid the course is no longer correct, you may need to tip things still further before you can begin to correct them." In her haste she had forgotten that she no longer had all her fingers, and so there was a gap not only in the raised hand but in its coverage, causing flickers of her chewing to be visible, but the others ignored that, as they had all been allies and partners for many years and were inclined to overlook each other's foibles when possible.

"It may be so," Narai agreed. He was not overly concerned for himself or his friends—though they all possessed first-rate aishone to grant themselves skill in appraisals, negotiations, and other related endeavors, they rarely used them. The relic bones were currency, after all. Why spend what amounted to a small fortune when you could train yourself to have the same skills and use them for free? No, the bones were reserved for when they needed that extra edge, or if they required a skill they did not have time or patience or natural talent to master, such as the warrior bone each of them kept in reserve in case they were attacked. The rest of the time, their own abilities would have to suffice—and, up until now, generally had.

"It might be a good time to invest in more aishone," Oritano suggested. "Their value could drop during the Saisaihyu, as people worry that this could be the start of a longer period of abstinence, perhaps even a permanent one."

"Or they could increase," Masute countered, "as people panic and grasp all the aishone they can, for fear they will all disappear during the interval."

"We will watch the markets," Yokori declared. "How the Senkousa behave will tell us whether to buy or sell, hoard or divest." The others nodded—the Bone Readers were essentially aishone merchants, using their strong aitachi to read bones and determine what knowledge and skills resided within each one, and thus what a relic bone might be worth. The group had carefully cultivated good relations with several of the city's more established Senkousa for just such a reason—it paid to know when there was a scarcity of potter's or baker's bones, or when suddenly there was a flood of bones with painter's and tailor's gifts.

"It will be an exciting time, this Saisaihyu," Narai commented, reaching for his cup and raising it to sip the hot, fragrant tea within. Ah, he had missed the comforts of home during their long wanderings! Thoughts of that trek—and the persistent twinge in his hip that forced him to shift position yet again, never quite able to be comfortable for more than a few moments—made him scowl and change topic slightly, to that which he had originally intended to broach before this decree had arrived to distract them. "And why did a certain young warrior not inform us of the event beforehand?" he asked the others and the very air, which seemed as likely to hold an answer. "Surely he knew of it, yet he said nothing."

All four of them were scowling or grimacing or frowning now, and each of them unconsciously rubbed their respective injuries, all of which had been caused by the man in question. "He does not answer to us anymore," Oritano pointed out carefully, for it was a sore point among the group. "If anything, we answer to him."

But Yokori was quick to disagree, her mind and tongue as sharp as ever despite being the eldest of them. "Not so," she argued, selecting another treat to gesture with. "It was that way on the road, yes, for then he had control, especially with those hoodlums of his." Another grievance—as they had journeyed back from the Tawasiri they had acquired more and more people in their train, men and women drawn to Kagiri's strength and skill and quiet confidence. Even their own guards had fallen under his spell, training with him and obeying his orders over their own. "But now we are back home," she pointed out, waving a hand at the sumptuous gardens they sat among. "We are strong here—we have friends, contacts, alliances. Wealth. Retainers. And what does he have?"

"A position in the emperor's court," Masute answered at once. "And, from what I've heard, his brother, back from the dead."

"Yes, yes," Yokori agreed, silencing him with a click of her fingers just before his nose. "But they are strangers here! They know no one! They have no friends, no money, no home—they must rely upon others for these things, at least for now!"

"Others like us," Narai added, nodding. "Yes. That is a very good point. We are Kagiri's sponsors, are we not? For that matter, we were Noniki's as well, before the unfortunate misunderstanding that led to our parting ways." That "misunderstanding" had been when the young man had refused to enter the haunted tower, of course, but it mattered not. "We are still the city residents Kagiri knows best, the ones he has worked with, traveled with, fought with. Why should he not turn to us for support and advice at a trying time like this?"

Yokori's smile was razor sharp. "And why should we not benefit from that relationship as well?" she asked, rubbing her narrow fingers together. "That seems only fair."

"Very fair," Oritano agreed around another dumpling. "A win-win."

"Precisely." Narai smiled. "We must invite him to dine with us at his earliest convenience. Surely he has questions about life here in the city—questions we can answer. We will advise him, counsel him, guide him—"

Masute laughed. "And in return, he will tell us what the emperor is planning, before anyone else hears of it, so that we may use that knowledge to our advantage." He raised his own glass—filled not with tea but with tsekuri—and the other three lifted theirs as well, all toasting this resumption of their plan.

Narai sipped his tea and smiled along with his friends. Yes, this presented quite the opportunity—and they would make sure they benefitted from it.

"He did it!" Jitu Kanai declared, jumping up and executing a small dance-like maneuver that clapped feet together in mid-air. "Noniki did it!" The sturdy potter's face was flushed, his smile wide.

"We don't know that," Minawa argued, though she could not keep a smile from her lined face. "It doesn't say anything about him here." She was holding the scroll in both hands and kept stealing glances down at it as if she feared it might disappear otherwise, or the wording somehow change to a different meaning.

But her friend could not be dissuaded. "Who else could it be?"

he asked, rubbing at his head and the few sparse hairs still sprinkled there. "We arrive here in Awaihinshi, Noniki goes to seek out the emperor to tell him that the Relicant Way needs to end, and a few days later the emperor declares that no one will be using aishone for a solid week! It has to be Noniki's work! He got through to him!"

Several of the others nodded. "It does seem that way," Isoro agreed, a smile lighting her otherwise plain face. "Otherwise, it would be quite the coincidence," the young herbalist added, twisting her long hair between her strong, slender fingers.

"I'm not saying it wasn't him," Minawa countered. "Just that we don't know for certain." She scowled, the fierce expression making the rest of the gathering chuckle, for after weeks traveling together they had all learned that the old woman was not as fierce or as unfriendly as she liked to pretend. Indeed, the next words out of her mouth—"Where is Seikoku?"—emerged as more concerned and petulant than angry.

"Not back yet," Ratal offered. The stocky fisherman rubbed his belly. "I hope she brings food when she does show. I'm starving!"

There was a murmur of agreement at that. They had only been in Awaihinshi a few days but they had used up all their money and most of their food getting here, with no clear plan on how they would survive once they did reach the city. Just faith in Noniki and belief in his teachings, that people could and should survive on their own merits rather than the bones they consumed and the talents of those long dead.

"There's a little stew still," Sanedi called, and Ratal hurried over to where the old basketweaver was tending a large pot over a fire. At least those they'd been helping recover from the attack had been giving them food as a way of showing thanks. That had kept them all fed these last few days. But they were nearly done with the repairs, which meant there would not be any more food from that source, either.

"We need to set up shop," Isoro stated. "I still have my herbs. That will bring in some money."

"I can weave," Sanedi agreed. "I just need dry straw and a place where I can sit to work."

Others chimed in. A few would have a harder time, like Ratal—difficult to fish when you were within a walled city!—or Otokai, who was a horsetrader without any horses. Even so, they had skills they could put to good use. They just needed a place to work from, and then to go out and find people willing to pay for their efforts.

"One good thing about all this," Minawa commented to no one in particular, though everyone listened, for she had shown a great deal of practical wisdom and had become, along with Kanai and Seikoku, one of the little community's leaders, keeping everyone together while Noniki focused on ideals and principles at a higher level. "If nobody's using their aishone, it means most people will be struggling to do even the simplest stuff, like baking bread or cooking rice or washing clothes. We can do that for 'em."

Everyone nodded. That was true! They had all sworn off the use of aishone since meeting Noniki, and their trek here had forced them to learn how to manage without the relic bones. As a result, they'd all learned a great many basic skills themselves—and now those could come in handy!

They were still discussing ideas, calling out things they could each do, when there was a stir from the front of the lot that had once held a granary and which they'd been using as their camp-ground. A moment later the crowd parted to reveal a young, attractive pair, both clad in simple but sturdy clothes, both lugging large sacks—and both with big smiles on their faces.

"Noniki!" Kanai shouted, charging forward to engulf the younger man in a hug. "You're back! And Seikoku!" She laughed as the potter turned to haul her into his embrace as well.

"Yes, we're back," Noniki agreed. "Sorry to have been away so long." He sighed and shrugged. "It's been a strange few days." He set his bag down on the ground and opened it to reveal a stack of woven containers from which mouth-watering smells began to waft. "We brought food."

The others all gathered round as he and Seikoku began to distribute the containers, each of which contained rice, fish, meat, greens, and other items. Her bag contained jugs of rice wine and others of tea, and those were passed around as well, creating a festive atmosphere.

"We've got some news, too," Seikoku stated once everyone was eating. Her eyes sparkled, making her even lovelier than usual. "Really amazing news!"

"If it's about this Saisaihyu, we already know," Minawa warned, nudging the scroll with her foot where it lay on the ground before her, set there to leave her hands free for food. "Did you do that?"

"Not entirely, no," Noniki admitted. "It was actually the emperor's idea—I'd never even heard of such a thing. But Kagiri and I agreed with him." He beamed. "It's amazing—we thought the emperor would be completely close-minded about the Relicant Touch but he's not at all! He hates it as much as we do! He knows it's poisoning the empire, and he wants to be rid of it! That's why he's doing this—it's sort of a test, to see how people manage without the bones for a few days at first."

"Noniki has been made one of the emperor's Rojiri," Seikoku explained, slinging an arm around his shoulders and making him flush with pride and embarrassment—and maybe something more as well. "It's a position that comes with a lot of perks—including his own estate!"

"Wait, what?" Kanai looked horrified. "You're leaving us? But you just came back!" There were tears in the man's eyes. He looked even more upset when Noniki and Seikoku both laughed at him, followed quickly by Minawa and a few of the more others, but they patted him on the back and smiled to show they were not ridiculing him in any way.

"I am leaving, yes," Noniki explained gently. "But you're coming with me! All of you are!" He grinned. "Don't you see? We're a family, and now we have a home—and it's big enough for all of us!"

That brought a cheer from the group, and it was in good spirits that they all dug into their food again, laughing and joking and chatting as they caught Noniki and Seikoku up on what they'd done and seen since the pair had been gone. They all talked late into the night, long after the food and wine and tea were gone, and when Noniki finally shook out his bedroll and lay down, he was happy.

CHAPTER SIX

Saisaihyu, Day One

Hibikitsu, the Echo of Victory, emperor of all Rimbaku, was engaged in one of the fiercest struggles of his young life. He battled with every ounce of his will, every fiber of his being, his every muscle taut, sweat beginning to bead across his forehead, but in the end it was no use. This was a contest he could not win.

At least he was able to raise his hand in time to hide his mouth from view as the yawn escaped.

The merchant—what was her name again? As yes, Obi Ren—did not notice, her head lowered in a bow that nearly brushed her forehead against the tiles of the floor. Nor did the rest of her entourage.

But, just to the side of the dais, Hibikitsu heard a faint cough, and felt his cheeks flush. Caught!

He did not acknowledge Kohori's gentle rebuke but instead struggled to pay attention to the woman in front of him, so that he could respond appropriately when she had finished her recitation.

And that was the only way to refer to it. Hers was a merchant house dedicated to fishing, to seafood, and she had, after making proper obeisance, launched into a lecture on the merits of various kinds of fish and other sea life, what made each one worthwhile and how to judge the value of individual specimens. Hibikitsu was certain he had never known so much about the scales of a salmon as he did now—and he truly hoped he never would again.

Still, when she finally paused for breath he declared, "That is fascinating, Madam, and we thank you for imparting such knowledge to us. Truly, you are an expert in your craft, and a credit to your profession."

A broad smile creased her face at once, and she bowed again.

"You honor me, your Imperial Majesty. I hope we may discuss sea life and its importance in even more depth at some later time."

Only if I have been captured and it is used upon me as a form of torture, the young emperor thought, but dipped his head and instead said, "We will look forward to such an opportunity. Thank you."

"Thank you." She bowed again, and then retreated, still facing him as was proper. "And I hope that you will enjoy the gifts." She had brought him a selection of her house's wares, from delicate silvery fish to gleaming eels to dappled crabs the size of a man's head, the first two conveyed in watertight woven baskets filled with water to keep the creatures alive until they were ready to be eaten and all bearing the faint salt tang of the sea.

Hibikitsu waited until the party had exited the throne room and disappeared down the hall before he allowed himself to sigh and slump in his throne, the carved and gilded wood as always an impressive sight but a less than comfortable seat. "Is that the last of them?" he asked, aware of the plaintiveness in his voice but unable to hide it. It had already been a very long day.

But the man to whom he had directed his question—Doiyu Soda—shook his head even as he bowed. "There is one more, your Imperial Majesty," the little scribe stated, his voice trembling as he spoke. "House Chohu."

Another sigh escaped before he could stop himself, but he straightened again and forced his face back into a semblance of regal dignity. "Very well," he declared once he was sure he was ready. "Allow them to approach us."

This would make the tenth merchant house he had granted audience to thus far today. It was a long and tedious process, but a necessary one if he was to find new Rojiri from among that class—especially since none of his current advisors could recommend anyone. Not that he was explaining the reason for these interviews—he had merely sent word to all the major merchant houses that they were invited to present themselves to their emperor. But it allowed him to meet with each of them, the heads of their respective houses, and to gauge their quality. Thus far he had spoken with fur traders, weavers, grain merchants, rice merchants, wine merchants, cloth merchants, carvers, sword dealers, and of course the noble house of Obi and their fish.

What distinguished between an artisan, a trader, and a merchant, Hibikitsu wondered as this latest house approached across the wide throne room. He would have assumed "merchant" meant "one who bought and sold and traded" rather than "one who created," yet House Ayano not only traded textiles, they crafted their own. Their gift to him had been a magnificent kisoni of a rich silk the burnished color and pattern of late afternoon clouds with a delicate echo of the tsodami hidden in the play of shadows between them, as sumptuous as any garment he owned, and the head of their house—a tiny man named Ayano Taketa with unusually long fingers and, unfortunately, almost equally long ears—had explained that they sold and traded both bolts of fabric and finished garments all across the empire. Surely that qualified them as a great merchant house? Their compound was in Sakiriti, it was true, but Master Taketa had mentioned a bit apologetically that the dyes they used could give off a powerful odor, and thus they had not sought to change locations because right now they were well situated to let the breezes carry those scents out over the water instead of in toward their neighbors.

He was drawn from these ruminations as this final house neared the dais. They were led by a man, large and fleshy but not fat, with a wide face and a beard so small it might have been painted on as an afterthought. His robes were gleaming satin, his cap heavily but cunningly embroidered, and jewels shone from the many rings on his fingers and from his earlobes. Ah, yes, Hibikitsu remembered. House Chohu. The gem merchants.

As with each merchant before him, the master of the house had arrived with several junior members in tow. They were a mix of men and women, all clearly attired in their best clothing and gems, but as they drew closer Hibikitsu found his gaze drawn toward one in particular. She was walking behind the master and some of the others, and so at first he had only tantalizing glimpses here and there—a flicker of raven-black hair, a flash of brilliant blue cloth, a peek of soft pink. Then the procession reached the spot some ten feet away that was as near as any were allowed to approach and spread out—and Hibikitsu sat back of a sudden, feeling the hard surface of the chair press into his back as he gasped for breath.

For the woman before him was perhaps the most beautiful he had ever seen.

She was of average height, and her kisoni—a full fumisoni, with long, sweeping sleeves that hung almost to the floor—clung to her body in a way that revealed rather than hid her lush curves. The fabric ranged in hue from deepest, almost midnight blue to the pale shade of a midday sky and was touched here and there with pale flowers in pink and white, their shades matching the petal-speckled obi encircling her narrow waist. Her hair was a perfect, inky black, its sheen demonstrating how soft and silky it must be, and was worn up to reveal her long, graceful neck and to allow focus on her features, which were flawless—heart-shaped face, small mouth with full lips, delicate nose, elegantly arched brow, and large eyes of a stunning emerald hue. Hibikitsu knew he was staring and struggled to compose himself as they bowed, the tiny smirk touching the woman's glorious lips and the sparkle in her eyes the only outward indication that she had noticed his reaction.

"Your Imperial Majesty," the man in front intoned, bowing deeply. "I am Master Eijiri, head of House Chohu, at your service." Straightening only once Hibikitsu had waved a hand toward him, the merchant beamed and gestured one of the men with him to step forward. "Please, accept this small token of our respect and admiration for you."

The man was holding a small case, which he relinquished to Doiyu Soda. The scribe carried it carefully over to Kohori, who inspected the box and its contents closely before nodding and allowing the little man to bring it to the dais, where Hibikitsu accepted it.

The box was beautiful, and heavy, made of silver carved and inlaid with mother of pearl and ivory and jade. It was entwined with dragons on every side and across the top, each scale picked out in a different stone but all matched so smoothly the differences in color seemed like the play of sunlight and shadow across the majestic creatures. Flipping the lid open, he reached inside and extracted the box's contents from where it nestled among velvet folds. It was an iniro, but one like he had never seen before. Typically, the little segmented containers were cylindrical and each segment was essentially a wide ring. What he held now, however, was a small coiled dragon crafted entirely from milky white jade, the stone cool and smooth to the touch, every element of the creature flawlessly carved and easily discerned despite the uniform shade. The segments fit cunningly together, coils overlapping here and tucking under there, so that when it was assembled no seams were visible, yet the sections came apart with a simple tug, revealing the compartments hollowed out within. It was indeed a princely gift, and a clear indicator of the merchant house's skill.

"It is fantastic," Hibikitsu told them honestly. "We have never seen anything as beautiful." Unbidden, his eyes flicked toward the young woman again, and her cheeks dimpled at the glance, which only made his own heat once more. "Thank you, Master Eijiri," he continued, forcing his gaze back to the head of house. "And thank you for accepting our invitation."

"Thank you for extending it," the merchant replied, bowing again. "It is truly our honor, though I will say we are still puzzled as to its purpose. I admit, I had hoped you wished to commission a work from us, for we would consider ourselves truly blessed to craft something for your Majesty, but"—and here the man paused, a gleam coming to his small, dark eyes and a sly expression to his face—"I cannot help but notice that we are not the first to attend you this day, and all our peers, though none our rivals."

So, the man was not stupid, nor shy. That was good, and Hibikitsu found himself nodding approvingly. "Just so, Master Eijiri," he agreed readily. "Though your work is exemplary, that was not our purpose in calling you here today. Rather, we feel that, between recent events and other matters, we have not taken the time to know all those within our kingdom, or even within our city. We seek to remedy this, and thus are pleased to invite our merchant houses to attend us so that we might become familiar with them."

Eijiri considered this, stroking the perfect point of his beard. "If I may say, Your Majesty, this strikes me as truly wise," the gem merchant offered, his tone neither obsequious nor arrogant but merely matter of fact. "Especially as you have done so on this, the first day of your Saisaihyu." He smirked, if only for an instant. "Thus you truly meet your merchants, as they are themselves, with no gilding."

"Indeed." Hibikitsu found himself liking this man—at least he was perceptive, and willing to speak his mind! What good would a Rojiri be if he were too afraid to voice his true opinions, or to dull to notice anything work having an opinion on? Now he leaned forward, allowing a bit more bite to emerge in his tone. "And what do you feel we should know of you, Master Eijiri, and of your house? For surely one who specializes in gems must dislike being laid so bare."

That drew a laugh from the man, though again it was polite and did not seem at all mocking. "Not so, sire," he stated, tapping his fingers together as he spoke. "Many who deal in gems and metals prefer such ornamentation, it is true. But House Chohu prides itself on quality and craftsmanship, the type that can be seen without any false embellishment. That is why, for example, the iniro you now hold has no paint, no gold leaf, and no other gems. The jade is flawless, as is the work, and needs nothing else— indeed, anything would merely detract from its brilliance." He bowed again. "I hope that I do not speak out of turn or appear too presumptuous by taking pride in my house and its members."

"Not at all, for your pride seems well-earned." Hibikitsu smiled, careful to keep his eyes from the woman in their midst. "Now tell us, what are your thoughts on how best to restore our city from its recent injuries, and to ensure that it continues to flourish?"

He listened as the merchant considered and then presented a sketchy but solid idea for beautifying while rebuilding, engaging the members of each level in the process so that they would feel more pride and investment in their surroundings. He had asked the same question of each merchant in turn, looking less for a fully developed proposal than for some sign that they were capable of independent thought and of thinking beyond themselves, their house, and their profits, and had the responses had been varied indeed. Master Eijiri's were among the most intriguing, and the most selfless, for there was nowhere in his suggestion any place for gems and jewelry.

After the man finished, Hibikitsu nodded, and favored him with a small smile. "We thank you, Master Eijiri," he declared. "You and the rest of your house." He glanced at each of the others in turn, acknowledging them individually, and was careful not to linger any longer on the woman than on the others, much as he wished it. "You have given us a great deal to think about, and we are grateful for your loyalty and your insight."

"It is our pleasure to serve in any way we might, Your Majesty," the merchant replied, dropping into a bow lower than any he had performed since his arrival. "Please know that House Chohu is always at your disposal." The others bowed as well, the woman flowing as smoothly as water poured into a basin, and then they were retreating from the room and the day's last audience was finally at an end.

"Ash and Bone, I am tired!" Hibikitsu declared, flinging himself from the throne and off the dais in a single prodigious leap that caused poor Doiyu Soda to squeal and stumble backward in fright. "You may retire," the emperor told him, and the scribe nodded, bowed to the floor, and then backed away as fast as his trembling legs could carry him.

That left only Kohori, and she chuckled, now that they were alone. "Are you?" his guard commander asked, leaning against one of the wide, carved columns that lined the room. "I'd have thought you were wide awake after that last meeting. You certainly seemed it when they entered."

I am the emperor, Hibikitsu reminded himself sternly as he rounded on the older woman. *I will not be taunted and teased by anyone, including my own Taikoro.* It was no use, however, for he could feel his face heating up and was horrified to discover his voice was squeaky when he declared, "We cannot imagine what you mean."

Kohori only laughed the harder. "You've got good taste, I'll grant you that," she told him with a grin. "That girl was stunning. Still, if you're of a mind to mate, I'd suggest you set your sights a bit higher than a mere shopgirl, no matter how tasty." He was reminded once again that the Taikoro was a warrior, with all the bluntness and indelicacy that often entailed—and that she had known him his whole life, having watched over him when he was still in swaddling clothes. There was no one more loyal, and no one he trusted more, but while he believed—he hoped—she respected him as a man and as her emperor, she would never hold him in awe.

Then again, that was probably for the best. He had learned the hard way that sycophants were as useless as manipulators. You needed people beside you who would be honest, even if that meant saying something you did not wish to hear.

Still—"Of a mind to mate," he repeated, glaring at her and earning only a raised eyebrow in reply. "Is that how you speak to your emperor?"

"It's how I speak to a young man who needs to start considering such things," Kohori informed him. "Your only two Rojiri so far are as young as you, so they won't know anything about this either, but I can tell you, you need to be thinking about your legacy and your line. That means an heir, hopefully more than one. Which means a wife." She winked at him. "You can enjoy your shopgirl on the side, if you like."

"I could have you banished to the farthest border of the empire, to walk a post among the mountains with nothing but a goat for company," Hibikitsu threatened, but the head of his Honteno only shook her head, executed a minimal bow, and walked away, chuckling again.

Despite the way she had said them, however, her words lingered, and the emperor found himself contemplating certain facts of life he had thus far managed to avoid.

Clearly, the time had come for more than one sort of change.

CHAPTER SEVEN

t was a magnificent view. Aihiri sat at the very pinnacle of the city, the highest of its levels, and from over its walls of the finest, purest white marble one could see out across the Edishu and Wagata rivers to the south, the mighty Tonawa to the east, and the vast expanse of the ocean itself to the west. You could also look down upon the whole of Awaihinshi, each successive layer spread out before you in widening circles until the ramshackle layer of Suranmui at the bottom on three sides, and the docks that thrust out into the Edishu along the remaining portion.

Of course, the walls were high and thick, so in order to see such things properly required being on the palace's second floor.

An even better vantage was the roof, balancing upon the terra cotta tiles and letting the breeze touch your cheeks as you gazed out upon the city below.

That was where Kagiri was at this moment, standing like an emerald beacon in his armor, feet securely planted, admiring this place that had become his new home. He stood completely still, taking in that sight and also the sounds and smells, but finally stirred at a discreet cough from somewhere just beyond the roof's edge.

"Dogenriku?" a voice called out hesitantly. "Are you there?"

It took him a second to remember that this title now referred to him, but then he answered, "I am here."

"Your Taisho are gathered and waiting, sir," the invisible speaker continued. "What shall I tell them?"

Kagiri sighed and shook himself. That was enough woolgathering! There was work to be done! Taking a step forward, he dropped feet-first over the edge, twisting his body around and raising his arms over his head to catch the carved wooden lip beneath the outermost row of tiles as he fell past them. His grip on that jerked his body to a stop and he used the remaining momentum to swing his legs in past the sill of the open window and, releasing his hold, to carry him the rest of the way into the room, where he landed on his feet with only a small thud. The man standing there gasped at the sudden intrusion and threw up his hands to shield his face. He was wearing the standard maikiro, Kagiri saw, but the war vest looked all but unused, its lacquered plates still shiny and undented. His jingaso looked equally pristine and he bore no spear, only a nihono stuck through his sash. The sword, at least, showed signs of both age and use, but Kagiri doubted any of those were recent, particularly given its haphazard placement.

"What is your name?" he demanded, and the soldier squeaked like a small mouse.

"Shosu Fuko Miyosi, sir," the man finally replied. "I am your clerk." The man did have a clerical look about him, with his pudgy build and round face. Certainly, he was no warrior!

"Are you?" Kagiri considered that. "I did not appoint you." Yet he knew no one in the army yet, for all that he was now in charge of them. So for now, at least, he would allow this timid mouse of a man to stay and assist him. "Where are the generals?"

"This way, sir." Miyosi led him out into the hall, down a flight of stairs, and along another hall to a door that he slid open before stepping aside. Kagiri found himself entering a pleasantly appointed room. The wooden floor was firm beneath his feet, the far wall opened wide to take in the view of one of the palace gardens as well as the fresh air and light, and the room simply furnished with an alcove—within which stood an empty guisuke kai atop what he assumed was an equally empty guisuke bitte, his predecessor's armor presumably having been placed upon him for his funeral—and a set of shelves side by side along one wall and a massive map of all Rimbaku taking up most of the wall opposite. A heavy desk of beautifully carved yanokai occupied a space slightly right of center, with a pair of chairs before it and a single chair behind it. The ceiling was not intricate, nor were the walls, bare wood rather than gilt, but they were well oiled and polished and glowed warmly in the light of the lanterns set in each corner. The room was made more crowded by the four men already standing within it, and all four turned to stare as Kagiri joined them and moved around to the far side of the desk. They each wore the armor of the aiashe, but far finer quality than a common soldier's, tailored to them individually, and gold-rimmed to denote their rank. Each carried a nihono as well, and Kagiri was pleased to see that those were at least worn correctly. Dare he hope these men truly knew how to use the blades, and how to command others who did as well?

"Gentlemen," he said, tapping his fingers against the object laid across the center of the desk, a sturdy chasai capped in gold shaped into the higeibara, its spidery petals trailing down onto the lacquered teak. "My name is Kagiri. I am the new Dogenriku."

"Kagiri?" one of them, a heavyset man with even heavier jowls and a flushed face, repeated, snapping the name off into a harsh bark. "What house is that, precisely? I am sure I've never heard of it!" He looked Kagiri up and down, taking in his armor in all its shades and streaks of green, with no insignia present and no household crest anywhere in sight.

"No house but my own," he answered, fixing this large, oafish man with a stern look until he finally turned away. "And who might you be, exactly?"

"Who am I?" The man puffed himself up even further, though the effect was spoiled by his being a full head shorter than Kagiri, if more than twice as wide. "I am Taisho Noboru Juniri! My family is among the oldest in Rimbaku!" He was all but quivering, which had the unfortunate effect of making his cheeks shake like jelly. "And I do not answer to some commoner! The emperor will hear of this!" And with that the man stomped out, his weight making the floor quake with each step.

Kagiri did not try to stop him—why should he? The man was under his command and pleading with the emperor would not change that. Indeed, Hibikitsu would only re-confirm Kagiri's appointment if the general did indeed ask. He would then return, and hopefully somewhat chastened. Instead of worrying about that Kagiri turned his attention to the other three. One was solidly built and stood at attention, crisp and straight. "What is your name, general?" Kagiri asked him.

The man saluted, fist against his chest, head bowed. "Taisho Daishin Nishoji, sir!" he replied, his words as clear and precise as his stance. "I live to serve the Empire!"

"As do we all," Kagiri replied, nodding and returning the salute. "Thank you, Taisho." He frowned, for the man's motion had caused a faint odor to waft across the desk, the smell of unwashed man and armor and something else. Horse, perhaps? "Where were you before this?"

"North, sir!" Daishin replied. "Assisting the emperor in fending off the Fyushan invasion!"

"Ah, of course. Good work." He had heard from Hibikitsu what had happened, how the Fyushans had taken control of several Rimbakan villages and were using the villagers as both hostage and shield—until the emperor himself ordered his soldiers to attack and spare no one, despite knowing innocents would die in the process. It had been a bold move, and no doubt a difficult decision, deliberately sacrificing some of his own people to eliminate the threat to all. And this Taisho had been there. He certainly seemed competent. It also explained the smell—the emperor had sailed back here but Daishin would have traveled on horseback at least part of the way, with the rest of his soldiers. Well, he didn't put on any airs, at least.

One of the other men saluted as Kagiri glanced his way. Tall, though not as tall as Kagiri himself, and whipcord thin, the general had dark hair beginning to silver at the temples and fine, narrow features. His armor showed some signs of wear, though to Kagiri's eye that appeared almost artfully done, as if it had been deliberately distressed to present the image of a hard-working soldier. "Taisho Atsumi Izo, at your service, sir," the man declared. "I was in Bezenkai, overseeing the placement of new guard forts." He stroked his upper lip. "We place them along the southern coast to watch for any potential threats from that direction." His smile was thin and nearly as cold as his eyes. "I can mark them on the map for you, if you'd like. And explain more about their purpose, and how many warriors each one holds." He spoke as if to a child, and Kagiri found himself bristling at the condescension dripping off each word.

"Thank you, Taisho Atsumi," he answered, biting off each word as it emerged and all but flinging them in the other man's face. "I believe I can locate them myself. I do know something of the south." The Tawasiri was in that region, standing upon the kingdom's southeast tip, and he was far more familiar with the Tower of Ghosts than this general could possibly have imagined.

That left the third man. Short and stocky, he was impeccably groomed and his armor shone as if it had been freshly polished. "Taisho Masagi Matsu," he stated, bowing low instead of saluting. "These past three months I have been in Tatsuma, training our troops. I won't bore you with the details." He straightened and glanced outside, past Kagiri, squinting up at the sun where it peeked through the clouds. "In fact, I'm afraid I must see to an urgent matter about those selfsame troops this very moment. Please do excuse me." And with and a quick, desultory salute, the general had stomped across the room to the outer doors and through them to the gardens, which promptly swallowed him from view.

Kagiri found he was grinding his teeth as he turned back to where the other two at least nominally still awaited his command. "Dismissed, for now," he told them, and turned his back as they quickly shuffled out. Only once the door had slid shut did he turn around, facing an empty room. Scooping the baton that was his badge of office up from the desk, he twirled it around him, testing its heft and reach but truly just wishing he had something he could attack with it. Bludgeoning something—or someone—until they were rid of any arrogance and condescension would be nice.

He knew, of course, that he had not been raised in the nobility, did not come from a distinguished family line, did not possess ancient honors and estates. Nor had he risen through the ranks of the military, learning its ins and outs, mastering its ways, and making a name for himself at greater and greater levels of command. But none of that should matter. He had been appointed by the emperor himself! What was more, he was Gensaiba, the conglomeration of a half dozen of the finest warriors this land had ever seen. As both that and Dogenriku he outranked those arrogant generals. Yet they had treated him as if he were still the same poor boy who had waited on tables and swept floors at the Happoa Kappua tavern back in Ginzai, eating table scraps and sleeping on the floor. And, faced with such utter disdain, he had indeed momentarily reverted to that child, unable to muster any sort of reply that could wipe away their sheer arrogance, which only made him feel more foolish and ill-used. Here he was, the finest warrior in the kingdom, and he had been cowed by harsh words and rude behavior!

Hurling himself through the outer doors, he leaped out into the gardens, thinking at least he might be able to roam the compound's perimeter enough to chase away the foul mood that had descended upon him from that awful encounter—and nearly crashed into someone, only avoiding the collision by twisting sideways and spinning in mid-air before landing on his feet. He glanced up, ready to snap at whomever had stepped into his path—and found himself facing a short, slight figure in the black enamel of the Honjofu, each piece of armor edged in gold. The face that turned to regard him, eyes narrowed in surprise, was a familiar one, and Kagiri found himself smiling.

"Taikoro Misataki!" He bowed, noting with approval how she had half-drawn her sword at his sudden approach but now sheathed it smoothly to return the gesture. Here, at least, was one who knew how to wield a blade! "I apologize. I did not mean to startle you."

"Rojiri Kagiri," she replied, returning the bow as an equal. "It is no matter."

For a second, they regarded each other warily—it had not been that long ago, after all, when they had battled in the throne room, each trying to kill the other—but Kagiri could stand it no longer and finally burst out, "How can you stand to deal with these people?" She arched an eyebrow at that but did not shush him, and so he continued, "I have just had a meeting with my Taisho, if you can even call them that. They are insufferable!" He banged the baton against his leg. "With men like that in charge, it's a wonder this kingdom is still standing!"

"Ah." She nodded. "Yes. Welcome to the realm of hereditary positions, where family is more important than ability." There was enough bitterness in her tone to indicate that she had experienced much the same prejudices, and Kagiri realized that she did not carry herself like a noblewoman. Could she be common-born as well? He could not bring himself to ask, however, as they were only barely acquainted.

Still, he appreciated that she not only understood his irritation but sympathized. "How do you deal with it?" he asked, tucking the baton beneath his arm to avoid swinging it in frustration.

The new head of the Honjofu considered that carefully. "I have always focused on obeying orders and doing my job to the best of my ability," she answered after a moment. Then she dipped her head. "But I have yet to face the challenge of leading the Honjofu, so perhaps I will find this new role as difficult as you find yours." She studied him, then broke into a smile. "One thing that helps me greatly is to work out my frustrations with exercise—or, if I am lucky enough to find someone willing, with swordwork." She tilted her head, and it took him a moment to register that this was an invitation.

When he finally did, Kagiri smiled as well. "Thank you, Taikoro Misataki," he stated, bowing again. "I would be delighted to cross blades with you again, and for no reason but exercise and venting external frustrations this time."

"In that case, follow me," she told him, and turned, leading the way around the side of the palace. "And my friends call me Shizumi."

"Shizumi." He grinned and lengthened his stride to keep up, his anger dissipating like the night fog upon the first touch of the morning sun.

CHAPTER EIGHT

Noniki stood and stared up at the wide, carved gates before him, which bore the image of a thundercloud in blue and gray, lightning flickering within it and picked out in gleaming silver. They were nearly as large as the entrance doors to Hibikitsu's throne room, and in some ways more daunting for being outside, with nothing above them but the curved double line of their supporting arch, and above that sky. To either side the walls stretched, high and sturdy, and clad in solid wood, though he could sense earth within that. The image was daunting, a forbidding front blocking all from access, and even moreso as he considered what lay within. But there was nothing to be gained from standing here gawking and so at least he stepped up to the gate and rapped upon it with one hand. The other clutched tight to a scroll he had received that morning, brought by way of an imperial courier. Within the rolled parchment was his future.

After a moment, a section of the gate slid open—so cunningly had it been crafted that he had not even realized it was movable until it began to shift. A man, wizened and tanned but still unbent enough to peer through the opening, glanced out at him. "Sir?" he asked, his voice rough.

Noniki cleared his throat. "My name is Noniki—" he began, lifting the scroll into view, but got no further, for the man's eyes had opened wide.

"Sir!" The panel slammed shut and an instant later the entire gate swung back instead, allowing the man to hurry out—and throw himself onto the ground at Noniki's feet, palms flat, forehead pressing the dirt. "I apologize for making you wait!"

"Please!" Noniki crouched and offered the man a hand, which

he accepted after a brief hesitation. "None of that." He helped lift the man up, then tucked the scroll into his own okube so he could brush dirt from the man's clothes, which were simple and sturdy and looked nearly as weathered as their owner. "Now, tell me your name."

"Ohiro, great Rojiri," the man answered, bowing so far from the waist Noniki feared he might tip over. "I am your gardener, an' it please you to keep me." There was a patch over the man's left breast where the cloth was brighter than the rest, as if it had been covered until recently, and looking more closely Noniki could see where threads had been pulled around the roughly circular space.

"You served the previous lord?" he asked, keeping his tone gentle to make clear that this was merely a question, not an accusation or an interrogation.

Ohiro dipped his head. "I did, lord. For fifty years, since I was a young man. My father was a gardener before me, a master with tree and bush and vine, and Lord Etsuya hired him away from his previous employer. I learned at my father's feet and took over for him when he became too old to continue."

Noniki frowned, peering past the man through the now-open gate, seeking any signs of movement. "Is there anyone else still here?" he asked, for he did not know exactly how such things worked.

"No, lord," Ohiro replied. "The rest were all kin to Lord Etsuya, and so all sentenced alike. My father never swore fealty, nor did I— we were paid in coin and aishone."

That explained it, then. It had been customary, when the head of a house committed treason or some other severe crime, to punish everyone equally. Hibikitsu had shown mercy and merely banished them from the city instead, allowing the family to retain any other estates beyond Awaihinshi's walls. If this man, like his father before him, had been only an employee rather than kin, he might have been considered exempt of such treatment. In the same way, the family might not have been required to care for him once they were cast out of this place.

Noniki studied his new acquaintance. He could tell from the roughness of his fingers and the calluses on his knees that Ohiro was no stranger to hard work, and the way he carried himself erect spoke of pride in those same efforts. Nor, once he'd urged against bowing and scraping, had the man been slow to accept that guideline and speak to him respectfully but directly. "I think I like you, Ohiro," he decided, clapping the gardener on the shoulder. "Will you stay and work for me? I'm sure I could use the help."

That brought a grin to the old man's face, and he nodded. "It would be my honor, great Rojiri."

"Good. None of that, though," Noniki warned, releasing him and stepping toward the gate. "It's just Noniki. Now, would you be so kind as to show me around my new home?"

This time the gardener even laughed. "I don't know the interior much, sir," he admitted, "but the outside, well, no one knows the place better." And he led the way under the arch that still bore the Etsuya name, in through the outer gates, then the inner ones, revealing a walled paradise.

Noniki had never seen anything like it. The Ikibanichari, where the Hakara Ikibanichi had healed him after his wanderings and had helped him re-center himself and start down the new path he had chosen, had been old and stately and meandering, the monastery occupying much of a mountain peak. Aihiri was lovely and too large to take in at once, with its massive central compound and outlying buildings all surrounded by gardens and ponds and bridges and finally the white marble walls protecting the entire level. This was something else entirely.

He could see clear across it, for one thing. It appeared to be roughly square, with those same thick walls all the way round, and he spotted what looked to be a smaller gate on the west wall, so directly opposite the entrance he had used. Spread before him to his left was a magnificent array of gardens and ponds and streams, linked by bridges and tiny islands all the way to the south wall. Ahead was a wide courtyard, its entire surface a single tile mosaic of the same thunderclouds emblazoned upon the gates. To his right, opening onto the courtyard, was a row of linked buildings, all a single story tall and all raised off the ground by stout wooden pillars. It was almost like they were built out on a dock or jetty, he mused, above water rather than solid earth, but he supposed that elevation allowed air to better circulate beneath. The roofs were clad in esuge shingles and rose to varying heights, the tallest being the biggest structure, which sat at the center of the row and had a wide set of stairs leading from a broad platform up to the building itself. All the structures were painted blue and gray, and the effect was that of a low stormfront rolling in, about to engulf the greenery arrayed before it.

He was about to say something to Ohiro when a flicker of motion caught his eye. Glancing to the right, he saw a small, dark figure racing along a covered walkway connecting the main building to the smaller one past it.

"I thought you said you were the only one still here?" he asked, breaking into a run in that direction.

"I am, sir!" the old man replied, huffing as he struggled to keep up. "I swear it!"

"Well, you're not alone now!" Noniki put on more speed, willing the air around him to propel him forward, and his feet lifted off the ground as he shot ahead of the gardener, flying across the courtyard. The figure had slipped under the rails of the walkway and into the courtyard, and now he could see that it was a boy, grubby and ragged, his small body hunched around something cradled in both arms. The boy glanced up as Noniki landed before him, his mouth falling open at the sight.

"It's all right," Noniki promised. "I'm not going to hurt you."

That seemed enough to shock the boy from his paralysis—and he lunged forward, a knife appearing as if by magic in one hand and stabbing toward Noniki's stomach!

He reacted instinctively, batting the weapon aside with magic as well as his hand. It flew from the boy's grip and flashed as it whirled to clatter almost all the way across the courtyard form them. The boy only snarled like an animal and raised his empty hand, the fingers with their dirty, jagged nails hooked as if into claws, as further threat.

Ohiro had finally caught up, wheezing for breath, and cursed when he saw the boy. "You again!" He gasped out, bent over nearly double with both hands on his legs for balance. "Sorry, sir. He's been in here before, stealing food that got left when the family departed. I've run him off, but he keeps coming back."

"That's all right." Noniki sank to his knees, which still put him a bit above the boy in terms of eye level but close enough that he could see the child's hallowed features, his sunken cheeks, his wide eyes and thin lips, his stringy hair. Had the boy ever known a decent meal or a proper night's sleep? "You're hungry, huh?" He could see now that the treasure the little thief held was nothing more than a loaf of bread and a hunk of what might be salted beef. "What's your name?"

The boy hissed in reply and batted at him when Noniki held out a hand.

"Not too friendly, are you?" He didn't take offense, though. He'd never been this bad off himself, but he'd worried it could come to that, back when he and Kagiri had left their village with only a handful of coins to their name. A few months living on the streets, begging and stealing for food, and would he have been any better than this? "Well, how about if we get you more food? Would that help any?"

"Sir," Ohiro said over his shoulder. "That's kind, but you shouldn't. They're like stray cats, urchins like this. You feed them and you'll never be rid of them." Noniki could tell without turning that the gardener was scowling at the boy. "Besides, I reckon he's stolen more than enough from you already."

"It isn't stealing if I give it to him freely," Noniki pointed out. He hadn't taken his eyes off the boy, and saw how he was sizing up him, Ohiro, their surroundings, everything, his gaze flicking here and there, never settling, like a fly or a gnat, constantly buzzing. "Would you like more food?" he asked again.

The boy just snarled again. Did he not know how to speak? Had he once known and forgotten? Or was he simply not willing to let his guard down enough to bring forth words?

With a sigh, Noniki rose to his feet. "Well, if you're not going to talk, and you won't accept my help, I suppose you'd best be on your way," he said. He took a step back, then another—and as if that had been the difference between safe and too close, the boy immediately bolted, making for the rear gate Noniki had noticed before. Ohiro started after him, but Noniki held out a hand and the older man instantly stopped.

"Let him go," he said, watching the boy as he streaked across the courtyard's back corner to the gate and then slipped through—he must have opened it to enter and left it cracked so he could make his escape.

"He'll be back," Ohiro warned.

"Maybe so," Noniki agreed, glancing at the other man now that the boy was gone. "And if he does, let me know at once—but don't chase him off, and don't hurt him. Perhaps if I let him in and feed him enough times he'll realize he's nothing to fear from me."

"You're not much like Lord Etsuya," the gardener said then, and there was wonder in his tone, and confusion, too. But not condemnation, Noniki noted, which at least was a start.

"No, I suppose I'm not," he agreed easily. "Now, let's finish that tour, shall we?" He glanced around them again, at the lavish estate that was now his, then turned to the older man and laughed. "Oh, and I should probably warn you," he began as they made their way toward the main building, now at a much more leisurely pace. "I've got a few friends who will be joining me here shortly. They're not much like Lord Etsuya, either."

That had Ohiro shaking his head, and Noniki was laughing as they started up the steps.

CHAPTER NINE

"Ash and bone!" Ratal muttered. "We're staying here?"

Seikoku couldn't help but agree with him. When she'd heard the emperor promise Noniki a former noble's estate she had pictured a grand house, like the mayor's back in Ginzai. She should have known better, perhaps, given the imperial compound, but that was practically a small city unto itself and most of the houses she'd seen so far in Awaihinshi had not been all that much more impressive than the finer homes she'd seen—and burgled— back home.

This, though—this was like nothing she'd ever seen before.

The walls around it had been so high and forbidding she'd felt they were entering a fortress. But now that they'd passed through the double gates it felt like they were in some sort of private haven instead.

Who had an entire lake behind their house? Or was that in front of it? And the courtyard, with its thundercloud pattern to match the gates—it was as large as most towns' central squares. Had this really been all for one family? Who could possibly need so much space? Or had that family been town-sized as well?

"Noniki!" Kanai called out, and Seikoku pulled from her thoughts to see the new Rojiri approaching, a huge grin on his face. As always, seeing him brightened her mood, and she found herself smiling in return.

"Welcome, all!" he called, reaching them. Kanai hugged him—the potter was always quick with the affectionate embrace, and so genuine about it that even the most standoffish or private in their little group could not take offense—and then Minawa did, so it seemed only right that Seikoku do so as well. She enjoyed the warmth emanating from him, the solid strength of his body, and his scent, which smelled faintly of sandalwood and pine and a cool breeze. Then she got embarrassed—had she been sniffing him?—and disengaged, stepping away and eyeing him awkwardly. Ugh, what was going on with her?

"This place is amazing," she said to cover any strangeness. "And huge!"

"I know!" he agreed, and it was as if all the seriousness he'd surrounded himself with of late, all the responsibility and worry, had washed away for the moment, leaving the enthusiastic boy she'd first met in a graveyard. "Did you see the lake?" He slapped himself in the head. "Of course you saw it, how could you miss it? Who has a private lake in front of their house?"

That made her laugh. "I guess...we do?"

"Yes!" Noniki grabbed her hands and spun around in a circle with her. "We do!" When they slowed to a stop again he was still grinning at her, and she felt her cheeks flush. *Stop it!* She told herself sternly. *He's your friend. Your best friend. Leave it at that. It's easier. Safer.*

But that was hard to do when he was looking at her like that, with his eyes so bright.

Minawa came to her rescue. "Where should we put everything?" the old woman asked. She had a bundle on her shoulder, and her husband, Sukame, was weighed down with two more. Most of the others were similarly laden—only a few of them, along with Sei-koku, Kanai, and Noniki himself, had started their long journey with little more than a small bag and the clothes on their backs. Isoro had an entire herbalist's shop on wheels stored carefully and neatly inside her sturdily constructed little wagon!

"Oh, good question." Noniki paused only a second before turning toward the house. "Ohiro!"

In response to his call, an old, suntanned man came trotting up, his skin the hue of well-polished teak, his hair heavily streaked with gray but still thick, his face lined but his eyes clear. "Sir!" The man replied, bowing, then turned to face the rest of them, his jaw dropping as he took in their numbers and their many burdens.

"This is Ohiro," Noniki explained. "He's the estate's gardener, and the only person who remained behind when it was vacated." He smiled and clapped the old man on the shoulder. "He's agreed to stay and help us take care of the place. He can help you get settled in."

"What about you?" Otokai asked, idly flicking his horsewhip against his side.

"Unfortunately, I have to get back to Aihiri." Noniki made a face. "The emperor wants to discuss some things with Kagiri and me. But I should be back in time for dinner." He smiled. "There's plenty of food in the pantry—Ohiro can show you. Back in a bit!" He waved and started off toward the gates.

"Noniki!" Seikoku hurried after him. "Wait!"

He slowed to a stop to let her catch up. "What's up? Is everything okay?"

"Oh." She twisted her hands together. "Yes, it's fine. Of course. No, it's great. It's just"—she took a deep breath. "What should we do with all this?" She waved at the house—or was it houses? She couldn't be sure—and the grounds.

This time his smile was smaller, quieter, sweeter—and meant just for her. "You'll figure it out," he said, and gave her a quick hug. "I trust you." He was gone through the gates before she'd recovered her senses.

"But—" There was no point, since he was already out of view, so Seikoku just sighed and returned to where the rest of their friends waited.

"What did he say?" Amon asked. "What's the plan? Where should we go?"

That, Seikoku thought, was a very good question. She looked at everyone, watching her and waiting for her to direct them, and pushed aside the doubts that had bubbled up again. Time for that later. For now— "Let's set everything over there," she stated, pointing at the broad platform leading from the courtyard to the steps up to the main house or center of the house or whatever it was. "Then let's check out this pantry and eat something. After that we'll tour the place and figure out what's what."

Everyone nodded, including Ohiro. "I can show you the way to the pantry," he promised, and added a wink. "I don't know my way around most of the interior rooms, but that one I do!"

Seikoku fell into step beside the man as they crossed the courtyard, Minawa next to her. "How long have you been here?" she asked, and he shrugged.

"Since I was a boy. More than sixty years."

"And you're the gardener? Do you use aishone in your work?" That was from Sanedi, and there was a collective hush from everyone as they waited on his answer.

"Not so much," he admitted to a sigh of relief all around. "My father left me his when he passed, of course, but I'd already learned from watching him and helping him and then taking over for him." He shook his head. "My daughter, she wasn't interested in plants, never was. She wanted to be a seamstress, sew fancy robes for fine folks. So when she was old enough, I sold all the aishone I had to get her into a sewing school with a few bones of her own." He smiled. "Haven't really felt the lack, myself. Though I guess that's not something to be said around most."

"It is with us," Seikoku assured him. "None of us use aishone. We don't believe in relying on the past—we'd rather create our own future." She could see why Noniki had asked the old man to stay. He'll fit in just fine, she decided.

She hoped the same would be true for the rest of them.

"Seikoku?" She glanced up to find Isoro standing at the foot of the little bridge she sat upon. The young herbalist had a hand upon the railing. "May I join you?"

"Of course." As the only two young women in their group, Seikoku had not been terribly surprised that the herbalist had started seeking her out for company from time to time. Especially after her mother had died, one of several who'd fallen victim to a saboteur and spy named Yori. "Is everything all right?"

Isoro smiled. "I was about to ask you the same thing."

"Everything—" Seikoku started to say "is fine," but stopped. These are your friends, she reminded herself. You don't have to lie to them. "I don't know," she admitted at last, staring out at the water—she'd stuck her legs between two of the supports and had her arms up on the railing, her chin resting on it as well as she stared out at the lake. It was peaceful here, and the air was sweet with the fragrance of the flowers all around but kept from being cloying by the presence of the water. "I just—I don't know what I'm doing."

"I think you're doing a very good job," her friend told her. "Everyone is settling in." They'd discovered from walking around that there were in fact six distinct buildings, though they were all connected by covered walkways which in some spots had been segmented into rooms as well. The big central building, while large enough to accommodate all of them if they slept as close together as they had in the old former granary, had only two real rooms to it past a large central space that would work nicely as a communal dining hall, and Seikoku had decided that there was no reason to all squeeze in together when they had so much space, so she had designated that as Noniki's and his brother's. It was flanked by two other buildings, both pavilion-like and only slightly smaller, with a third behind it, and she had assigned a third of their group to each of these. She and Isoro were in the same one, along the east side, along with Kuma and the other unmarried women. Ratal, Amon, Otokai, and the other unmarried men were in the building to the west, while Sukame and Minawa, Junko and Eiji, and the other married couples had the building to the north. It had seemed the fairest and easiest way to organize everyone.

"Thank you," Seikoku said. "But that's not exactly what I meant." She tilted her head, resting her cheek on the smooth wood, and studied her friend. "I don't know what I am doing. As in, I don't know what to do with myself." She pointed at Isoro. "You're an herbalist, like your mother was. You're planning to sell your wares and your services, yes?"

Her companion dipped her head in agreement. "I am." A small furrow wrinkled her brow. "Is that all right?"

"Of course it is! What I mean is, you know what you're doing. You know who you are. So does almost everybody else—Otokai's a horse-trader, Ratal's a fisherman, Kanai's a potter, and so on. But who am I?" She twisted her head to tap her forehead against the railing instead. "I was a thief, and a good one. But I don't want to do that anymore! New life and all that." She sighed. "But what else am I good for? What else can I do? Who am I, without all that?"

Isoro didn't reply right away. Then Seikoku was startled by the young woman's hand on her arm, for the herbalist was normally very reserved about contact with others. "I do not know what you will do," she said slowly. "But I do know who you *are*. You are a good person. A strong person. It's something I've always admired about you." She smiled. "I think whatever you do wind up doing, you will be good at it." She shrugged. "It may just take you some time to figure out what that may be."

Seikoku smiled. "Thanks." It might not be much of an answer, but she hadn't expected anyone else to provide that for her anyway. And knowing she had Isoro's support was comforting.

Approaching footsteps made her glance past her friend, in time to see Ratal and Otokai approach. The two men were arguing about something, and Seikoku sighed, hauling herself to her feet. "Something wrong?" she asked as the pair stomped onto the bridge, though Ratal paused and reddened when he saw Isoro there. He was utterly enamored of the quiet little herbalist, and Seikoku thought those feelings might not be entirely unrequited, though with Isoro it was difficult to be sure.

But the fisherman's ire overcame his infatuation, at least for the moment. "He took my spot!" he complained, gesturing at the horse-trader, who shook his head, a smirk upon his face. "I'd picked out my spot and went to get my bedding from the courtyard, but when I got back, he had his stuff laid out there instead!"

Otokai shrugged. "There was nothing there to mark it as claimed," he pointed out in a mild, reasonable tone. "So I set my things there."

"Well, now you know I did claim it, so you should move them," Ratal argued.

"But I'm already there," was the response. "And I like it. Since my stuff was there first, that makes it mine." He crossed his arms over his chest, the horsewhip trailing from his hand.

Seikoku glanced at Isoro, who rolled her eyes. "Let's go take a look and see what we can do," she suggested, leading both men back toward the west pavilion.

It looked like her quest to find herself would have to wait.

CHAPTER TEN

Kishin Narai rose to his feet and bowed as a servant showed Kagiri in. "Welcome," the merchant declared, approaching and grasping him by the upper arms for just a second before releasing him. "We are so glad you agreed to join us."

"Thank you." Kagiri dipped his head in return, and then nodded to the other merchants, all familiar to him. "To be honest, I was surprised by the invitation—not because I thought you would not want me to dine with you, but because I could not imagine why you would need to be so formal about it." He glanced at the long dining hall, which had been set with seats and, before each one, a trio of long ceramic trays, each of which stood upon a decorative stand and each of which was already heavily laden with food. "Now I see that this is far from the meals we shared along the road."

"Oh, very different indeed," Fujiko Oritano agreed cheerfully, stepping up and taking him by the elbow so that she could guide him to his seat, which was just beside Narai's. "This is a chunsin-inori, a proper feast. Have you ever been to one?"

He suspected she already knew the answer to that but saw no mockery in her face nor heard any in her tone, so he answered politely, "I have not, no," as he allowed himself to be settled upon the cushions. "Thank you." He was already glad that he had left his armor back in his study in Aihiri—though he felt almost naked without the mottled green pieces that had become his signature, the kitoro and ponmei he had found in a chest there and appropriated were certainly far more comfortable, especially for sitting cross-legged! Besides which, he felt the silk robe was quite handsome, with its smoky pattern against dusk blue like an approaching storm.

"It is not something we do every day, of course," Jiro Masute offered, taking a seat across from him and one space down. "But we felt the need to celebrate." As always, the severely thin merchant's hair was gorgeous, silky and smooth and flowing like a waterfall below his topknot, and his manner was languid but his eyes were sharp and bright.

"Indeed, there is much to celebrate," Narai agreed, arranging himself with a wince that almost made Kagiri feel guilty for inflicting that wound. Almost. Their host leaned forward to pluck a beautifully enameled cup off the tray before him and raised it in Kagiri's direction. "To our friend Kagiri, the newest of the emperor's Rojiri!"

The others toasted as well, and Kagiri lifted his own glass in return. It proved to contain a very fine tsekuri, sharp and rich and just barely sweet, and he drank it down, lowering the cup and releasing it just in time for a servant to refill it over his shoulder. "Thank you." He studied the leader of the group. "It is not precisely what we'd discussed, but upon meeting the emperor I realized this was a better way."

"A wise decision," Shizu Yokori agreed from Narai's other side. "Far less upheaval and you have the emperor's ear. That gives you a great deal of influence."

"Perhaps," Kagiri replied, eyes on the dishes before him as he tried to decipher exactly what he was seeing—and how best to tackle them appropriately. Each tray appeared to contain a bowl of soup as well as several other dishes and each was elevated above the one before it, so he chose a dish from the closest tray and brought it close, discovering that it appeared to be some sort of baked eggplant. He sampled it with the chopsticks that had been laid across the soup bowl, and found it to be simple but tasty, lightly salted and very fresh. "I mean, yes, I suppose I do."

"This Saisaihyu, for example," Narai stated, adding pickled ginger and pickled radish from a side dish to his first bowl of soup and then sipping at it. "That was a clever notion. Yours?"

"No, it was the emperor's, in fact," Kagiri answered, going for the soup himself. It was uridon and fried tofu in an adai broth, good and hearty, and he added raijo and atuma-yio as well. "But I think it's a good one. He wishes to make people see how they are too dependent upon aishone, and to help them learn to do without." Something occurred to him, and he tilted his head to the side, considering the food so handsomely arranged before him.

"Ha, do not worry," Yokori told him, correctly interpreting his look. "Narai's chefs were up before dawn preparing, and so they have not touched aishone since the sun came up and the Saisaihyu officially began."

Kagiri dipped his head in thanks for the answer and smiled. "Of course. I should have known and apologize for doubting." Now that he considered, he could see that his companions' hair and clothing were not quite as perfect as they might have been, though certainly still more precise and elaborate than during their travels together—he gathered that they had been dressed and coiffed before dawn as well, or had made do with their own skill and that of their servants without the benefit of the aishone.

"No offense taken," his host assured him, "And I agree it's an admirable goal. His Imperial Majesty has become more decisive since his return—which coincided with our own, from what I've heard."

"Yes." Kagiri decided to eschew more rice wine for the moment and took up the teacup beside it instead. The tea was jasmine, more floral than he tended to prefer but light and delicate. "He returned the same day, in fact." He smiled, remembering—it had been an extremely busy span of a few hours here in Awaihinshi! Starting with the emperor's return and followed rapidly by the attack, his own arrival, then Noniki's, and then the battle between them and the Silent Change. But all had worked out well in the end.

"And made you his Rojiri before nightfall," Yokori pointed out shrewdly, nibbling at what looked like cold noodles with shrimp and mushrooms. "Fast work."

"He does not waste time," Kagiri agreed. "Once his mind is made up, he acts. But he is not hasty, either—he considers carefully, just quickly." The more he saw of Hibikitsu, the more he liked this smart, serious young emperor, with his passion and his warm laugh. To think, he had meant to kill the man. That would have been a horrible waste.

"So you did not know about the Saisaihyu beforehand?" Oritano asked, dipping her fingers in a basin of water at her side before moving on to another dish.

"Not really, no." Kagiri frowned, studying the short, cheerful woman as she ate contentedly and with her usual gusto. What that what this was all about? "Even if I had, I could not have said anything," he said carefully. "The emperor wished for no one to know his decision until his decree was sent forth. To violate such a decision would be to disobey him, and although he is far kinder than I had expected I do not think he would look favorably upon such a betrayal."

"No, nor should he," Masute agreed, taking a drink of water from the third cup on his own tray. "But these decrees, they must have gone out in batches, yes? There are only so many runners, and there is a great deal of city to cover. It would not have broken any rule or order to have made sure one of those from the first batch reached us, would it?"

Kagiri considered that. "No, it would not," he agreed finally. "But would it have made any difference to have learned an hour or two earlier?"

"It might," Narai replied, sitting back with his teacup in hand. "It depends upon the situation, of course. With something like this? Not so much. But if, for example, the emperor decides to outlaw the sale of certain goods on the grounds that they are being imported from a neighboring land we are no longer on good terms with? Being among the first to know something like that could certainly have a significant effect."

"Besides which," Yokori cut in, "there is the appearance of the thing. If we are among the first to hear any official news, it becomes clear that we are favored. And that will make other merchants, craftsmen, and traders be more inclined to work with us, and to offer us beneficial terms in any agreement with them."

"I can see where that would be helpful," Kagiri admitted. Having now sampled everything on the first tray he moved to the second and was pleased to discover that the first dish there was rice balls and the second seared tuna with black pepper, soy sauce, and lemon. Glancing around at these men and women, he thought about what they were asking of him—and what they had done both for him and to him since he'd first met them back in Ginzai.

True, they had thrown him into the Tawasiri and had nearly killed him when he'd emerged seemingly empty-handed. But he had accepted their gold in exchange for promising to enter that haunted tower, and had balked upon seeing it, so though he did not approve of their methods he could not entirely argue with their wanting some recompense for their coin and their effort. And they had tried to poison him but that had only been after he had taken control, and at the time the Gensaiba had been influencing his actions and making him far more demanding and overbearing than he would have been otherwise. They had supported him the entire time, and since their return to the city as well, so perhaps he could allow some leeway on account of that, too.

"Very well," he stated finally. "Whenever we send out any official word, I will make sure you hear of it among the very first."

"Thank you," Narai told him. "That is very kind of you. I hope you understand that we do not wish to abuse our connection—but we would be foolish not to benefit from it, either, as long as we are not behaving improperly."

"We are merchants, after all," Masute agreed with a smile. "If we're not looking to make money somehow, something must be wrong!" He giggled at his own joke, and the others joined in, even Kagiri. It was true, after all. He could hardly expect a bird to change its tune or a cat to change its stripes!

"Now," Oritano said around a mouthful of the eggplant, "I hear the emperor gave you an estate of your own! Is that true? Are we neighbors now?"

"Yes and no," Kagiri answered. "He offered me one, but I didn't feel right about accepting it—I've only been in the city a few days and I don't feel I've accomplished much yet." He smiled, remembering the meeting. "But Noniki accepted for both of us, so I'll be staying with him." He had yet to see the estate, actually—he knew

Noniki and Seikoku had headed over there, but he'd remained behind in Aihiri, trying to make sense of the army reports he'd found piled in a cabinet behind his desk, and then had come straight here. He supposed he'd have to find the estate after this meal and hope someone had figured out where he was going to sleep. But probably Seikoku had. She seemed extremely practical, and as bright as she was lovely. He envied his brother a little.

Oritano was asking another question about the new estate, and Kagiri focused on her comment so that he could answer properly. The other merchants chimed in as well, and soon they were discussing various homes they had or had seen, features they'd liked or disliked, and recent innovations in some of the more forward-thinking dwellings here in the city. That took the focus off Kagiri and he found he was able to enjoy the rest of the meal—and there was a great deal of it, all excellently prepared—and the company. In fact, he could not remember the last time he had felt so comfortable with the merchants. When they'd first met, he'd been a little in awe of them, with their fine clothes and their money but even more with their confidence and the way they issued orders and expected immediate compliance. After becoming Gensaiba he had taken control, turning them into his subordinates instead of the other way round. But here, at least for tonight, it felt almost like they were equals—and friends.

It was a good, pleasant feeling. Noniki had Seikoku but also the other people who had followed him here, like their former customer from the tavern, Jitu Kanai—Kagiri had met most of them briefly the other day but didn't know them well enough yet to consider them acquaintances of his as well as his brother's. He felt as if he was beginning to build a connection with Misataki Shizumi, but it was very new and he was being careful not to presume too much. Same with Maniko Kohori, and even with the emperor himself. He'd been closest, in a way, with Joshi and Gento and the rest of the merchants' guards, and with people like Eisen and Ryoji who'd joined them on their way back to the city, but he hadn't seen any of them since arriving here. Kagiri reminded himself to ask after those people and everyone else they'd brought with them, and to make sure they had all found places here somewhere. They had chosen to follow him here, so he was responsible for them.

But he knew it was not Narai's favorite subject—most of those people had left their homes with no money and few possessions, and it had fallen to the merchants to make sure they were all properly fed, at Kagiri's insistence. If it turned out that they were still living off the merchants' generosity, he thought Narai would not be happy to be reminded of that fact, even if Kagiri could now offer to take those people back to his new estate with him.

Which is why he resolved to wait until after dinner to ask. No sense letting any of this excellent food go to waste, nor in diminishing his appetite or dimming his enjoyment of this feast!

He would absolutely remember to ask, though.

Right after dessert.

CHAPTER ELEVEN

Hajime glanced up as the bell above the door jangled. "Welcome!" he called out, but his focus remained upon the tray of sweets he had just set atop the counter, and from which he was now carefully cutting two pieces. The Ujiro were delicate and he prided himself upon each piece having clean, straight lines and sharp edges, and upon not damaging the rest of the sheet of the steamed cake. And all without aishone—for who could afford to waste them on something most would consider as minor as cutting a piece of dessert?—which he was especially glad of now, with the emperor's new edict in place.

Once he'd made the proper cuts he took a flat pane of frosted glass, set it over the rest of the tray, and—with a wink at his customer, a girl named Chiya and her mother who stopped in once a week—flipped the entire thing over, to the girl's thrilled gasp. The board held the rest of the cake in place and the two pieces he'd just sliced free dropped neatly onto the counter, directly in the center of the sheet of rice paper he'd laid there. A quick twist of his wrists and the tray was upright again, whereupon he set it down and folded the paper over the two pieces, fashioning it into a perfect origami swan.

Chiya clapped her hands in delight and her mother smiled at Hajime, as much in thanks for his entertaining the girl as for the desserts themselves. Not that she ever refused to get a piece for herself, of course.

"Thank you, as always," the woman told him, handing over a pair of silver coins as he passed the swan to Chiya, who beamed up at him. "We'll see you next week, I'm sure."

"Thank you, and enjoy," Hajime told her, bowing and winking

at Chiya again, which caused her to burst into giggles. "Have a good week!"

Once they'd exited the shop, he turned his attention to the newcomer, a sturdy woman with pale eyes and a strange mark on her cheek. "Sorry to keep you waiting," he told her, eyeing her helmet and cuirass. "I'm not in some sort of trouble, am I?"

She smiled at the joke. "Only if your wares do not taste as good as they look and smell." Her smile broadened. "I'm Chiyu Akaii."

"An honor to have you in my shop, Chuisu Chiyu," he told her, correctly reading the rank marks on her maikiro. "What's your favorite? I have all kinds." He gestured toward the counter, where most of his desserts were displayed. "Ujiro? Or perhaps you're more a fan of nigasi?" He indicated the dry sweets, which he'd shaped as flowers, animals, and even fruits and vegetables. "I have kibango as well, of course." He had the small, sweet dumplings arrayed on skewers, many in the traditional colors of green, white, and pink but some in wilder hues as well.

"Very nice," the aiashe commented, admiring the items, and Hajime beamed with pride. "Yes, I believe I'll take a kibango for now—that one there." The one she'd indicated was alternating black and yellow like a bumblebee, and Hajime retrieved one of the skewers and passed it over to her, wrapped in a bit of rice paper. She handed him a silver in return, and bit into the first dumpling with a quick flash of what looked to be unusually sharp teeth.

He watched as she devoured the treat and accepted the used stick back from her, where he deposited it in a small bin he kept for just that purpose. Many of his customers did not manage to exit the shop before their appetites got the better of them! He took that as high praise, though, and a welcome advertisement for the quality and lure of his wares, so he did not mind at all.

"That was excellent," the woman commented afterward. "Your reputation is well deserved." She glanced around the place. "It's a very nice space, too,' she observed. "You own or rent?"

"Oh, it's all mine," Hajime replied, look around as well. "The whole building—it's not big but it suits my needs nicely, and I don't have far to go to get to work each morning!"

When he'd bought the place, three years before, it had been a tailor's, crowded with bolts of silk and cotton and rolls of thread and ribbon and edging. There had been a front room for customers to examine both raw materials and finished garments, a fitting room where they could try on items, a small raised area with mirrors on three sides so they could examine themselves in the garment and where the tailor could make adjustments, and a back room where he could do his work.

The apartment upstairs was the same size and held only a small kitchen area, an even smaller sleeping alcove, and a moderate sitting room. But it was clean and private, the high ceilings and wide windows made it bright and airy, and it had its own small washroom. For Hajime, since he lived alone, it was perfect.

And the downstairs, once he had ripped everything out and transformed it into just the showroom in front and the kitchen in back, was perfect as well. He had painted the walls with a bright, cheerful image of dolphins cavorting in the waves, all greens and blues, and it was cool and comforting and set off the paler sweets nicely. There were shelves interspersed along the walls, holding both dried sweets and baskets and boxes that could be used for giving them as gifts, and of course the whole was dominated by the long counter with its glass front and top.

"Yes, I wouldn't change a thing," he said, looking about with some satisfaction. Going from a street cart to a shop had been a massive risk and had taken all the money he'd saved up for all those years, but it had definitely been worth it, and he'd never been happier.

"I can see why," the chuisu agreed. "You know, I believe I'll get one more kabingo, to go." She handed him another coin. "And I think I can safely say you'll see me again soon."

"Glad to hear it!" Hajime replied, tucking the silver away and reaching for the tray. "I'm always happy to gain a new regular customer!"

The sun was just beginning to set, its colors streaking the sky, when Hajime locked the front door and turned the little sign there to the side that said "Closed—see you tomorrow!" It had been a good day, filled with sales and happy chatter and smiles, and he was tired but pleased as he doused the lanterns and headed toward the back, toting the iron box that contained the day's sales. He needed to make another tray of the matcha ujiro—as always, that was one of his most popular items and tended to sell out fast— and work on a mold someone had commissioned for some nigasi shaped like a dolphin for their son's birthday. Then he could head upstairs, have some dinner, and relax.

He prepared the ujiro, setting the mixture in the usual square mold and placing that within the sehiro atop a pot of boiling water, and was just reaching for the mold when he heard a noise up front. "Hello?" he called, for it had sounded like someone try- ing the front door. "I'm sorry, I've closed up for the night! Come by tomorrow!" Then he went back to studying the mold. There was something slightly off about the profile, but he was having a hard time telling exactly what that was.

Another noise broke his concentration, and he frowned. Was whoever it was that desperate for one last sweet before bed? Set- ting the mold down, Hajime rose to his feet and stepped through the curtain separating kitchen from showroom. "Hello? Look, I'm sorry but I already told you—"

But there wasn't anyone standing outside the shop front. Night had fallen properly now, and the streets beyond were almost com- pletely empty—Bejinuri was mostly craftsfolk and artisans, and though many would still be working now they tended to close up shop to the public at dusk, just as he did. It made for a quiet neigh- borhood at nice, which was nice.

Just to be safe, Hajime checked the front door, but it was still closed securely. All right, then. Perhaps it had just been the wind rattling it. Or maybe something had blown up against it, a stick or some such. That could have been it. He'd check out front in the morning—he always did when he first opened for the day, wiping down the windows and sweeping away any litter that had accumulated there. No one wanted to get sweets from a dirty shop!

Chuckling at the thought of a sweets shop covered in litter and dirty handprints, he stepped back through the curtain—and froze as an arm locked around his neck. In the dark it seemed as if the restraining limb were made of darkness itself, shadows trailing off it like wisps of smoke curling up from a fire, but Hajime was more concerned with the iron strength of the arm, and with the sharp line of pain just above it that told him there was a knife held in his assailant's opposing hand.

It seemed he had heard someone after all.

"The money is in that box, there," he said, careful not to move his head but nudging the lockbox with his foot instead. "The key is here, around my neck. Just lift the cord over. Take it, I won't shout or try to fight." It was not the first time he'd been robbed, both on the street and since settling in here, and he'd learned that it was not worth it to struggle. Let them take the money. He could always make more.

He was surprised at the dry chuckle that sounded in his ear. It had a thin rasp to it, almost like a snake scraping across the floor. "I appreciate that, noble Hajime," his unseen attacker said, the words emerging as a cold, thin whisper that sent a shiver down his spine. "Unfortunately for you, what I require is a good deal more than the day's receipts."

The sharp crease along his throat intensified, burning enough to make him gasp and choke, and as his vision began to fade around the edges, the black closing in and his sight dwindling along with his life, Hajime realized that he would never get to finish that mold.

His last thought was a hope that his killer would remember to remove the ujiro from the stove before it burned.

The assassin straightened from the dessert-maker's corpse, which had already begun to blacken and shrivel, its salient features burned away. The eyes stared up from his palm, blank but still gleaming, not yet dulled. That was good. The quicker the transfer, the more he would retain.

A quick, convulsive motion brought hand to mouth and then, with a pair of strong gulps, the eyes vanished within, sliding past tongue and down throat. The assassin muttered under his breath and then began to change as the eyes gave up their secrets, the identity of their original owner bleeding out like dye tossed into a clear pool.

He writhed and jerked, unable to remain still as his body reshaped itself, shortening and widening, skin lightening, hair retaining a dark hue but gaining a silky sheen. The eyes came last as always, the shadows withdrawing from them reluctantly and leaving milky whites around a deep, warm brown.

"Hajime" studied himself in the reflective bottom of a wide pan and nodded. Yes, this was good. He had admired the dessert-maker's setup here, and it would give him a useful base from which to live and plan. He could travel the rings of the city easily, since the man often filled custom orders for people up above, and could gather information about current events from all the customers who entered his shop. And he did not have to share the space with anyone, so there was little risk of anyone seeing through his ruse.

With a smile, he lifted the sehiro's lid, checking the ujiro within. Another minute or two before it could be safely removed and allowed to cool. Then he picked up the mold and examined it closely.

Yes, the dolphin's nose was too wide and a touch too short. Picking up the short-bladed carving knife the original Hajime had set aside, he adjusted the carving with a quick flick.

Ah, yes, now it was perfect.

CHAPTER TWELVE

Saisaihyu, Day Two

Ibaru finally tugged his sleeve free of his brother's grasp when they at last came to a halt. "Was that truly necessary?" he demanded, shaking his arm to restore the circulation—their pace had been so rapid he had begun to lose feeling in the limb, and his shoulder ached from being yanked on so persistently.

"Sorry." At least Iraku had the decency to look chastened, if only for an instant. "But look!" Then he gestured eagerly across the street. "See?"

"What am I seeing, exactly?" Ibaru glanced in that direction but saw nothing out of the ordinary. Just a row of shops, with people walking to and fro before them. Still Iraku had been so excited, moreso than he had about almost anything in a very long time, so he tried not to be too harsh in his criticism.

Fortunately, his little brother had always been good at shaking off such things, though typically that was because his hatred for all around was so intense as to be nearly impenetrable. Not toward Ibaru, however. They were all each other had, and had been for most of their lives. There was no way they could ever truly stay mad at one another.

"There!" Iraku insisted, pointing again. "That shop! The one with the red door!"

Ibaru frowned and studied the edifice in question. "What about it?" Then his eye caught the understated plaque beside the door and widened upon reading the letters carved there. "Raku, are you joking?"

But his little brother had never been very good at jokes, nor was he laughing now. "Listen, Baru, it's perfect! It's an old man, he's there all alone, and he has the whole building! I've seen the lights downstairs go out and the ones upstairs turn on after he closes up for the night!"

"So you want to, what, rob him?" Ibaru rubbed his face with one hand. "I doubt he'll have much." This neighborhood—Bejinuri, it was called, with its walls the color of the red wisteria that grew along the gates—was mostly craftsmen, from what he'd been able to tell so far. Not as poor as the district below, Mazihini, where the laborers lived, but not all that much finer. "Why don't we go up a bit higher?" he suggested now, though gently so as not to hurt his sibling's feelings. "Richer pickings at one of those great big estates." Though of course those places would also have house warriors guarding the grounds and buildings and residents, which Iraku knew as well as he did.

"Well, what about a merchant's home?" he suggested next. "We could find one that wasn't too fancy and try our luck there." Truth be told, he was not all that enamored of the idea of breaking into someone's house—a lot harder to run away if things went horribly wrong. Better to continue stealing on the streets. It was surprising how simple that was when you could cause a purse's strings to crumble at your touch!

Iraku was already shaking his head. "I'm not talking about robbing it!" he insisted, for once remembering to keep his voice down—which was good, as a pair of soldiers strolled past, spears in one hand, the other resting on the hilts of their swords. Best not to draw their attention! "Look, what was it you said last night? When we were back in our room?"

He sighed as he recalled the conversation. "I said we could not stay here forever," he replied. Which was true. They had been able to find someone to rent them a room, using the money they'd stolen from their first real victim here in the city. And it was not a bad place, the bed big enough for them both and more comfortable than any they'd slept on since they were little, the roof solid, the floor dry and clean. But it was not theirs, and the owners slept just on the other side of the short hall. They could hardly sneak in and out, or plot their revenge, in a space like that!

Now he considered Iraku's find in a new light. "He's all alone there, and it's home as well as shop?" he asked, scratching his nose.

"Yes!" His brother was bouncing on his feet, his eyes alive, a grin stretching his narrow cheeks. "It's good, right?"

Ibaru nodded, patting him on the shoulder. "It's good." He glanced up, gauging the time of day. The sun still shone high overhead, not directly above but still lofty enough to not be obscured by the walls of the upper tiers, much less the horizon beyond. "We should wait," he concluded after a moment. "Until just before dusk. Wait until he's almost ready to close up shop."

Beside him, Iraku grinned wider. "Okay, sure. But then—we strike!"

"Correct," Ibaru said, his eyes on that red door but his thoughts back in another shop, a long time ago. "Then we strike."

A few hours later, they returned to the spot. It was growing dark now, the sun hidden by the city's heights, only gauzy tracers of its light still tingeing the farthest reaches of the sky, the rest already beginning to turn dark and cool. The streets were noticeably emptier, and most of the people still about were moving quickly, hurrying home for their evening meal. The brothers watched the red door for a time, but it did not budge. Finally Ibaru stepped out onto the street and crossed it quickly but not hastily, his brother right at his side.

A small bell jingled as they pushed the door open and stepped inside. "Hello?" a voice called from the back. "I'll be right with you!" It was tremulous, that voice, quavery with age, and matched the man who appeared a moment later, emerging from behind a screen. He might once have been taller than the brothers but age had bent him like a tree bowed down by its leaves, his spin curved like a bow, so that he entered the shop's front room with his bald, gleaming scalp leading the way. Only thin wisps of hair remained just above his ears, and a beard of similar transparency wafted from his chin. His brows were surprisingly dark and thick, however, as if they had been plucked whole from a younger man and set there above pale, watery eyes surrounded by a nest of wrinkles.

"How may I help you, young sirs?" the old man asked, wringing his hands together as he bowed, a motion that brought his head nearly to the reed mats covering the floor. "Were you looking to purchase new clothes, perhaps?" He eyed their attire, which was serviceable and moderately clean but little more, just some old workers' clothes they had swiped from a clothesline. "Or were you desiring that those be tailored to better suit you?" For the hantien and hosode did indeed hang loose over their thin frames, and while the torito were intended to be loose these barely stayed on, their waists cinched as tight as the drawstrings would allow.

But Iraku closed on the old man, grabbing his chin and forcing his head up so they could be eye to eye. "We're not here for clothes," he said sharply, giving the man's head a shake. "We're taking over. This place is ours now."

"What?" Those pale eyes grew wider, and the mouth above that thin beard began to tremble. "Please, I'm just a poor ishtaya, what do you want with me?"

Now Ibaru joined his brother, the two of them hemming the old man in on either side. "We don't want anything from you," he stated. "But we're taking your shop. Don't give us any trouble and we'll let you live."

"Let me live?" That struck a nerve, and the aged tailor straightened as best he could, glaring at them. "Go ahead and kill me, why don't you? This shop is all I have! If you toss me out, I'll die on the streets, anyway!"

"It'd serve you right!" Ibaru roared, making the tailor quake even more, like a leaf in a storm. "See how you like it for a change, being thrown out like so much garbage!"

A hand on his arm made him start, and he glanced up to see his brother's face, looking worried. "You all right, Baru?" he asked softly. "You know this isn't him, right?"

With an effort, he got control of himself once more. "I know," he agreed, his voice returning to a more normal volume. "Of course it's not. Thanks." But still it was hard to look at the elderly ishtaya and not see in his place another tailor of a similar age, only shorter and sturdier, with a thick shock of white hair carefully restrained in a neat bun. That shop had looked much like this one, with its long, low table for measuring out and cutting and stitching kitoros and kisonis, and its wall racks for hanging and drying them, and its shelves along the wall filled with roll upon roll of fine silk, a basket nearby holding spools of thread. Yes, he knew places like this all too well.

But the terror in the old man's face—that was something new. And although it might have been a slight improvement over the disgust and disappointment and disdain he had seen in such a face previously, Ibaru found he still did not care for it.

"I am sorry," he said finally, dipping his head in what could have been considered a bow. "I was...you just...well, never mind all that. We will not evict you from your own home." He smiled and clapped the old man on the shoulder. "But we have need of a place to stay, someplace private, where we can plan and discuss. This shop suits our needs. We do not object to your remaining here, and we can even"—he drew a pair of coins from within his sash and placed them in the old man's trembling hand, their weight and smooth edges revealing their golden nature even if the light from the lamps was too dim to elicit their telltale gleam—"repay you for your trouble." He tightened his grip a little, just enough to make the old tailor wince. "But we will require privacy, understand? You will tell no one we are here."

The man nodded. "Yes, of course, fine—whatever you say."

It was a good response, and Ibaru glanced over at his brother with a smile. "Well chosen, little brother." And it was. Iraku had been absolutely right. This shop was perfect for their needs—enough space to accommodate them and several more if need be, in a plain but decent part of town where guards would not be concerned about a pair of brothers roaming about, and far enough away from the imperial compound that even if that stranger did come looking he would never find them. They would leave the sign on the door turned to Closed and the door itself locked except when they needed food or any other supplies, in which case one of them would go and the other stay behind to make certain the old man did not try running to the guards or anything else equally foolish.

Besides which, it was ironic to wind up back in an ishtaya's after all these years. Only now they were the ones in charge, the ones deciding if anyone there was worthy of their notice, much less their concern. He tugged one of the rolls of silk free from its resting place on the shelf and watched as the glossy fabric dulled and faded and unraveled in his grasp, until only a few stray threads were left to drift in the air and waft gently toward the ground. The old man's cry of dismay, quickly stifled, elicited both a pang of sympathy and a burst of vicious glee.

Yes, this would do quite nicely.

CHAPTER THIRTEEN

Yuni tugged at Chimehara's arm, the older woman managing to giggle and not sound ridiculous at it. "Oh, you have to stay and have another drink with us!"

On her other side, Ritaru had latched on as well. "Yes, do stay!" The second cleaning lady lowered her voice conspiratorially. "We lucked into a very fine bottle—Master Kaznori brought it out the other night but got so drunk when he staggered off to bed he left it behind, still half-full!" She giggled as well. "Finders keepers!"

"That is quite the find," Chimehara agreed, smiling at the two older women even as she gently detached herself. "And I wish I could stay and help you finish it, I truly do. But I really must get back. Suda and Ruisoki must be getting worried." She patted the package she held, a present from the household staff, some of the same food the rest would be having for dinner shortly in the main dining hall. "And it's nearly time for their supper."

The mention of the children made her hangers-on slacken their grip slightly. The voice that lashed out from behind finished the job, making them leap back as if they'd been stung.

"Oh, let her go," Madam Ponsoi insisted, stepping up and resting a hand upon Chimehara's shoulder, the long, lacquered fingernails tapping gently but staying soft enough to never snag the fine silk of her robes. "But you really should come and spend at least one evening with us, my dear," the senior housekeeper continued as she guided Chimehara past the other two women and to the merchant house's front gates, angling away from the ponderous main entrance and toward the smaller side door instead. "It's lovely that you take such good care of them, but you must have time for yourself as well." She arched an elegant eyebrow, still a handsome woman despite age and hard work, and her cheeks dimpled in a small, arch smile. "And perhaps some company of a more adult nature, hm?" She had been careful to keep that last comment quiet enough that Yuni and Ritaru had not heard, which was kind of her, given their propensity toward gossip. As it was, Chimehara laughed, but not meanly.

"You may be right," she said, and patted her companion's hand. "Thank you, Madam Ponsoi. You always take such good care of me." There was a great deal of truth in that remark, too. She had befriended the household staff upon first arriving here, as a means to gain information and support, but had since come to regard the two cleaning ladies as actual friends and the head housekeeper as somewhere between a friend and a mentor, very nearly a confidante.

Not that Chimehara would ever confess her real activities to her, of course!

Still, she did regard Madam Ponsoi with genuine warmth, and that must have been evident in her face because the older woman smiled back and patted her cheek once before opening the door and letting her depart. "Another night, then," she said as Chimehara stepped through. "We will hold you to that, you know! But for now, have a good night, and tell those darling children we all send our best."

"I will," Chimehara promised, waving as the door shut again behind her. She adjusted her sorhu about her head and shoulders, then turned and began the short trek back to her home, her footsteps light and a smile on her face but her eyes and ears sharp and her free hand never far from the knife concealed along her thigh, where she could reach it in an instant through a carefully hidden slit in her robes. Though both Motohiri, where House Chohu stood and where she lived, and the neighboring level of Sakiriti, where she was headed to a particular sweets shop she knew to find a special treat for her pupils, were fairly safe, it never hurt to be careful.

She had just passed through the gates separating the two levels, peach giving way to rose—though there were guards stationed there, as always, they never bothered to restrict anyone who seemed to come and go with purpose, besides which Chimehara often shopped in Sakiriti and so had made a point to get to know each of them as well, such that they always smiled and waved and said hello whenever she passed—when she heard a sound somewhere nearby. To most it would have been nothing, a faint scuffing, but to Chimehara there was no mistaking the sound of someone being struck.

Part of her said to simply walk away. It was nothing to do with her, and she had her own life and that of her two young charges to worry about. But the rest of her suggested there could be opportunity here.

And Chimehara never walked away from an opportunity.

Zeroing in on the sound, she found herself moving toward a row of small shops—and, more specifically, the alley that separated two of them. Shadows were shifting there, far more than mere sunset could explain, and she reached the edge of the closer building and peered around it, not at all surprised to see two figures grappling there.

What did surprise her was that one of those two was no higher than her waist.

It was a boy, or at least so she surmised, for in the shadows all she could truly make out was narrow limbs and wild, snarled hair, ragged clothes and bare feet. He was struggling against a man of average height but broad shoulders and enormous hands, one of which had just cuffed the boy so that he staggered back, half spinning around as he slammed hard against the wall behind him.

"Get offa me!" The man shouted. Interesting, Chimehara thought. So he was not the aggressor here. Which made sense, given that the man's clothes, though not of the highest order or the finest cut, were still solid and decent and as clean as one might expect by the end of the day, nor was his topknot out of place or his cheeks unshaven. A respectable man, then, perhaps a merchant or some variety of craftsman—with those hands he could easily be a blacksmith or some other occupation that required strength as much as skill.

Which suggested that the boy had waylaid him. An attempted mugging gone wrong—for the mugger.

Except that the boy was apparently not ready to give up the attempt for lost. He leaped forward, pushing off the wall to gain momentum, and slammed his head into the man's stomach hard enough to double the man over, a loud *oomph* filling the night as the air burst from his lungs. That put the man's face within reach, and the boy clawed at him with both hands, making his victim scream and clutch at his eyes and cheeks, upon which Chimehara could see blood glistening.

"You little savage!" The man released his injured visage with one hand long enough to swat the boy away, again sending the little body reeling. "Leave me be!" He turned toward the mouth of the alley—and toward Chimehara. "Guards!" he shouted, raising his voice. "Guards!"

Up until now, she had been content to watch and see what occurred. But the call for a guard forced Chimehara to make a quick decision. Doing so, she stepped forward, putting herself in the man's way and also blocking off the light from the tall lanterns that ran along the street and were lit every night at dusk.

"Come now," she said soothingly, moving forward with a sway of her hips and a slow, sensual toss of her head. "There's no need for that, is there?"

"What?" The man stared, his eyes—which had not been gouged out, she saw now, only the cheeks below them torn—widening at the sight of her. She knew that he could not make out her features in the dark but that her form would be nicely silhouetted, her curves on display through the silk of her garments. When he smiled, confused but with growing interest, she knew that she had him.

It was a simple matter to move in close enough for him to gape at her perfect features—and continue to stare, eyes wide and rapidly dulling, as her knife took him between the ribs, the point driving deep into his heart and ending his life.

Even as the man slumped Chimehara was pulling her weapon free, pressing the blade between his arm and side so that the cloth there wiped it clean, and then sheathing it out of sight once more. The boy had watched all this, still as stone, and now she glanced his way.

"Back into the corner," she urged. "There, behind those bins. Quick!" He stared at her a second, but the sound of heavy feet approaching fast decided him and he ducked back where she'd indicated, vanishing into the shadows afforded by the baskets set out with refuse.

Just in time, too, as a pair of guards burst around the corner. They skidded to a halt upon seeing Chimehara standing there, a man dead at her feet—and she turned to them, her face streaked with tears.

"Oh, Emperor be praised!" She threw herself at the nearer of the two, a lanky fellow named Tokutomi, careful to avoid his long spear. "It's so horrible!" And she wept into his shoulder, the leather and metal of his maikiro scraping against her cheek.

"What happened?" the other guard, a woman named Akita, asked her. Her voice was not unkind but she was busy scanning the area as she spoke.

"I heard something," Chimehara answered, lifting her head from Tokutomi's shoulder. The guard had wrapped a protective arm around her, and she nestled into it even as she spoke with his partner. "I thought someone needed help. I saw two men fighting. That one called for help and the other—he stabbed him! Then he ran off!" She gestured down the hill, toward Bejinuri. "That way!" She shuddered. "I thought he'd hurt me too, but I ducked back and he didn't see me. I was so scared!" The guard stroked her hair and made soothing noises.

"We'd better see if we can find him," Akita muttered. She studied Chimehara. "Will you be all right getting home? I can send for some of the others to walk you there." Her eyes flicked to the dead man on the ground, blood seeping slowly from the wound at his side, though his robes had served to keep the spill small. "And to see to him."

"No, no, I'll be fine," Chimehara insisted bravely, straightening and brushing at her eyes. "Thank you. I'm sorry I'm such a mess." She had set her package down before entering the fray and now peered about as if unsure what had happened to it.

Akita retrieved it and offered it back to her. "Here you go. Head on home," the guard told her gruffly. "You were lucky he didn't see you." Then she nodded to Tokutomi and the two started off in the direction she'd indicated, their yanoi in hand.

Chimehara waited until she could no longer hear their footsteps before calling softly, "All right, you can come out now."

The boy appeared, quiet as a ghost, and quick as wind he crossed to the body. Crouching down, he began searching for the man's iniro, no doubt hoping for any aishone or coin he might have had on him, clearly unconcerned by the blood or the body's rigor.

"Leave it," Chimehara snapped, and the boy froze, glancing up at her. "I told them it was a fight. If you rob him, they'll know that was a lie. Now come on, we need to go before they send anyone back to collect him."

For a moment, the boy regarded her with big, dark eyes. He seemed to be weighing his options.

"Quickly," she insisted, not harsh but not a question, either. She held out her free hand, the same one that had wielded the knife but moments before. "Come on."

At last he rose to his feet and, crossing the distance between them, took her hand.

"Good." Chimehara led him out of the alley and back toward the gates above and her home. "Now, in future," she said as they walked, her voice soft enough that anyone else out and about would not hear her words, pitched just enough for the two of them alone, "if you are going to attack someone, either make sure they do not see you clearly enough to identify you later or do not leave them alive to do so. Understood?"

The boy frowned, considering, but after a moment he nodded.

"Excellent." She smiled down at him. How fortunate she had not let Yuni and Ritaru sway her into staying! "Now, let us talk about what we shall do next," she told her silent companion—for he had yet to utter a sound, she realized, not a word, not a grunt, nothing but the soft whisper of his breath. That, she felt, was a promising base upon which to build. She began to say more but fell quiet herself as she heard a rhythmic beat upon the cobblestones.

More guards? But no, this sounded solitary. Another resident, on their way home? Perhaps. To be safe, however, she steered her new friend over to one side and stopped to listen and to see. At least with this one she did not have to urge him to be quiet!

A figure appeared up the street, walking quickly and resolutely toward her. Tall, broad-shouldered, head shadowed beneath an irogaso, they moved with purpose, marching right past Chimehara without noticing her or her companion in the shadows. But as they passed the light from the nearest lantern struck their face for just an instant, and Chimehara started. She knew that woman!

For it had indeed been a woman, though a tall, powerfully built one. Not young but clearly still strong, with stern, even handsome features, gray hair, narrow eyes—where did she know her from? Not House Chohu, certainly. No, despite the common straw hat or the rough kaoni she'd had drawn about her, the woman's poise spoke of nobility, and also of martial training. Aha, that was where! In Aihiri, when Chimehara had accompanied Master Eijiri and some of the senior traders to wait upon the emperor. This woman had been there by his side, decked out in the red armor of the Honteno. She was part of his personal guard!

And now she was walking the streets of Sakiriti, clearly in disguise.

Interesting.

"We will be heading home soon, where I'll introduce you to the others and get you fed," Chimehara informed the boy beside her, starting off down the street—but not toward Motohiri. "But first, I need to see where that woman is going." He did not argue— did he even speak, she wondered—and scurried along at her side, two steps to every one of hers as she rushed herself, trying to keep the taller woman in sight. Ash, she walked fast!

In minutes they had crossed the rest of Sakiriti and were nearing the next set of gates. The guards there waved the tall woman through, but Chimehara frowned. She could pass, no question, but the boy beside her looked like a tiny akatai come to life, all rags and bones and hunger. With a sigh she tugged off her sorhu and wrapped the silk shawl around his head and shoulders, tapping him gently on the temple when he stiffened and recoiled from her touch. "Hold still," she warned, adjusting the disguise and then straightening and handing him the bag. "There." Fortunately he was a good deal smaller than her, so what for her draped just past her shoulders hung below his waist. Now, if one did not look too closely, he could be a small girl in a hooded kisoni helping her mother or older sister carry home their dinner.

The guards did not look too closely—Chimehara smiled prettily at them and they preened for her instead—and soon they were into Bejinuri, its pale violet walls looking blood-dark now at night. They had to hurry to gain sight of the woman again, and just in time, for she had stopped at a single-story building and, as they watched, she slid aside one of the pair of wide front doors and ducked through the opening thus created. The sign above the entrance read "Yue Judei." "Good times." Interesting. A brothel? But no, judging from the size and shape of the place, and the warm light she'd seen through the open door, as well as the burst of voices and laughter from within, Chimehara guessed it to be a different sort of establishment altogether. A zaihaya.

But what was one of the emperor's own guards doing slumming it like that, dressing in commoner's clothes and traipsing most of the way down the city, just to go drinking?

Intriguing indeed.

Chimehara smiled down at her companion, who peered back up at her. "I'll ponder that more later," she told him, laughing at the complete lack of response or even interest upon his face. "For now, let's head back, introduce you to the others, and have some dinner, yes?" She tapped him on the nose, and this time he did not flinch. Good, he was teachable after all. "My name is Chimehara," she said, dipping into a brief curtsey. "And what shall I call you, my fine little friend?"

He stared up at her, and at first she thought he still would not answer—or perhaps could not. But then, just as they had turned away to begin heading back toward Sakiriti, she heard what could have been merely a gasp upon the wind—but was not.

"Gou."

"Gou. Well, I'm very pleased to meet you, Gou." She laughed as she led the way back up to Motohiri. A third charge—for she no doubt now that she'd convince him to stay with her and the others—and a new mystery, one that could open a path into Aihiri itself.

Yes, this was shaping up to be a lovely evening!

CHAPTER FOURTEEN

Orita Sadachi glared at Amani Denbi, scowling at her peer's immaculate kitoro and kisoni and tidy taikamage. "How is it," she demanded, sinking onto a cushion beside the low table, "that you look flawless, like always, while I look like I slept in my clothes and rolled in a mud puddle?" In truth, the heavyset ex-Rojiri did not look *that* bad, but there was a marked contrast between her slightly wrinkled attire and the smooth silk of her friend's, and Sadachi's hair was a bit mussed as well.

"It's a wonder I even found this robe to wear," she groused, plucking at the fabric, whose darker blue color and abstract circular patterning surrounding her house's hummingbirds might have suited some but on her brought to mind a short, stout bottle bubbling over with newly pressed blueberry wine. "My servants had screwed up all the others—too much heat on one, not enough soap on another, and so on." She scooped up a steamed bun from the handsome ceramic platter gracing the center of the table, and took a prodigious bite, groaning in satisfaction and somehow also in outrage. "Even your food tastes better! My cook nearly burned my house down!"

Denbi settled herself on another cushion, selecting a sliver of sweet rice cake from another platter, and nibbled delicately at it, but even so a small laugh escaped her. "My dear Sadachi," she answered after swallowing both the tiny bite and a sip of tea from the cup near her other hand, "surely you don't mean you're actually participating in all this ridiculousness?"

Sadachi gaped at her hostess, as did Yoshino Narami, though the latter covered her mouth with one dainty hand to hide both that shocked expression and the giggle that escaped it. Domo

Harata did not bother for such subtlety—as the four of them were alone save some of Denbi's servants, he dropped onto a cushion with a loud guffaw.

"Oh, very good, Denbi!" he crowed, slapping his russet-clad knee, his green eyes glittering with glee—and malice. "Why not just defy an imperial edict? Where's the harm in that, eh?"

Their leader smiled again, though the expression was razor-sharp. "It is utter foolishness," she reminded her friends and co-conspirators, snipping off another morsel of cake with neat, sharp white teeth and chewing carefully as the others waited for her to finish, savoring the delicate flavor of rose and jasmine that rose to her nose even as it teased her tongue. "I will have no party to it," she continued finally. "Besides which, why should we? What will happen if we were found to be violating the Saisaihyu?"

"We would be executed!" Nanami whispered, eyes wide, which made her look even younger than usual.

"And if we fail at our intended goal?" Denbi pointed out, sipping her tea, its sharp, almost bitter flavor cutting the cake's sweetness, the steam from her cup curling up before but never obscuring her sharp eyes.

The others nodded. Yes, that was a fair point. When one was intending to overthrow the emperor, a crime of high treason punishable by death, what matter refusing to follow lesser rules?

"You're right," Sadachi exclaimed, shoving the rest of the bun into her mouth and already leaning forward to snatching another. "If we're not accepting his rule anymore, let's not accept it in all things."

"Indeed." Denbi nodded. "Besides which, we will need all our faculties, all our skills, if we are to succeed."

"What is our plan, for that matter?" Harata asked, refusing the sweets and reaching instead for the tsekuri Denbi had set out in a handsome little rough-glazed decanter for just that purpose. "The second day of this ritual is nearly over already, and we still sit here, eating your food and drinking your wine," he hoisted the bottle at that, "while the Echo of Victory remains secure in his imperial compound, surrounded by his many guards." He poured a full measure of the clear, pungent liquid into one of the tiny, glazed cups and tossed it back in a single long swallow, smacking his lips after. "How do we remedy that?"

Denbi frowned, but her eyes were not on her ill-mannered guest any longer. "You are correct," she said softly. "We need a way into Aihiri. But how, now that we have been barred from access?" As Rojiri they had come and gone as they pleased, having the run of the entire compound save only the emperor's private quarters—after all, their own council chamber had been in Aihiri as well, and how else could they advise the emperor whenever he desired if they were not always near at hand? Now, though, although Hibikitsu had magnanimously not stripped their lands or titles, he had removed them from their positions, meaning if they wished to speak with him they would need to petition through the proper channels, like any other noble. In some ways that rankled most of all, that they were now no better than the meanest lord from the most distant corner of Rimbaku, bowing and scraping for the mere chance to glimpse the emperor's hem!

She pounded a fist on the table, startling her colleagues and causing many of the dishes and cups there to jump and rattle about. How indeed would they get into Aihiri without being obvious about their intentions? They could try to fight their way in, of course, but they would be at a severe disadvantage, aishone aside. There was only the one gate in, and that would be heavily guarded, as always—even moreso, during this strange time. They might be able to battle their way through, but at what cost? None of them had large armies, and they had all lost warriors during the previous attempt, men and women they had not yet been able to replace.

No, something more subtle was called for here.

A motion caught her eye, and she glanced up to see Nanami raising her hand. The timid woman gulped when she saw Denbi's gaze fall upon her, but she lifted her chin and spoke, though the words came out as little more than a fluttering in the air, below even her normal whisper. She swallowed and tried again, loud enough that the others were able to strain to hear it: "What about Nagao?"

"Nagao? What about him?" Sadachi demanded. "He's dead, or soon will be! Fat lot of good he can do us!"

But Harata met Denbi's gaze and nodded. "You may have something there, Nanami," he said, stroking his chin. "What do you think, Denbi? Could Nagao be our way in?"

She was considering as well, and now she favored Nanami with a smile and an approving nod. "Very clever, Nanami! Yes, that just might work. We shall have to be careful, of course. It's a delicate line to walk. But I think it might be just the thing."

"What are you all talking about?" Sadachi burst out, scowling from one to the other. "How can Nagao help us? He's all locked up!"

"Yes, he is," Harata replied, openly laughing at her inability to see what he was seeing. "And soon to be executed. But he is still a nobleman of the highest order, at least for the moment. And that entitles him to certain privileges." He grinned. "Such as a visit from some of his closest friends, come to offer him comfort in his hour of need."

"Oh!" The sound was so explosive Nanami let loose a stream of giggles, like a delighted child. But Sadachi ignored her. "We send word that we'd like to pay last respects, of a sort, to dear old Nagao, our friend and colleague of many years..."

"And how could the noble and generous Hibikitsu refuse such a request?" Harata answered. "Yes! So he allows us to enter Aihiri, with a handful of personal guards as befits our rank. Not enough warriors to be any real threat, of course—"

"Unless his have no aishone, and ours do," Sadachi cut him off. "Which they will." She was laughing now as well, picturing a properly trained warrior carving his way through a dozen lesser foes.

"Precisely. We eliminate his Honteno and Honjofu, and then the great and mighty emperor of Rimbaku is at our mercy." Harata smacked his hands together like he was crushing a fly between them.

Denbi was already a step or two ahead, as usual. "This Saisaihyu plays right into our hands," she mused aloud now, rising to her feet and pacing the edge of the terrace, hands behind her back, posture as erect as ever. "The emperor has clearly become unhinged. And who can blame him, after all the horrific events that have occurred recently? Why, he might even have contracted some sort of illness while he was away, contributing to his erratic behavior. We, his loyal Rojiri, arrive to plead with him to stop this madness and let cooler heads prevail. But he has become irrational, nonsensical, almost bestial. He is on a rampage, and we are forced to defend ourselves, afraid for our very lives but also for the safety of our entire nation." She smiled now, turning back to the others, head held high. "We remove him, as one would excise a growth, and now the empire can once again return to normalcy, as it has ever been—with its wise and faithful counselors there to guide it every step of the way."

The others nodded. "We should send word at once," Harata suggested. "We do not know how quickly he will bother to receive our message, much less reply, and this only works during the Saisaihyu."

"Agreed." Denbi tapped a finger against her chin, thinking. "I will handle that part. The rest of you, go home and begin selecting who you would have accompany you. We can each bring no more than ten—beyond that and our true motives will be clear as the sun on a cloudless sky."

"Ten apiece, forty in all, each completely loyal to us, prepared to do what must be done, and armed with the best aishone available?" Sadachi grinned. "It will be more than enough."

"Let us hope so," Nanami whispered, the long strands of hair that hung down around her doll-like face swaying with her motion. "Because if it fails, we will wind up right next to Nagao, awaiting the very same fate."

Having that stated so openly sobered them all, washing away any remaining glee at the thoughts of revenging themselves on the emperor who had so callously dismissed them. It did nothing to dim their resolve, however, and when their quartet separated a few moments later, three of them rising to return to their own estates as evening fell, it was with quiet determination and a clear focus.

For her part, Denbi remained on the terrace, sipping her tea as she organized her thoughts. Then she called for her suzeri kabo to be brought to her and, once she'd received it, she drew forth a piece of fine, clean parchment, pinning it atop the table with several small figurines carved into the stars and moons of her family crest. Next she set out ferume, suzeri, mosi, and kogatano, along with a small dish of water. There was no haste to her motions, no agitation, as she used an eyedropper to add a few drops of water to the inkstone, then ground the inkstick against it, disintegrating the end of the dried cylinder and blending its flakes into the water there.

Then, fully prepared, she swept back her sleeves and, charging the tip of her brush in the ink she had just created, began to write.

CHAPTER FIFTEEN

Saisaihyu, Day Three

Noniki gazed about them as they walked. "I still cannot get over how large this place is," he said, admiring the tall walls they had just passed through, which were the soft, warm pink-gold of a perfect summer peach. "All of Ginzai would fit within a single level, maybe a few times over."

"Definitely a few times over," Seikoku agreed on his left, gauging the width of the street and height of the buildings. "I would never have believed it either, without seeing it." She spun in a tight circle, causing her sleeves and hem to flutter around her like a flight of butterflies, and Noniki smiled to see her so happy, so carefree.

"It's impressive," Kagiri agreed from his other side. "And note the way the gates are staggered. Smart. Very defensible. Plus, from the rooftops of one level you could fire arrows down upon invaders as they made their way through the level below it."

"Stop thinking like a soldier all the time," Noniki teased, cuffing his brother on the shoulder. It was a good thing he'd convinced him to change out of his armor for this little expedition, otherwise he might've hurt himself doing that.

Kagiri smiled and cuffed him back. "Can't help it," he replied. "I guess that's who I am now."

"That's not all you are, though, right?" Seikoku asked. "I mean, I know you've got the Gensaiba within you, but you're still you, too. Aren't you?"

"One way to find out," Noniki declared. There was a man selling skewers of meat and fish and vegetables from a small cart parked along the edge of the street and he hurried over, digging in his iniro for coins as he went. A moment later he was back and brandished three sticks at his brother. "Beef, eel, and shrimp," he declared. "Pick one."

Kagiri made a face as he selected the first option. "Eel? Seriously?"

"See, you're still you!" Noniki told him, laughing. "He hates eel, always has," he explained to Seikoku, offering her the remaining two and shrugging when she chose the eel for herself, leaving him the shrimp, which had been delicately spiced and grilled. "Ever since we were kids and he fell into a whole pile of them. Funniest thing you ever saw—here's Kagiri, usually all serious, and now he looks like he's made of seagrass or like an octopus stole his clothes, long eel bodies wriggling from his shirt sleeves, his pants legs, his collar..."

"Enough!" Kagiri shoved him, but not hard, and he was laughing as he did it. "She doesn't need to hear about that!"

"I don't mind," Seikoku told them, laughing as well as she nibbled her eel. "I'm an only child, so I think it's really nice that you two have stories like that to share."

A man brushed by them just then, grumbling and holding a large bag filled with something. Noniki got the distinctive odor of burnt bread as he passed. Odd.

"I'm glad you suggested this," Seikoku commented. "It's such a lovely day out, and I've been wanting to see more of Awaihinshi."

"Me too," Noniki agreed, beaming at her. They'd been so busy since they'd arrived—had it really been less than a week?—and whenever he'd been out and about before now it had been for a specific purpose, so he felt that he'd only seen very specific parts of the capital city. He really wanted to learn about the rest, and what better way to do that than with his best friend and his brother?

They walked past a small shop just as someone wailed from within. In an instant Kagiri was leaping toward the door, sword already flying from its sheath. Noniki and Seikoku were right behind him.

"What's wrong?" Kagiri demanded, bursting into the shop. From over his shoulder Noniki could see that it was what looked to be an artist's studio, with a skylight currently thrown open to the sun overhead and a low table directly below that holding a long roll of parchment. There was only one woman in the place, and she leaped up from the table now, startled. In her hand was a long, thick brush, its tip a vivid blue.

"What?" She stared at them a second before waving her brush. "Go away! What do you want?"

Seikoku eased past them both, gently pushing Kagiri's sword down with her hand as she went. "Sorry to burst in on you like this," she told the woman. "We heard you cry out and thought something was wrong."

"Something is wrong!" was the retort. "Just look!" And she gestured toward the parchment.

Now Noniki could see that there was a landscape taking shape there, with hills and rivers cleverly depicted by quick strokes that suggested without overstating. The rivers were in blue that matched the ink on her brush. "It looks amazing," he told her.

"Does it? And what about that!" She stabbed down toward one spot, where a river had turned from a delicate line to a wide, messy scrawl. "The whole thing's ruined!" She flung the brush across the room, narrowly missing another scroll that hung against the wall there. "If only I had my aishone, I'd have done it right!"

Noniki tilted his head, studying her. "Would you? Or would your great-uncle or grandfather or whoever learned to paint in the first place?" He waved his hand over the marred painting and the lady gasped as the blue splotch rose up from the paper and drifted lazily across the room like a tiny, vivid cloud, to settle back into the bowl holding the rest of that pigment. Kagiri and Seikoku had already backed out, and he followed them, shutting the door carefully behind him.

"I guess not everyone's as thrilled about the Saisaihyu," Kagiri commented as they resumed their trek. He frowned, eyeing the other people they saw on the street. "Everyone does look a bit harried. And a bit more haphazard."

"They'll get used to it," Noniki insisted. "It's only been a few days."

"True." They continued walking, passing through the rest of this section—Noniki had forgotten its name but knew it was mostly merchants and artists, which explained the painter—until they'd reached the next set of gates. There were guards gathered here, as they'd seen at the other entry points, but in addition to the usual gray of the aiashe he was surprised to see several warriors in black, including a large, scowling woman and a slender, narrow-faced man he was sure he recognized from around Aihiri. What were the Honjofu doing here?

He got the answer to that question as they approached and the warrior in front turned to face them. She was shorter than her companions, and slight, but they clearly deferred to her, automatically falling into a wedge formation behind and around her as she stepped forward. Though she was not smiling, she looked less stern than she had initially as she bowed.

"Rojiri Kagiri," she stated. "Rojiri Noniki. Miss Seikoku. A pleasure to see you again, and outside Aihiri." Behind her Noniki saw one of the guards start and stare at him and Giri, and was torn between a laugh and a sigh.

"Nice to see you again too, Taikoro Misataki," he replied, bowing in return. "But please, no need to stand on ceremony. It's just Noniki."

"And I've already told you to call me Kagiri," his brother added with a small smile. "We hadn't expected to see you here, Shizumi. Hope we're not interrupting."

The use of the Honjofu commander's first name made Noniki throw a sharp glance his brother's way. Since when were these two on such familiar terms? What had he missed?

She took the comment in stride, however, and did smile now. Though not what Noniki would have called pretty, the swordswoman did have an appealing face, he decided. Honest. No nonsense.

"Not at all," she told them. "We were simply out on patrol." She glanced about and then lowered her voice, and now her eyes did light up. "To be honest, I have been cooped up in Aihiri for the past several days and I was going out of my mind. I needed an excuse to get out and stretch my legs."

"Same here," Kagiri assured her with a chuckle. "That's why we decided to take a look around, see the other parts of the city."

He tapped his chin. "Would you care to join us?"

Shizumi stiffened. "*I* am on patrol, sir," she told him primly, and for a second Noniki thought she might actually be offended. But then she grinned. "*You* should join *me!*"

"We'd love to," Seikoku answered for the three of them, nudging Noniki's shoulder until he agreed as well. And so the two of them fell in behind Kagiri and Shizumi, with the other Honjofu bringing up the rear as they passed through the gates and down into the next level.

"What's going on between them, do you think?" Noniki whispered to Seikoku as they walked.

"No idea," she whispered back. "But I like her."

He nodded. No argument there.

"This is Bejinuri," Shizumi told them as they walked, glancing over her shoulder to make sure her words carried to the two of them as well. "It's mostly artists and craftsmen. You were just in Sakiriti, which is merchants and the most successful artists."

"Did you grow up here?" Kagiri asked her.

"No, far from it," she admitted. "I was born in Botetsu. That's out in Yunigiri. I joined the aiashe as soon as I was old enough, then came here when I was selected to join the Honjofu." She studied their surroundings, the clean, wide street and neat buildings lining it, and smiled. "But now it feels like home, as much as any place does." Noniki saw her steal a sidelong glance at her companion. "And what about you? You didn't grow up here, obviously."

Kagiri laughed. "No, definitely not. Niki and I are from a tiny little village down in Bezenkai. It didn't actually have a name. Never needed one." He sighed, and Noniki knew his brother was thinking about their childhood. Which, truth be told, had been a good one. Their mother had taken good care of them, and they'd had the run of the village, along with the handful of other children. Most of their days had been spent swimming and fishing and running the odd chore for this or that neighbor, with the occasional task at home added in.

And look at them now, he thought, peering about them again as they went on their way. Here in Awaihinshi, two of the Emperor's

Rojiri—his only two, at the moment, though that would hopefully change soon—and with their own estate! He glanced up toward the sky and the clouds, wondering if their mother could somehow see what they'd become.

If so, he hoped she'd be proud of them.

They'd passed clear through Bejinuri and then Mazihini, which Noniki and Seikoku already knew because that was where they had first arrived and where they'd been quartered initially while helping with repairs. At that point Shizumi paused. "If we go that way," she explained, gesturing to the north, "we'll wind up reaching the North Gate. Through that you'll find Suranmui. It's a shanty town, basically. Not a place you want to go most of the time—no real streets, no permanent structures, just a jumble of tents and makeshift shacks. Immigrants, mostly, people who show up here without a plan, no real usable skills, and no money." She shook her head. "Most of them never get out of there."

Noniki glanced at his brother and knew from his somber expression that they were thinking the selfsame thing—had things gone differently, that could have been their fate as well. Indeed, they had not been far from it when they'd wound up in Ginzai after leaving home, with only a few coins in their pockets, no aishone, and no skills to speak of, at least not that the towns-folk would care about.

"Is there nothing that can be done for them?" Noniki asked, and Seikoku squeezed his arm.

Shizumi shook her head again. "I wish there were," she said, and she seemed sincere. "But I'm not sure what. You could toss money at them, but what good would that do without them hav-ing proper jobs and proper places to live?" She looked as unhappy about that fact as Noniki felt, and then visibly shook herself. "But that's a problem for another day," she declared. "Because we're going this way instead." She turned to the south and smiled. "And I think you'll like this a whole lot more."

She led them around to the southern gate, which the others had all seen before, as they had all passed through it to enter the city just days before. The guards there saluted as they stood aside, allowing them to exit the city's outermost walls, which shaded from a deep, midnight blue to a pale blue like a mountain stream, onto the wide dock that jutted forward like a straight-lined wooden extension of the street they had just been traversing. Halfway along the dock stood a guardhouse, tall and gleaming with its sides open to allow a view in all directions, and Noniki could just make out the glitter of spearpoints in the sun that told him the post was currently manned. He was astonished, however, to see that the guards were not the only ones out here.

Indeed, the entire length of the dock was crowded with people of all sorts, from those wearing rough worker's clothes to a few in fine silk robes. Many of them had fishing poles propped against the railing, the lines trailing into the water where they were tugged this way and that by the current. Others leaned back against the same railing, facing upward instead of out, eyes closed as they enjoyed the sun upon their faces. Many simply stood around talking or watching those who had not been content to be near the water but instead felt the need to be in it or on it. The water was crowded with people splashing and swimming around the thick wooden columns supporting the dock's length, and out farther there were others rowing small boats. Past even them were more boats, but these were powered not by oars but by sails, their color-ful cloth catching the breeze and filling with wind that carried them along at a rapid pace.

"What is all this?" he breathed, his cheeks stretching into a grin, and Shizumi laughed, seeming more at ease now though he noticed how she still positioned herself with her back against the rail so that she could watch anyone approaching—and how Kagiri automatically did the same.

"It is Dayabei," the Honjofu commander pointed out. "Many of our shops and businesses close, and most children do not have lessons, so on this day each sihu, the dock is made available for all of Awaihinshi to use." She scowled. "It is a strategic nightmare, of course—so many people all crowded along its length at once, no discipline, no order, boats docking and pushing off constantly, no way to keep track of anyone." Then her face relaxed into what was, if not a full smile, at least a look of mild contentment. "But it is also a wonderful time for most people, and a chance for the entire city to enjoy something as one with no divisions of rank or money or power, and that is well worth it."

Noniki nodded—he could certainly appreciate that—but he was distracted by all the sights and sounds, and particularly by the boats. Their little village had not even had a boat—they had been too small to require one, and they had not traded with anyone, nor had anyone ever sought them out—so he had only seen a few in passing before beginning the long trek here. And never had he imagined boats like the little sailboats he saw now! They seemed so delicate, and so agile, like wooden fish that skimmed the water rather than swimming beneath it!

"Those are chayaburi," Shizumi explained, noticing the subject of his attention. "They are primarily used for pleasure, exactly as they are now, though they can also ferry important messages or couriers across the river." She turned toward the east and indicated the town on the Edishu's far side there where it met the Tonawa, really only a handful of small buildings clustered before a large barracks.

"Can anyone use one of these boats," Kagiri wondered beside her, also gazing out upon the water, "or are they strictly the province of the nobility?"

"They are not inexpensive," she admitted, "so you will primarily see them owned by nobles, yes. Though I have seen some groups that have gone in on a chayaburi together and share its use. And there are a few that can be rented for the day, as well." She frowned, turning to follow the direction of his eyes. "Why do you ask?"

Noniki was looking as well and understood at once. A cluster of the little sailboats was traveling as a pack, turning as one, like a cluster of birds might wheel together mid-flight. It was an elegant dance, and though a few of the boats were not handling the shifts and circles as neatly as they might, still it was impressive that they all stayed together so well.

Now that he looked more closely, however, he could see that his initial interpretation had been inaccurate. They were not a pack moving as one—they were a flock following the commands of a leader, for there was one chayaburi that sailed slightly behind the rest, the whole forming an inverted wedge so that this central boat could see and control the actions of all the rest, functioning as the pivot upon which they turned. Two men occupied that controlling vessel, one standing and the other sitting behind. Noniki could see that the one who was standing was wearing a kitoro all in orange and red like a sunset, and from his hair and his stance the man looked to be a lord of some sort.

"That would be Kazutai Katani," Shizumi reported. "He is a shugodiri. I do not know much else about him."

"He seems to enjoy the water a great deal," Kagiri pointed out. "And to handle himself well out there."

Noniki could tell what his brother was thinking and nodded. They did have need of more Rojiri, and also of a Dogenkaishu. And at least from here this lord Kazutai looked young, which might mean he was still open to new ideas. It was certainly an avenue worth pursuing. Noniki grinned.

What a glorious day!

CHAPTER SIXTEEN

Misataki Shizumi stood at ease despite her armor, one hand resting upon her sword scabbard, the other loosely curled around its silk cord-wrapped handle. "Remember," she said loudly, projecting her voice across the sand-filled square and to all the warriors gathered there, most of them with their armor as black as her own, "you have done this many, many times before. This is no different. Do not let your mind get in the way of your body—relax and trust your instincts. Your body knows what to do. If you allow it control, it will do what needs to be done."

She took a deep breath, let it out, took another, and, as she let this one out with a shouted "Hai!", drew her nihono, her other hand tugging the scabbard back so the blade could exit quickly and cleanly, whipping up in a classic first strike before carving a graceful arc and coming to rest before her, that second hand now free to encircle the chahito and add power and precision to her follow-up move.

Before her, the Honjofu—*her* Honjofu, with the handful that remained of Kohori's Honteno clustered in the back—echoed the maneuver, their shouts filling the practice yard and reverberating off the sturdy bamboo walls enclosing it. To Shizumi's experienced eye, there was a notable range of skill displayed among the warriors. Some drew cleanly but not quickly, no doubt worried about remembering each step in the process correctly. Others sacrificed precision for speed, drawing fast but clumsily, their blades rattling in their sheaths, the tips catching the edge and jittering upward in a haphazard swing. Then there were those who managed neither aspect entirely, moving too slowly and clumsily to boot. She sighed but carefully, so as not to let them see.

She had known this would be a long and difficult process.

Sheathing her own sword without a glance, her fingers guiding it unerringly home, she hopped down from the walkway that ran along the walls back into the barracks and that she was using as a makeshift stage. "Continue," she instructed, and before her the rows of warriors took a single large step forward, striking downward as they did. They would hold each pose for a moment before flowing through to the next, which did not give her a great deal of time. It would have to do.

Stepping over to the first person in front—Geniji, of course—Shizumi reached out and gently tapped the other woman's wrist. "Loosen your grip," she said, her voice now back to a more normal volume. "Control without restricting."

Geniji nodded, eyes straight ahead, and her fingers relaxed, allowing the sword more freedom and flexibility. Shizumi nodded and moved on, but in her mind she replayed that instant. Had she felt the other woman flinch at her touch? She could not be sure.

Next was Akino, and his grip was perfect but his arms were taut as if he were straining to hold a live snake at bay. "Relax," Shizumi told him. "Strong but not stiff. You can't move as fast if you're tense." He took a breath and visibly forced himself to unclench, and his arms settled slightly, into a more natural position. "Exactly." That earned her a small smile, though he did not shift his gaze from forward, where his imaginary foe waited.

She moved down the rows, offering tips to each warrior, adjusting their stances, their grips, their swings. Many seemed happy to follow her lead. Some scowled or frowned but still listened. And then there were those who acted as if they had not heard her at all, continuing through the exercises without so much as acknowledging her presence.

One of that third type was Dairamu, and Shizumi wanted to shake the woman after she ignored a second suggestion. She knew the Honjofu could hear her just fine. This was a deliberate snub, and she knew why all too well. Nor had she failed to anticipate such a reaction from some of her warriors—she just had not expected it from one of her own bantao!

A part of Shizumi wanted to ignore it and move on. Another part still wanted to shake Dairamu, to shout in her ear. But the first would simply allow such nascent resentment and distrust to grow, not just in her but throughout the ranks, for she could see the other warriors watching this exchange from the corners of their eyes. And the second would cast her as the villain, the child, the one who lost her control and her temper.

Neither of those would do, so Shizumi chose a third route instead.

Turning away, she marched a few paces toward the walkway. Then she pivoted, placing herself directly in front of Dairamu—and drew her sword.

The other woman's eyes widened at that, but she did not otherwise react. Instead she moved to the next stance in the exercise, an overhand parry designed to catch a downward strike exactly like the ones she had just enacted herself.

But this time her parry caught more than empty air. Shizumi's blade clanged down upon Dairamu's, the loud clash of metal on metal causing many of the warriors to jump and glance over. Dairamu herself started, and her sword wobbled in her hands, nearly banging against the top of her head.

"I told you to grip it more tightly," Shizumi explained, careful to keep her tone friendly, informative, rather than petulant or combative. "If you do not, you will not have the power to block an attack." She withdrew, back to a ready position, and waited. "Continue."

Now Dairamu was glaring, but she could hardly refuse a direct order from her commander so she proceeded to the next block, which was the same but from the opposite side, her hands on her right now instead of her left. And again, Shizumi struck, battering at the Honjofu's blade.

But this time Dairamu's hands were tighter, and her sword wavered but only barely, and stayed well clear of her head.

Shizumi nodded. "Better." She stepped back, sheathing her sword once more, and continued along the row to the next person, Isano, whose form was perfect but who was executing each motion at half speed. The rest of the Honjofu slowly returned to their own exercise, and the drill proceeded with no other interruptions.

After they had gone through the entire drill, Shizumi returned to the walkway to speak once more. "Very good," she told them. "You are already more proficient than you were yesterday, and that was better than the day before that. By the end of the Saisaihyu, you will not even need your aishone." She smiled to show them this was at least partially in jest, and a ripple of quiet, polite laughter carried across the ranks. "Now, those with evening posts proceed to them. The rest, you are at liberty until your next shift."

She hopped down from the platform, intending to catch either Geniji or Dairamu or both, but the two women had turned away almost as one and were already halfway across the practice yard, moving at a fast walk for the far entrance. Shizumi scowled and started after them, but a hand on her shoulder halted her mid-stride. She spun about, rather to shout at whomever had dared, but the words died in her throat when she saw it was Isano.

"Leave them be," the wiry archer warned, his tone making it clear this was meant as advice rather than threat. "Just give them time to process."

"You did not need time," Shizumi retorted, brushing his hand away.

He tilted his head, considering as he always did before speaking, and then smiled. "I already knew, so there was no need." His eyes flicked toward the far gate, which Geniji and Dairamu had already vanished through. "For others, it is more of a surprise."

There was little to say to that. She had wondered in the past whether Isano, whose sharp eyes missed nothing, had known she had no aitachi, that she had been merely faking aishone with ground-up chicken bones. More than once it had seemed he had, but if so that fact had clearly never bothered him. That question must have been visible in her gaze now, because he shrugged.

"You are who you are, same as you were," he told her. "If you are no different, why should I be?"

"Thank you," she said, and meant it. "That means a great deal to me."

He saluted, not a hint of mockery in the gesture, and turned to go, leaving her with her thoughts. If only all of them were as accepting about the revelation of her dark secret! But clearly that was not the case. The question was, what could she do about it?

Kohori might have some idea. Not that the other woman was a Mukanichi, or a commoner, but she was a fellow warrior, a fellow Taikoro, and a fellow woman—surely she had encountered prejudices in the past, especially in terms of taking command of the Honteno. She might be able to offer some suggestions on how Shizumi could win over the rest of her Honjofu.

She hurried around the side of the compound, away from the Honjofu's area and toward the section that held the Honteno, trailing behind the handful of crimson-plated warriors who had attended the training—she had offered to include them along with her own warriors, and their commander had happily accepted on their behalf. As she approached it, she spotted a tall, broad-shouldered figure walking away, and recognized the very object of her search by the gait. But where was she going, and why was she out of armor?

Catching up to the taller woman, Shizumi settled in beside her. "Kohori?"

The head came up, her irogaso casting long shadows across the face but not enough to mask her fully. When she saw who had spoken, though, Maniko Kohori relaxed, her hand leaving the sword she had grasped out of reflex. "Hello, Shizumi. What can I do for you?" If she felt any awkwardness at being spotted standing here in a rough kaoni and irogaso like some common worker, she did not show it.

"I apologize for interrupting you," Shizumi answered, bowing. "Clearly you have other plans. I had hoped you might have time to advise me, however. I find myself dealing with some difficulties and I do not know how to proceed."

Kohori sighed. "I'm sorry," she said. "You know I'm happy to talk with you about whatever, but it's been a long day and I was just headed out." A thought struck her, and she considered Shizumi again. "Would you like to come with me? You'd need to change into something less distinctive, but it's a bit of a walk and we could talk along the way." She smiled. "Besides, this place has excellent tsekuri."

For a moment, Shizumi was tempted. A night out did sound pleasant, and she suspected Kohori would be a fine drinking partner. But in the end she sighed and shook her head.

"Thank you," she told the older Taikoro. "I would be happy to take you up on that offer some other time, if it still stands. But I still have many things to do here before I can sleep, and if I go drinking with you I suspect I will be in no shape to do them properly after."

Kohori laughed. "No, probably not," she agreed. "And the invitation is definitely still open." She rested a hand on Shizumi's shoulder. "We can talk tomorrow, if you like."

"I would appreciate that." Shizumi watched the other woman go and wondered if this would now be her fate as well, having to disguise herself in order to get a simple drink in any kind of peace? She hoped not. Of course, as head of the Honjofu she could still expect to spend at least some of her time traveling about the nation, and on the road she expected that she could shed formalities and drink and eat with her fellow warriors, just as she always had. Time would tell if that were still true.

In the meantime, she still had no idea what do to about her problem—but there was one other person she could ask.

Circling further around the compound, she arrived at the side set aside for the aiashe, the aikaye, and, farther along, the Rojiri. Hopping up onto the walkway there, she strolled past several chambers, offices and meeting rooms and the like, before arriving at the one she sought. Its outer doors were open, fortunately, which confirmed that her target still resided within, seated cross-legged behind a long, low desk with a disorderly stack of scrolls covering its dark-lacquered surface.

Shizumi hesitated only a moment before rapping politely on the open doorframe. When the room's occupant glanced up, she bowed.

"I'm sorry to disturb you," she said, "but I was wondering if you had a moment to talk?"

Kagiri sat back and smiled at her. "Of course. Come right in."

CHAPTER SEVENTEEN

Maniko Kohori let out a sigh of relief as she stepped into the zaihaya, doffing her irogaso and holding it before her in both hands almost like a penitent. Ah, but that was how she sometimes felt upon entering here. As if she were seeking alms, only in this case that was not money but quiet and calm and peace of mind!

Oguro nodded at her as she approached the place's only permanent fixture, the hollow wooden square that served to shelter bar and cookstove both, and upon whose worn counters food could be set out for the servers to deliver. Kohori added a pair of coins to the bowl there, making sure he had registered her motion, and then glanced about for a place to sit. As always, the room was more than half-full, and many of the low tables had not a single empty cushion around them. There were still several spots available toward the back, however, including one at the very rearmost table that faced into the room. Perfect.

She nodded at several of the other regulars as she crossed the room, and each of them smiled and waved and nodded back. That was what she'd liked about this place, right from the first time she'd entered. Zaihayas were local establishments and in some of them you were treated coolly unless you were from that particular neighborhood. No outsiders welcome—tolerated, yes, as long as your money spent, but never encouraged. Yue Judei was not like that, however. Oguro treated everyone with the same slightly distant friendliness and the other patrons were only too happy to greet and include someone new.

Nor had any of them asked much of her beyond the same courtesy. She'd been asked her name, of course, if for no other reason than so the servers could call out when her food was ready. She'd given it as "Kori," which was close enough that she'd glance up upon hearing it but not enough for most to make the connection, and no one had ever pressed her on that, or where exactly in the city she lived, or what her occupation was. People here were happy to listen if you wished to share such details, but they wouldn't press you on it. They were more interested in talking about the weather, local events, food, drink, and other mild and unassuming topics.

One of the servers, a girl named Yuki whose looks might have been marred by her long nose if not for the brightness of her blue eyes, brought her a rough-glazed cup. It was empty, of course, but upon the table sat a short, tapered cylinder of a similar appearance and one of the other people sitting there lifted the bottle and poured tsekuri for her. She nodded her thanks, raising the cup in silent salute, and took a long, slow, appreciative sip. Ah! She hadn't been lying to Shizumi when she'd said that this place had excellent wine.

Thoughts of the younger Taikoro intruded, and Kohori frowned, but quickly erased that expression when she caught Yuki looking anxious. "Some heioki and some eioha to start," Kohori ordered with a smile, and the server nodded, seemingly reassured, and hurried away back toward the cookstove to pass the request to her employer. Meanwhile, making a conscious effort not to think about anything resembling her everyday life, Kohori turned to her companions and concentrated on their conversation, soon finding herself dragged into a discussion over the best type of brush to use for cleaning one's stovetop and how often one should change floor mats.

Several of her new tablemates she had seen here before, one or two of them frequently. A few of the others were new to her, however, including the woman to her immediate right. Though this neighbor had a pale blue sorhu wrapped around much of her face and hair, Kohori got the impression that she was young, and her movements were graceful. She had yet to speak, but a smile was visible even through the folds of her shawl, and that brief glimpse was lovely—and strangely familiar.

After Yuki returned and set down a pair of dishes, one with

the fried octopus balls and the other with the steamed dumplings, Kohori let her curiosity get the better of her. "Excuse me for being so forward," she said to the veiled woman, "but have we met?"

The woman dipped her head, and that enticing smile widened. "We have," she replied, and her voice was stunning, rich and warm and smooth like heated honey, "though I am flattered you remember, for it was extremely brief, and from a distance." She let the shawl fall away from her face, and Kohori was glad she had already swallowed or else she might have choked from surprise and sheer awe.

Her companion was beautiful! Extremely so, distractingly so, with stunningly perfect features and perhaps the loveliest eyes Kohori had ever seen, deep and dark as a midnight well, radiant as the moon. It was the sort of face that could stop a war—or start one—and of course she recognized it right away. This was the girl from the gem merchants, the same one she had teased Hibikitsu for being so smitten with. Though even then she had said that she could hardly fault his taste.

Now, respectful of the unspoken rules of a zaihaya, Kohori merely nodded and raised her cup. "In truth, you are not the sort of woman one forgets." She sipped her wine as the other woman bowed, eyes creasing and lips bowing up into a warm smile of acknowledgement and thanks.

"And what sort of woman is that?" she asked playfully, lifting her own cup in reply. Then she gestured at the plates. "May I?"

"Of course." As with many such establishments, the food here was communal, and included in the entrance fee, as was the wine. The woman—what had been her name? Had she even been introduced?—expertly speared one of the heioki, popping the entire sphere into her mouth without marring her deep red lipstick or scraping her perfect white teeth, and then chomped down with obvious gusto. "I have not seen you here before," Kohori remarked, keeping her tone light and selecting a dumpling herself to show that she was not fixated upon either the question or its awaited answer.

"No, for it is my first time here," the woman agreed, patting at

her lips with a napkin and only drawing attention to their lush-
ness by that motion. "May I be honest with you?" Those eyes studied her closely, an intense look lightened by the crinkling at their
corners.

"Of course."

Now that dangerous gaze turned away, directed downward for
a second but then rising again to spear her once more. "I followed
you."

"What?" Kohori shook her head, not sure she'd heard that
right, and her hand fell reflexively upon her sword. That, at least,
she had not set aside with the rest of her usual attire!

Her companion laughed, and it was as captivating as the rest
of her, light and musical like the ringing of a small, sweet bell.
"What I mean is, the other day I happened to see you walk past.
You will forgive me for saying, but you are...distinctive." Dimples
appeared on either side of that mouth. "I recognized you, despite
your change in attire, and was curious as to the cause. So I followed you." She glanced demurely down again. "I apologize. It was
rude of me to intrude. But when I saw where you had gone, I wondered, and resolved to see what about this particular place had
drawn you to it." Now her smile returned but it was wider, more
general in its approval. "And it is lovely here. I can see why you
chose it. But I have intruded upon your privacy, and I will beg your
forgiveness and be on my way." She made to rise.

"No!" Kohori held out a hand, almost taking the woman by
the arm but stopping just shy of her fingers brushing the silk of
that lady's kitoro. "I mean, please, do not leave on my account.
Truly, I do not mind." She smiled, and the smile she received in
return was like the sun breaking through the clouds, so bright it
warmed her through and through. "I am flattered you would be
so curious about my actions." Had she really just said that? She
cursed herself silently. Small talk and flirtation—and was this
flirting?—had never been her strong suit.

But her charming neighbor just smiled, tilting her head to one
side. "Are you surprised?" she asked softly, slender fingers picking
at the edges of her shawl. "I shouldn't have thought so."

Kohori did not know how to answer that, and saved herself from doing so by gulping down some of her wine, which the lady then kindly refilled. Another plate of food arrived, this time aragei and tukaiono, and she sampled both, as did her new companion. The conversation around them had shifted to talk of a new shop that had just opened nearby, one that sold both clothing and household textiles, and Kohori listened despite having nothing to contribute, both because she did not live on this level and because most of her own wardrobe and other needs were supplied by the Honteno. The woman beside her, whose name she still did not know, did join in, as if seeking to spare Kohori from the embarrassment of their recent discussion, but every now and then she glanced her way and smiled, a small, private gesture clearly meant just for her.

They continued that way for the next few hours. Some of their tablemates departed, only to be replaced by others, for Yue Judei was a popular establishment and never wanted for customers. Kohori and her new friend nibbled at dumplings and pickles and other foods, sipped tsekuri, and talked here and there between larger conversations with others. Even with her limited experience at such things Kohori became convinced that there was a marked difference between her lovely neighbor's looks and tone when directed just at her versus those shared with the rest of the table, and that thought warmed her more than all the rice wine she had consumed. But finally the hour grew late enough that she knew she could not stay any longer.

"This has been a pleasure," she said as she rose to her feet, moving carefully as she adjusted to being upright again after so long and also as she gauged how much alcohol she had consumed and how heavily it had affected her. "But the hour grows late, and so I am afraid I must depart." Collecting her hat from where she'd set it behind her, she bowed to the woman. "I hope to run into you again, and I thank you for a lovely evening."

"It was my pleasure," the lady answered with that same warm, bright smile, also rising to her feet. "I will certainly be back, perhaps even nightly, and I hope to see you here when I do." Again that look, which Kohori was sure was for her alone. An invitation?

"You will," she promised impulsively, then dared a smile of her own. "But only if you will tell me your name."

That earned her another rich laugh, and the reappearance of those devastating dimples. "Of course. It is Chimehara."

"Chimehara." Kohori grinned. "I will not forget it."

She turned to go, pleased to find that she had not drunk so much as to become clumsy, and made her way toward the door, waving farewell to Oguro as she passed him. Chimehara!

She was whistling to herself as she stepped out into the street, settled her irogaso atop her head, and began the long, winding path back up toward Aihiri, where her bed awaited. Somehow, she felt sure she would barely even notice the distance, or her fatigue, or much of anything else beyond the memory of those dark eyes and that bright smile.

What a splendid evening it had been!

CHAPTER EIGHTEEN

It was funny, Seikoku thought. Even after everything that had changed, she still felt most alive at night.

Oh, there was nothing wrong with daytime. She enjoyed the sun on her face, and the golden sparkle of it on the water of the Edishu, which was usually visible down below. She liked seeing people out and about, talking and laughing and working. She enjoyed the warmth in the air and the smell of baking bread and cooking rice and roasting meat and, yes, of people too—there was nothing wrong with the smell of sweat, it was good and clean and natural. It meant people were working and living, same as the chatter of conversation and the thrum of footsteps.

But, for all that, she still loved the night more.

There was just something about walking the streets when it was quiet, your footsteps the only sound besides the faint hiss of the wind, the moon and stars overhead casting a silvery glow about the world, turning everything mysterious and otherworldly. The smells changed, the scent of the water rising to the fore but still tinged with hints of people and their daily activities.

Mostly, she thought, it was the freedom. Here she was, strolling down the street on her own, only flickers of movement visible behind the windows she passed, a stray cat darting across her path once.

At times like this, she could pretend she was alone in Awaihinshi, that the entire city was hers to do with as she would.

Not that she would have any idea what to do with an entire city! It was fun to imagine, though, that she did have such free rein, at least. She could go anywhere she wanted. Turn down any street. Enter any building.

Like that one, there. It was two stories tall—few buildings in this city went above that, as additional floors would obscure the view from the upper levels and also, strategically, could allow someone to climb up a building and then over the wall into the neighborhood beyond. The first floor was locked up tight, its heavy wooden door shut and latched, its windows covered in sturdy shutters that had been carved into an intricate leaf and vine pattern to allow light and air through while still providing privacy and security.

Its upper floor, however—ah, the windows there were wide open to allow the evening breeze. They were a good ten feet off the ground, of course. But that was nothing, especially when the building had such lovely thick beams at the corners and across the windows and door! It would be child's play to scale those, swing up and catch hold of the roof, and then angle back down and in through the open window.

Seikoku stopped herself with a laugh, her hands already reaching for the gloves she'd tucked into her sleeves out of habit when she'd decided to step away from the estate. What was she doing? She wasn't a thief anymore! She couldn't just go around breaking into people's houses!

Though, if she wanted to, it would certainly be easy!

She sighed and forced her hands back to her sides as she turned away and moved on down the street. The next building had all its shutters drawn, upper and lower, but past that—that house's door was not even latched! She could tell by the way the door shifted with the wind, in and out like the house was breathing. How could its owners not notice? And why hadn't they done something about it? Didn't they realize that anyone could just walk in and rob them—or worse?

She realized she'd edged closer to the door in question, reflexively dropping into a half-crouch, her feet making no sound on the cobblestones. It would serve the occupants right if she slipped inside and removed something, just to show them how vulnerable they were. Maybe then they'd think to get their door fixed!

"No!" Seikoku exerted her will and straightened, pivoting so that she now had her back to that alluring door. She felt as if she could hear it calling out to her, urging her on, but she ignored that and stomped away instead. Oh, this was not good! She couldn't do things like that anymore. She was trying to be a new person now, a better person.

Plus, what would Noniki think?

For that matter, what would the emperor think if she broke into someone's house and got caught? She might not have any official role in his government but she had somehow found herself within Hibikitsu's inner circle, along with Noniki and Kagiri and the two warrior women, Kohori and Shizumi. She couldn't risk embarrassing him by abusing his trust in such a fashion.

Thinking like that helped, and she was able to almost ignore the next few buildings, despite a tempting overhang on one, an unfastened shutter on another, and an enticing back gate to a third. Somehow she was able to pass all three by with barely a second glance, though if she had to choose one she would have gone for the first building, as the second was showing lights and movement within and from the third she'd heard the particular creak of metal and leather rubbing together that indicated someone adjusting a sheathed sword.

Well, there was nothing wrong with keeping her skills and her senses sharp, was there? She wasn't breaking any laws or hurting anyone, and she wouldn't be much good at all if she let herself get slow and inobservant. Indeed, she should pay attention to all the little details. That was how to make sure she was still sharp enough to be helpful if anyone needed her.

She decided to make a game of it. Each house she passed, she would consider as if she were going to rob it. Study the front, the sides, the doors and windows, the roof. Imagine the possible interior layout. Gauge inhabitants, number and occupation and current state of alertness. Estimate what sort of valuables might wait within, where they could be, and what sort of protections they might have. Imagine how she would get in, retrieve those items, and get back out again unnoticed, if she decided to do such a thing.

Which she wouldn't. Obviously.

But it didn't hurt to go through the steps in her head.

Engrossed in these mental acrobatics, Seikoku almost didn't notice that she was no longer alone on the streets. But notice she did, subconsciously at first, her steps slowing as a shuffling somewhere up ahead began to intrude upon her deliberations. Someone else was walking about, it seemed. Someone a bit bigger and heavier than she was. Someone who did not care whether anyone knew they were out and about, most likely because they were a law-abiding citizen and had nothing to hide.

She smiled. Well, neither did she. But she still could not bring herself to make her footsteps ring out upon the pavement. It simply went against her nature.

That meant that, when a shadowy figure resolved itself out of the night, she saw that whoever it was did not pause in their own movement. They had not noticed she was here.

Hm.

Again Seikoku slipped back into the notion of a game. And why not? She would shadow this stranger, seeing how close she could get without them noticing her. It would be good practice for her, a way to recall the stealth and speed she had once relied upon so heavily and which was never bad to have at her disposal.

Creeping closer, she saw that the figure was a man, of middle years judging by the gray hairs that caught the light and the way he moved slowly, laboriously, with faint grunts of pain and effort. He wore what she judged to be hantien and torito, an irogaso hanging across his broad back and bouncing with each step, held there by a knotted cord. A worker returning home, perhaps? Or on his way home, since this was Sakiriti and it seemed unlikely someone with such coarse attire would live here among the merchants and artists. Though who was she to judge? Many of her own friends had clothing no less rough, and they were now in Atsani among the nobles. Still, the man seemed to be heading down, toward the gates that would lead through to Bejinuri, which suggested her initial supposition had been correct. He worked here and was now heading home for the night.

She followed along, matching her pace to his, any rustling of her feet swallowed up by the clatter of his, her body ensconced well within the wide shadow he cast. They were as one being, moving together, breathing together, and for all that she could have reached out a hand to tap him on the shoulder, he had no idea she was even there.

They had gone a dozen paces, two, before she realized she was not her new companion's only shadow.

This one was wholly separate, however. It emerged from a narrow gap between two buildings, slender and dark as a sliver of bark, winding its way across the street until it had met with the man's own, its forward edge diffusing and melting into the larger darkness. And now she caught a set of footsteps, approaching on the wings of that same shadow, small and light and quick. A whiff reached her nose, clean skin and good soap but a hint of dirt and metal and blood beneath that, and the shudder of motion resolved itself into a small boy or girl dressed in dark clothes and with even darker hair.

Whoever this was, they were nearing quickly, and their angle intersected with the man Seikoku was currently following. But why? Who was this child, and what did they want?

They were only a few feet away when she caught the gleam of metal in their hand, its edge catching the lamp light. The child had a knife!

Seikoku reacted instinctively. "Run!" she shouted, lunging forward and shoving the man ahead with both hands. He stumbled, gasping in surprise, and fear made him obey, quickening his step as he took off at a lumbering pace down the road, his breath heavy in the air. That left her with the child, who turned on her at once, snarling and showing off its yellowed teeth like a cornered animal.

"Now, listen—" she warned, raising her hands to show they were empty. Then she had to skip back as the child—a boy, she was almost certain—swiped at her with his knife. The blow was clumsy but quick, as someone inexperienced with combat but unconcerned about killing.

"Stop," she tried again, and again was forced to dodge a broad, arcing blow. "Look, put that down before somebody gets hurt!" she urged, and the boy chuckled, his large dark eyes never leaving her face, his mouth stretched into a wild, hungry grin. He advanced on her, his legs so short he took two strides to every one of hers, his limbs thin, his face drawn, but his eyes almost feverishly bright. He was enjoying this!

Against her will, Seikoku drew the kogotano from her sleeve. It had been part of a writing set she had stolen once—she had sold the rest of the set but kept the blade, liking the way it fit in her hand, liking how light and sharp it was, and most of all liking the delicate blue butterflies enameled along the handle. Now she held it the way she had been taught once by a young man who had wanted to impress her, hand angled down, blade back against her forearm. With her other hand she removed her scarf and wrapped it around that limb, hoping it might provide some protection from a knife thrust.

"He's already long gone," she told the boy. "I don't know if you meant to rob him or kill him or both, but that's over and done. And I'm not some slow laborer, tired from a long day's work. I have a knife of my own, and I know how to use it. Keep at this and you'll only get hurt."

The boy hissed in reply and lunged in, quick as a snake. Seikoku blocked the blow with her knife and slapped the side of his head with her free hand, causing him to reel back and stumble, nearly falling but righting himself just in time. She'd hoped the pain would make him realize the untenability of his current endeavor, but it seemed to only enrage him. He snarled, eyes wide, lips drawn back, foam flecking the corners of his mouth, and charged her, more wild animal than small boy.

Not wanting to hurt him if she could avoid it, Seikoku side-stepped, letting him roar past when he met no resistance. She aimed a kick at his backside as it sailed by, and the blow sent him staggering farther away and collapsing to his knees.

"Go home," she warned, careful to keep her distance even if from certain angles he looked small and weak and helpless. "There is nothing for you to gain here except more pain and humiliation."

But the face he turned to her was devoid of caution, devoid of shame, devoid of thought. It was fully feral, the eyes black pools, the mouth working as if already chewing her flesh, the nostrils flaring with each heaving breath. The boy pulled himself back to his feet, gripped his knife so tightly his fingers turned bone white, and screamed as he launched himself at her once more.

Enough of this, Seikoku thought. She dodged his crazed attack and dropped her knife to the ground so that she could grab the boy by the sleeve and collar and hurl him from her with all her strength. She'd hoped to stagger him, at least long enough for her to disappear, but had not counted on his being naught but skin and bone. He flew across the street, flailing through the air like a bird startled from its nest—and slammed headfirst into the nearest lamp post with a sickening crunch that seemed to fill the night and sink deep into her bones.

The boy slid down the iron post and crumpled at its base like so much discarded cloth. He twitched once or twice, then went still, a rattling whisper emerging from his mouth, and the air become redolent with the stench of a body having voided itself.

She knew without having to approach that he was dead.

For a moment, more, she just stood and stared at the tiny corpse huddled against the lamp post. She had just killed someone. Admittedly, he had been trying to kill her, and she had only meant to stun him, but still—he was dead. And she had killed him.

That was not anything she had intended to happen, nor anything she had even wanted. She had merely gone out for an evening stroll! How had that transformed into this?

Nor was she entirely sure what to do next. Should she alert someone? Should she run? No one had seen her, no one here even knew her, she could easily vanish and leave no one the wiser. But would it be better to alert the nearest guards? Would that get her in trouble or keep her out of it? She had no need to lie—the boy had attacked her, she had defended herself, he had hit the lamp post too hard and died. Surely anyone could see that?

But what if they couldn't? She was a stranger here. What if

this boy were a known quantity? Some sort of beloved local figure? And she had inadvertently caused his death. Would she find herself imprisoned for it? Would her actions reflect badly on Noniki—on the emperor himself? She did not truly think that likely, but found herself collecting her knife, unwinding her sorhu and resettling it about her head, and starting to retrace her steps back to the estate.

Perhaps it would be best to leave now. Just in case. There was nothing that could done to change what had happened, and little good to be had from staying here.

Besides, the night had lost its luster now. All it contained was a poor, dead boy, an inky spot beneath the circle of the lantern's light, like a deep well dragging Seikoku's spirit down into the depths of darkness and despair. Her pace quickened, walk becoming sprint becoming full-on flight, but she knew she would never be able to outrun that specter she herself had created.

CHAPTER NINETEEN

Saisaihyu, Day Four

The paper in his hand was fine, smooth as silk and with a delicate mottled pattern like a sun-dappled hill. The penmanship was also superb, the brush strokes strong and decisive yet still graceful, flowing smoothly through the characters. And the wording was precise, careful, polite, diplomatic, and very nearly poetic, each element chosen carefully to blend together into a seamless whole.

And still Hibikitsu snorted as he read it, torn between shock, amusement, irritation, anger, and sheer incredulity. Finally, upon reaching the last syllable he was able to tear his gaze away from the page and glance up at the two men waiting to either side of his throne.

"Did you read this?" he demanded, knowing full well that they had, for he had asked them to after reading it the first time himself, only to take it back and peruse it again afterward. "Can you believe it? The sheer nerve of that woman!"

Noniki frowned as he paced along the edge of the dais just before the rail, his arms behind him, hands folded together, like some tutor pondering what lesson to next apply to his pupil. "Is there any chance she is sincere?" he asked. "They were colleagues for a long time, weren't they?"

"Decades," the emperor agreed, leaning back in his chair and tossing the paper from him, then watching it drift lazily toward the lacquered wooden planks. Even that had a certain languid elegance to it, but he simply could not look past the names affixed by personal seal in the upper right corner. "But no. You never met her, but trust me, Amani Denbi has no care for anyone but herself." He shook his head, the motion causing his kanashi to rattle in his hair. "She is up to something."

"It seems noble, on the face of it," Kagiri offered. He was perched upon the rail, and not for the first time Hibikitsu marveled at the difference between the two brothers. He had no siblings himself, and so had grown up without ever knowing such companionship or such close kin, but was it common for siblings to be so different? The one seemed filled with energy all the time, almost constantly in motion to some degree, while the other was calmer, quieter, prone to complete stillness except when called into bursts of action. Yet they complemented one another, and both seemed at ease with the other's behavior. Curious. "What could be less honorable than visiting a friend in need?"

"Even when that friend is being held for treason?" his brother asked, pausing his perambulations. "Wouldn't the proper thing be to condemn his actions and disavow any and all contact with him as a result? And why ask to see him now? He has been held for nearly a week already, and this is the first time they've made such a request."

"It's the Saisaihyu," Hibikitsu agreed. "It has to be. That is why they've asked now, and not before. But why?"

Kagiri tapped his chin with a finger, thinking. "Your Honteno are still short-staffed," he pointed out, "and they and your Honjofu are not at full strength right now in other ways as well." He refrained from pointing out why, which was politic of him, though they all knew what he meant. "If I meant you harm, now would be the ideal time to attempt it." That brought a slight shiver to the young emperor, remembering how, not that long ago, this serious young man in his green armor had indeed meant him harm, and had nearly killed him. But the comment had clearly been made as an academic point, and the moment passed.

"If I allowed their request, it would get them through the gates," he agreed. "But what then? And their own warriors would be just as disadvantaged." He nudged the fallen document with one foot, the tip of his boot sending the paper fluttering off the dais and onto the tiled floor beyond.

"I wouldn't allow it," Kohori offered from her post just before the dais, her back set against the massive pillar there, arms crossed over her chest. "Amani's a mamusha, always has been, always will be. She's after something, most likely revenge or your throne or both. Don't play into her hands."

Hibikitsu nodded, his fingers resting idly on Kosshiki's hilt. There was little to gain from agreeing to the petition, and far too much potential for harm. "You are right," he said, acknowledging all three people's input with a general nod. "I will inform her that her request to see Nagao has been denied." He started to rise, intending to retrieve the paper in order to craft a reply, but Noniki stopped him, scooping it up instead.

"I know I'm not all that good at this courtroom stuff," he said with a grin, "but is it really right for the emperor to reply directly to a—what is she now? Jigekugi?"

"It is not." Kohori's grin was decidedly sharp. "In fact, it would be wildly inappropriate for you or your Rojiri to respond. You should delegate a minor noble to do it—another jigekugi would be ideal." There had never been any love lost between her and Amani, and he could hardly fault her now for enjoying the other woman's fall from grace. Nor was she wrong.

"Very well," he said. "Noniki, find someone to take care of that, please?" His young wizard bowed, accepting the charge. "Good. Now, shall we see the young man you've sent for?"

"Absolutely." Kagiri waved at the Honteno stationed on either side of the throne room's doors and the two saluted and stepped out of sight into the hall.

A moment later they returned, taking up their stations once more, as a small cluster of well-dressed men and women followed them into the room. They approached, their soft-soled shoes rustling across the intricate tilework of the floor, and paused some ten feet from the dais, as was proper. The man in front took another step or two forward and dipped into an elegant bow, the rest of his party following suit.

"Your Imperial Majesty." His voice was clear, his diction crisp. "I am honored to place myself at your disposal."

Hibikitsu studied the man. He had vaguely recognized the

family name, Kazutai, when the others had returned from their outing to the docks, but knew nothing more beyond that. This man, Kazutai Katani, was perhaps his own age, or within a few years of it, his hair thick and glossy, his mustache and beard neat, his shoulders slight but not stooped, his carriage good. He was dressed perhaps more flamboyantly than one might have expected from someone of a nautical bent, his robes a rich crimson decorated with orange leaves and white petals, his obi and underrobe a matching white, his cap a peaked black satin that blended with his hair, the ribbons securing it under his chin echoing his sideburns and matching his beard. Then again, he was not at sea now, and wouldn't one put on one's best attire when summoned to court?

"We are glad you accepted our invitation, Kazutai-san," he replied, steepling his hands before him. "We understand you were out upon the Edishu yesterday, among the waves."

"Indeed I was, sire," the nobleman confirmed, straightening. He was carrying a white fan and tapped that into his palm as he spoke. "I am often out there, as often as may be. I feel most alive upon the water, with a ship beneath my feet." He smiled, an expression that seemed genial enough. "Have you ever been out in a chayaburi, sire?"

That seemed an odd question, for surely most of Awaihinshi would already know the answer to that—the emperor rarely left Aihiri, let alone descended all the way to the outer walls and the river beyond! Still, he chose to accept the query at face value and shook his head. "Alas, we have not yet had that pleasure."

"Ah. Well." Kazutai leaned in a bit, as if conveying a secret. "It is truly an incomparable feeling, sire. Out there, the wind in your hair, the sun upon your face, the spray of the water against your lips as you race along, other boats chasing after but never quite able to catch up. An experience like no other."

Hibikitsu glanced at Noniki, who had taken up a position to his left perhaps ten paces away and now turned his head away from the lord to roll his eyes without being seen except by Hibikitsu himself and Kagiri, who was in a matching spot to the right. And, although he had to school himself not to laugh at the response, the emperor found he did not disagree. Incomparable? Surely racing a horse across the open plains would give rise to similar feelings, or even running yourself? And if the other chayaburi were manned by members of your household, wouldn't they be deliberately holding back so as not to embarrass their liege lord?

Still, he kept his face blandly interested and his tone engaged as he said, "We hope to experience that for ourselves one day, then, if it has won such praise from you. Tell us, though, when you are are sailing, what is your chiefest concern? What draws your greatest attention while you are out on your chayaburi."

"The sun," the nobleman answered at once, his tone confident. "You must be aware of the sun at all times, Your Majesty. It can blind you if you are not careful, and then you could easily wreck your boat on some unseen obstacle. Plus you will need to keep track of the tides, and the sun's place in the sky will reveal that to you."

A sound arose from somewhere behind Kazutai, so faint Hibikitsu thought at first he had imagined it. But then he saw how the young lord's brow furrowed for an instant, his lips setting into a scowl before that faded back into the pleasant smile he had worn throughout. Had it been someone clearing their throat? Perhaps.

"Interesting," he said, glossing over that errant noise. "We would have thought the wind would be of paramount importance, as without it your craft would surely founder." He was listening closely, and thus this time was sure he had heard the sound again. It had come from one of Kazutai's entourage. Curious.

"Of course, the wind is critical, sire," the young lord agreed, bowing. "There is no question." Very diplomatically put, Hibikitsu had to allow. One did not want to disagree directly with the emperor, after all, but at the same time the reply did not discount Kazutai's own answer or experience.

"Tell us, Kazutai-san," he asked next, "how are you finding the Saisaihyu?" He leaned forward, genuinely interested to hear the man's response.

Nor did he have to wait long. "Oh, I am enjoying it immensely, sire," his visitor stated at once, bowing again. "Such a fascinating exercise! And so valuable, I think, for the common folk to

understand how much they have to be grateful for! Without aishone, look what they become—little better than savages! After
a week without the benefit of their bones, they will once again
rejoice in being part of the glory that is the Relicant Empire!"

It was a pretty answer, to be sure, and one well designed to
flatter both Hibikitsu himself and his heritage. Pity it was exactly
the opposite of what he'd hoped to hear. Nor had he missed the
casual disdain with which Kazutai had said "the common folk."
Such a typical noble-born response, to consider himself better than
others solely because he had been born into wealth and power!

Hibikitsu decided he had heard enough. "We thank you for
your insight, and your loyalty, Kazutai-san," he declared, lowering his hands to his lap. "And we appreciate your attending us
today. May you enjoy the rest of the Saisaihyu, and may it bring
you purity and peace."

The lord was not slow to apprehend that the audience was now
over, and bowed more deeply, backing up until he was once again
surrounded by his companions. "It has been my honor and my
pleasure, Your Imperial Majesty," he intoned, kneeling and placing his forehead to the floor before rising to his feet, his entourage
mirroring the obeisance. "Please do not hesitate to call upon me
again if I may serve you in any way." He backed out, head bowed,
until he had passed over the threshold and disappeared from view.

"What a pokanu!" Noniki burst out. "I can't believe it! He
seemed completely different when we saw him out on the water!"

"He was not at all what I expected," Kagiri agreed. "I'm sorry.
We really thought he might be of use to you."

Hibikitsu was pondering that himself. Though he had only
known them a short time, he had already come to trust the brothers' judgement. For them to have been so wildly mistaken about
Kazutai seemed out of character. Coming to a decision, he rose
to his feet and, with two quick steps, had crossed to the front of
the dais. "Noniki, your kaoni," he demanded, and the young Rojiri
tugged off his coat and tossed it to him at once. Hibikitsu was
already hopping down and pulled the loose jacket on over his
robes as he hurried across the long room, Kohori falling into place

at his side. But that would never do. "Wait here," he instructed as he reached the throne room doors, and she reluctantly did as ordered, stopping beside the guards and watching as he continued on. He only hoped he was not too late!

Pausing a moment to listen, he was pleased to hear voices from somewhere nearby. There! The corridor led to the compound's front entrance but there were several hallways branching off it along the way, and the sounds had emanated from one such hall ahead and to the right. Hurrying forward, Hibikitsu reached the corner and glanced around it. Aha!

Kazutai Katani and his entourage had not yet departed. Instead, they were arrayed across the hall there as the young lord berated his men. Or, more precisely, one man in particular—a young fellow who, though clean-shaven, shared several features with his liege lord.

"You embarrassed me in front of the emperor!" Kazutai was saying, his face only inches away from the other man's. But if he'd thought to intimidate his subordinate with that maneuver, he was sadly mistaken.

"No more than you embarrassed yourself," the younger man retorted. "'The sun, Your Majesty. It can blind you.' Are you for true?" He snorted, and now Hibikitsu knew that was the sound he had heard, only unrestrained by propriety now.

"What was I supposed to say?" the nobleman demanded.

"The water, of course," came the reply. "What else? Sun, wind, rain—none of it matters if you cannot feel your way through the water! That is what true sailing is all about!"

"Fine!" Kazutai said, the word practically a bark. "If I am ever asked that again, that is how I shall answer. Does that satisfy you?" He snapped his fingers and the others straightened like soldiers undergoing review, turning as one to follow as he pivoted back toward the main doors. Fortunately, Hibikitsu had guessed the young lord's intent and had sprinted across the main corridor so that he was now tucked around a different bend as the little group made their way to the exit.

So, he thought, watching them depart. Interesting. Not the lord at all but…his brother? Cousin? Whoever he was, that young man seemed like the one he should be speaking with. He would have Kohori make some discreet inquiries.

He returned to the throne room, still considering what he had just seen, only to find Kohori, Kagiri, and Noniki waiting for him around the front of the dais. "Has something occurred?" he asked, absently shucking the kaoni and handing it back to his younger Rojiri. "You all look concerned."

"We've just received reports, sire," Kohori answered, all business. "There are emissaries making their way up through the city to see you."

He stared at his guard commander, trying to shift his thoughts from the recent audience to this strange news. "Emissaries? From where?"

"Fyushu," Kagiri answered.

"Yatamoro," Noniki added right after his brother.

"And Higinasi," Kohori finished.

"What?" Hibikitsu plopped down on the edge of the dais, unconcerned about appearing regal while he tried to digest this. All three of Rimbaku's neighboring nations were here to speak with him? After never having sent any sort of diplomat or ambassador before, all three were coming here now?

Suddenly he wished he could just take a chayaburi and escape. Nothing but him and the water and the wind and the sun, no worries about politics and diplomacy and caring for an entire empire!

But of course, he could no more abandon his responsibilities than Kazutai Katani could understand the value to "common folk."

"Very well," the emperor said, twisting about and getting his feet under him so he could rise already on the dais and from there return to his throne. "Let us ready ourselves for their arrival."

CHAPTER TWENTY

*C*oncentrate, Noniki told himself. *Feel the world around you. Let it flow through you. All are connected, rock and tree and ant and person—and you are linked to them all.*

He felt the wood beneath his hands. It was solid and unyielding, but it was also warmed from the sun's rays and he could still sense traces of the life that had once caused its beams to flourish into trees. He inhaled, taking in the distinctive tang of seasoned wood but also that hint of sunlight and soil and water and spreading leaves. All were connected.

Letting go of his sense of self, he allowed himself to fall into the wood, to immerse himself in its essence. It did not drown him—he was buoyed up, floating within it but still separate to some degree. Yet he was now closer than before and could feel it more intimately.

And, thus surrounded, he could influence it as well.

It was, in a way, similar to what he thought a potter must do, shaping clay as it spun upon the wheel. Only Noniki did not use his hands. Instead he shaped with his soul, his will guiding the wood into the form he wished, altering a touch here, a bit there, gentle and gradual but firm, allowing it to shift from old to new gracefully, organically, but still urging that change.

There was resistance at first, of course. He had expected that. The wood was old and set in its ways. Yet deep down it remembered life as individual trees, and thus each piece remembered what it was like to grow and flourish, to bend with the wind, to lean toward the light. He restored that, nurtured it like one encouraging a spark to catch and expand into a flame, and as it took, the wood began to accept his directions. There was even an undercurrent of excitement, if wood could be said to have such feelings, at growing and changing again after being still and silent for so long.

Opening his eyes, Noniki let his hands fall to his sides and stepped back, glancing up as the carved front gates of his estate began to writhe and change. It was like watching a puppet show, as the thunderclouds covering the two heavy sides began to recede, thinning and fading from a thick, ominous gray to a light, cheerful white, tinted a warm yellow in places by the sun that rose behind them, casting its golden rays across the whole. The lightning vanished altogether, and along the bottom edges vines arose, writhing and growing as if alive but still carved into the wood, a rich light green that danced from the gates to the walls beyond, forming a playful pattern that stretched from end to end and made the whole less forbidding and more like a stylized garden than a strict and foreboding wall.

That, he thought with a grin, was much better.

Pushing the gates open, he stepped into the space between those and the inner doors, which were flung wide open. Through them he could already see that the courtyard was a hive of activity, and he smiled to see his friends so busy. It seemed they were indeed making themselves at home in this, their new space. He could still see much of the tile mosaic there, however, and frowned, for it no longer matched the barriers he had just passed through. Nor did the buildings. While he understood the notion of keeping to a family emblem and colors, why would anyone wish to paint their entire estate in such gloomy blues and grays? How did that make it an inviting space, or a warm and welcoming home?

Well, that was all about to change. He trailed his hand along the right wall as he walked, and it responded to his touch, the alterations of the outside bleeding in to brighten the wood there, like dye spreading into a pool of water, the wood bleaching in some places and brightening in others until more bright, fluffy clouds danced within that space, their luminescence hinting at the sun from the gates. The ground was not immune either, and vines sprang up beneath his feet, following his steps as he made his way into the courtyard—not real stem and vine and leaf but versions of them captured within the tiles, the mosaic shifting its colors and patterns to become an intricate woven design of entwined greenery like some elaborate wreath, all centered around a bright sun with stylized rays warming the vines wherever the two intersected. The color and warmth crept up onto the buildings next, the blue lightening into that of a clear midday sky, the grays disappearing, white clouds and golden rays replacing them, and bright flowers curling up around the base. Now it was a happy place full of life and color, fit for his friends to enjoy!

Gasps had sprung up around the courtyard as the alterations had occurred and people had noticed the ground changing beneath their feet and the walls transforming behind them. After that, heads had turned, seeking the source they knew must be nearby, and so Noniki found himself surrounded by shouts of welcome and cheers and hugs and backslaps as he made his way toward the main house.

"Beautiful!" Isoro exclaimed, a rare smile brightening her face. She went so far as to twirl about, her sleeves trailing around her.

"It's lovely," Kuma agreed, hugging him. Despite all their travels her hands were still permanently roughened from years as a washer woman, but her arms were strong and her smile broad as she added, "thank you."

The others all thanked him as well, but there was one face Noniki was seeking in particular. And there she was, emerging from one of the walkways connecting the side buildings to the main structure. She looked so serious, even somber, in a way he had never seen before. And then, glancing up, her eyes met his. He watched as a smile blossomed, sparking her eyes to even greater brilliance until her gaze practically outshone the sun beneath his feet and the real one beaming down from the sky overhead, her gaze taking in the changes he had wrought.

"Oh!" Seikoku hurried down the broad front steps and onto the platform at their base, meeting Noniki just as he reached that same spot. "Noniki, it's wonderful!" He felt a dozen feet tall, seeing the warmth in her gaze. "Before, it felt as if we were staying in someone else's home," she told him, studying the light and green-ery emblazoned everywhere, her sharp eyes even noting the front gates where they still stood open. "Now it feels like this is really ours."

"Good." He ducked his head, his words escaping his grasp as they often did when confronted by her attention. "I'm glad." But his cheeks hurt from smiling so widely, and when she laughed, whatever had been upsetting her evidently forgotten, he knew that she did not mind his being so tongue-tied.

"I'm sorry I've been away so much," he told her next, rubbing the back of his head. "Hibikitsu is keeping me pretty busy."

"Good," she replied, then laughed again, waving away her own word. "Sorry, what I meant was, it's good that he values you so much. He should. Not good that you haven't been here." She reached out took both his hands in hers, her fingers warm in his. "But you're here now."

"I am." He could have lost himself in her eyes, and it was only with great effort that he looked away, to study the activity slowly resuming around them. "You've all been busy."

"We have! Come see!" And she dragged him back down onto the courtyard and around in a wide circuit. Many of their friends were out here, spaced slightly apart, yet that expansive space still had enough room for them all to fit easily. Isoro was first, her wag-on's wheels fixed in place by simple wooden blocks tied beneath them on both sides, the built-in cabin's back door open to display the neat rows of bottles and drawers that lined the inner walls and the countertop near the back, behind which she could sit and dispense herbs and instruction.

Next to her was Amon, his setup a good deal simpler as it con-sisted only of a low wooden stool and a massed heap of sturdy silk cord. He was already hard at work, knotting strands together to form the start of a net, but glanced up to smile at them as they passed. Noniki was amused to see that the simple netmender's stool was in fact elaborately lacquered and gilt and most likely worth more than Amon had earned in all his years of labor.

Junko and Eiji had found a small table, similar in design to

Amon's stool, and had upturned a pair of beautifully glazed tall pots for seats. The couple had brought various scraps and bundles of cloth with them among their things, and these were now spread out across the table, ready to be turned into clothes upon command.

Past them was Kanai, and Noniki stopped by his old friend and stared. "Where did you manage to find that?" he asked, for the potter was seated behind a pottery wheel. "I know you didn't pack it in your bag!"

"Ha, no, though that would have been impressive, no?" Kanai answered, laughing. "No, one of the places we helped repair down in the lower levels was a potter's. He had this wheel just sitting unused—it had been his apprentice's, he said, but she'd left to start her own shop and he felt he was too old to take on another." He shrugged his broad shoulders. "He said I could have it, so Ratal and I hauled it up here." The stool he sat upon was such a perfect match that it must have come with the piece, and it looked extremely solid.

Noniki admired the wheel. It was a simple, sturdy piece, carved of some heavy wood whose warm grain was visible even through years of caked-on porcelain dust, with a thick base and an equally thick top. His friend must have seen the question on his face because he laughed and demonstrated how it worked, using his bare feet to kick the base. The piece turned out to not be solid wood after all, because that section rotated with his kick, spinning around the central column and causing the top to spin as well.

"You have to keep up a steady rhythm," Kanai explained, his feet nudging the base repeatedly so that the top continued to spin evenly. "It's all about your breathing, and centering yourself, physically and spiritually." Though his words were often slow, Noniki was reminded yet again that his friend was far from dumb. And although he often appeared ungainly with his wide, slightly bowed stance, seated there now and chatting easily as he maintained the wheel's steady motion, it was clear that Kanai was in fact very good at his craft. "I will need to figure out something for a kiln, of course. The ovens here are nowhere near hot enough." He frowned a second, then smiled and shrugged. "I think I know how to make one, though. Just need the materials."

"We'll get you whatever you need," Noniki promised. He clapped his friend on the shoulder. "Don't worry about that."

Sanedi had simply spread a blanket—in reality an exquisite tapestry Noniki suspected had been left hanging on a wall somewhere—out upon the ground and was seated cross-legged on it, his nimble fingers already weaving reeds together into the base of a wide basket. "I should have this one done by tomorrow eve," he explained when Noniki and Seikoku stopped to admire his work. "It'll serve as my example while I make others to actually sell."

Not everyone was able to set up as easily, of course. Ratal was a fisherman, and that was going to prove difficult. Noniki made a mental note to ask Hibikitsu about that, or perhaps Kohori. Someone had to be providing fish for the imperial compound—perhaps he could get Ratal work with them? Kuma couldn't exactly display her washing skills. And they had no horses for Otokai to trade, though he had chosen a spot to sit and told them he would offer his services for appraising horses and for teaching training, care, and riding as well. That might prove valuable to the various nobles around them here.

In many ways, the courtyard now reminded Noniki of the market back in Ginzai. He mentioned that to Seikoku, who nodded. "That was exactly what I was thinking," she told him. "We have no stalls, but not everyone there did. And we have no roof, though perhaps we can fix that at some point, if things go well. Still, it's a chance for everyone to display and sell their wares and their services." She smiled at him. "And it is ours."

They came upon Minawa and her husband Sukame, who were walking in the opposite direction and clearly supervising the overall activities. "What of the two of you?" Noniki asked. He knew they had been farmers before deciding to join him and the others on their trek.

Sukame laughed. He was a quiet man who usually let his wife speak for them both. "Did you know there's soy growing in the back corner?" he asked, pointing back behind the buildings. "And beans and radishes and some other things as well. And there's trees, too—plum and pear and more." He smiled. "Ohiro's been handling all of this on his own for years. Past time he had some help."

"And Seikoku and I've taken charge of the household," Minawa put in. "Assuming that's acceptable to you." The old woman's shrewd gaze took in the pair of them standing before her, their hands linked, and she nodded, her face crinkling into a smile. "Good to see you," she said warmly, and Noniki felt there were layers to that simple statement, but all of them warm enough to make him feel slightly flushed.

"Good to see you too," he replied, "and of course it is. I always know I can count on all of you." He turned and glanced back across the wide space, with their friends all arrayed before them. "It's really coming together, isn't it?" He sighed happily.

"It is." Seikoku hugged him. "Thanks to you."

"Thanks to you, and to everyone," he countered. "Actually, to you most of all. I sort of dumped all this on you. I'm sorry."

"Don't be," she protested, starting forward as the older couple continued on their own way and leading Noniki out away from the courtyard, toward one of the bridges that linked it to the tiny islands dotting the lake. "It's good. It's kept me busy." For a second that sorrow returned, flitting across her face like a shadow, but then it vanished once more.

He studied her then, as best he could without pulling his hand free because that he found he did not want to. "You have been busy," he agreed, his heart pounding so loudly now he could barely hear his own words as they tumbled from his lips, his head turned so he could look upon her properly, his feet stilling because he knew he would stumble if he did not stop with so much of his attention focused so tightly upon his companion. "So maybe you could take a short break? Long enough for dinner?"

She smiled, and there was something hesitant about the expression that caught at his heart. "We'll eat in a little while," she stated. "It's Kuma and Amon's turn to cook, though, so don't expect anything fancy—you know what they're like." The whole group took turn with most of the basic chores, and some were more skilled at certain things than others. Ratal had proven a surprisingly good cook, especially when it came to grilled fish and hearty stews. Kuma and Amon were less talented at making meals, though at least what they produced was mostly edible.

"That's...not quite what I meant." He gulped in air and then plunged ahead, knowing he would falter if he did not. "I was hoping you might want to go to dinner. With me. Just us."

"Oh. Oh!" He saw the color flood into her cheeks as her eyes widened and her lips parted. "I..." He thought she was about to say no, to give some reason why not, and he felt a wash of terror and sorrow poised overhead, ready to crush him beneath its weight.

But then she smiled, and his world turned to sheer happiness.

"I would love to." The words came out in a rush, as if she did not trust herself with them any more than he had with his question, but her eyes were aglow and he found that his own had filled with tears. He could not speak, not even a word, but he nodded, hoping she saw how happy that made him, and from the way her gaze glistened, he thought perhaps she had.

They stayed that way a moment, just gazing into each other's eyes and smiling. Then they turned, as if upon some silent agreement, and began walking again, their hands still clasped, their feet thumping across the wood of the bridge, the sweet scent of the flowers all around tickling their noses.

And to Noniki, still connected to it all, it felt as if the whole word was singing with him.

CHAPTER TWENTY-ONE

Saisaihyu, Day Five

Kagiri sidled up beside his younger brother as they both entered the throne room. "You seem inordinately happy about something," he pointed out, keeping his voice low enough that the others would not hear. "What is it?"

Noniki shook his head, but the motion did nothing to wipe the grin from his face. "Nothing," he claimed, the word practically bubbling from his lips. "Nothing at all." Kagiri simply waited—all their lives his little brother had been the very soul of unrestraint, unable to contain thoughts, feelings, and actions for more than a few seconds, and though he had certainly grown and matured at least some of that inability to keep silent remained. Sure enough, after a second he burst out, "Only, Seikoku and I had dinner together last night!"

"Do you not dine together most nights?" Kagiri asked, feigning ignorance, though already a smile was tugging at his own lips as well. For that certainly explained the good mood, and he was of course happy for them both—and indeed, just from what he had seen since they had reunited, it was long overdue. Still, what was the point in being related if you could not occasionally tweak your sibling's nose, just for fun?

Sure enough, Noniki took the question seriously. "No, you do not understand," he insisted, his voice starting to rise slightly. "This was not all of us together. This was just the two of us. Dining. Alone. As a couple."

"Ah. And are you a couple now, then?" Kagiri was struggling hard to keep his face blank, though he knew it was not a battle he could win for long. Where were the skills of the Gensaiba when he needed them most?

"I..." His brother's grin faltered. "I think so? I do not know. How does one even determine such a thing?" There had not been many girls their age back in their village, and in Ginzai there had been no time to think of such things between work and sleep— though he did recall Noniki's rapt description of a certain beautiful Koshitsu he'd met when sneaking into the city cemetery. But Noniki had never been one to let his spirits be dampened for too long, and the grin returned, brighter than ever. "But I think so!" He was practically skipping now as they proceeded toward the dais where Hibikitsu already waited. "Isn't it wonderful?"

A new voice cut into their conversation, like cold water thrown onto a pair of quarreling cats, stilling them at once. "Joy is always a good thing," Kohori stated quietly without turning about. "But perhaps now is not the time to discuss or celebrate your newfound felicity?" Noniki's face fell like a chastened child, and as if somehow sensing that the Honteno commander did glance back, a smile creasing her face. "But I *am* happy for you."

They nodded, and, stepping up onto the wide platform, assumed their now-customary places on either side of the throne without another word. Though that drew a sharp glance from their emperor.

"Why so silent?" he asked them both, though his gaze quickly focused on Noniki. "You seemed to be all smiles when you entered, and now you are grim as a mountainside."

"He and Seikoku are together now," Kagiri confided, leaning in. "But Kohori felt he was being too boisterous." He did not think she had heard, but the glare she shot his way suggested that, at the very least, she had guessed what he was saying.

But Hibikitsu only laughed and slapped the arm of his ornate chair. "Why, that is excellent news!" he said, smiling at Noniki. "I am very happy for you, my friend. She is lovely, clever, capable, and it was clear from the first how much you two cared for each other. I wish you every joy."

Noniki smiled and bowed. "Thank you, sire," he replied, his good mood now fully restored. "I appreciate that. Though Kohori was right that perhaps I should show more restraint, given the setting and our current purpose."

The emperor waved that away. "You have noticed, no doubt, that I switch from 'I' to 'we' at times," he said. "Right now, with just us four present, we can be casual, friendly, and joyful. In a moment we will put on our public faces—but until then, grin away."

Studying the man as he spoke and seeing the kindness and generosity and honesty in his words and actions, Kagiri wondered again how he had ever thought of Hibikitsu as some unfeeling monster who needed to be deposed. What a fool he had been! And how lucky that he had been slowed enough in his original, bloody purpose to meet the emperor, to hear him, and to take his measure properly!

Which reminded him—"Where is Shizumi?" he asked, glancing about. For the head of the Honjofu was nowhere to be seen, and the room's energies felt off-kilter without her standing by the pillar opposite Kohori.

"I did not require her to be here for this," came the emperor's reply. "She is still settling into her new role, and had various details to handle this morning, and so begged off on attending." Now his eyes were drawn to Kagiri, and Kagiri regretted calling such attention to himself, for that gaze was knowing indeed. "Why do you ask?"

He did his best to shrug nonchalantly. "No reason—I am just accustomed to it being us five." He hoped he was convincing, and after a moment Hibikitsu shrugged as well, but on his other side Kagiri saw Noniki grin his way and knew he could expect some revenge for his earlier teasing.

Fortunately, they were all distracted by the Honteno at the door announcing, "Kazutai Takami!" and all turned as one to study the young man who approached alone across the tiled floor. It was like looking at a younger, slimmer, less polished version of Kazutai Katani, Kagiri thought, as if a few years and a few layers of polish had been stripped away. The young man wore, not elegant robes like his brother, but a hantien, the short coat open over shatage and ponmei. The clothes were all in red and orange with white accents, and the workmanship appeared fine, yet they were so simply adorned as to appear almost plain, especially when surrounded by the intricate decorations of the throne room. Kagiri appreciated the simplicity and practicality of the man's attire, seeing nothing in his bearing to indicate that the clothes had been worn as an insult, and gathered from the open face and posture of the emperor that he felt the same.

"Your Imperial Majesty." The younger Kazutai dropped to his knees, not gracefully but with the agility of a man accustomed to living by his reflexes and his footing, and lowered his head to the floor.

"Rise, Kazutai Takami," Hibikitsu intoned, and Kagiri saw at once what he had meant before. This was no longer merely their friend sitting in a jeweled chair but now the Emperor of all Rimbaku, the Echo of Victory himself, and his voice carried the weight of all his forebears and the full authority of a nation. "We thank you for responding so swiftly to our invitation."

Rising to his feet with the ease and vigor of youth, the young man nodded, though Kagiri thought he was forcibly suppressing a smile that, judging by the laugh lines already ingrained around the mouth, he suspected was a default expression. "Of course, sire. Though, in truth, who would dare delay from answering such a summons?"

The emperor answered that question with one of his own: "And do you always react at once to all such entreaties and requirements?"

"I certainly endeavor to do so," the junior Kazutai replied, "though I will admit, since you ask and duty compels me to be forthright, that curiosity may have also played a part in my alacrity." Kagiri noticed his brother smiling and nodded. The young man might dress rough, but he did seem to have a way with words!

"Curiosity?" Hibikitsu leaned forward. "And what were you curious about, sir?"

Now the young man bowed his head. "I hope I do not offend you, sire, for I am a loyal subject," he stated. "I was merely surprised to be asked to attend you alone, without my brother, and thus curious as to the reason why. Whatever it may be, I live to serve."

Now it was the emperor's turn to smile. "You have not offended us, Kazutai Takami," he declared, "and in truth we value your honesty. We wished merely to take your measure, for unless we are greatly mistaken, much of the credit we gave your brother for his skills upon the water should in truth belong to you."

This was of course, if not a trap, at least a test, and Kagiri watched closely, as did the others. The young man had been asked a pointed question by his emperor, one which made it clear they already knew the answer. Did he openly acknowledge it, being honest to his ruler but disloyal to his brother? Did he lie to protect the family name? Or would he somehow find a middle ground?

The young noble licked his lips before speaking. "I am but a humble servant to my brother, the lord of our house," he answered slowly, "and thus any skills I may possess and any honors I may accrue are rightfully due to him. It is his voice that commands us when we sail, and his directives that we follow."

"But it is your hand upon the tiller," Noniki cut in. "His voice may be the wind blowing you in one direction, but it is your skill that guides you safely along that path."

The younger Kazutai turned to face this declaration fully and bowed deeply. "You are wise, great Rojiri," he stated, "and you see much." A clever way to acknowledge that statement without saying so directly!

Kagiri decided to weigh in as well. "Who would you say is the better sailor," he asked, "you or your brother?" He saw the man stiffen, eyes widening as the net was fully cast upon him, knowing there was no good way to wriggle free without exposure or injury, and wondered if he had been too direct, but Hibikitsu nodded approvingly beside him.

"I would have to say," the nobleman answered, each word emerging slowly and precisely, "that I am the better sailor, for that is a lower skill. My brother is the captain, the commander—I am merely his hands, his instrument enacting his will."

The laugh that erupted from the emperor surprised Kagiri only a little, but it made the man before them jump nearly out of his skin. "Oh, well put!" Hibikitsu told him, slapping his knee. "You answer perfectly—no offense can be taken by any party!" His humor cut off abruptly as he tapped his chin. "Now, answer us this—what would you do, if you were captain of your own fleet? How would you fare?"

"Your Majesty?" It was clear that this was not a question the young lord had expected.

"If you were not bound to serve your brother," Noniki explained gently, his eyes kind, "but were put in charge of ships wholly under your command, what would you do?"

"Ah." Kazutai Takami straightened, chin up, and in that instant was every bit the noble, not by dint of blood but by courage and dedication. "I would command from the front, my lords. I would never require any ship, any sailor, to face any threat I was not willing to encounter first myself. I would know every inch of every vessel, every name of every sailor, every scrap of sail and every nail and plank. And I would train my sailors to respond to wind and wave as one, to work with nature rather than against it, to honor and respect river and sea and live as one with them."

It was a dangerous statement, for it was a clear condemnation of his brother's method of command, directing from the rear. Yet he had not mentioned his liege lord in all that and so could not fully be called out as insulting him. Still, it was a bold move, and even Kohori was nodding in appreciation of his honesty and his courage in taking such a strong stance.

"We understand," Hibikitsu commented, leaning back in his chair, his fingers stroking the delicate carvings of dragons coiled along the arms, "that your late father bequeathed all to your older brother, leaving you nothing but your name. Is this not so?"

The young man bowed. "It is, Your Majesty," he acknowledged, his voice and face carefully neutral. "My father did not approve of my passion for sailing. He felt I would only squander any wealth and holdings left to me and so gave them all to my brother instead, and my loyalty with them."

"Not even any aishone?" Noniki asked, carefully casual, and the young lord nodded.

"That is correct, sir," he replied. "Though," his eyes narrowed a second, clearly considering, before he took a deep breath and continued, committing himself, "if I am to be wholly honest, I have not felt the lack. Indeed, having been forced to master such skills for myself instead of relying upon the skills of others, I believe I have a better understanding and appreciation for them than many." He raised his chin. "And I would hazard a guess that the Saisaihyu we are currently observing indicates you do not disagree." He bowed again. "If I overstep, please forgive me."

Kagiri had frowned during the first part of that response. He and Noniki had always shared everything and there had been no question, when their mother had died and they had sold her bones for a few small coins, that they would share in those as well. The notion of one brother being so utterly beholden to another was anathema to him, and he failed to see how it could harbor anything but entitlement on the one side and resentment on the other. He was now even more impressed by the younger Kazutai's bearing and particularly his discretion, to maintain such seeming equanimity in the face of such a one-sided relationship. He also admired the young man's willingness to go against tradition by declaring his lack of reliance upon any aishone.

Of course, Kagiri also knew what was coming next and now, having listened closely throughout the interview, took great pleasure in nodding when Hibikitsu glanced his way. Noniki did likewise, as did Kohori, and it was with a mischievous gleam in his eye but a studiously nonchalant expression that the emperor continued.

"You do not offend us," he replied, "and we hope our questions likewise caused no harm or ill will. We asked after your inheritance and allegiance," and now he affected an almost bored tone, as if discussing his next meal, "because we have a particular need right now. You have no doubt noticed we are reduced in our Rojiri, and though our two advisors are wise and offer excellent counsel we feel we must expand their numbers. We also have need for a new Dogenkaishu, and desire this to be, not merely one who has inherited the role, but one who truly has a passion for the water and for sailing upon it. Such a dual role—Rojiri and Dogenkaishu—would require someone who is dedicated to the empire, who is willing to speak plainly even when their statements may not be those we wish to hear, and who is able to put aside personal pride or greed or ambition to focus on what is best for the nation as a whole. Kazutai Takami, we call upon you, and charge you to answer with all honesty and gravity—is this a task you are willing to accept?"

"I?" For a moment, the young man stood before them, utterly frozen, all propriety forgotten, his mouth hanging open like that of a fish gulping for water. Then he dropped to the ground, controlling his fall at the last second so that his knees hit with only a dull thud and his forehead with barely any sound. "I live to serve," he declared, his voice strong and clear and rich with emotion, only partially muffled by the tiles it projected against. "I am yours to command, my emperor, and if I may serve you in any way, I shall do so, with all my heart and soul. If you desire my counsel, you shall have it, honest and unfettered even though it go against propriety or rote obedience, and if you were to grant me the task of command I would give my life before dishonoring your faith in me."

"That is all we could ask and more," Hibikitsu announced, rising to his feet. "Rise, noble Takami, Rojiri and Dogenkaishu, and accept my blessing and my thanks." He smiled down at the young man as he stood and faced the emperor proudly, eyes bright. "To you we grant the estates and titles once held by the Fujibuki, who sadly are no more. Carry them with honor. You may take on their name and crest or create one of your own, as you choose, but you are no longer reliant upon your brother, nor upon anyone but myself, and that only insofar as I will require your counsel, your service, and your loyalty." He hopped down to the main floor and, covering the distance between them in his usual strong stride, startled the young man by clapping a hand upon his shoulder. "Welcome, Takami," he said. "I am very pleased to have you join us."

Takami nodded, still visibly stunned by this strange turn of events, and Kagiri exchanged a smile with his brother.

Now they were three.

CHAPTER TWENTY-TWO

Iraku swiped at the length of silk where it hung draped over a panel, the edge of his blade slicing through the fine blue fabric but not cleanly, its edge snagging on the threads and tugging the entire roll tumbled to the floor at his feet. Behind him he heard a grumbling, and then Aganaka was there, scooping up the tangled pile and clutching it to him as if he were a mother and the silk his only child.

"Will you stop that?" the aged ishtaya demanded petulantly, his bushy eyebrows drawn down so far over his pale eyes it was a wonder he could see to scold. "I've asked you not to! I never should have let you have the sword in the first place!"

"As if you could've stopped me," Iraku replied, waving the old chokoto at the even older man. But if he'd thought the gesture would intimidate the tailor, he was very wrong—the man just snorted at him, ignoring the straight edge and sharp point lingering mere inches from his face.

"Find something useful to do, why don't you?" Aganaka suggested, carrying the silk over to his worktable and lay it out, tsking under his breath as he took up a pair of long, sharp scissors and neatly cut the fabric where Iraku's sword had done such a ragged job before. The bulk of the silk he then rolled neatly back up, restoring it to its place among the shelves that lined one wall of the shop before returning to the worktable and trimming the edges of the cut piece, then folding that up as well. "Like your brother," he added, glancing over his shoulder. "At least he's doing something productive!"

Iraku glared, first at the old man and then in the direction he'd indicated, toward the back of the shop and the small yard behind it. There he could just make out a mop of dark hair, bent over something he could not see but had no doubt was green and leafy. "It's just a bunch of old plants," he muttered, more out of jealousy than anything else.

Not that he wanted to be back there. He could have been— Ibaru had offered more than once. But plants did not interest him. They never had except insofar as they could be eaten. His brother, however, was an altogether different story. The very first day they'd been here, they'd explored the entire space to make sure of what was where and what was useful. When they had slid back the panel separating the interior from its outdoor component, Ibaru had given a ragged little cry. "What in the First Emperor's name?" he'd declared.

"My wife's garden," the old man had stated behind them, his voice still tinged with fear but now also with regret and even irritation. "She loved it, spent half her time out there." He'd shaken his head. "I'm no good with plants, never was. When she died"— he'd lowered his head— "I just let it go."

Ibaru had said nothing more at the time, though his lips had tightened into a disapproving scowl. But the next day he'd rolled up his sleeves, stepped outside, and gone to work. Since then he'd spent a great deal of his time out in the tiny fenced area, weeding and planting and pruning. And Iraku had to admit, it did look a thousand times better, all the disarray tamed, the soil tilled, most of the plants tiny and weak but green and starting to thrive from his brother's careful attentions.

Which was all well and good, but it meant Ibaru was not focusing on what they needed to be doing, which was seeking revenge.

Plus, it left Iraku at loose ends. Aganaka had suggested, none too subtly, that he could help clean up the shop but that brought back too many bitter memories and besides, they were supposed to be in charge here! Fortunately, he had, when rummaging through closets in search of any hidden valuables, discovered this old chokoto leaned in a corner. "It was Denaya's," the old tailor had explained when confronted with it. "She was a soldier for a time, before we met and she gave all that up." Which certainly made more sense than the thought that Aganaka himself could have been the owner, since the idea of fighting back had never even seemed to occur to him. Iraku had claimed the blade and had spent much of his days since swinging it about, much to the ishtaya's alarm and the walls' detriment.

That didn't further their goals much either, of course. But at least it made him feel better.

The sound of footsteps made him turn, to see Ibaru stepping back inside, drying his hands on a towel. "They're coming along nicely," he announced to no one in particular, a rare smile creasing his face. "I recognize some herbs in there, and some radishes, a few other vegetables. It'll be months yet, but eventually they'll be edible."

"Wonderful," Iraku groused. "We can make ourselves a salad and celebrate rotting away doing nothing."

"We're not doing nothing," his brother corrected. "We're biding our time."

"For what, exactly?" Iraku asked, sheathing the sword before stepping up to confront him. "For some magical plan to just land in our laps? How's that going to happen while we're hiding away, playing at gardener and soldier?"

Ibaru studied him a moment but finally sighed. "Perhaps you're right," he admitted. "This isn't getting us anywhere. Though..." he hesitated a second before continuing, "I feel more at peace than I have in...well, maybe ever." He frowned. "Or at least since before our parents died."

"Well, I don't," Iraku insisted, scowling and shrugging it off when his brother tried resting a hand on his shoulder. "I'm not peaceful at all!" Deep down, though, he knew that was not entirely true, and he suspected his brother knew that as well. Before they'd arrived in Awaihinshi it had been a very long time since they'd slept more than a few nights in a single place, and most often that had been by the side of the road or in an old barn or, if they were lucky, on someone's floor. Even the room they'd had after first reaching the city had been a significant step up, with a proper bed and a door and a wash basin all their own. But this! Here they had a whole house to themselves! Themselves and Aganaka, who had somehow gone from being their captive to being more like their irritable uncle and landlord. Still, it was more space, more comfort, more privacy, then ever before. How could that not have an effect on them?

Though one thing it didn't have much of was food. The old man evidently didn't eat a great deal—indeed, it seemed before they'd arrived he'd subsisted mainly on hot tea and rice and bits of dried mushroom he pulled from a large jar. What little else he'd had the brothers had quickly consumed and then been faced with the question of where to get more food—proper food—without using up what little money they had left.

Fortunately, that had been a relatively easy problem to solve. The day after they'd forcibly moved in Iraku had volunteered to find them sustenance, and had only gone as far as next door, which he'd already known was a bakery from the constant smell of fresh bread and buns that filled the shop and set his stomach to grumbling at all hours. It was a warm, clean, sunny little shop, and set out on the counter were all manner of buns and breads and dumplings, enough to make his mouth water. There had been a few other people already in line to purchase things, and so Iraku had waited until they had gone, turning as if to go himself as the last of the customers filed out. Then he'd shut the door behind them and turned the sign upon it to read Closed.

"Excuse me?" the woman behind the counter had called out, coming around to see what he was doing. "Leave that alone, please!" She was nearly twice his size, with thick arms full of muscle from kneading dough all day long, and the fact that her face and hands were spattered here and there with white bursts of flour did not make her any less imposing, especially with a heavy wooden roller in her hand. "If you're not going to buy anything, go ahead and get out," she had warned, hefting that roller in his direction.

"I am not going to buy anything," Iraku had agreed. "And I'll go. After you load all of that into a bag for me." And he glanced past her, toward the heavily laden counter.

That had made her laugh. "And why should I do that?" she'd

asked, looking him up and down, clearly noting his narrow frame and rough clothes. "Get out of here before I thrash you!"

"I think not." Quick as a snake he'd darted out his hand and caught the rolling pin, not trying to yank it free of her grasp but just holding it. Then he'd concentrated.

It was a strange feeling, a bit like trying to force yourself to cough something up, he decided. He could sense the energy, the magic, still within him, but buried deep and cold, like a slumbering lizard. He had to coax it awake, shake it into motion, warm it with his thoughts and his will and drag it back up and out, into his eyes and most importantly his hands.

In this case, one hand in particular.

Once it was jarred back into activity, it rose quickly, swirling up through him like heat from a cup of strong rice wine, filling him and lifting him, giving him strength and purpose. The skin of his hand had paled, all the color draining away until it was ghostly white, and under his touch the sturdy rolling pin had begun to crumble, the heavy wood flaking away like dried leaves, like ash, until it had dissolved to dust in his hand.

The woman had gaped at him, her empty hand falling to her side, and Iraku had smiled at her. "Now, about that bag," he'd prompted, stretching his white hand slowly toward her head, and she'd started and backed away quickly, nodding as she'd hurried to comply.

He'd been grinning ear to ear when he'd returned to the ishtaya's with an entire sack stuffed with food and doled some out to his brother and the old man. He'd been even more pleased when he'd explained what had happened and Ibaru had laughed and hugged him.

"Now, that's thinking, little brother!" he complimented, making Iraku swell with pride. "Excellent! We'll visit each of our neighbors, introduce ourselves, and let them know what we'll be expecting from them. If they don't have food themselves, we'll accept coin instead. Nothing too fancy, not enough to ruin them, but enough to keep us going comfortably."

"By stealing from those around you," Aganaka had accused,

but he'd done it quietly, and he'd not refused the red bean bun when it'd been offered to him a second time.

They had established a pattern, and every day one of them went out to collect from people: meat here, buns there, rice and vegetables and fruit and coin. They now had the entire street under their control, and more food than they could eat themselves, even with the old man grudgingly accepting some.

But that was still just sitting here, wasting time. It was not getting them any closer to their vengeance.

They were still mulling that over when there was a knock on the front door. Iraku exchanged a glance with his brother and the two of them moved as one, flanking the entrance, Iraku drawing his sword again and holding it in what he hoped was a useful position. "Yes?" his brother called.

"I'd like to speak with you," someone replied from the other side. A woman, from the sound of it, with a strong, cultured voice. "May I enter?"

Ibaru frowned by unbolted the door and swung it open, revealing the speaker to be a tall, slender woman in fine robes patterned with stars and crescents, her silver hair pulled back in a tight bun atop her head, her face lined but dignified, even commanding. She swept inside and nodded politely to them, her sharp eyes not missing Aganaka scowling from behind his worktable.

"Thank you," she said, stepping further in so Ibaru could shut the door behind her. If she had any concerns about being closed in with them, she did not show it. "My name is Amani Denbi. And I do not know your names but I have seen you before—in Aihiri, a week or so ago. The day of the invasion." Her eyes trapped them both like the strands of a spider's web, dark as a pit and twice as deep. "I was just departing the compound as you were entering with your...companion."

Iraku stiffened, shooting a glance at his brother. She had seen them with Kaemusei! They had thought no one had save the stranger, the emerald warrior, the two soldiers, and the emperor himself. They had in fact been counting on that anonymity to give them the time to formulate some sort of plan!

He shifted slightly, raising his sword, but the woman—Amani Denbi—only smiled. "There is no need for that," she promised, her voice soothing and calm. "I am here to talk. I believe, from what I saw and from what I have heard is occurring in this neighborhood of late, that the two of you may have some particular talents. And I believe we may have a common goal, or at least complementary ones. I think we may be able to help each other get what we want." She glanced toward the far side of the room, where a low table sat ready with teapot and three cups, as well as a small selection from the day's haul. "May I?"

Iraku looked to his brother, for Ibaru had always been the wiser of them. And after a moment he nodded and stepped aside, allowing this strange visitor to pass. "Please do," he said, draping an arm over his brother's shoulder as they both moved to follow. "You may be exactly what we were waiting for."

CHAPTER TWENTY-THREE

Saisaihyu, Day Six

Hibikitsu nodded his approval as the four figures entered the throne room and advanced across the floor, admiring the stately way in which they moved and the rich, deep purple of their matching robes, broken only by a single golden higeibara upon the left breast. "Ah, excellent!" he exclaimed, pounding a fist upon the arm of his throne. "Now you are truly Rojiri!"

"If you say so," Noniki commented, tugging at his round collar. "I certainly feel different in this thing!"

"Let's just hope I'm not called upon to defend you while wearing it," Kagiri added, frowning as he almost tripped himself, his long legs constrained by the garment's starched silk and sewn sides. "I can barely move."

"The eikono is not designed for combat," Hibikitsu replied loftily, suppressing a very un-emperor-like giggle. "It is a formal garment, and its style and color denote that you four are my imperial councilors. It is a mark of great honor to be granted it, and you should wear it accordingly." That only made Noniki pull another face and Kagiri sigh, and Hibikitsu had to cough into his hand to hide the laughter struggling to escape. The brothers looked so miserable!

At least his other two advisors were facing their new attire with more equanimity. Master Eijiri was advancing at a steady, unhurried pace, his lined face unconcerned. On his other side, Takami was taking small, careful steps, feeling his way in the unfamiliar garb, but his face showed only concentration, not irritation. Then again, for them it was their first foray as his Rojiri. He wondered if they, too, would become more casual toward him in time. He hoped so, for he had no desire to foster the same stiff formality he'd experienced with his previous advisors.

"Welcome, Master Eijiri," he declared as the quartet finally reached the dais. "I am grateful you chose to accept the appointment to Rojiri."

The master jeweler bowed deeply. "You honor me, Your Imperial Majesty," he replied. "I can do no less than promise you that I serve you and the empire and will do so with all my heart."

Hibikitsu accepted this with a gentle nod, then turned to his other new advisor. "And greetings, Fujitai Takami," he said. "I am pleased you have joined us, and appreciate your choice of house name, for it shows both a respect for the past and a desire to move toward the future." Takami had opted to merge the name of the original estate-holder's family, Fujibuki, with that of his own birth family, Kazutai, and had taken for his crest the image of an otter among the waves, which was extremely fitting and highly auspicious for his new Dogenkaishu.

"Thank you, sire," Takami answered, bowing as well. "I am happy it meets with your approval."

"So," Noniki asked, still fiddling with his collar, "will we be expected to wear these all the time now?"

That broke the dam of his self-control and Hibikitsu did laugh, which the young wizard shared easily. "For formal occasions such as this, yes," he admitted. "When you are meeting in your council chambers, no, you will not need them, nor if I summon you to my study for a private conversation."

Kagiri nudged his brother in the side, none too subtly. "That's more than reasonable. And wise for us to present a unified image." As always, the emperor thought, the older sibling was the very voice of reason and restraint, while the younger was all optimism and enthusiasm. How glad he was to have found these two, or to have had them find him.

Standing in her customary place by the righthand pillar closest to the dais, Kohori cleared her throat. "I believe the first of the emissaries approaches, Your Majesty," she said pointedly, raising an eyebrow, and the four Rojiri hurriedly climbed up onto the platform and took places to either side of the throne, Kagiri and

Eijiri on the right, Noniki and Takami on the left. With the four of them beside him and Kohori and Shizumi by the two closest pillars, Hibikitsu felt well-fortified to face these foreign dignitaries, and nodded to the guards to announce the first of them.

"Presenting the Lady Nihiro Omeshi of Fyushu, and Makono Takari if Fyushu!" one of the guards declared loudly, him and his partner standing at attention, yanoi upright, as the pair stepped up to the open doors, paused, and then proceeded across the room, gliding gracefully past the massive pillars to either side. As they approached Hibikitsu could see that the woman was older, her face lined and her hair almost completely silver, her eyes dark and shrewd. In many ways she reminded him of Amani Denbi, which put him on edge, though the Lady Nihiro was smaller and more wizened and did not carry herself with the same haughtiness. Her companion was of average height and stocky build, with sloping shoulders and a round belly visible even through his robes—his face was equally plump and he wore spectacles over pale blue eyes.

"Your Imperial Majesty," Lady Nihiro declared upon reaching the spot even with the last two pillars and all but throwing herself to the floor, pressing her forehead to the tiles there. "I bring greetings from your fellow monarch, the Empress Rilani, and warm wishes." The man beside her had not been as quick to lower himself, and she gave a sharp, vicious tug upon his robes to force him down.

"Indeed?" Hibikitsu leaned back in his chair, fingers tapping his chin, and frowned at the pair. "This is a vastly different greeting than the last we received from Her Majesty, though we grant it is more polite." He was, of course, referring to the recent attempted invasion, which he himself had put down, sending the Fyushan Dogenriku, Yanitai Lai, back in two separate boxes.

Before him, Lady Nihiro ground her head against the floor, but her words rose clearly across the distance. "That was a regrettable incident, Your Imperial Majesty," she agreed, "and the Empress sends her apologies. Yanitai Lai overstepped herself, misunderstanding her orders or perhaps choosing to ignore them."

"Ah, we see." It was boldfaced lie, of course, for the field marshal had brought the full forces of her nation with her, along with several generals. That could not have happened without the empress's approval. But the polite fiction allowed them all to pretend their two nations had not just been at war mere weeks ago. "And to what do we owe the pleasure of your visit, Lady Nihiro?" he asked, adding belatedly, "You may rise."

She did so, slowly, with the creaks and groans of advanced age, and Hibikitsu wondered that she had been sent here. Was this an attempt to gain sympathy? Or a show that there would be no renewed hostilities, sending two who were so obviously not warriors? Or both? Rilani was nothing if not conniving, so he was sure she had considered her choices very carefully.

And indeed, after expressing her thanks, Lady Nihiro's next words revealed her purpose. "I come to beg for mercy and aid, sire," she explained humbly, bowing her aged head. "For you must know that Fyushu starves. We cannot feed our people, and thus we must rely upon the kindness of our neighbors if we are to survive."

"That is unfortunate, and we grieve for your people," he told her. "We had offered Yanitai Lai to sell food to Fyushu at a reasonable price, and we stand by that offer—we would not see anyone suffer needlessly and have no desire to profit off your nation's misfortunes."

The emissary bowed once more. "Thank you, Your Majesty," she intoned. "Rimbaku has ever been admired for its generous spirt and kind nature. I will relay these words to the Empress, and if I may, will await her reply here, for I am sure she will be eager to begin a conversation on how we can satisfy both our nations."

"You and yours are most welcome to remain as our honored guests," Hibikitsu assured her. "We look forward to discussing the matter further." He waved his hand, granting her permission to withdraw, and she did so, retreating and bowing the whole way, as did Makono Takari beside her. He had not said a single word the entire time.

The minute they were out of the room, Shizumi exploded. "Ha!" she declared, circling the column to face Hibikitsu and the others. "So they attack us, try to conquer us, and when we drive them back—when *you* drive them back, sire, and deliver them a decisive defeat—they come crawling back begging to buy grain and rice? I've known snakes who'd not dare such effrontery!"

But Master Eijiri shook his head. "Begging your pardon," he started, waiting until Hibikitsu had gestured for him to continue, "but I took it very differently. This is Fyushu's way of saying, 'we lost and we know it, now we are at your mercy.' It is a public embarrassment, and one they have chosen to embrace, demonstrating the depths of their defeat."

Noniki nodded. "That's why they sent those two," he agreed. "An old woman and a scribe? No threat at all, no show of strength, humble as eel pie."

To her credit, Shizumi gave that due consideration. "I had not seen it that way," she admitted after a moment. "Thank you." Hibikitsu admired her even more for being willing to acknowledge when she was wrong, and when she apologized to him for speaking so angrily he waved it away.

"I value all six of you for your honesty and your devotion, and your willingness to speak your mind," he reminded them gently, leaning forward to speak with them more easily. "We all have much to learn from each other, and how else can we do so but by saying what we think and hearing from others? We will be wrong from time to time—I will, too. But as long as we can accept that and learn from it, we will be better off in the long run." He smiled at Master Eijiri. "I think your interpretation is the correct one, and I am pleased to see your presence here already adding a new dimension to our counsel. Thank you." He sighed and sat back again. "Now, let us proceed to the next visitor, hm?"

That proved to be a slightly larger delegation, four honor guards marching in tight formation around a trio of men, all tall and slender with long, black hair pulled back in a tight braid and wearing long, close-fitting, high-collared robes of yellow satin edged in black embroidery and patterned with the winged serpent of Yatamoro. Behind them came four more guards, these each bearing the weight of a pole supporting a large, intricately carved metal cask between them.

"Your Imperial Majesty," the robed man in front declared, stopping at the appropriate spot and bowing deeply but remaining upright. "We bring greetings from the High Council of Yatamoro." He smiled, though it was an oily expression. "I am Hu Yongian, Chief Ambassador to Rimbaku. My companions are Shen Liang and Wei Bingwen." The two men behind him bowed as well.

"Welcome, Hu Yongian, Shen Liang, and Wei Bingwen," Hibikitsu replied. "To what do we owe this unexpected visit? For we rarely hear from our eastern neighbors." He saw Kohori scowl and Shizumi stiffen slightly, and knew that, like him, they were thinking of the last visitor they'd had from Yatamoro—the shadow assassin who had infiltrated his court, killing several nobles and taking on their identities. At the last he had posed as Fujibuki Haro, the head of the Honjofu and Shizumi's direct superior, and if not for her and Kohori's quick action the false Haro would have killed him right here upon his own throne.

Of course, there was no mention of that now as Hu Yongian bowed again. "Indeed, we regret that lack," he explained with a faint smile, hands clasped behind his back, "and the High Council hopes to address and rectify it. We wish to open more cordial relations with our neighbors and thus have been sent here in the hopes of establishing a permanent diplomatic channel." He pivoted to the side, his two companions sliding away with him, to allow the four bearers to step forward and set the cask down with a loud clatter of metal upon tile. "Please accept this small token of friendship from our nation to yours." At a gesture the guards undid the clasp, which looked to be gold, and flipped open the heavy lid, revealing a satin-lined interior filled with gold, gems, and pearls.

Hibikitsu inclined his head. "We thank you for this noble gift, men of Yatamoro," he said, for he did not know what form of address to use for residents of a country which had long ago abolished its nobility. "And we agree, it would be good to know one another better, and to be able to discuss matters freely. We share a border, and surely must have common interests along it, and perhaps beyond."

"That is our thought as well," Hu Yongian agreed, facing forward once more.

"Please accept our hospitality, as our guests," Hibikitsu stated formally. "We will look forward to conversing with you more, and to opening this new era of communication between our two lands."

"Thank you, sire. We look forward to it as well and will await your convenience." With that the Yatamorans bowed and backed away, leaving the open cask behind.

No sooner had they gone than Master Eijiri was off the platform, leaping down and hurrying across the room with all the vigor of a much younger man. "This is a princely gift," he exclaimed, studying the gems with a sharp eye. "Yatamoro is rich in gems, including diamond, sapphire, and agate. None of those are native to Rimbaku, so their value is even greater here."

"I don't like it," Kohori stated, frowning. "They sent that assassin"—this brought gasps from several of the others, who had not heard of the event—"and now they wish to be friends? And have those three here full-time? They cannot be trusted."

"Maybe not," Noniki countered, "but wouldn't it be useful to get a sense of who they are and how they think? I know I'm not court-educated or anything, but I don't know a thing about Yatamoro except that it's west of us."

"No one knows much about them," Takami agreed, speaking up for the first time. "I've sailed clear up the Zinyang as far as you can go, then tried hiking the mountains in the hopes it would broaden out again on the far side. Guards stopped me before I could cross over into Yatamoro and sent me packing—they were inoffensive but resolute. No one enters their nation without their express permission." He shrugged. "I think, as long as we are careful what we say around them and what we let them do and see, we could learn a great deal from having them here."

Hibikitsu tapped his chin. "Agreed. We will let them stay and see how it goes. But we will be careful, and I will have guards with me any time I meet with them." He grimaced. "I'm not going to give them a second chance to slit my throat."

The others all nodded, and Eijiri asked the guards to send

someone to remove the cask. Once that was done, they all resumed their places to meet the third and final foreign delegation.

"Lord and Lady Yakami Morinaga of Higinasi and entourage," the guards announced, and a small procession entered. At the front marched the couple in question, both in formal court attire in the greens and blues and whites of Higinasi, the nation's stylized wave crest upon his round satin cap and patterned across her silk shawl. Behind them came several men and women in similar but less elaborate garb, clearly assistants and other minor functionaries.

The pair stopped and bowed. They were a handsome couple, Hibikitsu saw, both tall and well-featured, not quite young but still strong and graceful. "Your Imperial Majesty," Lord Yakami declared, bowing low, and his wife flowed into an elegant curtsy. "We bring you greetings from the King and Queen of Higinasi and wishes for health and happiness to you and all your people."

"Thank you, and welcome, Lord Yakami," Hibikitsu replied. "We appreciate those wishes and return them with all sincerity, for ever has Higinasi been a friend to us." Which was certainly true, as far as such things went. They had never been at war, had never squabbled over their shared border, had never had cause to seek redress from one another. And though their contact had been infrequent it had always been cordial. The two nations kept to themselves and did not worry one another—in the realm of world politics, was that not a friend?

"We are glad you feel so, sire," the ambassador stated, smiling pleasantly, "for our only aim is a fervent wish to improve such relations. Our king and queen feel that there is much to be gained by a closer alliance between our two nations and have given us the happy task of broaching such a possibility."

"Oh?" Now he leaned forward, hands upon his knees. "And what form does such a possibility take?"

The lord smiled and, turning, nodded to his lady, who curtseyed in return. Then she spun about and offered her hand to the woman behind her, guiding the lady forward. This woman was younger, Hibikitsu saw at once, and pleasantly featured if not stunningly so, with a perfectly composed expression that spoke of years of court training. Her movements were also precise and perfect, her curtsey smooth, and now he noted that her clothing was a finer cut than even the ambassadors', and her robes were all over patterned with the Higinasi crest. A strange pit opened in his stomach, and he found himself almost dreading what might occur as the foreign lord opened his mouth to speak once more.

"Your Imperial Majesty," Lord Yakami declared in ringing tones, his words echoing around the room, "may I present Her Highness, Ogawa Tsuni, sister to our king, His Majesty Ogawa Kunetai." He bowed again, but there was no mistaking the smirk on his face when he straightened and continued, "it is our king's most fervent wish that you will consider taking his sister as your bride and uniting our two nations by the ties of kinship and blood."

Hibikitsu was very glad then that he had his Rojiri beside him, and Kohori and Shizumi near as well. He might need all of them to catch him if he fainted dead away and toppled from his throne.

CHAPTER TWENTY-FOUR

Shizumi was only able to contain herself until they had left the throne room—her and Kohori heading for the hallway toward their respective barracks, the Rojiri retiring to their council chamber, and the emperor retreating to the safety of his private study. But once it was just her and her fellow Taikoro out in the hall, with some distance safely between them and the others, she burst out laughing.

"He looked like a fish I once caught!" she exclaimed, hugging herself as she laughed. "Mouth wide open, eyes bulging, and that look of, 'I can't believe this just happened to me!'"

"That is our esteemed emperor, the very spirit of our nation, you are comparing to a fish," the older woman pointed out, yet her lips were twitching as she said it, and after a second a loud guffaw escaped her as well. "But he really did, didn't he?"

They shared their amusement for a moment before getting it back under control. "I don't blame him, mind," Shizumi added once she'd composed herself again. "I'd have been shocked too, if someone had shown up for a meeting with me and said, 'oh, by the way, here's someone you've never met, I think you should marry him!'"

"No, that was certainly a surprise to us all," Kohori agreed. "Though, to be fair, it would be an advantageous match on both sides. We would gain access to their streams and lakes, their farms, their vineyards and orchards. They would gain access to our granaries, our rivers, and most importantly our warriors." Higinasi had never had any military might of its own—surrounded by mountains to the north and the west and water to the south and east, it was difficult to assail, and its greatest riches were its fruits and vegetables so it was hardly a rich prize for most would-be conquerors. But that did not mean no one had ever eyed its lush fields with envy, and of course Yatamoro was becoming increasingly rapacious. Allying with Rimbaku would indeed be a way to keep Higinasi safe.

"I understand that, strategically speaking," Shizumi agreed now. "But wouldn't it have been more diplomatic, not to mention more considerate, to broach the subject first, *then* bring the prospective bride? Rather than the other way round?"

Her companion nodded. "It would. But I suppose this way makes it harder to refuse gracefully." She shook her head. "I am glad I have never been important enough to merit such manipulation."

"What? But you're Taikoro of the Honteno," Shizumi protested with a grin. "You stand beside the emperor himself! You must have suitors beating down your doors!" They both chuckled at that, as only two lifelong soldiers could, not to mention two women who had never been praised as great beauties. Fortunately, their careers did not depend upon their looks.

Thinking about careers brought Shizumi back to another matter. "Norio Shinjuru should arrive in the next day or two," she said, "with the recruits. As soon as he does, I'll send for you. And..." She frowned, struggling to recall the names of her counterpart's two chuisu. "Itamon and Reizei as well."

"Thank you," Kohori told her. "I do appreciate that." She smiled. "And I promise not to steal all the best ones." She turned and fixed Shizumi with a sharp, steady gaze. "How is everything else? I know you wanted to talk the other day, and I'm sorry about that, and that we've both been so busy since." She shrugged. "But we're both here now."

Shizumi nodded. "We are, yes." She sighed, stopping and turning to put her back against the wall, leaning her head back to rest it against the smooth paneling there. "I am...managing, I suppose. To be honest, I never dreamed I'd be here. Taikoro of the Honjofu! It's mad. I'm not a noble, I'm a woman...and I'm Mukanichi!" She had still had trouble openly admitting that last one. "The first should have barred me from ever advancing past gunso. The second wouldn't have stopped me in and of itself, but compounded with the first it would have cemented my inability to rise higher. And the last—well, that should have been ground for immediate expulsion, maybe even incarceration for falsifying aitachi." She laughed, and even to her own ears the sound was bitter, hollow. "Yet here I am, much to my own disbelief—and that of many others."

As always, the head of the Honteno heard the truth within the words. "That's the real problem, isn't it?" she asked now, setting herself against the opposite wall—this was one of the more private passageways, narrow enough that they were still only a few feet apart and could converse easily, not like the major halls where they'd have had to shout if they'd stood in such positions. "There are people who are questioning your appointment." Shizumi could feel the older woman's eyes upon her, even though she kept her own gaze on the delicately painted ceiling. "Your own Honjofu. Dissension within the ranks."

"I cannot entirely blame them," Shizumi admitted, shutting her eyes and breathing in the scent of the palace, the lemon oil used to polish the wood and the hint of sandalwood burned in alcoves to freshen the air and, behind it all, the faint hint of soil and grass from the gardens and yards beyond. "I did lie. And my appointment does violate all tradition, all the rules they have always lived by."

"Do you think you don't deserve it?" The question was quiet, and Shizumi blinked, tilting her head down to meet Kohori's gaze and seeing that she was serious—not mocking, not insulting, just genuinely curious.

That felt like it deserved an honest answer, and after considering, and setting aside both foolish pride and false modesty, Shizumi was finally able to say, "No, I do deserve it. I am an exceptional warrior, a strong leader, an able planner, and the best-suited among the Honjofu to take command." Coming to that realization felt like a weight had been lifted from her chest, and she smiled, knowing it to be true.

Her companion smiled back. "Good. I agree. As did our emperor, or he would not have appointed you. So trust in yourself, and in him, and never let anyone tell you different." Her face grew more somber. "There will always be those who try to tear you down, Shizumi. Don't let them. Show them what you can do. If they're decent at all, they'll learn to accept that. If not—" She shrugged. "Then they are not worth your time."

"You're right." She levered herself off the wall and saluted, hand to her chest. "Thank you, Kohori. I appreciate the advice, and even more just being able to ask for it."

The older woman returned the gesture of respect. "My pleasure." Then she clapped Shizumi on the shoulder. "I'll see you later, yes? And we really must go for that drink some time."

"Absolutely." Shizumi smiled at her, and turned, for they were near the place where their paths would part. "But right now I think I have some soldiers I need to speak with."

She found Geniji and Dairamu in the barracks as usual, playing at cards with Akino, Isano, Diritan, and Nioko. All six stood and saluted when she entered, and she waved them off. "At ease," she insisted, pulling up a stool beside the table. "Who is winning?"

For a moment none of them spoke, still standing there not quite at attention but certainly not at ease. Then Isano shrugged and folded himself back onto his seat. "I am, of course," he answered with a smirk. The pile of coins before him confirmed his claim. Not that she was surprised—she'd been foolish enough to play cards with the archer once or twice before and had regretted it every time.

"Hai," Diritan agreed, the burly warrior as loud as always. "It is not right that one man should be so lucky—especially when it is not me!"

The others laughed, and Akino and Nioko both relaxed and took their seats again. Geniji and Dairamu sat as well, but more stiffly, and both women kept glancing at Shizumi from the corners of their eyes.

"Look," Shizumi announced with a sigh. "I wanted to apologize, especially to you four." That was directed at her former bantao, her trusted squad. "I am sorry I lied to you, even if it was just by omission. I know you can understand why, but still I hated not being able to be honest with you all."

"Why couldn't you?" Akino asked bluntly. "We wouldn't have cared."

She smiled at him. "Thank you. I appreciate that. But we both know that not everyone would...not everyone *does* feel the same way." She was careful not to look at Geniji or Dairamu as she said that. "What I did, it wasn't illegal but it flew in the face of tradition. And what's more, some of you might have worried about my command if you'd known. You all trusted that I was relying upon decades, centuries of experience each time I led you into battle. Instead, it was always just me."

"'Just you' saved our asses countless times," Isano pointed out after a moment, his words as unhurried as always. "You're clever, brave, and not afraid to take risks, and we all know you'd never ask us to do something you wouldn't do yourself, and that you'd gladly die for us. I'd trust all that—and you—over some old bones any day." Akino pounded the table in agreement, and Diritan and Nioko nodded, even though they had not served under her as much as the other four.

Shizumi grinned and ducked her head to hide the tears that had sprung up in her eyes at what she knew was a heartfelt declaration. "Thank you. And I want you all to know that I trust you, too. With my life. I'm glad my secret is out now, I'm sorry I ever felt I had to keep it from you, and I promise you that none of this has changed me, or my respect for all of you. I am still the same person I always was."

"Just with a bit more gold on your armor now," Diritan said with a grin. Most of the others laughed at that, as did Shizumi—and, after a second, so did Geniji.

"So," the big woman said, clapping Shizumi on the shoulder. "Are you going to try your luck with us again? Or is the big bad Taikoro afraid of looking foolish when she loses all her money to some lowly Honjofu?"

It took every ounce of will Shizumi had to keep her voice steady as she replied, "Bring it on—this Taikoro is going to clean you out!"

She wound up barely able to see the cards she got dealt, her eyes were so misty. Not that it mattered. Isano won the hand and took her coins along with everyone else's—but Shizumi still grinned until her cheeks hurt, knowing she'd been the real winner here.

CHAPTER TWENTY-FIVE

Chimehara started when the hand landed on her shoulder, her free hand reaching reflexively for the concealed slit in her robes—and the knife sheathed just beneath. Fortunately, awareness overrode instinct and she settled for resting that hand upon her hip as the person beside her began kneading her shoulders, now with two hands that, despite their wrinkles and lines and the long, heavily lacquered nails, were still strong and supple.

"You're so tense!" Madam Ponsoi said, massaging her shoulders through the silk. "Is everything all right, dear?"

Chimehara nodded. "I'm so sorry," she told the head housekeeper, reaching up to pat her hand. "Thank you. I'm just tired. I've not been sleeping all that well."

That earned a snort. "Who has, with all this going on?" The older woman freed one hand to wave it at the world around them. "A Saisaihyu, of all things! And you with not one but two younglings at home now! How are dear Suda and poor Ruisoki holding up during all this strangeness?"

"They are well, thank you," Chimehara replied. She knew her friend's interest and concern were genuine and had begun to appreciate that—before being here she had never had anyone who had truly cared about her before, only about what she could do for them or what they could get from her. "It is taking a little time to adjust, of course."

An adjustment made both harder and easier by the disappearance of her third charge, the feral boy named Gou.

That was what had really been keeping her up at nights, and even now she ground her teeth thinking about it. She had been so sure she'd won him over. He had followed her home docilely enough, no doubt mainly for the promise of food. He had seemed interested to see the two apartments she occupied, and had reacted to the other children with, if not enthusiasm, at least guarded curiosity.

She had insisted he bathe before she set out the food they'd brought back with them, and afterward he had seemed less a wild beast and more just another poor, starved child left to fend for himself on the streets. He had not lunged for the food but had instead reached carefully, eyeing the rest of them closely, hunched over the rice and fish and vegetables and buns as if he thought they might steal everything from him if given a chance. Ruisoki had laughed at that, but then he'd grown up in the care of House Chohu. He had never had to fight for every scrap. Suda and Chimehara herself both had, and they understood exactly what the cadaverous little boy was thinking.

After he had sated his appetite somewhat—and she'd been pleased to see that he hadn't gorged himself, either—she had explained their situation and offered to let him join them. Food and lodging, clothing and care, protection and training, all in exchange for listening to her and doing as she instructed. Gou had considered it carefully and had finally nodded. Satisfied with that, Chimehara had fixed up a bedroll for him on the living room floor, not too far from the others but far enough away that he would not feel crowded, and that had been that. When she had left for work the next morning, she had instructed Suda and Ruisoki to answer any questions their new classmate might have but also to give him space, let him get acclimated.

By the time she had returned home, he was gone.

"He just got up and left," Suda had insisted when asked. "I told him not to, I told him to stay and wait here for you, but he didn't listen." She shook her head. "When I reached for him, he hissed at me. So I let him go." The little girl had looked miserable. "I'm sorry."

"Don't be," Chimehara had assured her. "You didn't do anything wrong. We can't make him stay here if he doesn't want to. And you could've gotten hurt if you'd tried to stop him." She remembered the way he had attacked that man on the street. Yes,

Gou was dangerous. The question was, had he left to get some air, to assert some independence, to be alone for a bit? Or had he gone for good?

Unfortunately, he now knew about Chimehara and her little school—and he knew where they lived. Which meant she couldn't just let him wander off. They'd have to find him and either convince him to come back, be convinced he would keep their secret, or make sure he could never expose them to anyone. "Let's go look for him, shall we?" was all she'd said, but she'd guessed by the children's grim expressions that they'd figured out those options for themselves, and all three of them were armed when they'd left the apartment.

They had searched for several hours before giving up for the night. And had continued to do so every night since. But thus far they'd found not a single trace of the wild little boy. It was possible he'd slipped through to one of the other levels, though Chimehara considered that unlikely—even in the clothes he'd borrowed from Ruisoki, Gou still looked like a hungry spirit made flesh, far too unhealthy for the guards to just let past without questioning. And she already knew how he reacted to confrontation. No, more likely he'd found some place to hole up, some hiding spot she'd yet to uncover.

She would, though. It was just a matter of time.

Of course, it did not help that she was also spending several hours each night down at Yue Judei, drinking with Kohori.

A smile touched her lips at that one. She had always known, since she was very young, the effect she had on men. And she'd also learned, not too much later, that some women found her attractive as well. But none of them had been anything like the grizzled but still hearty guard commander. Such a fascinating figure! She had to admit, she was enjoying her time with the older woman. As yet it had been nothing but food, drink, and some mild flirtation. Still, there was a great deal of promise there, and it was certainly a pleasant way to pass the time.

It did, however, mean that she was currently operating on too little sleep. Again.

Madam Ponsoi paused in her ministrations, lowering her hands and giving Chimehara a quick hug. "Well, if you need anything, you know you have but to ask," she promised warmly.

"I do. Thank you." Chimehara returned the hug. Then, with a sigh, she disengaged from the older woman and continued into the compound, heading toward the trading room. She had several recent orders to go over, and a few other potential deals she needed to follow up on. She had not been a trader for long, and was still very junior at it, but it was exciting, using her natural skill at coaxing and manipulating to draw in clients and convince them to buy jewels and gemwork from the house.

She was proving to be very, very good at it.

Some hours later, Chimehara was studying a list of requirements for one possible project—a noble who wanted a present for his son and heir's coming of age and was still trying to decide between a set of kanashi with matching combs, a fine iniro, or a full suzeri kabo, and had asked for how much each option would cost and how long each would take to create—when movement outside the trading room made her glance up. A tall, handsome woman was gliding past behind Madam Ponsoi, walking in that manner some had that was both elegant and purposeful, like a soldier mingled with a dancer. The woman was older, with silvered hair pulled back in a neat taikamage, and her face was lined but strong and aristocratic, chin automatically tilted up at that slight angle that said she was better than her surroundings and the people who filled them. Her clothes were very fine, a pattern of stars and moons picked out upon them, and though she wore little in the way of jewelry Chimehara noted that her few adornments were of exceptional quality and looked, at this distance, to be of advanced age as well, heirlooms and the like. And she was heading straight for Master Eijiri's private office. Interesting.

After they'd passed, Chimehara rose to her feet, stretched, collected some things from her workspace, and made her way toward the hall. Turning right would bring her to that same office, but she had no excuse for going there at the moment. Instead she turned left, walking along past several small meeting rooms until she reached the main hall. That led her to the dining area, where she was able to refill her teacup from the pot that was always kept boiling there. Ah! She was tired enough that the first gulp of hot tea was like a splash of cold water to the face, jolting her back to full alertness even as the delicate jasmine scent cleared her head. Much better!

And on her way back to her desk who should she run into but Madam Ponsoi? The housekeeper wasted no time taking her arm and pulling her to the side. "Did you see who that was just now?" she asked in an excited whisper. "That was Amani Denbi!"

Chimehara frowned. The house name sounded familiar, though she could not place it right off. No doubt due to her current fatigue and foggyheadedness. Tea could only do so much!

When she did not otherwise react, her friend hurried to fill her in. "She was the head of the emperor's Rojiri!" she explained quickly, glancing down the hall in case the woman in question should overhear. "Until he removed her, and all the rest, the same night as the invasion."

"Ah. Of course." That made sense. She had heard about that— indeed, the whole city had been in a mild uproar over it, for the emperor had demoted all his advisors to the lowest rank of nobility. Then he had replaced them with a pair of young men no one in the city knew anything about, and all this the same day the emperor himself had returned from somewhere beyond Awaihinshi's walls—and the day those bizarre, gigantic skeletal creatures had attacked.

Which begged the question—what was the former head of the Rojiri doing here?

Chimehara could guess, of course. Master Eijiri had called the entire house together just the previous morning to make a grand announcement. "It is with great pleasure and much humility," their master had declared, "that I inform you that I have been invited to become one of the emperor's new Rojiri!" That had caused a wave of surprise to ripple through the assembled crowd, and he had smiled good-naturedly. "Yes, I too was surprised," he'd told them. "But it seems the Echo of Victory, long may he reign, has decided he should be advised by not just nobles but merchants and even those of lower birth. I have of course accepted, as it is a great honor, and I only hope I may live up to His Imperial Majesty's faith in me." He'd chuckled a little. "I will only be up in Aihiri for sessions and any time I am summoned to give counsel, so do not worry, I will still be here with you much of the time. And, of course, Madam Ponsoi will maintain the house whenever I am absent." He'd favored them all with a proud glance. "This is a great day for our house and can only improve our status and our fortunes in future." Everyone had agreed and had gone up to congratulate him afterward.

And now the woman who had formerly held that position was here, a day later. No doubt to see for herself this merchant who dared take on her old title.

Chimehara returned to her station, and her work. She was not back there long, however—her tea had only just cooled enough to be truly drinkable—when a shadow fell across her desk. She glanced up, lips parting to ask whomever it was to refrain from blocking the light, only to find Amani Denbi standing before her.

"Ah." The former Rojiri was studying her, sharp eyes missing no detail, and Chimehara's own narrowed slightly, her chin lifting in response. "Yes, I can certainly understand why Master Eijiri would bring you with him. No doubt you made a favorable impression upon our young, handsome, lonely emperor?"

"I hope the emperor found favor with me," she replied, bowing her head, for there was no denying the woman she faced was nobility, and she was not. "I am Chimehara."

"Amani Denbi." It was clear from her manner that the noble lady had no doubt her identity was already known. "And how did you find the Echo of Victory?" she asked next, the words and tone casual but that gaze like a quisuin, coiled and ready to strike.

"The emperor is a great man," Chimehara stated carefully, eyes demurely downcast. "We were honored that he requested we attend him."

"I'm sure you were." The woman was still watching her closely. "Although it is your master he chose for his Rojiri, not you." There was an insult hidden within that statement, but so subtle it was more the ghost of an insult, like the faintest tinge of the sea upon a weak breeze.

Still, Chimehara raised her head and met the other woman's gaze square on. "I am but a junior trader," she pointed out, her own tone sharpening. "Master Eijiri is the head of our house, and renowned for his wisdom. I applaud the emperor's choice."

Now Amani Denbi smiled, a slow, self-satisfied expression like a cat who had just caught a mouse. "Ah, so there is some fire to you, after all! Good—it would be a shame for such beauty to be wasted upon one without a spine." She glanced around then, taking in the rest of the room. "A well-appointed space," she commented. "And you are in a fine spot within it, I notice."

Which was true. Chimehara had seen at once upon being promoted to trader that the two best locations in the common trading room were the ones closest to the outer doors, where you could look out upon the central gardens and feel the sun and the wind upon your face, and the two in the middle, where your space was turned so that you had a wall at your back. The worst two were the ones closest to the door, where anyone could walk up behind you without your noticing them. She had not felt justified in trying for one of the two front positions—not yet, at any rate—but had felt no qualms at coaxing one of the other traders into swapping with her so that she could be in the middle. She had chosen the desk to the left of the room's central aisle, so that she had more sunlight and more of the breeze, and was happy with the position. She was impressed, though, that this woman had discerned so much. And even moreso when she added, "But you are the most junior trader in the room, are you not? How fortunate for you, then, that you were able to secure such a good location. Normally I would have expected placement to go in order of seniority."

"Yes, well," Chimehara smiled, "Master Atunobu was kind enough to allow me to take this place after I explained that being confined to the shadows tended to make me sneeze." It had not hurt, of course, that the fleshy trader had not been able to take his beady little eyes off Chimehara, or more precisely off that cleft where her robes parted ever so slightly to hint at her bosom, and he had quickly realized that if he gave up his middle space to her, he would then be positioned to ogle her all day long. She did not mind—it cost her nothing for him to get an eyeful, and a few bright smiles and lingering stretches each day kept him more than willing to do whatever she wanted. A happy arrangement for all.

Now Amani Denbi laughed, the sound one of dry amusement, even some approval. "I see," she said. "Yes, well done." Her eyes narrowed. "You seem to me to be a young woman of sharp eyes and deep ambitions," she commented quietly, her voice low enough that Chimehara doubted any of the other traders could make out the words. "Between that and your other virtues, I suspect you could go far, provided you are not the type to balk at taking chances. Are you?"

Chimehara recognized the question within that question, and set aside all dissembling long enough to answer, "I am willing to do what must be done."

The ex-Rojiri nodded. "Yes, I believe you are. I think you may be able to help me, Chimehara. And I can help you in return." She dipped her head just a notch, that of a noble to her social inferior, but not dismissively or intended to insult. "If you like, you should stop by some time for tea. I am sure we would have much to discuss."

She turned and headed for the hall without another word. Chimehara watched her go, weighing the older woman's words and what they could mean. These were strange times indeed, but she knew one thing for certain—she would be visiting House Amani soon. Very soon.

Because yes, she had grand ambitions. And if Amani Denbi could help her realize them, so much the better.

CHAPTER TWENTY-SIX

Noniki arrived at the front of his estate to discover a crowd gathered before him. They were massed around the open outer gates, and among the throng he saw people in the rough clothing of laborers, those in finer ponmei and shatage and either hantien or kaoni, and some in kitoro and kisoni, the last group ranging from simpler robes to truly elegant ones. It was rare to see such a mingling of ranks, and even more so to find them not arguing with one another, but at the moment everyone's attention seemed directed toward his own home.

And the mood he was picking up was not congenial.

One of those toward the back spotted him first. "Who're you?" the man demanded, turning and stepping forward to confront him as he walked up. "Go on home. There's nothing for you here!" He was big and broad, with thick arms and no coat to hide them, just a sleeveless cotton shirt belted above coarse but sturdy torito and dusty boots. His hands looked as large as Noniki's head, and his broad features were set in a scowl.

But Noniki had faced far worse than some burly worker and refused to be cowed. "I will be the judge of that," he said calmly. "Kindly step aside and let me through."

"Didn't you hear what I just said?" the man snapped, leaning in to tower over him. "I said go away!" And he raised one of those enormous hands to shove Noniki back.

That, Noniki decided, was a step too far. He shook his head and a wind swept up from behind him, flowing past and ruffling his hair as it forced the big man back one step, then another, then finally carried him clear off his feet until he collided with the estate's outer walls hard enough to knock the breath clean from his lungs. "You should be more polite," Noniki instructed. "You never know when you will threaten the wrong person."

The little confrontation had not gone unnoticed, and several of those watching retreated a pace or two, creating space around him. There were whispers through the crowd as well, and many of the people shied back, fear in their eyes.

Not everyone was so effected, however. One man, for example, stomped forward to take the large laborer's place. This was no mere worker, however. Instead Noniki found himself facing a heavyset man only a little older than himself but attired in sumptuous silks of a deep, rich red, emblazoned with the black silhouettes and paw prints of a large bear. "Your trickery reveals your identity," the man stated loudly, waving an elaborate fan before shutting it with a decisive snap. "You are that new Rojiri, the foreigner." The man's manner was elegant but arrogant, his eyes narrowed as if he had already decided to take offense, and there was about him a scent of candied orange that verged on the overripe.

"I am Noniki," Noniki admitted easily enough. "And I have the honor and responsibility of being one of the emperor's new Rojiri. I am no foreigner, however. I was born and raised in Bezenkai, not far from Ginzai." He nodded politely but saw the stranger's nostrils flare, for it had been the greeting of one to his equal or even someone of lesser rank. "Now if you will excuse me?"

"There can be no excuse!" the nobleman retorted, tapping Noniki on the shoulder with that fan. "You are to blame for this! Fix it at once!" And he stalked off with a huff, a smaller man in a more modest and muted version of the same colors hurrying after him.

"I don't even know what 'this' is!" Noniki protested, more to himself than to the lord's retreating form.

"They are objecting to business being conducted here," a voice responded, and Noniki swiveled back around to find a woman before him. She was tall and thin, with a long face and a long nose, but at least she was not scowling, nor blocking his path. Instead, she was regarding him with some curiosity, her head tilted to the side in a manner that seemed remarkably like the blue and green swallows decorating her robes. "This is Atsani, after all. Only the richest and most powerful nobles reside upon this level. To do anything as common as offering services or selling wares would be crass." There was a quirk to her lips that suggested she found all this amusing, which intrigued Noniki in turn.

"You disagree with them?" he asked, folding his arms over his chest.

The woman shrugged. "I am not from Awaihinshi either," she explained, matching his posture, her hands disappearing into the sleeves of her kitoro. "Thus, I am perhaps less concerned about maintaining the sanctity of the neighborhood."

He nodded. "Thank you for explaining it to me. I will speak with my friends and see if there is some way we can ease everyone's concerns."

"Good luck." She bowed and turned, gliding back to clear the path fully for him, and Noniki returned the bow before continuing past her.

The rest of the crowd had remained pulled back, and so he was able to reach the gates without further obstacle. He noticed as he approached, however, that something had changed. When he had altered the design on the gates, he had removed the Etsuya name from the arches above, leaving the curved double expanse clean and blank. Now, however, that stretch was covered by a scroll that had been tied to both sides. He suspected the long parchment bore some sort of painting on it and had recently hung in one of the rooms within the estate, but someone had reversed it and painted upon the blank back in blocky but serviceable script, "Sorainasei."

"Those without bones."

Noniki smiled. He rather liked that.

Passing through the more entryway, he saw that the estate's courtyard was more crowded than it had been when he'd left this morning. Now it was not merely his friends who were spread out across the tiled expanse. There were other people wandering about, chatting with this resident or that, and in a few places they had gathered in small clusters. A man walked past Noniki carrying a woven basket, and another exited holding a small sachet of something that smelled deeply floral. Noniki's smile broadened. It seemed his friends were faring well in their new endeavors.

A figure hurried toward him, and he felt his cheeks flush and his heart race as he saw it was Seikoku. Would he ever stop feeling such a rush at the mere sight of her? He hoped not.

"There you are!" she exclaimed as she reached him, giving him a quick hug but pulling back almost at once so she could speak more easily. "I'm sorry to call you away from your own work, but I was worried."

"It's all right," he promised, catching her hands in his and marveling at how slender and agile they were. "I'm here now." He glanced back over his shoulder, where the crowd had thinned and seemed more confused now than angry but had not dissipated fully. "I take it that was the reason for your concern?"

She nodded. "We've had a steady flow of people in since we opened the gates at dawn," she explained, leading him back toward the others. "Many seemed thrilled that they could now purchase goods or services without having to leave their own neighborhood." She sighed. "But then some of the people they'd been buying from showed up, and they were a good deal less pleased to see us setting up shop here. They told us we couldn't do that, that this neighborhood is for nobles only, that we didn't belong!" She was as angry as he'd ever seen her, and he tried to push aside how lovely her eyes were when they flashed like that, or how that flush showed off the delicate curve of her cheek.

"Yes, I met some of them out there," he answered, squeezing her hands in what he hoped was a reassuring manner. "You are correct, they are not pleased at having us here." He frowned, both because he hated to see anyone upset—especially people he cared about—but also because he could see the locals' point. If you were a baker and lived down in Bejinuri but made your living selling and delivering your baked goods here in Atsani, and someone opened a shop in the neighborhood selling the same sorts of breads and buns and treats as you, would you not feel threatened? And cheated, since you would never have had the opportunity to start a business here yourself?

He explained his thinking to Seikoku, who sighed. "Yes, I can see that as well," she admitted. "But at the same time, it is not our fault that those bakers and weavers and potters and whomever else were not allowed to set up shop here! And if their goods and services are better than ours, or equally as good but at a better price, wouldn't the nobles around us still use the same people they always have instead of choosing us instead? Does that not suggest that we are offering better goods, better value? And are we to blame for that?"

Noniki did not fail to note how she said "we" even though she was not providing any of those goods or services herself. He understood completely, however. They were a community, a family, and so they were all looking out for each other's best interests.

"No, you are right," he agreed. "That is not our fault. We have been given this estate, and I have never been told that we were not allowed to sell things from within it, so we are not breaking any rules except perhaps those of long tradition. And we must find ways to be productive and to provide for ourselves." He released one of her hands to scratch his chin. "But perhaps there is some way we can be more considerate toward our neighbors, and the people who have been providing for them all this time, while still taking care of ourselves."

"If we can do both, that would be lovely," Seikoku said. "But how do we manage that, exactly?"

He hated to look into those beautiful eyes and give this reply, but he refused to lie to her. "I do not know," he said finally. He offered her a small smile. "But I promise you, together we will do our best to figure that out."

She smiled back, her fingers still twined with his, and Noniki felt a surge of happiness and confidence. Together with her, how could there be anything they could not accomplish? He laughed from sheer joy, and her smile widened into a grin in response. "Now," he told her, "why don't we see how all our friends are faring? And," he added, raising an eyebrow, "perhaps you can tell me about how you renamed our home in my absence."

That made her laugh, and always it was a delight to hear, clear and bright like sunlight made into sound. "Sorry," she said. "Do you hate it? It's just we needed to be able to tell people something besides 'come find me at what used to be House Etsuya' and it seemed appropriate."

"It is perfect," he assured her, swinging their joined hands gently back and forth as they walked. "I was only surprised, is all."

"Well, I promise not to rename or rearrange the rest of the place without at least warning you first," she stated impishly, and they were both laughing as they reached the first of their friends' makeshift shops, their troubles momentarily forgotten.

CHAPTER TWENTY-SEVEN

Saisaihyu, Day Seven

Kagiri sighed and pushed away from his desk, letting himself fall onto his back just long enough to arch up, tucking his knees into his chest and then propelling them back down so that his feet hit the ground and shot him to his feet, where he stretched widely, his mouth parting in a massive yawn. Bones, but he was tired! And utterly fed up with being cooped in here all day.

He glanced down at the paperwork spread across his writing surface and scowled. Why had he never realized that being in charge of the nation's armies would largely be a matter of reading and signing reports, issuing orders, and poring over budgets, forms, and maps? He had, of course, held in his head an idealized image of leading troops into battle, riding a massive horse and charging into foes, but in reality there were few foes to be had, and with Fyushu so utterly defeated none who would dare face them in open battle.

No, for the moment the people opposing him most severely were his own generals. It was maddening, and every time Kagiri thought about it he wanted to scream. What was wrong with these men? Did they not understand that he was now their superior, appointed by the emperor himself, and that he was trying to keep the realm safe?

But he knew exactly what the problem was. He was not one of them. Not only was he not a scion of one of Rimbaku's leading families, he was not even noble-born. Ash, he wasn't even of the merchant class! He and Noniki were from a tiny fishing village. They were peasant stock, pure and simple, and the taishos, who were all members of ancient bloodlines, took that as a personal insult of the highest order.

He twisted back and forth, feeling his shoulders and side pop, and grunted. In the past few days, since their initial meeting, he had spoken with Daishin Nishoji twice, finding him far and away the most amenable of the four generals. In fact, Daishin had been the only one to respond to his summons by actually appearing—Masagi Matsu and Atsumi Izo had both begged off, claiming urgent business, and Noboru Juniri had not bothered to dignify him with a response. That would have to change, and soon.

Now was not the time, however. It had been a long day, and he had been invited to an early dinner by Kishin Narai and the other merchants. Though he suspected they wanted something from him, Kagiri still felt he owed it to them to accept.

Besides which, although Noniki and Seikoku's friends had welcomed him, he still did not feel entirely a part of their small community. Those people had traveled together, spending days and weeks walking and riding beside each other along the road, nights sleeping near one another under the stars—they had faced wind and rain and drought and hunger and poverty and bandits and all manner of other obstacles together. The experiences had bonded them, as such things would, and now they were more family than friends.

Whereas he only knew Niki, really. Even Seikoku he had only spent a short time with since meeting her here in Awaihinshi, and although Kagiri liked the pretty former thief—and could see exactly why his little brother was so smitten with her—he felt they were still getting to know each other. It was a process that would take time. Nor was he unwilling to try, both with her and with the others at the estate where they now all lived together.

But Narai and the rest, those were people he had traveled with and bonded with, albeit in odd ways. So in some ways, despite their attempts at manipulation, Kagiri felt that dining with them tonight would be a more relaxed affair for him than trying to keep Isoro and Sanedi and Minawa and the others straight.

With those thoughts in his head, he took up his sword from the stand, sliding it through his okube and then stepping out onto the open balcony, from which he hopped down onto the grass. It was good to feel the earth beneath his boots once more. He was smiling as he strode toward the outer gates that would allow him to descend from Aihiri to Atsani and then Motohiri. It had poured for a period earlier but the sky was clear now, the air pleasantly crisp and lightly scented with river water and wet grass, and the walk would do him good.

"So," Kishin Narai commented as they finished their meal—not as elaborate as the feast they'd had previously but still excellent. The broad-shouldered merchant had his cup in hand and was ever so gently swirling the tea within it, causing hints of lemongrass to reach Kagiri's nose. "How are you finding your new accommodations?"

"The estate is beautiful," Kagiri replied honestly, sipping his own tea, which was a more robust megaita, and enjoying the roasted flavor. "I've never seen anything like it, much less lived there." It was taking some getting used to, of course—as a boy he'd grown up sharing a tiny hut with Niki and their mother, then the two of them had lived in the tap room of the Happoa Kappua, sleeping under the tables at night, and then he had been on the road. Now they had an entire enormous estate, with several large buildings and an entire small lake. And he and Niki shared the largest building just between them—admittedly, much of the space was a tremendous dining and meeting hall, but they each had their own of a pair of good-sized rooms behind that. Though he did realize being in that room kept him still a bit separated from the rest of the community, who were all divided between the three outlying buildings, Kagiri still appreciated having some privacy, and a space to call his own.

"Yes, the Etsuya estate is lovely," Shizu Yokori agreed. "Though I understand the decorations have been modified a bit, hm?" Her eyes and her tongue were as sharp as ever, but the question was mostly innocuous, and Kagiri saw no reason not to answer it honestly.

"They have, yes." He shook his head. "From what I understand, it was all thunderclouds before, very foreboding. Niki brightened the place up a bit, that's all."

"Brightened it—and turned it into an open-air market," Jiro Masute commented, drinking what Kagiri suspected was water again. The frightfully thin merchant might eat like ten men, but he rarely touched tsekuri or any other form of liquor. "A bold decision, but one that has angered many of your new neighbors, I suspect."

"It has," Kagiri agreed with a frown. He'd wondered when the merchants would get to the real reason for the dinner invitation and sensed that they were now beginning to skirt it. "But the others are merely trying to be productive citizens of Awaihinshi, and of the estate. They wish to contribute, and to use the talents and skills they possess. I see nothing wrong with that."

"Oh, nor do we," Fujiko Oritano agreed, smiling as she selected a kibango from the platter before her, holding the small, sweet dumpling pinned between her eating sticks as she spoke. "Quite the opposite. Good for them for defying convention!"

"Precisely," Narai agreed. "We admire that sort of innovation. And I suspect the emperor does as well. He has not put a stop to their little endeavor after all?" That last was partially a question, and Kagiri dipped his head acknowledging it.

"No, the emperor has not said anything against their activities," he allowed. "Nor has he spoken out in approval. I believe he is leaving it up to us, and particularly Noniki, to handle. They are his friends, after all." In a way it was their first real test as Rojiri. Privately, Kagiri wondered if they were up to the task—bandits and skeletal beasts he could handle, but nobles and merchants? First Emperor preserve him!

"Well, the Echo of Victory is proving to be surprisingly forward-thinking," Yokori offered, the steam from her teacup rising from her hands to almost but not quite obscure her bright eyes. "I wonder, do you think he is equally amenable to setting aside other foolish traditions?"

Ah, now we were getting to the meat of it, Kagiri thought, setting his cup down and folding his hands before him. "Perhaps," he replied carefully. "Are there particular traditions you had in mind?"

Masute chuckled. "You know us well!" he stated, tossing his long hair back over his shoulders. "There is one, yes. An old and foolish tradition, but one crafted by imperial decree and never repealed."

"It has to do with patents," Oritano explained, taking up the thread. "The nobility has certain exclusive rights." She shook her head. "It makes no sense today, though I can see where it might have, long ago, as a way to reward loyalty and service."

Kagiri frowned, studying the four merchants. "What rights, precisely?" he asked, his tone making it clear he wished for a direct and succinct answer.

Narai leaned forward, signaling that he would handle the reply. "Only the nobility, and only those of the highest rank, are allowed to grow rice and cotton, harvest silk, and mine iron," he stated clearly, his eyes locked on Kagiri's. "Rimbaku's greatest resources, and all entirely under the nobles' control!" A grimace flickered across his wide face, and for once he did not bother to school himself back to his usual genial expression instead. "It is intolerable! Everyone else, from merchants to craftsmen, to even other nobles, must purchase those materials from the oldest families, at a significantly increased price."

Something struck Kagiri, a fleeting memory, and he tilted his head. "I am sure I have seen families growing their own rice," he stated, "and others harvesting their own silk, as well."

"You have," Narai confirmed. "That is allowed, below a certain amount intended for personal use. Anything larger, however, can only be done by those same nobles."

"I see." He considered that. It did not surprise him, truly, given how deeply entrenched the nobles were in the power structure of the kingdom. And, as Oritano had said, he could understand why early emperors might have granted such rights—and the wealth that would flow from them—to their most loyal and valuable followers, who had then gone on to found the oldest and most influential families. But was it still right that their descendants should hold such control, simply because their ancestors had?

"You are right, that does not seem fair or just," he said slowly. "I can mention that to the emperor." But then he had a different idea. "Or perhaps," he added, "I will suggest that he invite you to speak with him yourself." That was directed at Kishin Narai, who straightened, unable to completely hide the shock on his face—or the smile that followed. "I feel you would make a far better case for this than I."

"I would be honored to do so," the merchant replied, bowing his head in thanks. "And we truly appreciate your willingness to hear us out, and to make such an introduction on our behalf."

The others all nodded, raising their glasses to toast him, and Kagiri returned the gesture. He was not sure Hibikitsu would wish to meet with Narai, but he might. At the very least, he could say he had honestly tried. But the point was not without merit, and the emperor was certainly proving willing to consider revamping many of those old and outdated ideas and structures.

Kagiri only wished he could address his own problems as easily. Though he now realized he had a ready source of advice before him, should he choose to utilize it. "I wonder," he began, lowering the cup to his tray once more and lacing his fingers together, "if you all might be able to help me in turn. I am faced with a question, and I am curious how you would handle it."

He found he had four rapt listeners. "We would be happy to help if we can," Oritano promised, and the other three readily agreed.

"How would you deal with a subordinate who refused to listen to you?" Kagiri asked.

There was a moment of silence as his audience considered.

Masute was the first to speak. "Fire them," he stated, "and promote someone who will listen."

"No, don't fire them," Yokori countered. "Demote them, give them the most menial tasks imaginable, make an example of them so that no one will dare refuse in future."

Oritano nodded, but Narai had not yet weighed in—the head of the little group was stroking his chin, still pondering the question. At least he spoke.

"I would make an example of them, yes," he offered. "But I

would neither fire nor demote them—not right away. Instead, make them lose face somehow. Show them to be your inferiors to everyone else, so that it is clear who is in control." The look he gave Kagiri was half admiring and half reproachful. "That is something I know you are fully capable of."

Kagiri felt his face flush at the reminder of his own past behavior, but he nodded. Yes, they knew all too well that he was not one to be crossed. Of course, that had been a Gensaiba against five merchants. There had been no question as to who would win.

But was that a question now, either? If he were being truly honest about the capabilities of the men who ostensibly served him?

He smiled. "Thank you. I believe you have given me much to think about." An idea was already forming, and although he was sure it flew in the face of all tradition, he found himself liking it very much.

If nothing else, it would afford him some much-needed exercise.

CHAPTER TWENTY-EIGHT

Yamana Muiada was huffing and puffing as he pushed the door aside, the bell above it jangling merrily at the motion. "Sorry, so sorry!" he all but shouted as he rushed through the opening he had just created. "I know, it's late and you're near to closing, I meant to get here much earlier!" Now that he was safely inside, he finally took the time to bend at the waist, hands on his thighs, as he gasped and struggled to slow his ragged breathing back to a more respectable pace and volume.

Fortunately, the man behind the counter only chuckled at his behavior, seemingly unoffended by his haste, his tardiness, or his loudness. "It is fine, Muiada," he promised, restoring a tray of kabingo to their rightful place beneath the glass countertop, where they could safely wink up at him with their alternating bright colors. "I have not closed up yet. Though you were cutting it close this time." He squinted to Muiada's side, where the wide windows, their shutters still thrown open, showed the darkening shade that was beginning to creep over the street outside. "Another ten minutes and I'd have been locked up tight, and then you'd have come all this way for nothing."

"I'd have battered your door down," Muiada claimed, though in truth he'd have done no such thing. "Nothing can keep me from my one true love!" More or less recovered from his swift jog here, he straightened and made his way between displays to the front counter, where he set both hands on the glass to peer down at the object of his affections. He was relieved to see there were any left at this hour!

Across from him, Hajime laughed. "The usual, then?" He was already reaching for the tray, sliding it off the shelf and lifting it up onto the glass.

"Of course." Muiada closed his eyes and sniffed, his mouth widening into a smile as the familiar scents of sugar and red beans and green tea hit him. Ah! He opened them again to watch as the sweet-seller began quickly and expertly cutting several squares from the tray of matcha ujiro. Here was a true craftsman! "I really wish you would take me up on my offer," he said absently, his eyes fixed on the sweets that would soon be his. "Then I wouldn't have to come down here from Aihiri every time. And it would be good for you too, of course," he added hastily. "Sweets-maker to the emperor! What could be better?"

For just an instant, in the act of lifting the tray and the pane of glass, the shop owner paused. "It does have a nice ring to it," he admitted slowly. Then he shook himself and smiled. "I like it here, though. I have my own shop, set my own hours, am my own boss—I can't do that if I'm working for someone else, even if it is the emperor!"

"Well, no," Muiada was forced to agree. "But it's not like we're slave drivers up there! You would be able to make all your lovely desserts each morning and then that would be that—you would probably have the rest of your time to yourself. Mostly." The pieces dropped from the tray, landing perfectly onto the rice paper, and he sighed happily. There were other sweets shops in the city, of course, and at least a few that were closer to him, but no one made ujiro like Hajime!

"And what would I do with so much free time?" the man asked with a laugh, flipping the tray back over and setting it aside to take up the corners of the paper. "I am sure I could hardly wander the imperial compound at will!"

Muiada frowned. "Perhaps not," he was forced to concede. "Not at first, at least. They are so serious up there, the whole lot of those Honteno and Honjofu! Especially right now, during the Saisaihyu, always marching about, swords and spears in hand! Always practicing fighting." He tutted a bit, his thick fingers tapping absently at the glass. "I would not be surprised if they make me open my lovely package so they can inspect my ujiro, make sure I am not smuggling some sort of knife or other weapon within them!" He shuddered at the notion of one of the guards manhandling the delicate sweets, destroying their clean lines and elegant layers just to paw through it. How awful!

"So, you are saying," Hajime commented, folding the paper here and there, bending it and turning it, until the three pieces of ujiro were completely concealed within the perfect semblance of a bear wrought in red and black striped rice paper, "that once I have been there as long as you, then I can roam freely, but before then I'd be restricted and closely watched?"

"Something like that." Muiada smiled. "I have been head chef to His Imperial Majesty for the past two years, after all, and a part of the kitchen staff for another six before that. Everyone there knows me and likes me—and they had better, if they do not want fish bones in their stew and feathers in their dumplings! Once they got to know you, my dear Hajime—and especially once they'd had your lovely kabingo and nigasi and, of course, your amazing ujiro—believe me, you would all but rule the place!" He was very nearly salivating as the other man slid the neat little origami package across to him.

"You make a compelling argument," Hajime told him, which was the closest he had ever come to even considering the offer. "I imagine it is quite nice, being able to walk wherever you will up there, with no one to question you or stop you."

"It is," Muiada assured him. "There are so many little hidden spots, gardens and walkways and the like, where you can go for some peace and quiet. A few places—the Rojiri's chambers, the emperor's private study and bedchamber—are off-limits, of course, but nearly everywhere else I can walk freely." He inspected his nails, which still had traces of rice flour under them. Well, signs of his craft were nothing to be ashamed of.

A sudden chill took him then, and he glanced up. Where had that come from? The lanterns outside were being lit, and in the flare of light Hajime's shadow seemed to stretch and twist, becoming tall and lean and terrifying, its long arms extending toward Muiada as if to snatch him up and gobble him down just like one of the shop's sweets. Ash and Bone! He glanced at Hajime himself, and Muiada's throat tightened as, for an instant, the little shop-keeper seemed to loom large, his features vanishing into the sudden gloom and leaving only bright eyes and the flash of sharp teeth in a narrow face. What in the First Emperor's name was going on here?

Muiada gulped, closing his eyes and blinking them open again, and nearly wept when he saw that the shadow now looked normal again, and that the friendly shopkeeper was his usual self as well. It must have been a trick of the light, mixed with his own imagination and no doubt fed by his haste in getting here, which had unbalanced his humors. That was all. Nonetheless, he fumbled the coins as he pulled them from his iniro and nearly bobbled the package of ujiro as he scooped that up, cradling it protectively to his chest.

"I had best be getting back," he said, the words flying from his lips even as he backed toward the door. "I need to make sure my lazy assistants have not burned the soup!" He bowed, hand on the doorframe. "Thank you, Hajime. Take care. I'll see you again soon."

"Yes, I'm sure you will," the shop owner agreed as Muiada slid the door open once more and hurried through it, not bothering to shut it again behind him. "I'm sure you will."

The man who was now Hajime watched the fat chef go, scurrying away on thick legs, his whole body shaking and swaying with each step. A chef up in Aihiri, eh? Interesting!

He had to admit, a part of him had been tempted to take Muiada right here and now. Claim his eyes and his identity and walk into the imperial compound, bold as brass and easy as a summer breeze. But he had held back. Why?

Because that had been Zhen Shu's method. He had jumped at every chance, taken each and every person who came his way. It had been a rapid process, and risky, though it had almost paid off—certainly it had put him in the throne room in a surprisingly short time, and the target within striking distance. The fact that he had failed seemed more to do with the quality of the emperor's guards than with any lack on his part.

But this was why it paid to be thorough. He, Dai Yi, was not about to make his late partner's mistakes. He would be slow and steady and careful. He would advance at his own pace, no one else's. And he would let targets pass unharmed if he could not see a way to use them right away.

That was why he had allowed Yamana Muiada to continue on his way, never realizing how close he had come to bleeding out right here on the sweet shop's floor. But what would be the point in that? True, if he killed the chef, he could take the man's place. But how long before someone caught on to what he had done, to who he truly was? And if he became Muiada, Hajime's shop would go empty. Word of that would spread quickly and might make some of the guards remember seeing Chiyu Akaii enter here once, and recently. He could not have them track back through the various lives he had stolen and identities he had taken since he'd arrived here, nor could he risk putting them on higher alert by being careless and wasteful.

He could afford to wait, to be patient. What he could not afford was to get found out before he was ready.

For now, being Hajime suited his purposes. He had this shop, and the apartment above, and no one to order him about, which gave him time and space to plan.

And now, when he was ready for it, he had the name of someone who could get in and out of Aihiri with ease: Yamana Muiada. He even had a way to get to Muiada—indeed, the rotund little chef would come to him, all on his own!

That was the key, the piece he had been waiting for to open the path.

He just needed to decide the exact right time to insert that key into the lock and give it a good hard twist.

CHAPTER TWENTY-NINE

Kohori smiled as she entered Yue Judei, her gaze going automatically to the table at the back—and saw Chimehara already there, waiting for her, an empty seat reserved at her side. This had become a nightly ritual for the two of them to meet here, and the bright point of each day, but tonight she was later than usual, and typically she was here first, rather than rushing to catch up.

"I am sorry I am late," she stated once she'd paid Oguro and hurried over to claim that cushion before anyone else could attempt it, pulling her sword free and leaning it against the wall behind her with her hat hooked over its handle. "It has been a long day."

"Not at all," her beautiful companion replied, lifting the bottle and pouring tsekuri into her cup. "But I am glad you are here." Her smile, as always, was warmth itself.

"So am I," Kohori assured her, saluting her with the cup before taking a long sip. Ah, that helped! As did, she had to admit privately, the excellent company.

For it had been a long day. They were well into the Saisaihyu now, and indeed only a few days from its end, and in some ways her Honteno had become used to the idea of operating without aishone. They were learning to compensate for that lack, relying upon themselves rather than the bones, just as Hibikitsu had hoped. But they were still undermanned, and a week was not nearly enough time to fill in the gaps in their training and skill that the lack of aishone had left. It also didn't help that Reizei had taken a sword strike to the leg during the battles with the former Rojiri and thus was still on limited duty. As a result of all that, Kohori spent every day on constant alert, patrolling the grounds herself and checking in on each of her remaining warriors, worried that any minute some enemy might try to exploit the Saisaihyu for their own benefit, knowing that she and her guards would be at a severe disadvantage.

She had Shizumi's support, of course, and was grateful for that. Without the Honjofu to back them up and cover some of their patrols and guard posts, there was no way she would have been able to protect Aihiri. But of course the Honjofu were in the same situation as her Honteno, off-balance and out of confidence because they were being denied their precious relic bones. Only Shizumi herself was immune to those concerns, and she was but one woman, no matter how skilled.

A hand landed upon Kohori's arm, gentle as a butterfly, and she started slightly, glancing up—to find Chimehara watching her closely, those breathtaking eyes narrowed ever so slightly, the perfect brows lowered in concern.

"Are you all right?" she asked softly, the words reaching her ears alone. "You were clearly somewhere else, and judging by the frown it was not a pleasant experience." There was no judgement in that statement or the look accompanying it, but still Kohori flushed.

"I apologize," she said, ducking her head. "I am fine. As I said, a long day."

"But you are here now," Chimehara pointed out with a small smile. "The day is behind you." She held up her own cup. "Let us forget it and relax and enjoy ourselves, yes?"

"Yes. Definitely. Thank you." Kohori matched the gesture, and the smile, and forced herself to focus on the here and now. After all, the problems of her work would still be there in the morning. In the meantime, she was sitting here with the most beautiful woman she had ever met, sharing excellent wine and, soon, excellent food and equally excellent conversation. That should have her full attention.

Yuki brought over a platter with several plates, all her usual favorites, and smiled a hello as she set them down on the table, the rich smells of fried food wafting over them. "I ordered them,"

Chimehara explained as the server retreated, for Kohori had not done so. "I hope you do not mind." She raised her eating sticks like spears and then stabbed down, claiming one of the heioki with a mischievous grin. "But you will need to be quick about it if you hope to have any!"

That made Kohori laugh and she quickly took one of the other fried spheres, popping it into her mouth and relishing the rich, salty flavors that coated her tongue at once. "Oh, I believe I am up to the challenge!" she promised, her dark mood chased away for now. Then there was no time for anything else but eating and drinking and laughing.

It was several hours later, and they had nearly polished off the latest plates of food, as well as the most recent carafe of wine, when Chimehara blurted out, "Do you sleep there, or elsewhere?" Then she blushed, the delicate shades blooming across her face like a sunset all in rose hues, and glanced away, wringing her fingers together. "I am sorry. That was rude of me. Please, forget I asked."

But Kohori, mellowed by the wine and the food and the company, smiled. "It is all right," she replied. "Truly." Even though the rule of the zaihaya was that you not intrude upon another customer's privacy, she could not imagine being upset with this lovely and charming young woman over anything, much less over expressing an interest in her! "But yes, to answer your question, I sleep there." She laughed. "In truth, I have never had another home, not since I left my parents to seek my own way in the world and signed up as a soldier for no other reason than that I was big and could hold my own in a fight." She shook her head, remembering the many years since then. "I was in the general barracks, then the officers' quarters, and then repeated the process when I joined the Honteno. I've never needed a home of my own, and if I had one I would rarely be there anyway."

"You have always been a soldier, then?" Chimehara asked, arms coming to rest on the table as she leaned in a bit—which had the unsettling effect of causing her kitoro to shift as well, revealing a long expanse of flawless porcelain skin. "But you said officers' quarters, so you at least have a space of your own? I find privacy to be so important at times."

Kohori gulped and wished there as more wine so she could distract herself from this beguiling lady whose voice had somehow gone husky in a way that made her pulse race. "Yes, I do have my own quarters," she agreed. "They are in the Honteno's barracks, but separate from the rest, with a private entrance as well as one that opens onto the general area."

Her companion glanced about as if assuring herself no one else was listening. "I must admit," she said then, "what I saw of Aihiri was lovely, but that was really only the path to the palace and then through it to the throne room itself."

"The throne room is one of the most beautiful places in the entire compound," Kohori answered, glad to shift the attention from her sleeping arrangements. "But there are other parts that are amazing as well."

"What is your favorite?" came the next question, and again she found herself all but drowning in those luminous eyes.

"There is a tiny garden," she found herself answering, unable to look away, "tucked away just behind the practice grounds. It belonged to a previous emperor's wife and has been all but forgotten now, though the groundskeepers still tend to it from time to time. I like it because it is secluded and private and I can slip away there when I need to be completely by myself."

She had stumbled upon the spot more or less by accident back when she had first become Honteno and had determined to walk every inch of Aihiri and know it backwards and forwards. The garden was walled on all sides, and she had circled it more than once before realizing something did not match between the wall's circumference and the spaces she knew existed within. Then it was a matter of locating the hidden door into the garden and prevailing upon one of the groundskeepers to unlatch it for her. When that barrier had swung open and she had gazed upon the small space for the first time, with its trees and its flat stepping

stones laid out in a shallow pond and its weathered wooden panels broken by bamboo screens over shallow ledges, she had been
awestruck. The fact that it had been allowed to become slightly
overgrown, the trees and bushes stretching forth their limbs and
leaves toward the sun in glorious disarray, had only made it more
perfect.

She had taken to frequenting the spot whenever she could,
wheedling a key from the groundskeepers so that she could enter
at will. No one else seemed to remember the tiny garden existed,
and so she could escape there and not be bothered by anyone.
Within those walls, surrounded by rock and wood and water, she
could forget that she was a Taikoro, forget that she was a warrior,
and simply be one with the world and with nature, all her troubles
and thoughts sliding away on the wind.

"It sounds amazing," Chimehara remarked, her own eyes shining, and Kohori blinked, realizing with a shock that she had been
speaking aloud this whole time. But if she was worried that her
companion would think her mad, she needn't have—instead the
younger woman seemed entranced. "Everyone should have a private refuge like that," was all she said, and reached out to squeeze
Kohori's hand, her skin silky soft against battle callouses. "I am
happy you have found yours."

"Would you like to see it?" Kohori had blurted the words out
before she had even registered the thought, and caught her breath,
afraid that she had overstepped, shattering whatever this strange
and wonderful thing was that had spun up between them, delicate
as a spiderweb. "I mean—"

But her dining companion smiled, the gesture sweet and
lovely, her dimples once more presenting themselves. "I would love
to," she agreed, gentle fingers stroking the back of Kohori's hand
and sending shivers up her arm. "But are you certain that would
be allowed?"

"Of course it would," Kohori replied, forcing a laugh to cover
her discomfort. How did a mere look and touch serve to shatter
her composure so? "After all, I am the one in charge of security."
Since she was certain she would lose her nerve if she waited, she

added, "We could go now, if you like. It is lovely by moonlight."

In response Chimehara rose to her feet, graceful as a flower unbending with the morn. "If you are sure it would not be any trouble, yes, I would be delighted." She was already lifting her sorhu to settle it over her head, an act that only served to frame her lovely features.

"Oh? Oh. Yes, of course. I mean, no, not at all. I mean—let's go!" Kohori surged to her own feet, nearly knocking the table over in her haste, and reached back for her sword and hat, almost tossing one or both on the ground but catching them in time. Her face was aflame as she led the way out, nodding to Oguro and Yuki on her way. What a fool she must look!

But once they were outside Chimehara smiled and settled a hand on the arm of her kaoni and Kohori forgot any hint of embarrassment. Instead she felt light as air and carefree as a leaf, for the night was cool and clear, the stars and moon bright, and she had never felt more alive than now, with this beautiful woman at her side.

"Come on," she said, and together they began wending their way back up through the city, toward where Aihiri shone above like a second moon, its walls glowing a pale, perfect white. She found that her cheeks were hurting from smiling so much, and her steps were light and eager, nearly skipping, as they walked, so much so that her companion laughed, though not meanly. The sound only raised Kohori's spirits further, and she could barely even remember the mood she had been in when she had first entered the zaihaya that evening. It had only been a few hours ago, yet it felt as if it were an entire world away.

CHAPTER THIRTY

Shizumi stood, tense but relaxed, alert but distant, eyes sharp yet unfocused, her feet apart, knees slightly bent, back straight, with her nihono held perfectly upright, one hand just below the tehuya, the other lower with the bottom fingers loosely curled around the chahito, the blade's edge catching the light of the lanterns flickering at the edges of the practice yard. Her opponent faced her in a similar posture, the mottled green of his armor gleaming as he stood, as motionless as if he'd been cast in bronze, and waited.

He has the reach advantage, she reminded herself yet again. *Those damnably long arms of his! If I let him keep me at bay, I've got no chance.*

Accordingly, she screamed out a challenge and charged, arms pulling the blade back as she leaped forward, coiling like a snake so that she could then swing out and down with all the force she could muster, her blade slashing through the air as if it could slice the very night breeze in twain.

His own sword floated up, seemingly casual but so fast it seemed to merely be one place, then the other, and caught hers just below his guard. A quick twist of his wrists and he had knocked her blade aside, spinning his around with deceptive ease to slash down and across in a move designed to split her from shoulder to hip. But she had kept her grip on her weapon, merely backpedaling, and thus was able to bring the nihono up in time to block his attack. She retreated, returning to the same spot she had stood in before, her bare feet settling back into the same indentations in the sand, and she returned to her ready position, watching him with narrowed eyes.

He smiled.

"Ash and bone, stop making this look so easy!" she ground out, scowling to keep from smiling in return. She advanced again, more cautiously this time, and feinted an overhand blow, then pressed inward with her lower hand to tilt the sword suddenly, swinging it in a swift sideways arc instead. He merely ducked under that, bending his knees enough to let the blow slide above his head despite his ridiculous height, and then thrust upward, catching her sword from behind and keeping it pinned away from her, her arms extended and unable to pull back.

But Shizumi was no stranger to combat, nor to facing taller, stronger opponents, and she knew how to deal with such tricks. One foot lashed out, catching him squarely in the groin, and despite the armor plates there he groaned and stumbled back, his sword dipping as he momentarily lost control of his limbs. She did not pursue the opening, for that would have dishonorable. She simply waited a moment, letting him catch his breath again. Then, when he straightened slightly from his instinctive huddle, she struck.

This time he did not attempt to match her blade for blade. Instead he let go of his nihono with one hand and simply grabbed her wrists with the other, his hand large enough to snare both at once, his gauntlets grating against her own. She struggled to free herself but he was too strong and laughed as she tried. That made Shizumi's blood boil, and she bared her teeth at him. Enough!

Hanketo were made to fit comfortably and to not slip or slide or loosen in combat. But that did not mean they were impossible to get out of, especially for someone with small hands. Flexing her fingers, Shizumi slid her hands free of the armored gauntlets, leaving her opponent clutching the empty shells and the sword still trapped between them. A kick to his midsection dazed him, but her nihono was too tangled up in his hand and her hanketo for her to retrieve quickly—so she grabbed his sword, which dangled from his other hand. Her two hands proved more than a match for his one, especially when he was stunned, and she pulled the weapon free, quickly spinning the longer blade around to rest it against his neck, right where the plates of his karute would have ended and his deo began. A quick twist and the sharp edge would slide between those two armor pieces and bite deep into his unprotected neck. Of course, he was not wearing his helmet right now and so he had nothing to stop the blade's advance.

"Yield," she demanded, her voice low and rough, her breathing heavy in her own ears, her hair sweat-soaked and falling into her eyes.

"I yield!' Kagiri declared, letting her gloves and sword fall to the ground between them and raising both his hands. "I yield."

For a moment they stood frozen like that, their faces only inches apart. She could see again how young he was, younger than her, his face almost completely unlined. It was not an unattractive face—not so handsome as his brother's, longer, slimmer, more serious, yet not unappealing for all that. Right now his dark eyes were studying her just as intensely, but his mouth was twitching with the beginnings of a smile.

"Hibikitsu might not be happy with you if you slaughtered one of his Rojiri," he pointed out softly, and she snorted and finally lowered the weapon, letting its unfamiliar weight drag it down until its tip rested upon the ground. "Ah, much better," Kagiri continued, straightening up and brushing a hand against the spot where the sword had hovered. "Thank you." He brought his hand to his chest, then, and bowed deeply.

Shizumi returned the gesture and laughed. "For trouncing you soundly? You're welcome." She reversed the sword and offered it to him, blade down. It would have been safer to use baraken, of course, but somehow it was never quite the same, for all that the practice swords could be made to have the exact same weight as a real nihono. Besides which, they both trusted each other's mastery enough to duel with live steel.

"Well, I wouldn't go so far as to say 'trounced,'" he replied, accepting the sword back and sliding it into its sheath without a glance. "At least, I believe there was some mutual trouncing going on."

"You're the one who almost lost his head, not me," she argued, scooping up her sword and hanketo. She didn't bother to pull the gauntlets back on but instead crossed the yard to the low platform alongside it, where she had set her boots. Dropping the hanketo beside them she shucked her deo next, unbuckling the breastplate along one side and pulling it off and over from the other. After that came the suneoto and haidoto, all dropped in a heap on the bamboo planks she then hauled herself up onto, stretching out on her back in only hakami and hosode, face up toward the sky. She was breathing heavily and her entire body felt wrung out but it was a good tired, the fatigue that followed strong exercise. The night air felt refreshing on her skin, cooling the sweat that stuck her clothes to her, and she relaxed, shutting her eyes and letting her heart calm and her lungs quiet.

When she felt fully in control again, she glanced up—to find Kagiri watching her, a strange look upon his face. "What?" she demanded.

"Nothing," he replied quickly, glancing away. In the lantern light his face looked flushed. Had she embarrassed him somehow?

He was still in his armor, and now started to remove it, moving slowly but with the grace of long practice, his fingers finding each buckle without fumbling, the well-oiled leather slipping free without difficulty. He too wore only light, close-fitting pants and shirt, and she did not bother to hide her admiration for his physique, which was long and lean. He had shown the foresight to bring a kisoni, however, the silk robe dark green and patterned with the silhouettes of golden leaves, and slipped that on, belting it around his waist with a dappled golden-brown sash and slipping his sword through that. The parts of his armor went into a neat stack, deo at the bottom, and he gathered that up in his arms before turning back to her.

"I should go return this to its stand," he explained. "I won't be long."

"I wasn't planning on moving again any time soon," she replied, and he laughed as he drifted away.

He was a strange man, Shizumi thought. In some ways he seemed little more than a boy, or at least a young man with a boy's enthusiasm and optimism still. So unlike the grizzled soldiers she was often surrounded by, who had seen all of life's horrors and survived but with that spark of hope and light now tamped down or extinguished entirely. But then there was the Gensaiba, the warrior of legend, with all the skills and knowledge and fierce practicality of a half dozen ancient fighters. It was an odd combination—and, she had to admit, an intriguing one.

She lay there, her eyes closed, enjoying the mild breeze and the scent of flowers and trees mingled with sweat, until she heard footsteps approaching. Then she levered herself upright, hand coming to rest near her sword just in case. But it was Kagiri returned, and this time he had in his hands a woven basket.

"Hungry?" he asked and she nodded, her stomach growling its own reply. Sparring always made her work up an appetite, especially against so skilled an opponent! "Good. Come on." And once she'd hopped down and scooped up her gear, he led the way across the yard to its far end, and through that into a decorative garden. Paths and bridges crisscrossed the space, over and around ponds and bushes and trees, with benches set aside for moments of quiet reflection. A few firepits had also been placed in small hollows, and Kagiri stopped by one of these, sinking to a crouch as he set the basket on the ground at his side and took up the kindling already resting in the pit, striking flint to it to create a spark.

"I'm impressed," Shizumi admitted, settling down cross-legged on the basket's other side. "Did you get that skill from the Gensaiba?"

He laughed again. "Starting a fire? No, that is all my own. Necessary when you live in a small village." He pulled skewers from the basket, chunks of beef and marinated chicken alternated with onions and peppers and mushrooms, and set them over the fire that now leapt about merrily, casting its flickering shadows across his face and emphasizing the cut of his cheeks and the clean line of his jaw. "And you?" he asked, glancing over at her, a grin on his lips. "I'm guessing that kick wasn't something you learned in training!"

"More like 'learned fending off my older brothers,'" she agreed, grinning back. "But it's come in handy."

"I can imagine!" He tended the skewers, turning them so they would cook evenly, and when he looked her way again his smile was gentler, almost hesitant. "I really...I mean, thank you for sparring with me these past few days. I've really enjoyed it."

"So have I." She grimaced. "It was always difficult enough finding anyone who would, back when everyone was concerned over wasting aishone over something like mere practice." She remembered Fujubuki Haro sneering at her over just such a thing, more than once. "And now, with my new rank and everyone knowing I'm Mukanichi, it's been even worse." She smiled. "But you don't seem to care."

He shrugged. "Why should I? I'm new to this whole rank thing as well. And I can hardly complain about someone's aitachi or lack thereof, when I'm such an oddity myself."

"What is it like?" she asked then, leaning forward to see his face more clearly. "Having the Gensaiba within you? Do you hear them? Do they speak to you?" It was something she had wondered since he had first told who he was and what had happened to him but had not dared to ask. Until now.

For a moment he did not answer, and she feared she had offended him. But when he did his tone was thoughtful rather than aggrieved. "It was at first," he admitted, tearing free a blade of grass and tossing it into the flame, which had already begun to yield the mouth-watering scents of grilled meat and vegetables. "It was like being trapped in a small room with a group of people who were constantly shouting in your ear, arguing with each other, trying to tell you what to do." He shrugged. "But that faded over time. Long before I reached here they had stopped being actual voices. Now they are just like impulses, memories, instincts—the same way, if you reach your hand toward the fire, your own reason says, 'don't, you'll get burned'? Now when I use something from one of them it just feels like something I've always known how to do."

He plucked the skewers out then, offering her one and taking the other for himself. It smelled perfect, the meat charred outside but still tender and juicy when she bit into it, the onions and peppers crisped, the mushrooms slightly shriveled and dried out enough to not drip everywhere, and she ate with enthusiasm, happily accepting the wineskin he offered her and taking large gulps of tsekuri to wash everything down. They chatted as they ate, but not about anything consequential—a maneuver one of them had used while sparring earlier, a trick for stacking armor neatly, which types of mushrooms were best grilled versus for soup, the time she and her squadmates had snuck wine on a patrol by pouring it into their iniro, only to have it drip down their legs as they marched, leaving a sticky trail behind them and a drove of enthusiastic ants and flies following in their wake.

By the time they had finished eating—and nearly finished the wineskin as well—the moon was high overhead and the night sky was a dark, rich blue, broken by the twinkling of many stars. "We'd best be off to bed," Shizumi said, stretching, and Kagiri, who had been taking one last sip of wine, choked, gasping until she slapped him hard on the back. "Are you all right?"

"Yes, fine," he wheezed, setting the bag down and thumping his chest. "Fine." He gathered up the debris from the meal, stuffing it back in the basket, and rose awkwardly to his feet, his usual grace deserting him for once. "Shall we?"

She was unsure what had bothered him but stood as well, brushing grass and leaves from her clothes and hair and collecting the armor and sword she'd laid on the ground beside her. "Yes, let's." It did not take them long to retrace their steps out of the garden, and then around to the side where the Honjofu barracks lay. "Thank you for this," she said, turning to face him. "Good night."

For a second, there in the shadows, Shizumi thought she saw something flicker across his face, in his eyes, but she was not sure what and it vanished an instant later. "Yes, good night," he responded, giving her a smile. He was still standing there as she turned away and headed into the barracks, and then up toward her own bedchamber.

Yes, he was a strange one, she decided as she walked.

Still, strange was not always bad. And he certainly made her life more interesting.

CHAPTER THIRTY-ONE

For the fourth night in a row, Seikoku found herself in the same place. A quiet part of Sakiriti, a narrow street branching off ahead from the main road, houses and buildings all around but not crowded in shoulder to shoulder, and right before her a lamp post, the stout iron column tapering as it rose from its base until it widened again at the top to support the oil lantern there.

The recent rain had washed away most traces, but she thought she could still make out a slight indentation in the post at about shoulder height, and the graceful curves of the post's base contained hints of something darker than water, something that had pooled there and refused to be removed.

Much like the guilt she had been carrying since the incident.

Try as she might, she could not rid herself of the memories of what had happened here. She saw it all again every time she tried to sleep—the man walking down the road, the strange little boy who emerged from between those buildings across the way, silent as a ghost, dark as a shadow, eyes wide and hungry, hand clutching the knife. The way he had hissed at her like some wild beast, how he had flung himself at her—and how she had tossed him aside like an old coat.

The sound it had made when his skull had cracked against the lamp post.

The ragged little pile of his broken body huddled at its base.

And how she had fled the scene like a coward, like a criminal. Like a murderer.

Because, after all, that was exactly what she was. A murderer. A killer. She had killed that little boy.

Yes, he had been trying to kill her. Yes, he had no doubt meant to kill that man. And no, she had not meant to hurt him, or anyone.

But it did not change what had happened. Or what she had done.

For days she had struggled with it. She had wanted to tell someone, anyone—Minawa, Isoro, Jitu Kanai.

Noniki.

That was who she really wanted to tell. He was her best friend! And more, it seemed—unbidden, a smile touched her lips, followed by her fingers, gently resting there where his own lips had been just that evening. He had kissed her! And she had kissed him back, still unsure—not about her feelings, no, she knew those well enough, but about his, about what this meant for them, about whether this would cost them what they already had.

But when she'd felt his mouth against hers, well, she had forgotten all of that. His lips were so soft, and warm, and sweet, and the way he had kissed her, gently but firmly, showing that he had been carefully restraining himself from going too far, too fast, had assured her that he felt the same way she did. And that had made her very heart sing and her entire body thrum with happiness.

Of course, he did not know that he had been kissing a killer.

What would he think, if he knew? But how could she not tell him? How could she lie to him, especially about something so terrible? What did it mean about her, about them, if she hid this from him?

And what if she did tell him, and it tore them apart just as they were finally beginning to knit together?

She still did not know. And that was part of why she found herself back here every night, staring at this lamp post as if it could somehow answer her questions.

It never did, though. It just stood, as mute and immovable as before, a constant reminder of her wrongdoing, a silent testament to her guilt.

A sound behind her made her start, and Seikoku whipped about, raising her cane. She had found it among the items left behind on the estate, a sturdy bamboo stick carved into birds and deer and other strange, fanciful creatures chasing one another in a rising loop around and around until at last, at the very tip, it became the head of a bear. She was not sure why she had taken to carrying it with her but it had a pleasing weight to it, a solidity—it would serve nicely as a weapon yet was handsome enough to be dismissed as a mere accessory. And now she found herself wielding it, that bear-head top held high—against a young boy.

For just an instant, her mind showed her a picture of a small, starved, feral child, hair and eyes wild, mouth open in a snarl, crouched low over his knife. Then reality intruded and her vision replaced that with the sight of the youth standing before her now, reassuring her.

This was not the same boy.

In fact, the two could not have been more different. That one had been small, narrow, with enormous eyes in a pinched face. This boy was significantly taller and looked older, with a stout frame and equally wide face and features, the largest of which were his thick lips. He was neatly dressed in a dark jacket and pants, and his hair was not only neatly trimmed but glossy with proper washing and care. His eyes were the only narrow thing about him, and those looked sharp but oddly flat, almost disinterested.

"I beg your pardon," he told her, his voice clear and with that quiet, measured pace that spoke of a good education. "I did not mean to startle you."

"No, that's all right," Seikoku replied, quickly lowering her cane and straightening. "I'm sorry." She glanced about, and up— the moon was well past its apex, indicating a late hour. "Should you be out this late? Where are your parents?"

"It is late, you are right," he agreed, studying her closely in a way that made her vaguely uneasy. "But actually, I was hoping you might help me. You see, I am out here because I am looking for someone."

"Oh?" He came a bit closer, and she guessed that he was perhaps ten or eleven. His hands were burrowed deep in his jacket pockets, as if to keep warm, though the night was not cold.

"Yes. My brother. Have you seen him?" He continued to approach, only stopping a few feet away, and she could see now that she had been right about his gaze. Seikoku had dealt with arrogant nobles, with vicious women, with bored guards, with violent thugs. In each of those, some, though not all, had a true detachment from others, seeing anyone not their equal as not worth their time or consideration, as not even human. It was the way a man looked upon a small bug, as an irritation and nothing more, to be snuffed out if it should bother him or simply because he chose to do so.

She saw that same dispassion in this boy's eyes. He did not see her as an equal, not even as a person, but merely as an object, to be used or toyed with or discarded as he saw fit.

She shivered despite herself, then remembered that she had not yet replied to his question. "Your brother?" she asked. "What does he look like?" In her mind's eye an image arose, of a boy much like this one, only shorter and heavier, cheeks rounded and plump.

"Oh, he and I are not much alike," this strange boy warned, as if somehow reading her thoughts. "He is much smaller than me, and slight, with a narrow face and large eyes."

That description of course brought the first child back to mind, and Seikoku gulped, glancing away. "Oh? Did the two of you get separated?" For surely he had only been out here searching for a short time?

"Not precisely." She felt, more than saw, this boy sidle closer, so close she imagined she could feel the heat from his body warming the side of her nearest to him. "He disappeared several days ago, I'm sorry to say." He sighed, and she glanced over, to see his eyes downcast. "I am forced to admit that he is not entirely in his right mind. He was very sick, feverish, and when that finally broke, the healers said it had damaged him in his head. He does not speak, has forgotten much, and is little better than a wild beast now." He shook his head. "But he is still my brother, and so I continue searching for him, in the hopes that he can be found and given the help and care he needs."

"Oh." The sound came out as almost a sob, and Seikoku raised a hand to her mouth, turning away quickly lest he see the tears gathering in her eyes. "I'm so sorry." Her motion had spun her around to face the lamp post, and again she saw the boy—the very one this child described—as he slammed into it, head-first, and then slid down it, his eyes already going dull even as he fell. She began to shake, and wrapped her arms around herself, the cane's top digging into her upper arm as she struggled not to dissolve right here on the street.

"Thank you." The boy had slid around her, his footsteps soft, but rather than glancing her way his attention went the same place hers was so focused, to the post. Dropping into a crouch, he studied the iron pillar, raising a thick-fingered hand to touch the very spot where the paint had been scraped by impact. Then he dipped the fingers of that same hand down along the base, into the droplets pooled there.

When he raised his hand, those fingers were red with blood.

"I see." He stared at his fingers, at those stains, and those his face was turned mostly away from her Seikoku thought he looked more fascinated than horrified. No, not fascinated—interested, but still in that distant manner. "Interesting. Did he attack you?"

That made her start again, and stare. How had he known? "Yes," she admitted, relieved to do so. "He was stalking a man. I interrupted him and he turned on me instead. He had a knife," she added, as if that somehow excused everything she had done.

"Yes." The boy had still not moved. "And you threw him into the post here?" He might have been asking after the weather, or whether she had enjoyed a poem or a recent meal, for all the emotion in his voice.

Even so, she found she could not stop, did not want to stop— now that she had started to recount it, she wanted to air it all, to hold nothing back. "Yes. He threw himself at me. I tossed him away. I didn't mean for him to hit the post—to hit anything, really. Especially so hard. But he was so light, and I didn't realize—I'm so sorry." The tears were flowing freely now, dripping their way down her cheeks, but she felt calmer, lighter, than she had in days.

"I would not worry about it much." That made her gaze snap back to this boy, back to the here and now, as he wiped his fingers on his pants leg and rose, slowly to his feet. "He was an odious little creature. I'm quite pleased not to have to deal with him anymore."

"What?" Seikoku stared as the boy turned to face her. "But he was your brother!"

"Not really, no," came the offhand reply. "Not by blood. We had been taken in by the same woman, that is all. The same teacher." He was staring at her again, and his eyes were still so cold as he sighed and added, "She will not be pleased, however."

The things he was saying made little sense to her, and Seikoku stared at him, trying to piece them together. She barely noticed as he took a step, then another, until he was right in front of her, the top of his head just below her chin. His lips were moving, and she leaned in slightly, trying to make out what he was saying:

"This will, perhaps, make her feel slightly better about his fate, knowing you have joined him."

Seikoku had spent years training herself to react to danger, to adversity, to obstacles. Those reflexes kicked in now and she flung herself to the side, twisting as she moved. Her arms, which had been wrapped so tightly around her, loosened, spinning outward as she turned, and the cane spun out with them—and sent a shock through her arm as it collided with the boy's arm where he had thrust forward, the knife blade a glittering point extending from the circle of his fist.

He was trying to kill her!

"Stop!" she pleaded, planting her feet to halt her gyrations, legs slightly bent, arms wide apart, cane held out before. "You don't have to do this!" The scene took her back to the first incident, only now the boy facing her was calm and cold.

"I do," he replied, and there was no regret in his voice but no glee either. This was a chore for him, a task, nothing more. "But I will attempt to end it quickly." He took several quick steps forward and stabbed again, but she batted his attempt aside with her cane. He was not as fast as his...the first boy, she noted with the part of her brain that was still able to observe such things. Nor was his grip on the knife as sure, for all that his handling of it might be the more technically correct. It was as if he had studied knife-fighting but had never attempted it himself.

"You're not going to end anything," she warned, regaining some of her own equilibrium as the initial shock ebbed away and her hands stopped shaking. "But you might get hurt if you keep it up."

"Like Gou, you mean?" he asked, advancing again, a smile spreading across those thick lips. "That was his name, you know. The boy you killed."

I know what you are trying to do, she thought, shifting her footing and sidling to the side, forcing him to turn to keep her in front of him. *Telling me his name. You're trying to make me break down, to give you an opening.* It was not working, however. If anything, his calculating attempt was irritating her but helping her to focus. Whatever the full story, the first boy had been ready to kill her and this one clearly was as well. That fact helped ease her guilt a little, just enough to allow her to breathe and concentrate on the problem at hand.

A problem that kept lunging at her with his knife. She was able to knock his clumsy attempts aside with her cane each time, but eventually he might get lucky and injure her.

She could run, of course. She had longer legs and no doubt she could outpace him. But now that they had met, now that he knew her face, he would simply keep looking for her. Eventually they would find themselves back in this situation. Better to simply deal with the matter now.

The only question was, how did she deal with it? He seemed intent upon killing her. Was there anything she could say or do to convince him to stop?

Her attention had wandered as she pondered, and he had evidently noticed that, because suddenly she found him inside her guard, his knife sweeping wide in an arc that intersected with her throat. There was neither time nor room to raise her cane again, so she dropped it. Instead, she threw herself backward, flipping over completely to land safely several feet away—

—and, in doing so, one foot caught the boy solidly under the chin.

His head snapped back and he toppled, hitting the cobbled street hard with an explosive grunt. His knife flew from his grip, spinning up before plummeting back down, turning end over end as it fell, gaining momentum as it dropped—to slam into the boy's right leg along his upper thigh.

"Ah!" he screamed in pain—the first sound he'd made with any emotion to it at all—and thrashed about, hands groping for the blade embedded in his leg.

"No, don't!" Seikoku shouted, hurrying forward, but too late—the boy had found the knife handle and yanked it free, causing blood to jet from the wound. His pants absorbed some of it but not enough to stop the flow, darkening rapidly as the stain spread. She dropped to her knees beside him, pressing her hands against the spot, trying to staunch it, but the blood welled up beneath her fingers, and the boy's motions slowed as his life bled out under her touch.

What felt like only seconds later, he jerked once, twice, and then expired, his last breath rattling from his lungs as his body stiffened and then went limp.

Seikoku stayed there a moment, unable to move, staring at this second boy who had died because of her. But finally she pulled herself to her feet and stiffly, woodenly retrieved her cane. Whatever she had thought after the first death, things had clearly escalated here and could not be allowed to continue. She would have to take steps, and quickly.

A small basin sat upon a pedestal not far away, collected rainwater there for anyone to use, and she splashed some on her hands and then washed her hands, scrubbing away the blood that had collected there. Then, once she was sure she was presentable again, she made her way quickly back up toward Motohori and then Atsani.

The guards at both gates let her through without more than an appreciative glance, and soon she was back at the estate. The main gates were closed but she had left the rear gate unlocked and circled around to that, slipping through and into the courtyard. From there it was a simple matter to climb the wide steps, enter the main building, and then cross the wide room and rap on the door of one of the two inner chambers.

As soon as the door slid open, before she could convince herself otherwise, Seikoku said, "Noniki, there's something I need to tell you about."

He smiled at her, but sobered, no doubt from whatever expression was carved onto her face. She could not feel it herself. "Of course," he said, and he reached out and took her hands in his. "Whatever it is," he stated then, "we will figure it out together."

CHAPTER THIRTY-TWO

Amani Denbi was not accustomed to being disturbed.

One of the advantages of possessing power, she had always felt, was the ability to control one's surroundings. You ate what you liked, wore what you wished, and saw only who you wanted—when you wanted them.

Even her husband had understood this basic rule, that Denbi would determine the time and place and duration of your interactions. You would simply accede to her demands. Once he had accepted that, their marriage had gone far more smoothly, and she had even experienced some small regret when he had passed away over a dozen years ago. Their children, of course, had taken the lesson far more quickly, as it had been drilled into them from birth, and they had rarely interrupted her, especially as they had grown old enough to understand.

Thus, when a hand landed on her shoulder and gently shook her, she did not at first react. The shaking continued, slowly dragging her from sleep, and Denbi glanced about, eyes still more than half-closed, brain still foggy enough that she did not immediately know where she was. "What?" she managed, lifting her head to squint at the figure crouched beside her bed.

That figure soon resolved itself into the small, slight, tidy form of Tanekate, the head of her household staff. "A thousand apologies, Amani-sama," he said softly. "I would never dream of disturbing you but...we appear to have a situation."

Sitting up, Denbi gathered her wits around her along with the folds of her sleeping robe, which had slipped clear off one shoulder. She did not worry about Tanekate seeing, of course—he had witnessed far more, in his time, and one of the reasons she employed him for was for his circumspection—but she did not like being so disheveled. It made her feel like she was not in control. "What sort of situation, exactly?" she snapped at last, though her throat was so dry doing so hurt as the words rasped their way clear.

Her major domo dipped his head in further apology—and held up a small silver platter, upon which rested a cup of tea. Ah, Tanekate! The light aroma of rose tickled her nose, stirring her to further wakefulness, and she accepted the cup with a nod of thanks, sipping from it and nearly sighing aloud as the steaming hot liquid soothed her throat.

"There is a young lady here to see you," her servant replied. "She is quite insistent upon seeing you this very instant, or as soon as may be."

Denbi had known Tanekate for more than two decades—she had hand-picked him after removing the previous head of staff for an embarrassing lapse in tact and civility. The man had been invaluable, and she had long since learned to read his expressions and posture as easily as she might a child's crude poem. But right now, she had to admit—to herself alone, of course—that she was puzzled. His eyes were wide, his breathing rapid, his face slightly flushed, as if he were excited. Yet there was nothing here to elicit such a response, and besides that his tone and his hands were as steady as ever.

"And what is this young woman like?" she asked, draining the cup and returning it to the platter before rising to her feet and tying her robe in place. There was a mirror hung to one side, over a low table, and Denbi moved to that, quickly taking up brush and comb to smooth her hair so that she could draw it up into its customary bun.

Behind her, Tanekate took a moment to reply. "She is…lovely, madam," he answered finally. "Uncommonly so, one might say." He swallowed. "Yet she is also…agitated, it seems. Fume was barely able to restrain her, and she injured both Ushi and Tane when they would not allow her entrance at first." He bowed his head. "They will recover, and the young lady is calmer now, but I must urge caution."

Aha! That explained his strange reaction, then—lust mixed with fear—and revealed the identity of her mysterious caller! Denbi smiled as she finished with her hair. So, the beautiful and mysterious Chimehara had chosen to make good on her invitation, had she? Excellent! But why at such an odd hour? A glance through the windows confirmed that it was indeed still night out. And why in such a state? She must be every bit as formidable as Denbi had suspected, to fight her way past two of her guards like that, but why bother to do so when she could have simply waited until dawn and then been allowed in without trouble? Strange.

Nonetheless, this was not an opportunity Denbi planned to waste. "I am sure it will be fine, Tanekate. See her to the alabaster room," she instructed, "and inform her that I will be there shortly." Tanekate bowed and rose, moving away at his usual quick but unhurried pace to do her bidding and Denbi returned her attention to her appearance. Though she could never hope to match her visitor's sheer beauty, there was no call to show herself before she was at least presentable.

A short time later, Amani Denbi swept into the alabaster room. The walls here were paneled in ash that had been layered with alabaster carved away to create delicate seascapes, the iridescent white shell forming hauntingly luminous waves as well as the moon and stars above. A light repast, tea and sweets, had been set out upon the elegantly carved table in the small room's center, yet she found her guest not sitting and relaxing but pacing, her garb—not a kisoni or kitoro, Denbi saw at once, but ponmei and shatage and hantien, all dark and without obvious embellishment—catching at the table's edge as she swished past time and again. When Denbi entered the woman turned, and for a second she was taken aback by the face that confronted her there.

Chimehara was as beautiful as ever, of course. In all her years, Denbi was not sure she had ever seen such perfect features, nor such captivating eyes. Even the simple clothing she wore only accentuated her appearance, its clinging fabric showing off her curves to perfection. But that was not what had stopped her. Before, at the gem house, Chimehara had seemed calm, cool, utterly self-collected. Now there was a fire in those arresting eyes, a flush upon those smooth cheeks, and a tremble to those lush lips. What had her worked into such a state, Denbi wondered.

She did not have to wait long to find out. "At last!" the younger woman declared upon seeing her. "I have been waiting for ages!"

"I apologize for any delay," Denbi replied smoothly, gliding around the other side of the table and taking her favorite seat, on the cushions facing the door. "But I am here now. Please, dear—you seem worked up." She glanced past them, to where Fume stood watch just past the door, arms crossed and a fearsome expression on her face. "Sit and tell me what has upset you so."

"What has upset me?" Chimehara glowered down at her, fists clenched at her sides. "They're dead, that is what!"

"Dead? Who is dead?" Denbi reached for the teapot and calmly poured herself a cup. She rarely drank so much tea this late at night but, then again, she was rarely up this late, and the tea would help fortify her. She had the feeling she might need it.

"My pupils," the young woman stated, sinking onto the cushion to her right. "First Gou and now Ruisoki! They're both dead!" She seemed almost beside herself, but Denbi could not say for certain that it was entirely grief. Anger, perhaps?

"What happened, exactly?" she urged. Leaning forward, she poured a second cup and then set that before her guest, the steam curling up around her breathtaking features in quiet invitation. "Tell me everything."

Chimehara nodded, her hands extending to wrap around the teacup. "Gou—he disappeared several nights ago," she started, talking to the cup as much as to Denbi, some of her long, silky hair coming loose from its looped knot to fall forward, framing her face. "He was not with me long—only one night, in fact. He was gone the next and I thought perhaps he had simply run away, back to the streets where I found him. We searched and searched, but to no avail."

Denbi nodded. She had no idea why the younger woman had taken in a child off the streets in the first place, but doubted it was out of simple charity. She had already guessed, from their conversation the other day, that Chimehara left little to chance and did nothing without an eye toward how it might benefit her. Both of which were traits Denbi herself shared and admired in others—provided she could use them.

"Ruisoki, though," her lovely guest continued. "He was different. He has technically only been with me a week himself, but we knew each other before that and we had an understanding." She sighed, and the cup shook where her grip on it had tightened. "And now he's dead, too!"

"Are you certain they are both dead?" Denbi asked then, after another sip of her tea. "You said the first boy ran off—perhaps you just have not found him yet?"

But Chimehara shook her head. "No." There was sharp certainty in her voice. "I was still out searching when I saw guards marching past. More than you usually see this late, and it was not yet time for a shift change at the gates." Interesting that she would know that, Denbi observed, hiding a smile. There was certainly a good deal more to her guest than your average gem merchant. "I followed, and they led me to a spot in Sakiriti. I saw a man and a woman there, and the guards were speaking to them, but respectfully. At their feet was what looked like a bundle of old clothes—but I recognized the garments at once. And the body within them. It was Ruisoki. And he was dead."

Denbi frowned. "Did you hear them say what had happened to him?"

"No. I was too far away to make out their conversation," the younger woman admitted. "I did not want to risk them seeing me and asking what I was doing there." She tapped her fingernails on the cup, one after another, up one side and then the other. "But as they were leaving I heard one guard saying how strange it was, two little boys wandering the street with murderous intent in so short a span, and another agreeing that it was sad, especially considering their shared fate."

"Dead, then," Denbi agreed. "Exactly as you said. Did you get a look at the man and the woman?" She wondered who they might be, and what their involvement was.

"Of course." There was no arrogance there, just a simple statement of calm confidence. "Both of them were young, and neither was tall. He was handsome, clean-shaven. She was pretty, slim, athletic. Simple clothes but solid, well made. The guards were focused more on him than her and bowed deeply when they left." She frowned. "I have not seen them before, and neither of them wore any sort of house crest."

"Hm. I wonder..." There were two who might fit that description, and whose presence would explain the guards' reaction. But what would one of Hibikitsu's new Rojiri be doing in Sakiriti in the middle of the night, conferring with guards about a dead boy in the street? Curious.

She returned her attention to her guest, who was watching her closely now. Something in that gaze reminded Denbi of a cat, readying to leap. "I am very sorry for your loss, my dear," she stated over the rim of her cup. "But I fail to see why you came here, and at such an hour—and were so determined to see me that you injured several of my staff to gain entry. What can I do for you, precisely?"

"Help me!" Chimehara demanded, rising to her feet, her eyes flashing. Ash, but she was stunning! Denbi wished she could have had such looks—she could have conquered the realm without ever needing to draw a single blade. "Help me find out who did this. Help me eliminate them!" She frowned. "And help me protect Suda. I can't let them get her too!"

Denbi nodded. "Ah, I see. You have one pupil remaining? Yes, of course she must be protected at all costs. And you as well, my dear, in case this is somehow meant as a way to get to you through them." She saw the younger woman's eyes narrow at that idea. Good. She was sharp, this one, and dangerous, but she could still be molded, still guided. Still led.

Of course, that also suggested there was something she was hiding, something that she felt could make her the target of such ire. Denbi did not need to know what it was—yet. For now, simply knowing such a secret existed was enough.

Rising to her feet, she reached out and took Chimehara's hands in hers, feeling how slender the fingers were, and how smooth the skin. "I will help you, my dear," she promised in her most reassuring tone, her face composed in what she referred to her as her "kindly old aunt" pose. "Of course I will. Why, you are welcome to stay here, if you like, and Suda as well. No one will bother you here. And together we will find out who did this, and we will make them pay." She smiled at her guest. "And you must help me in return. Though I think, really, you will be helping yourself at the same time. For it seems to me that we share common interests and common goals, and therefore our enemies must be the same as well."

Chimehara was watching her closely, but she nodded, and a small, sweet smile blossomed on her lips. "Thank you," she said, blushing and dipping into a curtsy. "I already feel worlds better. I am sorry about your guards—I did not mean to cause such trouble." She glanced up through her long lashes. "I was so upset, though. That's why I had to come here—I knew you could help me. And of course, I will help you however I can."

She is like a poisonous flower, Denbi thought, smiling back. Beautiful and beguiling—and utterly deadly.

Well, all the better. She could use such a flower. Precisely how was unclear yet, but between this delicate and lethal lady and those two odd but powerful brothers, Denbi was beginning to feel she had exactly the tools she needed to finally set things into motion.

The time was fast approaching, and when it came, she would be ready.

CHAPTER THIRTY-THREE

Saisaihyu, Day Eight

Hibikitsu considered the man standing before them. Clever, he decided. Very clever. He wore a kitoro, of course, but one that had been unusually tailored, its lapels rising higher than was normal and curving inward more, so that instead of the usual V at the front the robes presented a semi-circle around the neck. The robes were longer in back as well and were of a midnight blue that almost held hints of red and purple, especially in the shadows. Higeibara were imprinted across it in a dark silvery gray, so that they were only visible in certain light.

All in all, it called to mind nothing so much as the eikono of the Rojiri arrayed before him, making Kishin Narai appear almost to be one of their number.

How had he known what the royal councilors wore, Hibikitsu wondered. Had Kagiri told him? But no, that seemed unlikely—glancing at the young man to his side, he saw a slight frown, as if the Gensaiba was trying to decipher what game the merchant might be playing. No, if the information had come from there it had been unwilling, even unconscious. Hibikitsu had certainly seen men and women who could draw forth critical details in seemingly casual conversation, asking apparently innocuous questions that led to information best kept hidden.

Which meant this merchant was likely good with words, good at shaping them, good at utilizing them. He had learned what the Rojiri wore, and had deliberately patterned his own attire after theirs, to present a more favorable impression.

Yes, definitely clever. Well, Hibikitsu did not object to clever, especially if it were used in his service. For now, he reserved judgement, keeping his face blank as the merchant approached to the

requisite distance and then knelt, favoring one hip as he prostrated himself and lowered his forehead to the floor.

"Thank you for seeing me, Your Imperial Majesty," Kishin
Narai intoned, his voice clear and strong, each word precise. Yes,
this one was good at speaking. "You honor me."

"Welcome, Kishin Narai," Hibikitsu replied. "You may rise.
Our faithful advisor informs us that you have a matter you wish
to present to us." He had to stifle a yawn as he spoke. Bones, he
was tired! He had already met with the ambassadors this morning, and that had nearly done him in. So much to do, and so much
care that had to be taken when speaking with them, since each
was here as the formal representative of their nation.

In some ways, dealing with Fyushu was proving to be the
easiest. As Master Eijiri had pointed out, Lady Nihiro was here
as a supplicant, admitted defeat and begging for aid. That put
them in a weakened position, and thus it behooved them to be as
accommodating as possible. They were still awaiting word from
the Empress, but the elderly ambassador had assured him that
her mistress would be eager to begin negotiating to purchase food
and would do so in good faith.

The Yatamorans were more complicated, in part because
they had thus far asked for nothing beyond the chance to speak
together. With no clear goal in sight, it was harder to interpret
their intentions and thus plan accordingly. In addition, there was
that shadow of the assassination attempt casting a pall over any
interactions, not to mention that Hu Yongian and his two companions had a strange air about them, disdainful of traditional
roles and rituals. They made Hibikitsu uneasy, and he was careful
to have Kohori and several other Honteno with him whenever he
did meet the visiting trio, to be safe.

Then there were the Higinasi. That one made the Yatamorans
appear as simple as a straight line! He had met with the Lord
and Lady Yakami once since their arrival—and with the Princess
Ogawa, of course. They had exchanged pleasantries but the question they had posed, that of his marrying Ogawa, hung over all
their heads, like a mamusha coiled about a tree branch rearing

back any moment to strike, and the conversation had been tense. They had not brought up their king's proposal, and neither had Hibikitsu, but clearly it would have to be addressed at some point soon.

Of course, Kohori had been telling him just a few days before that he would need to consider the issue of taking a bride at some point soon. But he had not expected it to be thrust upon him so abruptly! Nor did he find the young lady objectionable, and politically there was much to recommend their union. Still, he needed time to consider it—and, if he chose to decline, to find a way to do so without angering his royal neighbors and plunging the kingdom once more into war over something as foolish as his own pride.

A muted cough to his side made him glance over at Noniki, who raised an eyebrow and glanced toward the floor beyond the dais. Ash, had he been lost in his thoughts and left the man standing there waiting on him? Though he was the emperor, he did not wish to treat people so. Now he turned and focused his attention on Kishin Narai, who had returned to his feet and was waiting patiently.

Yet a part of his mind could not help also noting that Noniki had looked tired, far more than usual. The youngest Rojiri had said something when he'd arrived, his lady friend being attacked by a child on the streets? He would have to ask after that later.

Right now, however, the merchant was speaking. "Your Imperial Majesty," he began, "as I recently noted to Kagiri"—here he nodded at the Gensaiba, who did not return the gesture despite the obvious attempt to establish that there was a relationship there— "many of us greatly appreciate the changes you have made recently. We feel, and I hope I may say so without seeming presumptuous, that you are demonstrating a willingness to move beyond tradition, to break the stagnation that has bound our nation for too long and to seek new ways to move forward to the benefit of all."

Hibikitsu nodded. "We are pleased that you and yours find it so," he stated, "for indeed, that is our intent. Are we to take it, then, that your presentation is focused on another such method of progress?" He was pleased with that turn of phrase and saw his Rojiri smiling amongst themselves as well. This merchant was not the only one who could be good with words!

"Indeed it is, sire," Kishin Narai agreed. He was not a small man, broad rather than tall, with a wide face to match, yet his features were relatively fine and his eyes were very alert as he clasped his hands behind his back, assuming the stance of a tutor about to impart a lesson. "There has long been an...I hesitate to label it 'injustice,' though in truth it is, for it has prevented any but a select few from benefiting, and I feel that has been a detriment to the whole." He paused and frowned. "Is Your Majesty aware that certain forms of production here in Rimbaku are restricted to the nobility, and indeed even within that to a dozen or fewer of the oldest families?"

"We are aware that certain patents were awarded by our ancestors, for loyalty and service to the throne," Hibikitsu agreed slowly. "It has never been brought to our attention that there might be a problem with this arrangement."

"Nor would it," the man before him agreed, "for the nobles wished it to remain so and no one else had the audacity to gainsay them." He smiled. "But I am hopeful that such imbalances could now be redressed." He cleared his throat. "I hope I am not telling you things you already know, sire, and I apologize if I appear pedantic, but are you aware that the average farmer is not even allowed to own their own tienbao? They can possess only half a rice paddy, enough to feed their own family with a small amount beyond."

Hibikitsu frowned and glanced at his Rojiri. "Is this true?" he asked them.

Surprisingly, it was Noniki who nodded. "It is, sire," the young matekai agreed. "I spent some time in a monastery before coming here, and I remember the brothers speaking of this when nearby villagers would come begging for food. Imperial law states that each family may grow rice on only half a tan, because that produces enough to feed them for a year. To grow more than that would mean you are producing rice to sell, and that is not allowed."

"Precisely," Kishin Narai agreed from the floor, nodding at Noniki like a teacher pleased with his student's recitation. "This rule was established because only ten noble families—among them the Amani, the Watane, the Orita, the Yoshino, the Domo, and until recently the Etsuya and the Ieyuki—are allowed to grow more rice than they need for their own use. These houses control all rice production within Rimbaku—they sell the rice to merchants such as myself and we distribute it to the rest of the country, and to neighboring nations."

"We see." Hibikitsu mulled this over. "So these ten families set the price, and everyone else is forced to abide by it."

"Yes, exactly so. And it is not just rice," the merchant hastened to add. "It is also cotton, silk, and iron. Our nation's four greatest resources, and all controlled by a handful of noble houses." He bowed deeply. "And although those houses ultimately owe their loyalty to Your Majesty, I can only assume they do not pass along the profits from these sales, beyond a set amount for tithes."

This time it was Fujitai Takami who confirmed the statement. "I remember seeing my father going over the family accounts," he stated softly. "No matter the profits from our estates and holdings and ventures, only a set amount was tithed to the throne." He bowed in apology, though it had not been him at fault. Nor his father either, if that had been the rules established long ago—the man, and the other nobles, had merely taken advantage of a situation designed to benefit them.

"Thank you for bringing this to our attention," Hibikitsu told the merchant, who bowed again. "You are correct that this matter seems inequitable, and one of the many old traditions which should be re-examined and perhaps expunged." He tapped his chin in thought. "You appear to us to be a man who looks to the future, Kishin Narai," he stated at last. "And one who is not unwilling to make changes, should they benefit our nation." Glancing about him, he gauged the responses of the four men at his side: Kagiri wore a slight frown, not unusual for him; Noniki was nodding, however, as was Takami, and Master Eijiri gave a single nod as well when Hibikitsu's eyes reached him. "Perhaps you would be willing to offer such suggestions as this, and other counsel, as needed?"

"Of course, sire," Kishin Narai replied, bowing even more deeply. "It would be my honor. You have only to call upon me and I shall attend with all speed."

Hibikitsu smiled. "We are pleased to hear that," he stated, "but we had something more permanent in mind. Kishin Narai, will you accept the call of your emperor and take on the role of Rojiri, pledging to advise us, along with your fellow counselors, on this and diverse other matters, speaking honestly your opinion upon the governance of the nation and the welfare of its people?"

The merchant dropped to his knees—still favoring one side, Hibikitsu noted, and did not miss a flicker of something like sorrow or guilt across Kagiri's face—and pressed his forehead to the tiles there once more. "I would be honored, Your Imperial Majesty," he stated, "and I swear to place the empire first and foremost, and to do my utmost to help you guide us to new heights of prosperity and happiness."

Yes, clever, Hibikitsu decided as the man rose and the other Rojiri hopped down from the dais to welcome him into their ranks, Kagiri neither first nor last among them. Well, they would see if that cleverness could truly be turned to their advantage or if it was too focused on the advancement of its owner. Time would tell.

CHAPTER THIRTY-FOUR

Noboru Juniri huffed, blowing out his heavy cheeks and causing his wisp of a mustache to dance above his thick lips. "Explain to me again why we are here," he demanded, rubbing his hands together and glancing apprehensively behind him, where the walls of Bejinuri rose like a lavender cascade, their color lightening as they reached up around that district. "I have never been below Sakiriti in my life!"

"Then it is high time you rectified that," Kagiri commented from where he stood at the front of the wide platform he'd had erected at one end of the city's widest square, whose side was bordered by Awaihinshi's massive front gates. These were currently open, as it was still morning, and traders and travelers glanced about as they entered the space, surprised at the number of soldiers standing at attention in neat rows before that platform. Kagiri had considered barring the square to everyone except his aiashe but had decided in the end to let people come and go freely. He had no wish to hide his actions, after all. Far from it, the more who saw the better, and so he was pleased to note that around the square's edges many of the common aiashe had gathered, curious to see why the new lord commander had summoned all their officers.

Because those in rows were all ranked chuisu or above, Kagiri knew these were only the officers currently stationed in and around the city, but he was still impressed. There had to be at least fifty of them here, not counting himself or the four men standing behind him.

It was more than enough to make sure what happened today was known to all.

"Officers of the aiashe," he declared, projecting his words to make sure they carried across the entire square. "Welcome. I am Kagiri, your new Dogenriku. And, as you might have guessed from both my name and my armor, I am not exactly what you expected." There was a ripple of uneasy laughter across the ranks, as the officers tried to decide if that had been a joke or not. He hoped that his own smile reassured them but they had no doubt noted his lack of a family name, and his armor, which remained the same mottled green save for the singular addition of a stylized gold higeibara as his modato. He also carried his chasai, currently clasped behind him with both hands, but his sash was empty—he had chosen for today to leave his nihono behind.

Now he continued, "You also may have guessed, from the Saisaihyu that we are currently enjoying, that the emperor, long may he reign, has an eye toward shaking some of the rust off our society, pulling down some of the ancient scaffolding that has covered over much of our past achievements and at the same time prevented us from appreciating or expanding upon what we have now." He glanced at the officers before him—his officers. "I feel the same. For too long we have relied upon past glories, placed too much stock in history and lineage and not enough in ability and loyalty and courage. We are not historians! We are warriors! And warriors should be judged by their skill with spear and sword, their talent for leading on the battlefield, not who their forefathers were or where their estates stand!"

That brought cheers—not so much from the assembled officers as from the soldiers on the outskirts, though he saw many of the officers had perked up at his statement as well. After all, many of them were from lesser noble families, houses that had offered enough money to buy them a commission but who lacked the wealth or prestige to secure them a higher rank. Others, of course, seemed less thrilled with his comments, and he could all but feel the glares from at least three of his four taisho heating the plates upon his back.

"I know," he told the men and women standing in front of him, "that many of you carry the blades of your ancestors, heirlooms of your house. But not all." Here and there he could see choko-tos instead, mainly among the chuisu, since anyone without a nihono was either not noble-born or a second or third child and thus unlikely to ever rise above that level. But some of those with nihono were nodding as well, smiles lighting their faces, and it was toward them in particular that Kagiri directed his next statement: "From now on, when you defeat an opponent in battle, his or her nihono is yours, no matter your birth. You have earned that weapon and you should carry it with pride, for you won it—not your grandsire but you, and you alone!"

The soldiers around the square erupted in even louder cheers over that, and many of the junior officers clapped as well. The more senior officers were mixed in their response—some looked intrigued, others openly pleased, and then many others were scowling and shaking their heads. Those, no doubt, were the ones who had achieved their place through family connections alone. Well, they were about to be in for an even greater shock.

"Along those same lines," he stated, "from this time forward all promotions will be based upon merit alone. I do not care if you are from one of the oldest families in Rimbaku, with an estate spitting distance from Aihiri itself. I do not care if you are from a farming family out in Nariyari and had nothing to your name when you joined our ranks. Those who prove themselves capable and loyal will rise! Those who demonstrate incompetence and disloyalty will fall!" That brought collective gasps, but he was not done. Instead, he pivoted on his heel, turning so that his back was to the crowd and he now faced his four generals instead.

"Gentlemen," he told them, shouting so that his words would still be heard by the collective assemblage behind him. "You see that I have no nihono with me, only the chasai of my office. More than one of you have questioned my appointment as your commanding officer. Now is your chance to rectify that situation. You will kneel and present your sword as a sign of your loyalty, swearing upon it to follow my orders. Or you will draw your blade and attack me." He freed his left hand so the baton fell to his right side, tapping against his thigh. "Should you defeat me, this baton and the office it denotes are yours." He smiled at them, though he knew it was no expression of joy but rather one of grim determination, perhaps closer to a smirk. "These are your only two options," he informed them, lifting his menatu from where it had hung open and hooking it into place across his face. Once that was done, he raised his chasai and pointed it loosely in their direction, shifting his legs farther apart into a ready stance. "Begin."

At first all four men gaped at him. Then Noboru Juniri's eyes narrowed, all but disappearing between cheek and brow. "House Noboru!" the big man bellowed, yanking his sword free of its scabbard and charging, the blade lifted high in both hands. The platform shook with his approach, and Kagiri's greatest concern was that he might lose his footing from the tremors thus produced. He held fast, however, and stood his ground as the overweight Taisho bore down upon him.

Just as Noboru Juniri slashed downward, Kagiri exploded into action. His hand shot up, the sturdy baton knocking the descending nihono to the side so that it fell well clear of his shoulders. At the same time, he shoved the general hard in the chest with his free hand, the impact vibrating up his arm even as he hooked one foot behind the man's leg and kicked outward. Thus off-balance, Noboru Juniri toppled backward, startlement splashing across his face like a burst of rain, his arms flailing as he fell. His back hit the platform with a thunderous report and he grunted as the air fled his lungs, leaving him red-faced and gasping, his arms and legs thrashing about, looking like nothing so much as a turtle that had been flipped onto its shell and could not right itself. The impact had knocked his sword free of his grip. Kagiri stepped over and retrieved it, returning to place the edge of the blade against the struggling man's neck.

"Yield," he instructed, pressing with just enough force to crease the skin and part the outer layers.

"I yield," the man at his feet stammered out. Kagiri stepped back and waited as he levered himself to one side and then sat up, chest still heaving and face still flushed. "The emperor will hear of this!"

"He already has," Kagiri replied. He reached down and plucked the scabbard from the other man's okube, sheathing the blade and sliding into his own sash. "Noboru Juniri," he announced loudly, "you are hereby judged unfit for the role of Taisho and are thus stripped of that rank and any responsibilities and privileges thereof. If you wish to remain in the aiashe you will do so at the rank of taisu until such time as you have proven yourself. Or you may retire now." That brought more murmuring from the crowd, for the descent from general to captain was a massive one. There was some scattered applause as well, though, and much laughter. It did not surprise Kagiri that Noboru had not been well-liked.

Vibrations through the wooden planks alerted him, and Kagiri spun about in time to see not one but two blades slicing toward him, one from either side. He raised the chasai with both hands, blocking the twin strikes, the solid teak of the baton easily resisting the force of those swords, and shook his head at the two attackers. "Was your intent to share the role of Dogenriku between you?" he asked Atsumi Izo and Masagi Matsu as the pair circled around him, seeking an opening. "And how would that work? Each of you taking control on alternate days?"

"As long as it removes you from office, we will figure it out later," Atsumi snarled. He stabbed forward, but Kagiri countered the blow with ease. He had never seen the slender taisho so emotional, his usual good looks contorted by hatred. The man had some speed to him as well, but no real power, plus his attacks were sloppy and not helped by his rage.

On the other side, Masagi said nothing, his eyes narrowed in concentration. He did not seem as angry, and his strikes were more careful, suggesting this was less about taking personal affront and more about seizing an opportunity.

Well, no matter. Kagiri would deal with them both equally. The problem with fighting two on one was that you had to worry about your ally as much as your opponent, and it was clear that neither general had trained in paired combat. They both tried to move to the spot directly in front of Kagiri, instead of moving away to widen the span he needed to defend. They bumped

into one another in the process, Masagi's broader build and lower
height putting his shoulder solidly into Atsumi's chest and shoving
the taller man back. When that happened, Kagiri lunged in, quick
as lightning. He aimed, not for the swords themselves, but for the
hands that held them—a quick, hard rap on Masagi's fingers and
the man yelped with pain, dropping his sword and then stumbling
away as he received a blow to his helmet that left his head ringing.

Atsumi now found himself facing Kagiri alone and made the
mistake of trying a diagonal slash across the body. Kagiri stepped
into the blow, using one hand to catch the other man's arms and
force them up and away, preventing the strike from ever falling.
With his other he beat a rapid pattern against Atsumi's chest
and head, the heavy baton sending him staggering to the ground
where Noboru had been a moment before.

Kagiri had stripped the sword from Atsumi's hands as the
man fell. Now he turned to Masagi—and found the man dropping to his knees before him.

"I yield, Dogenriku," the stocky general declared, raising his
blade in both hands before him and bowing his head to the metal.
"I yield and pledge my service to you and to the empire."

Kagiri nodded. "Rise, Taisho Masagi," he replied. "I accept
your pledge and your service." Turning away, he retrieved Atsumi's
scabbard and, a moment later, placed the sheathed blade at his
belt alongside Noboru's. "Atsumi Izo," he said, "you are hereby
judged unfit for the role of Taisho, and—"

"Schism take you!" The disgraced former general snarled, all
but spitting the words as he pulled himself to his feet. "I'll have
none of this farce!" He stomped off the platform, his attempts at
retaining dignity disarmed by the laughter that rose at his exit and
the applause and cheering accompanying it.

That left only one, and Kagiri was not surprised to turn and
find Daishin Nishoji already on his knees with his sword held
before him. The sturdy general was still in the same spot he had
been standing before, and Kagiri had little doubt the man had
prostrated himself the moment the challenge had been issued.

"I pledge my service to you and to the empire, Dogenriku Kagiri,"

Daishin stated clearly, "and I am honored to serve beneath you."

Kagiri nodded and unhooked his face mask to smile down at the man. "Rise, Taisho Daishin," he said. "I happily accept your pledge and your service."

That done, he turned and stepped toward the front of the platform once more. The men and women watching him were utterly silent, eyes wide, many faces flushed or pale, but whether from excitement or fear he could not yet tell. "At its current size, the aiashe requires five taisho," he informed them. "I have but two remaining. That means there are now three openings for general."

He studied the officers now hanging on his every word and nodded. "Anyone ranked taisu or above who wishes to present themselves for consideration as taisho may do so, regardless of birth. I will require that at least one superior or officer of your same rank recommend you, and at least one officer or soldier of lesser rank as well. I will also expect you to stand against me in combat, though"—and here he smiled—"I will not require you to defeat me." That brought laughter and some signs of relief among the crowd, and he surveyed them a moment or two more before adding, "I look forward to leading you. Thank you."

When he turned away, dismissing them, the cheers that arose were as loud as a storm, and the square shook from them. Kagiri carefully kept his back to the dispersing soldiers—he was not sure if letting them see him grinning ear to ear would help his attempted image of the strong, stern commanding officer. He nearly lost his composure, however, when he glanced to the side and saw, standing just to the side of the platform, a young, well-built man in sturdy clothes, hair cut short, a broad smile on his handsome face—and then did laugh when Noniki put a fist to his chest and saluted him, as one warrior to another.

CHAPTER THIRTY-FIVE

Norio Shinjuru was not a large man. Indeed, he was barely taller than Shizumi herself. Yet his shoulders were broad, his arms and chest thick with muscle, so much so that he always seemed to swagger when he walked. In truth it was only his build that caused such a stride, for she had always found him to be a calm, even quiet man—at least, when he was not shouting orders.

Which he was doing at this very moment.

"First position!" He bellowed, and the rows of men and women before him drew their nihono—no chokotos here—and swept them forward and up, bringing the swords down in a line before them, both hands spaced properly apart along the hilt. "Second!" The warriors shouted "Hai!" in a ragged chorus and took a single large step forward, bring their blades up parallel to the ground, edge upward, tip to the left. "Third!" They reversed their swords so the tip was now to the right. "Fourth!" A spin and a slice as the blades arced down, returning to the original position.

That done, the Honjofu sergeant turned to Shizumi, who was standing behind him, and saluted both her and Kohori beside her, fist banging against his prodigious chest. "They are little better than monkeys with pointed sticks," he stated, "but at least I have taught them enough that they should not poke their own eyes out. Mostly."

Shizumi felt her lips twitching at the assessment and schooled herself to show only calm as she nodded to her subordinate. "Thank you, Gunso Norio," she replied, saluting him in return. "I am sure your teaching has produced excellent warriors, as always." She glanced at Kohori and grinned before shifting back toward the waiting recruits. "But perhaps we should put that to the test."

And with that she hopped off the walkway and down onto the sand of the practice yard.

"Warriors," she called out as she approached the first rank. "You wish to be the elite of Rimbaku, yes? To be part of her finest warrior cadres?" She drew her sword. "Then you have but one objective—stop me!" And she leaped toward the two nearest her, lashing out with her blade at the one on the right even as she kicked out at the one on the left.

Both cried out in surprise and stumbled backward, the first propelled by the impact of hardwood against her chest—for Shizumi was carrying, not her own nihono, but a baraken fashioned in its image out of smooth teak—and the second by her foot. She was already past them before they had even hit the ground, attacking the next two, who at least had absorbed what was happening enough to defend themselves. Neither was confident in their strokes, however, and Shizumi batted both swords aside, dealing punishing blows even as she slid between them and spun, attacking the one now behind her and circling around him to strike the warrior on his right. That put her at the back corner of the recruits' ranks, and she paused a moment, adjusting stance and grip as she waited to see what these younglings would do next. She was breathing heavily and could smell her own sweat along with the familiar scents of wood and leather and oil from her armor, but she had never felt more alive than moments like this.

One of the recruits nearby, a tall, slender woman with large hands, had evidently decided that enough was enough. With a cry she launched herself at Shizumi, sword high and already sweeping down. Shizumi blocked the blow, knocking it aside and stabbing forward in return, but the tall girl backpedaled and evaded, recovering control of her nihono in time to block with that as well. Good. This one had promise, Shizumi noted, trading a few quick blows with the recruit before disarming her with a devilish twisting blade-bind and then catching her behind the knees, driving her to the ground.

The next two were little challenge, but at least the two of them thought to coordinate their attacks, approaching Shizumi from either side, and she was forced to give ground. One of the recently fallen was still behind her, however, just stumbling back to his feet, and a swift kick sent him lurching backward into one of the pair, who dropped his sword rather than stab his fellow. That left Shizumi the other recruit, and she dispatched him easily enough. Still, it had been a good effort.

Only a handful were still standing—Norio had brought eighteen in all, only those he had felt were ready to at least join ranks and begin learning as they went. Three of those were standing back-to-back, facing Shizumi and covering their flanks as well, and she nodded. A sound strategy, especially against a single foe. One of the remaining two attacked recklessly, and a simple sidestep and gliding cut across the middle left him doubled over on the ground, coughing as he tried to recover his breath. Shizumi scooped up his fallen sword and lobbed it at the waiting trio, right at head level, the blade spinning like a top as it cut through the air, whistling with the force of its passage. The recruits cried out and scattered, avoiding the renegade weapon—Shizumi tripped one and thwacked him across the back of the head as he fell, feinted another and then batted her blade aside to deliver a ringing blow to the cheek, and then disarmed the third one with an overhand strike powerful enough to drive his sword from his numbed fingers.

That left only the last recruit. She had been watching, and stood waiting, a smug little smile on her face. A few inches taller than Shizumi, and rounder where it counted. Prettier, too. That, and the way she stood, told Shizumi that the girl believed she was something special. "Show me," she commanded, and the girl saluted, hand going to her sword and its scabbard. Yet still she did not draw.

Shizumi snorted. "You can't wait forever, girl," she pointed out. She advanced one step, two, but still the recruit held her ground and her patience. *She is counting on her draw,* Shizumi thought. *She must be good if she is willing to risk everything on that. She anticipates she is faster than me, fast enough to strike before I can close.*

She took another careful step, then another, marching slowly, methodically forward—and then, instead of a third, she suddenly leaped, leg flinging out and straightening, foot flat, other leg bent beneath her, sword pointed forward as if to guide her on her path. The recruit's eyes widened and she grabbed for her blade, but it was too late as Shizumi slammed into her, her kick connecting with the girl's chest and flinging her backward. She landed hard, and an instant later Shizumi was kneeling over her, baraken at her throat. "No rules on the battlefield," she pointed out, pressing hard enough to make the girl's eyes bulge a second before she backed off. "Next time, don't posture. Just fight." The girl nodded, and in her eyes Shizumi saw a flicker of anger and hurt pride but also understanding and acceptance. Good. This one was willing to learn.

Standing and sliding the baraken back into her okube, she returned to the platform, leaping back up onto it with ease. Kohori was waiting, arms crossed. "Well?" she asked the head of the Honteno as she brushed herself off and tossed her sweat-slicked hair back from her face.

"Your way of testing is certainly interesting," the older Taikoro remarked with an almost straight face. "Effective, though." She nodded. "Most of them are good. A few are better than that. And a few—" She shrugged. "They will learn."

"I agree." Shizumi accepted a waterskin from Geniji, who had joined them at some point during the exercise along with Akino and Isano and now stood along the back of the platform, opposite Itamon and Reizei. "So? How many do you want?"

Kohori considered that, pursing her lips. "I do not want to strip away all your new recruits—" she started, but Shizumi held up a hand, stopping that sentence as she gulped water.

"We have more back on Iwikaru," she pointed out once she'd swallowed. "These were merely the ones Norio felt were ready. Take what you need."

"I could use six," Kohori admitted with a dip of her head. "That would fill out my ranks somewhat and give me time to find the rest myself."

"It shall be done." Shizumi swiveled around to face the recruits, who had been milling about, unsure what to do after and still recovering from her strange assault. "Form up!" she bellowed, and they leapt to obey, hastily forming ranks again. "You were brought here with the intent to be Honjofu," she told them, "but for some of you I offer a different path. This is Maniko Kohori, Taikoro of the Honteno, the emperor's own personal guard. She has need of warriors to join her ranks. It is a great honor to serve among the Honteno, and you may be called upon to lay down your life for your emperor. Unlike the Honjofu, however, you will live and patrol within these walls. No travel but no sleeping on the ground, either." She glanced at the young warriors. "If you are willing to be considered for such a place, step forward. If you are not—and there will be no dishonor cast upon you for such a choice—step back."

After a moment where no one moved, the three who had joined forces against her stepped forward. So did the two who had fought together, the one who had charged her, and two others. The tall girl and the pretty one both stepped back, along with the remainder.

"I will take those three," Kohori commented, pointing at the trio, "and those two—I like the fact that they already know how to work together." Shizumi nodded. "And that one." She gestured at the one who had charged. "A little reckless, but his form was good and I can teach him restraint." She turned then and saluted Shizumi. "Thank you, Taikoro Misataki," she declared loudly. "I am in your debt and hope this is merely the first in many steps that see the Honteno and the Honjofu working closely together as two sides of the same coin, the emperor's elite forces."

"You are very welcome, Taikoro Maniko," Shizumi replied, returning the salute. "And I hope so as well."

With that Kohori hopped down, her two lieutenants right behind her—the one helping the other down, since her injury still made such maneuvers difficult—and beckoned the six she'd chosen to follow her. "Come with us, you lot," she instructed. "Bring your gear and we'll show you the barracks, introduce you around, and tell you what to expect as a Honteno." A smile creased her weathered face then. "And we'll get you fitted for some proper armor." The recruits were all in gray, as they had not yet earned the right to wear the Honjofu black.

Shizumi waited until they had gone before glancing behind her. "Norio Shinjuru," she stated, and the Honjofu presented himself and saluted. "You have done an exemplary job, as always," she declared. "Your talent is equaled only by your dedication, and it is my honor to promote you to chuisu."

The new lieutenant started for only a second before bowing deeply. "I live to serve, Taikoro," he announced. "Thank you." His eyes had creased into one of his rare smiles.

"Geniji," she called next. "Akino." The two members of her bantao straightened and saluted. "I am promoting both of you to gunso." She smiled at Isano, who raised a brow. "I only wish we were large enough to require a third."

The archer shrugged. "Happy not to have to give orders," he stated laconically, which made her laugh.

"Are you sure?" Geniji asked, her brow furrowed. "I mean—"

"Are you questioning your Taikoro?" Shizumi asked, but not loud, and she laughed immediately after. "Of course I am sure!" she said, stepping forward and clapping a hand to each of the two's shoulders. "You two are my most trusted, my most capable, my most loyal. You more than deserve it, and I'd be a fool not to find some way to keep you around."

Now the big woman's face broke into a smile. "You know I'm still going to keep watch over you," she warned even as she saluted.

"I'd expect nothing less." Shizumi saluted back. "Now please take our new recruits to the barracks and get them settled." She sighed, her eyes going to the empty space between Akino and Isano. "It seems I have one last person to speak with."

"She is in the gardens," Akino told her as he saluted and stepped away to begin giving orders to the recruits. The rest of them mercifully left Shizumi alone as she followed the walkway to its far end and then stepped down, cutting across the lawn and toward the gardens that arose between the buildings and the outer walls. They were beautiful, but they also served as a way to conceal Honteno should the household guard need to defend against attackers—there they could cut down foes unseen, leaving the remainder to stumble out onto open ground.

She found Dairamu sitting on a bench in one of the small clearings within the sculpted bushes and flowering hedges and trees. "You missed seeing the new recruits," Shizumi started, taking a seat at the other end, careful to leave some space between them. "Some of them are good, too. Or will be."

"I have no doubt," the other woman replied, studying her own hands, which were as sturdy as the rest of her. "Norio knows his job well."

Shizumi waited, and after a moment Dairamu sighed.

"I'm sorry," she said. "I know why you did it, I understand your reasonings, I get all of that, but I still cannot get past it." She lifted her eyes to Shizumi, half glaring and half entreating. "All that time, putting my life in your hands, I thought you had the wisdom of the ages behind you! And you didn't! You never did!"

"No, I didn't," Shizumi agreed, folding her own hands on her lap. "It was only ever me."

"And you are amazing," her friend said. "You are. But I still— I cannot help it, I still feel betrayed somehow. It's stupid, I know that. But that is where I am." She hung her head. "So, what now?"

Shizumi sighed. "There are three paths I can see," she said slowly, carefully. "The first is that you simply carry on as best you can. You stay with the Honjofu. I have promoted Norio to chuisu, and Geniji and Akino to gunso. You can take orders from them and rarely have to deal with me directly. It would be awkward, but we could manage." She paused a second before continuing. "You could leave the Honjofu," she offered. "Join the aiashe or simply find some other occupation. You are still young, and I would offer whatever support I could. Find something that makes you happy."

Dairamu nodded, but looked miserable, and Shizumi understood that completely. They were both military women. They lived for the discipline, the structure—and the combat.

"There is a third option," she added now. "As you know, the Honteno have been sorely depleted by recent events. I have just given their Taikoro first pick of our new recruits, and she has taken a half dozen of them. But they are all young and green. I am sure she would welcome the addition of a seasoned veteran, one of our finest."

The other woman's head came up at that. "You would allow me to transfer to her?"

"Of course." Shizumi had to blink away sudden tears. "You are my friend, Dairamu. No matter what. I want you to be happy." She smiled. "You would be a tremendous asset to the Honteno, and still able to play cards with Isano and the others, still able to reside here in Aihiri." *But you would not have to serve under me,* she added silently.

Dairamu considered that. "I think that would be the best for everyone," she said finally. "Thank you. And I truly am sorry I could not—" she let that trail off, the rest unsaid but still hanging in the air.

"I understand." Shizumi stood. "I hope that we can still be friends, at least. In the meantime, I will let Kohori know that she is stealing away one of my best."

She turned on her heel and hurried away before the tears could break free and blind her completely. Some stern Taikoro that would be.

CHAPTER THIRTY-SIX

Seikoku was back on that same street in Sakiriti again, back under the same lamp post, but this time there was a difference.

This time, she was looking for trouble.

She was, she freely admitted to herself, in a foul mood. And why shouldn't she be? She flashed back to the conversation she had had with Noniki just hours earlier, and her blood boiled at the very memory of it all.

They had met for dinner in this very district, just the two of them. It was still thrilling and nerve-wracking and confusing and exhilarating, this thing between them, and they were trying hard to find the proper balance—they had been friends first, and still were, but they also lived together and looked after the enclave together, plus now they were becoming something a good deal more than just friends. It was all very complicated, and only made worse by the recent troubles with their neighbors.

Noniki had started in on that as soon as they'd been seated and served tea. "I spoke with the other Rojiri today," he'd begun, the fingers of one hand curling around his cup, the other loosely entwined with hers across the table. "And with the karo, as well."

"The karo?" She'd asked. There had been a karo back in Ginzai, the regional governor choosing to make his home there in its largest city. But why would you need someone like that here, in the emperor's own capital?

As it turned out, there were five of them, one for each level of Awaihinshi save Aihiri itself. Those five governors were responsible for keeping their districts clean and safe and prosperous. They worked together with each other and the aiashe to keep the gates manned and the streets clear and to solve any problems that might extended beyond a single level.

Problems like a group of new arrivals setting up shop in Atsani, for example.

"It has a lot of people upset," Noniki had explained carefully, his thumb stroking the back of her hand in a decidedly distracting manner. "Atsani has always been home to the oldest, most powerful families, and none of them would ever even think of selling goods or services from their home, so it's a bit shocking." He'd sighed. "And since the estate is technically mine, I have to be very careful to not seem like I am simply granting myself and my friends special privileges."

"We are not breaking any laws," she'd replied sharply, pulling her hand away and cradling it in her lap instead. A waiter had hovered anxiously nearby but she'd ignored him, focusing on the man across from her instead, willing him to listen, to understand. "We just want to contribute, that's all. What is wrong with that?"

"Nothing," he'd agreed quickly, retrieving his own spurned limb and wrapping that hand around his cup as well, the steam rising from it and curling about itself like a coiled snake rather than blocking his intent gaze. "But we don't want to upset everyone around us, either. That can't end well. We have to proceed cautiously." He'd smiled. "We'll find a way through this."

"We?" She'd snorted at him—very ladylike, of course, but she hadn't been too concerned with manners at that precise moment. "You mean you. I wasn't at this meeting, was I?"

That had made his smile disappear like the sun ducking behind clouds. "Well, no," he'd said slowly. "As I said, it was myself and the other Rojiri and the karo. That's all. You—"

"Have no official standing anywhere, with anyone," she'd snapped, shoving her chair back and springing to her feet. "So why should I have been there? I obviously have nothing to contribute." And she'd stormed out, leaving him to gape and call after her. But she hadn't paused, hadn't even looked back, and mercifully he had chosen not to follow after.

Seikoku had stomped about for a while, this way and that, even climbing a tree or two, scaling a wall, balancing her way across a roof. But eventually she had wound up back here again.

Her anger had faded now. She wasn't even really angry at him, she knew. He meant well—he always did, he was the kindest person she knew. And of course it had been an official meeting, and of course she had no official rank or standing, and of course inviting her to join them would have been seen as the very favoritism he was trying to avoid.

But she was still frustrated, not at him so much as at the entire situation. She'd worked so hard! It was not easy, keeping close to thirty people living together and working together in harmony. She was not managing it all alone, of course—Minawa and Jitu Kanai were invaluable, and she could rely on a few of the others like Isoro and Kuma and Sanedi to be reasonable and follow her lead, but even so, most of the decisions fell to her. And she did not mind that, not at all—but it had felt like Noniki and the others had been dismissing her efforts, dismissing her, making a decision about her friends, her family, without even asking for her input. And that had infuriated her.

So, she thought, staring hard at the lamp post. Focus on something else instead. The boy she had met here—the boy she had killed here—had said something about his teacher. "We had been taken in by the same woman," he'd told her. But had he just meant himself and the first boy, Gou?

Or were there more murderous little children lurking about in the shadows, knives at the ready?

Because she could not believe that whoever had taken both boys in had just happened to find two with a similar tendency toward violence. In truth, though Gou had shown an eagerness, the second boy—whose name Seikoku had never learned—had treated the entire encounter as merely an exercise, something to be done quickly so that it was finished and he could move on to the next task. That—and his suggestion that this mysterious woman would feel better about Gou's death if Seikoku died as well—suggested that the killing was not an aberration but a feature.

That this strange teacher was in fact training these children to kill.

Seikoku did not approve of using children in any way. And particularly in using them for something this vile. She might not be able to solve her family's problems right now, or to speak with the Rojiri and the karo on equal terms. This, however—this was something she could handle.

She would find out who this woman was, and if she had any other pupils. And then she would find a way to take those children away from her, so they would not be forced to commit any more murders.

The only problem was, Seikoku had absolutely no idea how to go about that.

She circled the lamp post several times, but no more children emerged from the dark corners and alleys. No one spoke from the shadows. No knives emerged, no footsteps echoed out to her, no smell of soap arose on the still night air.

She was utterly alone.

After a few more moments, Seikoku sighed. What was the point? She had no clue what she was doing, not the faintest idea where or how to start looking. It was just another failure.

Turning, she began trudging back home. Already she was dreading what she would say, because she knew Noniki would be waiting up for her. She could already see him sitting there on the front steps, his handsome face so earnest, a hesitant smile touching his lips as she stepped in through the gate and he rose to meet her. He would have forgiven her by now, of course—he was too kind not to. But that did not change things any, nor did it invalidate what she had said, harsh though it had been. So where would they go from here?

She mulled that over, her eyes not focused on the road before her, her feet carrying her home out of habit, she had walked this way enough times in the past week. Even without conscious thought, her steps were still light, her soft boots barely whispering against the cobblestones.

It was that very quiet that saved her.

There was a whisper, leather on stone, the same as her own steps made—but not perfectly in synch with them. Close, very close, but it lingered just a little longer than her echo had and started just before her own feet made contact again. Someone else was here, and they were working very hard to disguise their footfalls within hers.

Even as that registered, Seikoku was throwing herself forward, arms out, hands striking the ground and propelling her up so her lower body swung around, legs curling over as she pushed up, bringing her torso under and around and then back up again as she flipped and brought her feet back down to the ground again. She'd left the cane behind tonight but was pulling her kogotano from her sleeve even as she twisted about—just barely in time to block a knife thrust that came from below at an angle, intending to drive up between her ribs and into her heart.

Ash, but this one was fast!

"This one" proved to be a little girl, short and slight of build, with enormous eyes in a narrow face. Those eyes were currently narrowed intently, and her mouth was pursed in a tight little grimace as she advanced, knife weaving hypnotically before her. She wore dark clothes like both boys had, and her thick hair was pulled back in a loose bun meant only to keep it out of her face.

Evidently Seikoku had been right about there being more students than just those two!

"Why don't we talk about this?" she tried now, backing up to keep the girl from being able to stab easily. Though not exactly tall herself, Seikoku had a clear height advantage over her current assailant and was not about to give that up if she could avoid it. "Look, this is all just one big misunderstanding."

The girl did not say a word. Nor did she stop moving in. Her eyes were focused, fierce, and Seikoku knew at once that there would be no reasoning with her. This one might not be as completely vicious as Gou, but she enjoyed the kill.

She was also fast, a fact she proved again as she lunged once more, nearly catching Seikoku in the stomach. There was only one thing to do.

Seikoku turned and ran.

The gates between here and Motohiri were less than a third

of the way around from her current location. There were always at least two guards on duty there—if she could reach them, they could help her deal with this miniature assassin.

She just had to get to them before the girl caught up with her.

She could hear the rapid pounding of footsteps behind her. The girl had given up on stealth in favor of speed, same as her. Fine. Seikoku was confident she could outrun the girl.

Then something solid struck her in the back of her legs. She toppled with a cry, rolling with the impact, and was back on her feet again a moment later, but the damage had been done. She had lost all her momentum, and the girl had closed the distance once more. The object in question had been a heavy wooden bucket, no doubt left outside to collect rainwater.

Which was exactly when it started raining.

This was no mere shower, either. The water began pouring from the sky, obscuring moon and stars and the imperial compound as well. The heavy thrum of water hitting buildings, trees, and the street would also serve to muffle any cries for help, and even if she were close to the gates the guards wouldn't be able to see her, much less help her, until she was practically on top of them.

It looked like she was going to have to handle this one all on her own.

The girl had stopped just out of striking distance and was circling around Seikoku now, body low, arms wide, knife at the ready. This one was a trained killer.

She struck like a snake, lightning-fast and with no warning. Seikoku barely blocked the blow in time, and the girl was already skipping back, just out of reach. One foot slipped on the suddenly slick tiles, but it was obvious she was not about to stop now. Not when she was already so close she could probably taste it.

Which meant Seikoku had no choice but to stop—to *kill*—this vicious girl if she wanted to survive herself.

Darting to the side, she scooped up the bucket and clutched it in both hands, hugging it to her chest. It was heavy, made of rough wood that scratched at her skin. It was also full of rainwater now, sloshing about as she shifted her grip.

The girl glared at her with those big, dark eyes—so Seikoku glared back.

Then she flung the contents of the bucket straight at her assailant's face.

It might have been only water, but the girl had not been expecting to have an entire bucketful suddenly thrown at her. She blinked, gasping for air, and took a step back—

—and that was when Seikoku smacked the girl full in the face with the bucket, as hard as she could.

Sturdy wood met flesh and blood with a meaty thunk. The girl groaned and sank to her knees, shaking her head, her knife dragging on the ground, its point vanishing into a puddle. This was the perfect time to kill her, while she was dazed and defenseless.

But Seikoku knew she couldn't do it.

Instead she lowered the bucket and retreated a step herself, waiting to see what the girl might attempt next. She hoped that the combination of water and wood might make her stop and consider and realize that this was futile.

When the girl struggled back to her feet, raising the knife again, Seikoku knew that she had been wrong. First Emperor, what did it take to make this girl quit?

The girl took a step forward, her boots squelching in the puddles caused by the sudden downpour. She was swaying slightly, her blade wavering, and blood was running down the side of her face, seeming black in the stark light of the lantern.

But still she did not stop.

"Just walk away," Seikoku warned, but the girl advanced instead, stabbing at her. The attack was weaker than before, though, and slower, sloppier. "Walk away now." Another attempt, which she blocked with the bucket. "This will not end well for you."

That at least got the girl's attention. She glared up at Seikoku, her face contorted into a fierce scowl. "You may have beaten the others," she stated proudly, drawing herself up to her full height, "but you won't beat me!"

And she flung herself at Seikoku, knife hand raised, blade pointed downward to strike from above.

Enough, Seikoku decided. Enough with the worry, enough with the guilt—and enough with letting any of that paralyze her. She was done. She stopped thinking about it. Instead, giving in to reflex and intuition, she spun, lashing out with one leg as she pivoted on the other, the heel of her foot catching the girl full in the chest. Her torso followed the motion, the bucket in her alternate hand whipping around to smash into the girl's head a second time.

With a loud crack, the bucket shattered. And with a faint whimper, the girl crumpled to the ground.

The rain stopped as suddenly as it had begun. The street was still slick with water but the air was clear and quiet as Seikoku stepped closer to the girl, her knife in her hand, ready for treachery.

But the puddles around the girl's head were far darker than their neighbors, from the blood pouring from both sides of her face now, and her eyes were open but unfocused, the knife fallen from nerveless fingers.

"No one beats me," the girl whispered, her voice faint even in the silence. Then she gasped, shuddered, and went limp, her eyes still open, her features and body going slack as the life left her.

With a sigh that was almost a sob, Seikoku sank to the ground not far away, crossing her legs beneath her, the rainwater soaking into her ponmei as she stared at the little dead girl across from her. Three children in under a week. She felt like a monster, even though each of those children had attacked her first.

No, she told herself firmly. *Stop thinking like that. They attacked you. They tried to kill you. You defended yourself. That doesn't make you anything more than a survivor.* She could not entirely blame the children, however. They were too young to really understand what they had been doing. No, the real monster was this woman who had trained them.

Well, Seikoku silently informed the night, *whoever you are, wherever you are, I will find you.*

And I will make you pay. Pay for what you did to these children, turning them into little killers—and pay for forcing me to kill them before they could kill me.

CHAPTER THIRTY-SEVEN

Chimehara sank to her knees beside the small form laying there upon the ground, the lantern light overhead casting its light to highlight the pallor of her skin and the dark shade of the blood pooling around her. In death, Suda looked so frail, so helpless, not at all like the fierce little creature who had once sought to rob her at knifepoint. Those large eyes, which had always watched her with such gravity, such sincerity—such trust—were still open but now vacant, the light gone from them forever.

She had nearly reached her in time.

She had been out walking the city, as they had every night since Gou had disappeared. No longer searching for him, however—not since she had learned of his and Ruisoki's deaths. No, since then she and Suda had haunted the streets at night with a different purpose—

To find the one who had done this, and to avenge the two boys.

Tonight had been no different. After meeting Kohori for dinner yet again, Chimehara had begged off and headed home, where she had changed, collected her remaining pupil, and then returned to Sakiriti to prowl about, seeking this elusive child-killer. They had started by the lantern where the boys had both died—the very one she sat beneath now, cradling Suda in her arms—and had then each gone in different directions, widening their search with each step.

But Suda must have doubled back. Clever girl, always so clever. And clearly upon returning to the scene of the crime she had found the one they had both sought.

Chimehara had been blocks away when faint sounds reached her on the night breeze: the slap of flesh against stone, the grunts and gasps of heavy exertion, the smack of something hard against something more yielding.

She had tossed aside any hope of stealth then and had run back as fast as her legs could carry her, her long hair coming undone and streaming behind her like an ebon pennant, her knife already clasped in one hand. The rain had taken her by surprise, slowing her a second as she slammed into the downpour like it was a wall, but then she had taken a deep breath and pushed on through, her clothes soaked in an instant and clinging to her like a second skin, her hair plastered down around her face so that she had to shove the heavy strands aside to see.

It had stopped, as suddenly as if someone had slammed down a barrier against it, just in time for her to hear the fading echoes of a fearsome impact up ahead.

She had burst into the circle of light shed by that lantern just in time to see someone disappearing from it, a slender figure vanishing into the shadows beyond, quick as a cat. A woman, by her retreating form. Chimehara started to pursue—and then she had seen Suda and her knees had simply given out, along with the rest of her.

Now she held the dear girl cradling her close, rocking her like a mother might her babe or a child her doll, crooning softly to her. Her long hair, still sodden from the rain, hung down over them both, forming a thick canopy, sheltering them safely within.

But Suda did not move. Would never move again.

At length Chimehara rose stiffly to her feet. Bending down, she gathered the girl up in her arms. She collected both their knives as well, sheathing those from view.

And then she turned and began to walk. Not toward home— no, there would be no comfort found there, in those empty apartments where children had once quarreled and fought and sometimes even laughed.

No, she had a different destination in mind tonight.

"This is becoming a habit," Amani Denbi commented once Chimehara had been shown in to see her. The older woman was dressed in a simple gray kitoro patterned in her usual stars and moons, her hair pulled back in its customary bun, and Chimehara knew she must look frightful by comparison, her hair twisted into a loose knot at her back, her clothes still damp even after that walk in the brisk night air. Yet her hostess did not look dismayed or disgusted, or even particularly put out. More...intrigued.

And probably not least by the dead girl clasped in Chimehara's arms.

"They killed her," she explained, lowering the little body to the low table before her and arranging her so that she seemed merely asleep now, those large eyes closed forever, the blood washed away by handfuls of gathered rainwater. That was how she had gotten past the guards at each gate, saying something about how her niece had fallen asleep over dinner and needed to be put to bed at once. Astonishing what sort of stories people would believe when told by a beautiful woman!

"Who did?" Denbi asked, coming closer to study Suda. Not squeamish, that one! "The same two you mentioned before? The man and woman?"

"The woman, certainly," Chimehara confirmed. "I saw her from a distance, fleeing as I approached. I should have gone after her, paid her back in kind, but..." She glanced at the girl who had been her first and best pupil. "I could not leave her behind."

"No, of course not." An arm came down around her shoulders and squeezed, not painfully, nor lecherously, but reassuringly. "I quite understand." Denbi sighed then. "I am so sorry, Chimehara. I can only imagine how you must feel right now."

"Feel?" Shrugging free, she turned to face the former Rojiri. "I am furious! I want to kill someone! To burn things to the ground! To tear down this whole blasted city!" She glared. "Will you help me, or must I do it alone?"

"Of course I will help you, dear," Denbi promised. "But who are we after here, hm? Did you get a good look at the woman? Do you know her name? Where she lives?"

"I don't care!" Chimehara snapped, pounding her fists against her sides. "I will just start killing if I have to, until either I find her or she finds me!" That was not her usual method, of course—she preferred the quiet kill, the stealthy death, the carefully planned murder. But right now she was too angry, too wound up, and yes, too upset, to care.

But the old woman laid a hand on her arm. "I understand that," she said soothingly, "but you know you would not get far like that. The aiashe would come for you, and then you would never avenge them. No, we must be smart about this."

Chimehara did not want to be smart. She had been smart before, and careful, and patient, and where had that got her? Here, with a dead girl at her feet! Still, she had come here for help, and so she forced herself to be patient and listen.

"There is a way I could help," Denbi offered at last. "If I had the right resources, the right influence, I could find this woman easily. I could have her brought to me, where you could take her and do as you saw fit." She smiled. "But that would require certain...sacrifices."

Her meaning was plain enough, for they had talked the other night, discussing recent events and current activities and future goals. Now Chimehara bit back a surprising swell of reluctance and nodded. "I am ready," she declared, straightening and brushing her hair back from where it had drifted in front of her face.

"Good." Her hostess studied her a moment, then nodded. "Yes, I think it is finally time." She patted Chimehara on the arm again. "But you will need to be at your best for this. So, a good night's sleep tonight, a warm bath tomorrow, and then we will begin." She clapped her hands and the manservant appeared in the doorway as if he had been a spirit summoned into being by the sound. "Tanekate will make up a guest room for you," Denbi instructed. "I will see to your young charge's final resting place and make a few other arrangements as well." There was a hungry gleam in her eyes as she smiled again, the expression purely predatory. "And tomorrow—tomorrow we will make our move at last."

Chimehara nodded and allowed herself to be led away, with

only one last glance back at poor dead Suda. *I will avenge you,* she promised the girl. *I will bathe this city in blood in your name. The walls will run red with it, and all for you.*

They will remember you for a thousand years, she swore to herself and to the sad little body laying broken behind her. *You will live on forever—the girl whose death caused an empire to fall.*

CHAPTER THIRTY-EIGHT

Saisaihyu, Day Nine

Kohori was bent over her desk, studying the papers detailing her new recruits and her one transfer—the administrative details a distasteful part of her job, to be sure, but one she had long since learned to accept—when a discreet cough made her glance up. Manari stood at the open outer door to her study, his long frame not quite at full attention but not slouching either, his thin lips quirking up at the ends, as if laughing at some private joke. "Yes?" she asked, straightening with a sigh of relief.

"There seems to be a disturbance over by the practice yard," the tall Honteno answered, raising fist to chest in the traditional salute. "You might want to come have a look."

She was frowning as she rose to her feet, reaching reflexively to lift her nihono from its stand and sliding the sheathed blade into her sash as she crossed the room to join him, collecting her karute and setting that on her head before pulling her hanketo from her belt and tugging those on as well. "What manner of disturbance?" she inquired, curious as to why whatever it was should require her personal attention.

"We have an intruder," he replied, already leading the way down off the walkway into the practice yard itself and then across it. Several warriors were sparring, and they each saluted as she passed. Kohori returned the gesture, but her eyes were on the far side of the wide square, where walls rose up to separate the sandy expanse from the grounds beyond. Something pricked in her thoughts and her gaze honed in on a particular spot near the corner—where, even from this distance, she could see that a section of the wall was no longer aligned with the rest, its wooden planks outward slightly, leaving a gap there.

Or a door.

"And who might this intruder be?" she asked, her heart racing as she guessed the answer. And, indeed, Manari smiled, reaching that door and pushing it open but not passing through it himself, instead stepping back and gesturing for her to walk on ahead.

"Enjoy yourself," he whispered as she pushed past him. "You deserve it." Then he was shutting the door behind her, trapping Kohori in the tiny garden—but not alone.

"I'm sorry," Chimehara said, rising to her feet from where she had been sitting on the little ledge. "I hope I didn't do anything wrong—and please, don't blame your warriors. I told them I wanted to surprise you, that's all." She smiled and held her arms out, turning in a slow circle to show off the patterning of her kitoro, which was black with golden sweeps and swirls and red circles behind some of them, splashed about with small black, red, and gold flowers here and there, the whole of it highlighting the glossy black of her hair and the deep black of her eyes, as well as the lush red of her lip gloss. "I assure you, they made sure I was unarmed."

"Ha!" Kohori crossed the small garden quickly, managing to set her feet on the stepping stones rather than in the pond around them even though she had yet to take her eyes off the stunning young woman before her. When she reached the far side, stepping over the low rock lip around the water and onto sand instead, she did not know quite what to do with herself, for suddenly they were very close indeed, and with the walls just behind Chimehara and the water behind her there was nowhere either of them could retreat safely. "No, you did nothing wrong. I was just surprised, is all—pleasantly so." After an instant's hesitation she embraced her guest, who laughed and returned the gesture. She smelled lovely, like plum but also pepper—sweet and spicy both.

"I am glad you are pleased," Chimehara teased as they parted. "I would hate to be thrown in prison just for bringing you—this!" She pivoted, somehow contriving to slide one arm around Kohori's waist as she did, and swept the other toward the ledge—and the beautifully lacquered box that stood there.

"What is it?" Kohori asked, taking a step closer, her own arm reflexively sliding up to match her companion's and settling around her waist in return. Even in her armor she could feel the heat of Chimehara's body against hers, and their proximity was making her slightly light-headed. She focused on the box, which had no sides—instead she could see that it was essentially a framework holding a smaller stacked box on the left and a pair of glazed bottles on the right, with even a single smaller box over the bottles and some sort of narrow sheet above the stack. The whole was beautifully finished, black with designs of leaf and fish and tree and water, and a handle at the very top allowed it all to be carried as a single unit.

"What is it?" The younger woman laughed and rapped a knuckle playfully against her deo. "Why, it is lunch, of course! I thought we might have a picnic here—in my new favorite place, with my new favorite person." Her eyes were bright as the sun, a flush tinting her cheeks, and there were dimples as she smiled, her lips ever so slightly parted. "Please?" she asked, her voice dropping into the lower, husky register that took Kohori's breath away.

She nodded. What else could she do? It was a lovely surprise, and perhaps Manari was right—she had earned the right to enjoy herself, hadn't she?

"What can I do to help?" she asked when she had finally recovered herself enough to speak.

"Nothing," came the quick reply. "Sit and enjoy. Only"—and here her beautiful guest effected a pout that was as stunning as it was clearly fake—"perhaps you could do away with all that?" She tapped the armor with a red-lacquered fingernail and winked at her. "I promise not to stab you while we eat."

Kohori laughed along with her, lifting the helmet off and tucking it under one arm, but the sound faded away as she glanced down at herself. "I don't—" she started. "I do not have a robe handy," she explained carefully, eyes downcast still. "I have only hosode and hakami beneath this." *And I am old, and scarred, and even when I was young and fresh I was not even a shade as lovely as you,* she thought but did not say, and once again wondered about it all. Why would anyone be so interested in her, especially a woman as beautiful and desirable as Chimehara.

She started when a hand gently tapped her under the chin, nudging her face up to meet her guest's eyes. "I do not mind," Chimehara promised, and now her smile was small and soft and sweet. "Not at all." Her lips parted, revealing neat white teeth, which now nibbled at her lower lip, and her long lashes fluttered down over her eyes as her cheeks darkened. *Embarrassed*, Kohori noted. *But why? I am the one who should be embarrassed.*

Or is it because she worries that she has been too forward?

Ah, First Emperor, enough of this! Pushing such worries aside, she smiled as well, and shrugged. "All right, then." She set her karute on the far end of the ledge, where it would not be in the way, and tugged her sword free, leaning it against the sturdy beams supporting that ledge and the wall beside it. The hanketo went next, the gauntlets tucked in under the helmet, followed by her kazure. Then, taking a deep breath before committing herself to this, she reached up to loosen the straps holding her deo in place, unbuckling both sides so she could remove the two halves and set them down beside the nihono. After that it was quick work to remove her suneoto and add them to the pile. "Better?" she asked, holding her arms out slightly as if presenting herself for inspection. The midday breeze caused goosebumps along her exposed arms and the back of her neck, but she felt flushed despite that, awaiting Chimehara's verdict.

The younger woman studied her critically for a moment, those dark eyes sliding across her broad shoulders and strong arms, her unimpressive chest, her flat stomach, her well-muscled legs, all of her more or less on display in her thin shirt and equally thin pants.

When Chimehara smiled, it was like the sun had just burst through the clouds and bathed her in light.

"Much," she declared. "Now come, sit, and let us eat and drink." She smirked, showing those dimples. "And afterward, we'll see whether I can persuade you to leave that armor off a bit longer."

Kohori could barely hear her, the way her pulse was pounding in her ear. But she sank onto the ledge nonetheless, sidling over to make room as her companion, instead of sitting on the box's other side, slid in against her instead. The younger woman's body felt almost too hot to touch, even through the silk layers of her robes, but Kohori would not have moved for the First Emperor himself.

The bottles proved to contain a very fine tsekuri, the stacked boxes all manner of small, elegant foods, the single box tiny containers of various dipping sauces and also small cups for the rice wine, and the shelf a pair of trays. Chimehara insisted upon preparing everything herself, twisting around each time to select this morsel or that to set on Kohori's tray, each motion bringing her supple form up against the older woman. They talked as they ate, about nothing consequential, and the time passed quickly. Before long the boxes were empty, as were the bottles, and Kohori was feeling both pleasantly full and mildly fuzzy, her thoughts pleasant and slow and soft around the edges.

Everything snapped into crystal focus, however, when Chimehara took her empty try, sliding it back into its place in the box, and then turned back around to say, "Now, what shall we do with ourselves next?"

She was so close, her face only inches from Kohori's own, those long lashes practically brushing against her cheeks. Bones, but she was glorious! Kohori gazed down at her and gulped, her throat suddenly dry, for all that her palms were inexplicably damp.

"What would you like?" she managed to croak out, the words barely audible, little more than a hiss in the air. But they were so close, and the garden so still and quiet, her companion heard her anyway. And smiled.

"It occurs to me," she whispered back, her breath tickling Kohori's chin, warm and sweet, "that I have you at a disadvantage here."

"Oh?" *If you mean stunned by your eyes, your lips, your scent, your skin, your voice, yes, you certainly do,* she thought, but could not bring herself to say.

"Well, yes." Chimehara tapped her own chin with one finger, head tilting slightly to the side, eyes sparkling, those dimples once more in full evidence. "Here you are, stripped of all your fierce armor, in nothing but a thin hosode and hakami," she pointed out.

"While I am still securely wrapped inside my kitoro. That hardly seems fair, does it? So"—and with a single twist of her hips in one direction and her arms and shoulders in the other, she wriggled free of the robes down to her waist, exposing a black hosode that strained to contain her breasts, which struggled to burst free from the thin fabric.

"There," she breathed, for it could hardly be called speaking, the word was so soft, so gentle—as gentle as the hand she laid on Kohori's chest, right between her own breasts, directly over her madly beating heart. "Better."

Then her face—that perfect face—was angling upward, those eyes so large and deep Kohori thought she could happily drown in them—those crimson lips parting. It was a clear invitation, and all doubt and reservation fled as Kohori. Brought her own face down, her lips meeting the younger woman's in a searing kiss.

"Better," she agreed after a moment, when they broke for air. She smiled, and her battle-scarred, age-roughened hands came up to caress Chimehara's shoulders, gliding down her silk-smooth arms, then back up, along her delicate neck, to cup her face.

They kissed again, and Kohori forgot about everything else for a time. Nothing mattered, nothing but the young woman in her arms, the two of them entwined together, here in their hidden garden.

Sometime later—it felt like hours, though the sun still hung in the sky, lower but not yet ready to disappear for the night—Kohori stirred. They had dozed afterward, there on the ledge—astonishingly, it had proven wide enough to accommodate them both, though only because they had been so closely wrapped up in each other. She still had her arms around Chimehara, who lay back against her, head just below her chin, so that she could bury her nose in that silky hair and breathe in that intoxicating scent.

"That," she said softly, "was lovely." Her entire body felt both relaxed and energized, her nerve and fiber singing yet utterly languid. Ash, but it had been far too long!

"It was," the younger woman agreed. She had her arms resting on Kohori's, their hands knotted together, and gently stroked the backs of her fingers. "I wish we could just stay here forever, hidden away like this, just the two of us."

"That would be nice," Kohori agreed with a sigh, leaning her head back against the worn wood panels behind her. "Sadly, people would eventually come looking for us." She squinted up at the sky again. It was perhaps a little later than she'd first thought. "Especially me, when the shifts change in just a few minutes." She knew she should get up, put her clothes back on, her armor, her sword.

But she just wanted to stay here a moment or two longer.

The woman in her arms shifted, however, and sat up, pulling free of the embrace. "Yes, I suppose they would," she agreed, and there was something so sad in her voice, far more than the sentiment seemed to warrant. Reaching toward the discarded pile that was her robes, she retrieved a small tube of something from them. It was lip gloss, Kohori saw as the younger woman applied it, but not the same crimson she already wore—no, this was a vivid blue and she did not coat her lips entirely but merely swiped it up the middle, leaving a single slash there against the red. Then she turned and, with a smile, leaned in for one last kiss.

Kohori met that happily, and afterward she sat back with a contented sigh. If anyone had ever suggested to her that she might find happiness at such a late stage in life, she would have laughed at them. She was Maniko Kohori, Taikoro of the Honteno. Her work was her life.

But now she saw that there was so much more.

Chimehara rested a hand on her cheek, and she was surprised to see tears in the younger woman's eyes. "I am so sorry," she whispered. "And I want you to know, I truly did care for you."

The way she said that—the tone, and the tense—made Kohori stiffen, warning bells beginning to sound in her head.

Then she realized that she had not stiffened solely out of alarm, but because her body was tensing up without her control. And not just tensing—her throat was closing up, her heart stuttering, all the strength washing out of her. She tried to ask why but could not move her lips or tongue enough to speak. She watched, through a darkening haze, as Chimehara rose to her feet, using a small cloth to wipe the blue from her lips. The young woman studied her, still nude, and Kohori drank in the sight of her killer's tremendous beauty, her perfect features and gorgeous body.

At least, she thought as her sight began to dim and her heart seized, everything starting to fade, *the last sight I see is the most glorious one I can imagine. The most beautiful woman in the world—a woman I have just made love to—right here in my favorite place.*

Her lips were still frozen in a smile as her heart stopped and her body shivered, giving up its last shred of life.

CHAPTER THIRTY-NINE

Kagiri paused mid-stroke, his nihono still a foot or more above Shizumi's head, much of him in shadow with the flickering light of the lanterns behind him, his entire body going utterly still in an instant as if someone had transformed him to stone. "Do you hear that?" he whispered.

Shizumi started to retort something about excuses and tricks but the words died in her throat. Yes. Yes, she had heard something. But what? It took her a second to process—it had been a creak, distant but close enough to be clear, a ponderous sound of wood and metal sliding along one another in a very familiar way, a particular noise she had heard many times before, and one that carried with it associated scents of rust and oil and varnish, with a hint of grass and flowers underneath.

The outer gates.

Dropping her own sword—which had been rising to a guard position—to her side, she turned, glancing away from her sparring partner, toward the outer edge of the practice yard and beyond, where the gates to Aihiri stood. That was the only way in or out of the imperial compound, save the imperial gates that led into the covered passageway which ran all the way to the very base of the city, and the hinges on the massive iron doors were deliberately kept from being oiled too well so that there would be a noticeable sound every time they were opened.

Like now.

But it was sunset. Why were the gates being opened? No one would be making deliveries at this hour, and anyone leaving the compound would most likely be of sufficient rank to use the smaller, quieter imperial gate instead.

Straightening from her half-crouch, she spun about and began trotting across the yard, Kagiri quickly falling into place beside her. She did not make for the wide archway that opened onto the outer grounds, however—instead she angled toward the palace, hopping up onto the raised walkway that ran around its outer edge and then slipping through the small corner gate there which separated the yard's section from the rest of the bamboo path. From this vantage she would be able to see clear to the gates, whereas on the ground she would have only seen the hedges and trees of the gardens that stood between here and there.

She stepped through, glancing across—and froze, staring in utter shock.

For the gates were indeed open—and warriors were pouring into the grounds. Warriors whose colors and crests she could not make out from here in the dimming light of dusk, save to be certain that they were neither black nor crimson. Which could only mean one thing.

"Intruders!" Kagiri shouted just behind her, his voice booming over her head. Clearly he had come to the same conclusion. Confident that he could handle the hue and cry, Shizumi took two swift steps to the side, farther along the walkway. Hanging from the roof beams just there past the corner was a large brass gong, its lower rim secured by a sturdy chain so that it would not sound if brushed against or shaken by the wind. The chain was looped around a heavy wooden mallet thrust into a hole in the floor and Shizumi reached down, yanking the mallet free of both plank and chain and then straightening to slam it into the now-freed gong, sending a vibration up her arm and a powerful clang echoing across the compound. These gongs were placed at each corner of the building, inside and out, and in most of the major rooms, and were to be sounded for one reason and one reason only—if Aihiri itself were under attack. Exactly as it was right now.

Almost at once she heard the rushing of armored feet coming from within the buildings, as her Honjofu and Kohori's Honteno hurried to answer the call to arms. And it occurred to Shizumi to wonder, where was her fellow Taikoro? Normally she would have expected the older woman to be the first to notice anything was wrong.

Well, no time to worry about that now. Banging the gong once more, Shizumi dropped the mallet at her feet and leaped down to the ground, making for the gates at a full run. A tall, lean figure in green armor joined her before she had gone three steps.

"Last. Day. Of the. Saisaihyu," Kagiri managed between gasps. "Smart."

"Very," Shizumi agreed, tightening her grip on her sword. Someone had planned this carefully. Including a way to somehow get in past the guards.

As she neared the gates, she saw a pair of red-clad figures on the ground, and two more battling the first of the intruders. Between them were four figures not in armor—two women and two men. One of the women, long glossy hair done up in an untidy knot but shapely and dressed in a beautiful kitoro of black and red and gold, had her back to Shizumi and appeared to be greeting the other, a tall, elegant older woman in silvery gray and midnight blue who she recognized at once with an angry hiss.

It was Amani Denbi. She might have known.

The two men were strangers to Shizumi. Both looked to be young, and neither was armed. They were dressed in plain, service-able clothing, and had dark, ragged hair and pale skin. Something about them seemed vaguely familiar as well, though she could not place them.

No matter. They were strangers without weapons or apparent influence, and therefore not her first concern. That would have to be the traitorous ex-Rojiri standing in the midst of all this chaos. Clearly, she was the one behind all this.

Shizumi slowed as she neared, for crashing into combat at full speed was reckless and dangerous. Sure enough, just as she approached Denbi a woman stepped in her way, this one closer to her own size and fully armored in the silver and blue of House Amani. Two other warriors were flanking her, and quickly spread out, trying to surround Shizumi.

Something about the way they moved, easily and gracefully

even in their armor, and the way they held their nihono so expertly, sent a chill down her spine. These warriors had aishone!

As if sensing her thoughts, the woman smiled, a slow, unpleasant expression that promised pain and defeat. "Yes, we have aishone," she stated, her voice low and thick. "And you do not. Surrender now and we will let you live."

Shizumi laughed and, having come to a full stop, leveled her blade at her opponent. "I need no aishone to deal with the likes of you," she declared, and saw the other woman's eyes widen beneath her karute. She had not expected such defiance, and that had her nervous. Good. Nervous people made mistakes.

There were more warriors marching in through the gates than just these three, of course. And not all of them in the same colors. A quick survey of the area showed that Kagiri had faced off against four in the yellow and black of House Yoshino. Several warriors circling around the pair of them were clad in the brilliant blue of House Orita, and she spied others behind and beyond those in the russet of House Domo. So. Four of the five ex-Rojiri were here—only House Watane was missing. This was more than a single slighted former councilor's personal revenge, then.

It was a full-blown attempted coup. And, aishone aside, more warriors than Shizumi believed even she and Kagiri could handle by themselves.

Fortunately, they were not alone. The night had been alive with shouts and with the clatter of armor and weapons ever since they had first sounded the alarm, and even as she and Denbi's warriors sized each other up, figures began to emerge from the shadows at her back. Only, these melted from it in armor black as the night itself, with a speckling of crimson-garbed warriors gliding among them like a sprinkling of blood upon a bed of coal.

Not far away, Kagiri laughed. It was not out of bloodlust, for he had no desire to kill anyone, though of course he would do what was needed to defend himself and the emperor. No, this was from the sheer joy of battle, the thrill of combat—and the excitement at, for the first time, fighting beside Shizumi. For the past several days they had been sparring each night, and he had come to know and respect and like the fierce Honjofu commander more and more each time. Now here they were, fighting not each other but side by side, and not holding back—no more worries about hurting one another, this was actual battle and every stroke, every strike had to count.

"Yield or die," one of the men facing him demanded, leveling his sword, and Kagiri smiled, even though he knew they would only see that expression by the crinkling of his eyes over his deep green menatu.

"Yield?" he replied, laughing again. "You face the Gensaiba and the Taikoro of the Honjofu, the two finest warriors in all Rimbaku. *You* yield!" With a single quick twisting thrust he had batted the other man's sword aside and had the chiseled tip of his own nihono nestled into that hollow in the throat where neck met chest—the one gap, besides the eyes, that the stranger's yellow-and-black armor failed to cover. The man froze, knowing his death was brushing against his skin at that very second, and the others with him stilled as well. The very air seemed to shift, crackling with possibility, as if Kagiri's words were rippling out over the intruders, causing them to lose their previous arrogance and wonder how the balance had suddenly shifted out of their control.

Kagiri retrieved his sword, sliding easily into ready position once more, and waited. They had been warned, and now honor demanded he give them a chance to retreat. They would not receive such mercy a second time.

Shizumi, hearing that exchange, caught the eye of the woman before her and smiled, knowing hers was every bit as sharp-edged as the one she had received. "You have already lost the element of surprise," she explained lightly as her Honjofu formed up behind her, spreading out to block all the others who had entered from getting any farther into the grounds, though she had lost sight of Denbi, the other woman, and those two strange men. Still, she kept her focus on her current opponent as she continued, "Now, unless you lay down your arms at once, you will lose a good deal more."

The woman laughed, either not hearing Kagiri's words or choosing to disbelieve them. "Brave words from one with no bones to rely upon," she snarled instead, drawing her blade back over her head with one hand, the other extended forward as if pointing the way to her attack. Shizumi merely shook her head, seeing that further attempts at reasoning would be useless, and loosened her stance, hands on her sword, blade up in front of her, waiting.

She did not have to wait long. With a cry of "House Amani!" the woman charged forward, her two companions advancing just as quickly on either side. There were other names shouted to either side and, all along the ragged line, the intruders attacked.

Shizumi took a long, slow breath and let it out, then another. She forced her limbs to relax, untensing so they would be limber and ready to respond.

Then the other woman's blade came leaping toward her face and she stopped thinking altogether, letting her body simply respond, her sword rising to knock the blow aside before dipping to the side and sweeping around in a punishing arc of its own.

And all around her, with cries and screams and shouts and the stomp of feet on hard dirt and grass and the clash of metal on metal, the battle was joined.

CHAPTER FORTY

Noniki looked somewhere between embarrassed, perturbed, and scandalized, and Hibikitsu had to admit to himself that he was amused by it all. He was used to his youngest Rojiri being, if not confident, at least upbeat and optimistic about everything, and willing to consider almost anything. At the moment, however, he appeared to have met his match—in more ways than one.

"Seikoku!" the young matekai was complaining, digging in his heels as his slender companion tried dragging him the rest of the way across the throne room to where Hibikitsu still sat upon his throne, having just finished conferring with Doiyu Soda and several of the other scribes and clerks on various administrative matters. "Please, stop! This is inappropriate!"

"Why?" the young woman demanded, not slowing her stride or ceasing her efforts to budge him—which were working, for those he was sturdy and well-built it was clear she was also in excellent condition. "Because he's the emperor? That makes it completely appropriate—it's his city, after all!"

"Yes, but he should not have to be confronted with such things, especially like this!" Noniki continued to argue, his boots squeaking as he was hauled across the tiled floor inches at a time. "This is a matter for the karos and the Rojiri, at best!"

"None of you have come up with any sort of solution, and meanwhile our friends are suffering!" she snapped, her eyes flashing fire, and not for the first time Hibikitsu wished he could meet a woman with passion and wit and intelligence like hers. Preferably who was also a noble, or foreign royalty. He envied his friend and advisor at having earned the interest of the spirited Seikoku, even as he despaired at ever doing so himself—and hid a laugh at this proof that there was occasionally a downside to a partner with such strong opinions.

They were nearly to the dais now, and Seikoku had turned her attention toward him, a quick glance upward followed by a demure lowering of that gaze. "Your Imperial Majesty," she began, sinking to her knees. She had released Noniki's hand in the process, and he huffed for a second, straightening himself and his robes before also dropping down into a deep bow.

"Oh, none of that," Hibikitsu insisted, waving for them both to stand and gesturing for them to come closer. They both started forward—and were halted midmotion by a sudden loud clanging that arose from somewhere nearby.

"What is that?" Seikoku asked. She had instinctively dropped into a half-crouch, legs sliding apart, feet shifted so she was balanced on the balls of her feet, and a small but clearly very pointed little knife had somehow appeared in her hand as she swept her gaze across the room, alert for trouble. Noniki had also tensed and had turned to put his back to hers, automatically working with her to cover the space more effectively.

"It's the gongs," Hibikitsu explained, rising to his feet and lifting Kosshiki from its stand at his side. "It means Aihiri is under attack." He made to hop down and join them, but his advisor held up a hand.

"No, you should stay here," he warned. "This is the safest room in the palace, correct?" Hibikitsu considered that a second before nodding. There were only two ways into the throne room, and the front doors were guarded by Honteno, as were the palace doors that opened onto the grand hall leading to them—and those would have been barred the moment they heard the alarm, with the guards taking up position behind it to defend should the barrier be breached. The other entrance was through his private study, which no one but him and occasionally his Honteno were allowed to use.

"Good. Stay here, then," Noniki confirmed. "We will see what is happening." And, taking Seikoku's hand, he turned away and began retracing his steps from the room. She glanced back once over her shoulder, giving Hibikitsu a reassuring smile, but did not argue and matched her pace to her partner's, their swift strides carrying them rapidly back through the main doors and out of sight down the hall.

With a sigh, Hibikitsu sank back down onto his throne, laying Kosshiki across the heavily gilded and carved arms and resting his own forearms on the sword's jewel-encrusted scabbard. He yearned to charge from the room after his friends and had nearly done so—he was the emperor, after all! But he also knew that Noniki had been correct. It was smarter to wait here, where it was safe, and let the others find out what had occurred. Smarter, safer—but much more annoying.

Who could be attacking, he wondered as he sat there, tapping his fingers on Kosshiki's silk-wrapped hilt. Whoever it was, they had clearly chosen their timing very carefully. It was the last day of the Saisaihyu—the purification period would end at dusk. Would it not have been better to make an attempt a day or two earlier, to avoid the risk of running up against the end, he pondered, but quickly corrected himself. No, because he knew Kohori and Shizumi had been concerned about just such a situation and had been on high alert the entire time. Now, with the end in sight, was when people started to relax, to get careless. The moments right before a shift change were always when those standing watch began to stop paying attention, he had learned during his time on the road with his Honjofu, because they were already looking ahead to when they would be off-duty and the watch became someone else's problem. This was the same on a grander scale.

A mighty crash from somewhere up ahead caused him to start and look up, though he could not see anything that might have caused that noise. It sounded as if it had come from the hallway beyond—could it have been the palace's front doors? He strained to listen, wanting to rush to see but heeding Noniki's warning and staying put on the dais instead. After a moment he could make out a sound, but it was not loud, nor terrible. Merely the soft tapping of feet upon the fine wood of the hallway floor. But that sound was growing closer by the second.

Hibikitsu forced himself to stay seated, his entire body tensed for action should it be needed, and nearly sagged in relief as two figures finally stepped in through the grand arches of the front doors. Because the throne room was so large, he could not make out much more than their number but judging by the sounds of their footsteps he believed the pair were not armored, nor did he see any visible weapons. As they drew closer, he saw that he was correct, for both wore fine kitoro. Indeed, both were women, he now discerned, the one taller and slimmer, the other with visible curves even through her robes. The latter also had dark hair, while the former's was paler, perhaps graying? Their clothes began to take on more definition as they approached at a steady but unhurried pace, the taller one in silver and blue, the shorter in black and red and gold. He did not recognize the colors or patterns of the second, but the first was a combination he knew all too well and he was unsurprised when she finally came near enough for him to make out the stars and moons of her crest, or her composed features, set beneath her usual tight silvery taikamage.

"Amani Denbi," he stated, leaning back and feeling the carvings along the chair pressing into his spine. "We did not summon you to us."

"No, you did not," the ex-Rojiri agreed. "Fortunately, I made my own arrangements. You can thank Chimehara here for that." She gestured at her companion, and now that he looked at her properly Hibikitsu was astonished. It was the beautiful young woman who worked for Master Eijiri! Was House Chohu involved in this plot, whatever it was?

The stunning young lady bowed, as graceful as ever, though there was something about her expression that seemed sad. "Your Imperial Majesty," she stated in that gloriously rich voice of hers. "It is a pleasure to meet you properly at last."

Denbi laughed at that, a sharp, bitter little bark. "'At last,'" she repeated, a smirk upon her thin lips. "How apt."

Hibikitsu frowned down at her. "What is it you wish of us, Denbi," he demanded, "that you would intrude upon us in this way?" His eyes flicked behind her toward the doors, but there were no guards in evidence. At least there were no other warriors there, either, though he suspected that might only be a matter of time.

She had seen the direction of his gaze, and her smirk widened. "The guards are trapped beneath the weight of the palace doors, Your Majesty," she stated with another little laugh. "Kohori, dear, sweet Maniko Kohori, is, shall we say, permanently indisposed. And the rest of your loyal soldiers are still busy outside. They are desperately attempting to hold off my household guard, and that of the other Rojiri you so callously cast aside. Sadly, they are badly outnumbered. And then, of course, there is the matter of aishone—which they are not using, and my forces are." She grinned, showing her teeth. "I must thank you for the Saisaihyu—it presented such a perfect opportunity I simply could not resist."

"An opportunity to do what, exactly?" he asked. As of yet she had not advanced past the last two columns, where everyone was required to stop unless and until he granted them permission to step forward. He knew the weight of years of tradition and at least outwardly loyal service were holding her to that demarcation, but also suspected she was working herself up toward overcoming that internal restriction. There were two of them to one of him, but neither of them were warriors, and neither armed or armored—he wore only his court robes, which might provide some protection with the jewels and metal discs sewn into the fabric, but more importantly he had his sword, whereas at best they each carried knives. That should more than make up for their being able to approach from either side.

Still, the longer he could stall them, the better.

As he'd hoped and suspected, Denbi could not resist showing off—or declaiming. "Why, to redress old wrongs, of course," she announced, hands going to her hips and a scowl displacing her previous smirk. "You threw away centuries of tradition when you spurned and insulted those families that had given generations of devoted service to the Empire," she informed him loftily. "You did more than just shun us, you turned your back on the sanctity of your own government, showing how little regard you had for its history or continuity. That is not something that can be borne."

Now she crossed her arms over her chest, resuming the role of stern teacher lecturing a backward pupil. "You have forfeited your right to rule this nation, Hibikitsu," she stated, each word sharp as a knife and hurled at him with as much force as an arrow shot from a bow. "You have surrendered any divine privileges your rank or blood might have granted. You have——"

Denbi straightened all at once, narrowed eyes going wide with outrage, arms dropping to her side, her lips twitching and then parting to continue her diatribe, but no sound emerging. Hibikitsu watched, frowning, hands resting on his sword, alert for some trick, but his former advisor merely swayed, still silent.

He just had time to notice the dark splotch spreading along her side before Amani Denbi's knees gave out and she crumpled to the ground in a pile of shimmering silk, the former head of the Rojiri's eyes rolling back in her head and a final, unseemly croak emerging from her lips.

"I am so sorry to interrupt you, dear," Chimehara commented sweetly, bending down to wipe her bloody knife on the robes of the very woman she had just stabbed in the side. "But even though we hadn't known each other long, I could tell you were the type who loved to hear yourself speak. And"—she rose and glanced up at the center of the room's vaulted ceiling, where the colored panes that made up the intricate skylight revealed the sun's steady progress across the sky, more than half the glass already in shadow as the sun slipped down closer to the horizon—"I am on a bit of a tight schedule here."

Then she turned to Hibikitsu and stepped forward, deliberately crossing that invisible line of respect and obedience, her knife glittering in her hand, a focused expression of great intent writ upon her stunning features. "And now, your majesty, I am afraid it is time for you to die."

CHAPTER FORTY-ONE

Noniki stopped just outside the throne room, seeing the way barred up ahead. That was good—the palace doors were made of solid iron that had been clad in gold and lacquer and paint, and with them shut and the heavy wooden beam across them an entire army would have difficulty getting past. It did mean, however, that he and Seikoku could not go that way, and so he turned down one of the side corridors instead, leading her away from the main hall until they could reach one of the smaller entrances used by staff and guards.

He was still trying to shift his mind to what was going on. The past few days had been so chaotic, especially after their fight the other night. He had not even understood at first exactly why she had been so angry with him, when he had only been trying to help! But she had stormed out anyway, and after a few moments when he was sure she was not going to return he had left as well, heading back toward the estate they both called their home. How strange to fight at all, but especially with someone who lived with you!

He had not even reached the gates to Motohiri before rapid footsteps had warned of someone approaching in haste and had turned only barely in time to catch Seikoku as she had flung herself into his arms. She was soaked from the brief downpour that had just occurred, her hair plastered down around her face, and was shivering, but after listening to her sob out a brief explanation into his shoulder he'd realized that last reaction had not been solely due to the cold. Another child! What was the meaning of it all? After calming her down, he'd followed her back to that same fateful spot—perhaps they should just have that lamp post removed altogether, its once cheery light now seemed so tainted by the ill omens that had collected around it!

But there had been nothing there! Only the shattered remnants of a heavy bucket had given any sort of proof to her words. Not that Noniki hadn't believed her, of course. But where had the child's body gone?

Regardless, they had gone home, their earlier argument forgotten in the face of this new situation—or so he had thought. But today she had turned up here in Aihiri and had demanded that they speak to the emperor himself about the matter of their enclave and its current reception from its neighbors, which remained chilly and hostile. He had tried to dissuade her, but once Seikoku set her mind to a thing, she saw it through. It was one of the many things he loved about her.

Love. That word nearly brought him up short, as it struck him like a thunderbolt, blasting its way through every fiber of his body. Yes, he loved her. How long had that been the case? And did she love him too?

But that was a question for later. They had reached the outer door, a small sliding panel that, if you did not know about it, would have simply seemed another spot on the wall both inside and out. "I don't know what we'll find outside," he warned her, his hand on the frame. She nodded, squeezing his free hand with hers, and he slid the door aside and stepped through, with her close behind him.

At once the sounds of fighting inundated them: the clash of metal on metal, the creak of armor plate and leather strap, the grunts and cries of men and women. The noises were coming from around the corner, back in front of the main doors—the direction of the main gates. Good. That meant the Honjofu and Honteno might already have the threat contained. Nonetheless he stepped onto the walkway that ran all the way around the building and followed it forward, moving quickly but trying not to make too much noise in case there was trouble about.

When he reached the corner, however, he saw that the trouble was paying him no mind.

A battle was indeed raging by the gates, and he could make out the emerald of Kagiri's armor amidst the black and red of the guards and various other colors he assumed belonged to the intruders. But what caught his gaze was motion to his left, at the end of the same path he now stood upon, where it widened out into a broad semicircular platform before those same main doors he had already seen barred. A quartet stood there, none of them armored that he could see, but two of those had stepped forward and placed their hands to either side of the doors.

Even at this distance, Noniki sensed the sudden presence of some dark magic, swirling like a knot within his stomach and rising up to his throat.

"We have to stop them!" he shouted, breaking into a run, his feet pounding on the bamboo planks as he raced toward the doors. Seikoku was right beside him, without even a second's hesitation, and again he felt his heart sing at the realization of a second earlier. Yes, he loved this woman.

They were halfway there when the doors collapsed inward with a tumultuous crash, the impact shaking the platform and the entire building. The two figures in front moved back and their two companions advanced instead, stepping up as they passed under the door arches, presumably to clamber up onto the fallen doors and across them.

"We need to get back to Hibikitsu!" he said, still rushing forward, but Seikoku shook her head.

"I'll see to him!" she countered. "You deal with them!" And she pointed at the two, who they could now see were young men with dark hair and pale skin.

After an instant Noniki nodded. They had been the source of the magic, he was sure of it, which meant Seikoku was right. He was the only person who could counter them.

At their approach the two men turned, no doubt hearing the heavy footfalls echoing up and down the walkway, and raised their hands, clearly ready for a fight. But Noniki was having none of that. He waved a hand and the wind swept in, carrying the intruders off the walkway and onto the grounds beyond, where they tumbled across the grass. "Be careful!" he shouted, about to leap down and pursue, but a slim hand on his shoulder stopped him short. He turned—right into Seikoku's kiss.

"You be careful," she instructed softly after they'd pulled apart again, his lips still tingling from the contact. "I am not done with you yet." Then, before he could reply, she had hurried past and disappeared through the open doors back into the palace.

Noniki smiled as he hopped down from the walkway, one hand going absently to his lips. She was not done with him yet. That had to mean she loved him too—didn't it?

Ibaru grunted and rose to his feet, dusting himself off. The nicely retailored clothes Aganaka had altered to fit them were now covered in dirt and grass. He hoped they would not stain. "Are you all right?" he asked his brother, who was pulling himself upright as well.

"Fine," Iraku replied, shaking his head to dislodge some grass that had settled there. "I'd say we've found the person we were after."

"Indeed." They both turned to face the young man who was now approaching at a steady pace. Though they had only seen him once before, the night of the previous attack, it was easy to recognize him, with his solid build and his expansive, attractive features. He was still dressed nearly as simply as they were, though his clothes seemed perhaps better made, and he held no weapons in his outstretched hands.

Then again, neither did they.

"At last," Iraku said, flexing his fingers, and Ibaru nodded. When that woman, Amani Denbi, had told them of her plans to depose the emperor, they had agreed to help, but really, what did they care who sat upon the throne? They had taken down the doors for her, a simple enough task, but then had not followed her inside. After all, they had done as she had asked, she could handle the rest on her own. Their interest had been entirely in locating this man, the one who had dispatched their former master. Now here he was, willingly coming to them, and they would finally have their revenge.

As he got closer, however, he slowed, and his brows rose, his lips quirking slightly. "Do I know you?" he asked, finally coming to a stop a few feet away. Just out of arm's reach, Ibaru judged, which was a shame, but a quick lunge forward would take care of that.

Still, there was something about the man, the way he spoke, his face, his voice, that did indeed seem familiar. They all studied one another, and then after a second Iraku gasped.

"You gave us food!" he blurted out, and with that the memory came flooding back. They had been out on the road, hungry and tired and more than a little lost, having recently been beaten for the simple crime of being Mukanichi. They had stumbled upon a traveling party of some sort, a large group with guards and many tents, and had been desperate enough to approach, begging for food. Most of the men had sneered at them, of course, as had their clearly wealthy employers. But there had been two—brothers, by the look of them, not much older than Ibaru himself and in only slightly better clothing, who had not. They had told the guards to stand down and had offered them food. Only—

"You flinched and would have sent us away once you knew what we were!" Ibaru accused. "It was your brother who gave us the food anyway!"

That made this thrice-met stranger flinch again, but he did not turn away this time. "Yes, I did," he admitted, his voice steady. "And I am sorry for that. It was wrong of me. I have learned a great deal since then." He studied them, frowning. "As, it appears, have you."

"We learned from our master, Kaemusei," Iraku agreed. "Before you destroyed it!"

"It?" The man's face puckered in a frown, then cleared. "Oh, you mean that strange cloud that followed you? Kaemusei? Interesting. But no, I did not destroy it—I freed it. Or, rather, them." He smiled suddenly, and it was such a warm, open expression Ibaru could not help but relax slightly. "Here, I will show you." He glanced around them, then behind them—and his gaze fell upon a smooth brass gong hanging from the edge of the roof not far from the front doors. "Come." And, without a second glance, he turned and began making his way back toward that spot.

Iraku sidled up beside his brother. "We should finish him now, while he's distracted," he warned, but even he did not sound wholly convinced, and he did not argue when Ibaru shook his head and followed this strange man, falling in beside his brother as he always did.

By the time they reached the gong, the man had laid a hand on it and its surface had shifted somehow, becoming even smoother and more reflective, as if it were now made of glass. But the image it showed was not the grounds and the battle behind them. Instead Ibaru saw the throne room within, and a strange, swirling mass of color and energy floating above the floor. Kaemusei!

There were figures arrayed before it, including the man standing with them now. As they watched, he joined hands with another in mottled green armor, the same who was currently battling by the gates—his brother, Ibaru was sure. "What you call the Silent Change was in fact the remnants of the matekai from just before the Schism," the young man explained. "Their spirits had all been trapped in the Tawasiri but when my brother Kagiri entered and absorbed the essence of their gensaiba matekan, it somehow released them. But they were all jumbled together, confused, not in their right minds—and drawn to me because I was the first new matekai and they could sense my magic." He shrugged. "Once we figured that out, we were able to separate the spirits so that they could each go to their final rest." And, in the images, the brothers saw exactly that—they watched as the warrior called out each name in turn, describing each long-passed wizard, its spirit arising from the cloud until six faces floated there, peering down at them.

Then another man stepped forward—the emperor, judging by his garb but also his demeanor, his palpable authority. He said something to the faces, bowed deeply—and, one by one, they nodded or smiled in return and then vanished.

Ibaru felt as if a weight had been lifted from him. Now that he was able to consider it clearly, he realized he did not want revenge. Perhaps he never had. Or maybe he had at first, but matters had changed since then. He had changed. Now all he truly wanted was a new life, preferably one working with plants. That was where he was truly happy.

Yet still, within him, he felt an ache, an emptiness. "I feel hollow," he said aloud, and beside him his brother nodded.

"Like before, when we were always so hungry," he agreed. "A pit that could never be filled." There was anguish on Iraku's face, and Ibaru embraced him, wishing he could take that pain from his little brother, wanting to protect him as he always had.

It was that impulse that made him turn to this stranger, this matekai, and say, "Can you help us?"

The man considered a moment, tapping his chin, but finally smiled. "I think so." He held out his hands, and instinctively Ibaru took one and Iraku the other, their other hands still linked together so the three of them now formed a small circle. "Concentrate on that empty feeling," the man urged. "Focus on it. Remember it at its worst."

Ibaru closed his eyes and did so, remembering that deep, overwhelming hunger that had driven him to do horrible things in an attempt to fill it, even for an instant. It was an ache deep in his bones, one that left him feeling both weak and somehow beyond weakness or pain, and he trembled slightly, but he was grounded by his brother's hand and this stranger's.

"Good." All at once he felt a tingle in his hand, as if it were falling asleep. That spread up his arm, across his shoulder, into his chest, up and down until his entire body was awash with the strange sensation. It swirled into that old void like water poured over a sponge, finding and filling every crack and crevice, and when it finally subsided he felt…full. Sated.

Whole.

"What did you do?" Iraku whispered, awe in his voice, and looking at him Ibaru saw that his brother's eyes were clear again, for the first time since they had first fallen under the cloud's influence, devoid of those strange dark whorls that had denoted its power. "I feel...alive." And he smiled and laughed, sounding like his old self again. No, not even that, for some of the ever-present anger seemed to have vanished as well, leaving him lighter than before.

"That force within you was unnatural," their savior explained, releasing their hands now. "I called forth nature to replace it. You are now free of its touch." He frowned. "Can I trust that you no longer mean me or anyone else here harm?"

Ibaru glanced at his brother, who nodded, before nodding himself. "We have no wish to hurt anyone," he said, and meant it. "I'm sorry," he added.

Surprisingly, the young man seemed to accept that. "I'm sure we'll need to talk about some things later," he pointed out, "but for now I'll ask that you just sit here and wait." He turned more serious as he continued, with a glance inside, "I need to go check on some people I care about."

"We will wait," Ibaru promised, lowering himself to perch on the walkway's edge, his legs dangling over the side, the tips of his boots just brushing the grass below. His brother joined him, and after one last look the man nodded and turned away, climbing over the palace doors.

"What now?" Iraku asked, but he did not sound overly concerned.

"Now we wait," his brother answered, glancing out toward the front gates, where it seemed a pair of warriors, a shorter one in black and a taller one in green, had cut down many of those who had entered with them, and were making short work of the remainder, backed by more in black and a few in red. "And after that? We shall see."

For the first time since his youth, though, he thought there might actually be a future for them. For the first time since he was a child, he dared to hope.

CHAPTER FORTY-TWO

Chimehara studied the man before her as she approached, step-by-step—no hurry, though the sun was beginning to set she still had more than enough time to accomplish this task she had long ago set for herself. He was young, she saw, perhaps her own age. Handsome enough, with clean, almost sharp features, good cheekbones, a strong chin, and bright eyes that were now focused on her beneath a lowered brow. Well built, unless his robes had been padded somehow to grant him such an appearance, but he did not strike her as vain enough to engage in such trickery. And, for all that she had just killed someone right in front of him, calm—not completely unafraid, which showed he was not a fool, but not panicked, either, his eyes only flickering once to where Amani Denbi's body already lay cooling before returning to lock onto her once more.

That woman! Chimehara had to struggle not to grind her teeth at the audacity of it. Time running away from them, the Saisaihyu nearly over—and with it, their window of opportunity—and she had wanted to stand there and lecture. Idiot! Kill him first, then you could rant all you liked while standing over his corpse! But the former Rojiri had been too used to getting her own way, to being free to speak whenever she wanted, for as long as she wanted. She never would have abided by the suggestion to hurry things along, especially since she had clearly viewed Chimehara as little more than a servant, a handy tool to be used and then, if necessary discarded.

Much as she had used and discarded Kohori.

Thoughts of the Honteno commander nearly paused Chimehara, her steps faltering as if synched to her stuttering heart. She had not lied when she had told the older woman how much she cared for her, or how sorry she was. She had never felt that way about anyone before. Perhaps she never would again. There were always people waiting to be smitten by her, but Kohori had genuinely listened, had truly cared not just about how she looked but about what she thought and felt!

It was just awful luck and worse timing that she should be their way into Aihiri—and the kind of woman who would never have sat still during this little coup. She could not have been left alive. And later, when she had the time, Chimehara would weep for that.

But not right now. Right now, the emperor of Rimbaku sat, transfixed at her approach like a mouse watching a mamusha glide toward it, unable to look away or move as she stepped slowly, so slowly toward him, her knife ready.

Then he blinked.

"Tell me," he said, the words raspy at first as if his throat had dried from disuse, "why should I not just cut you down where you stand?" He tapped the scabbarded sword that lay across his chair arms before him. "You have no armor, and Kosshiki will slice through skin and bone as easily as silk." His one hand tightened upon the sword's corded handle.

But Chimehara was prepared for this. "Surely, your Imperial Majesty," she replied, adding additional breath to her voice so that it thrummed deeply, richly, across the narrowing space between them, "you would not draw your ancient and noble sword against an unarmed woman?" And she dropped her knife at her feet, clanging upon the swirls and patterns of the mosaiced floor as she smiled her sweetest smile for him, the one that she knew brought her dimples out in full force.

His eyes widened as the full effect of her smile slammed into him like a tidal wave, and his breathing caught in his throat. Impressively, he recovered himself enough to frown, though he was gulping for air—but after a second of scowling he shook his head and loosened his grip upon the blade. Just as she had expected. He had too much honor to harm her while she was defenseless. And that, of course, would be his undoing.

She advanced another step, now only a few paces from the gilded railing along the platform's front edge, and her hand dipped into her sash, drawing forth the tube of lip gloss once more. "A single kiss," she told him, deliberately parting her lips and licking the lower one with just the tip of her tongue, causing him to gasp once more. "And then I will leave you alone. You have my word."

The tube was only inches from her lips when something slammed into her back, sending her flying off her feet to crash into that same railing hard enough to crack it. Chimehara stumbled back, the lip gloss bouncing free to roll upon the dais's lacquered floor, and turned, wincing from the force of the blow and the impact with the railing—

And found a woman standing there, arms crossed over her chest.

"I don't know who you are or what you want," she stated, "but you need to leave, now."

Chimehara laughed, studying the stranger. She was young and pretty, though not in her league by any stretch. More slightly built, and her arms showed more muscle than most found seemly in a woman, but then her clothing was simple enough to indicate she was not concerned about such things. Looking more closely, Chimehara frowned. Young, pretty, athletic, simple clothing—"I know you!" she burst out, her hands curling into claws. "You killed my students!"

Now the other woman's eyes narrowed. "Those murderous little beasts were yours?" She freed her arms and shook them loose. "They tried to kill me!" She frowned. "What kind of monster trains children to be killers?"

"The kind that kills!" Chimehara shouted back and flung herself at her new foe. Her intended task, killing the emperor who symbolized this city and this kingdom that had hurt her and others like her with its callous indifference, was all but forgotten beneath the blinding hatred of her new goal, to avenge Suda and Ruisoki and even poor little Gou. Their killer must die!

She lashed out with both hands, trying to claw out the other woman's eyes, but her target stepped back and to the side, one foot licking out to tap Chimehara in the ankle, and suddenly she was falling, her feet tangled together with each other and the hem of her kitoro. She hit the ground hard, shoulder and arm and side banging against the cold tiles, and rolled quickly to the side, old instincts rising up once more. You moved out of the way of the expected kick, curled into a ball, protected head and throat and stomach.

But this was not some abusive adult beating on a child, and when no additional blows landed she uncoiled and pushed herself back up to glare at the other woman, who was watching from a few paces away. "I don't want to fight you," she stated. "But I will if I have to."

A glint to the side caught Chimehara's eye and she smiled as she extended her leg and hooked it with her foot, dragging it toward her until it was close enough for her to reach out and snatch up. Her knife. Then she rose to her feet, weapon in hand.

"You don't have to fight at all," she said, raising it so the razor-sharp blade jutted between them. "You can just die where you are." And she lunged again, this time lashing out with something a good deal more deadly than her nails.

The other woman—Chimehara didn't even know her name and did not particularly care—twisted as if she were performing some sort of dance, gracefully avoiding the attack. One hand lashed out as she spun about, catching Chimehara on the back of the neck, hard enough to send her crashing to the ground again. But rage brought her back to her feet more quickly this time, fueling her limbs with a strength that let her ignore the pain. "Stand still and fight!" she demanded. Some of her hair had come loose from its knot again, draping around her face and sticking to her cheeks and neck, and she knew that she must look frightful, but for once she did not care. There was no one here to see her but two dead people, anyway—or at least they soon would be.

"I told you I didn't want to fight," the first of them insisted, but she did at least draw a small knife from her sleeve. Chimehara almost laughed at the sight of it. It was only a kogotano, its blade perhaps as long as her little finger. That was not a weapon!

"How do you expect to fight at all with that?" she asked, a giggle bubbling up despite herself. She waved her own knife, whose blade was as long as her hand and as thick as her thumb at its base. "This is a proper knife. That is for opening letters." And, to prove her point, she slashed at the woman's throat, a powerful stroke with as much force as she could muster behind it.

Her foe did not attempt to block it—if she had, her little kogotano would have snapped in two. Instead, she flung herself backward, flipping over completely—and kicked Chimehara in the jaw, snapping her mouth shut and drawing blood where she bit her own tongue. Curse her! Spitting blood, Chimehara snarled and attacked again, swinging wildly, but somehow the other woman moved like water, like air, always managing to twist and dip and duck and slide away from her knife, delivering kicks and punches and slaps in return.

"Enough, bones take you!" Chimehara screamed. She charged forward, arms wide, planning to wrap them around the woman and hold her still while she stabbed her in the chest, the back, the side, wherever she could manage. But her opponent ducked under the intended embrace and this time her little knife licked out, catching Chimehara across the throat and leaving a stinging line where the narrow little blade had slit the skin. It burned, and Chimehara knew it was weeping blood, the edge of her kitoro sticking to her neck, but it was not enough to stop her.

"Fight properly!" she cried, slicing the air with her knife but hitting nothing more than that. Her breath was coming in great heaving gasps, her skin sticky with sweat, her fingers slipping on the knife handle, droplets falling into her eyes so that she could barely see but still she staggered forward, unwilling to back down, unable to do anything but kill.

That was all she had ever really been good at, after all.

"Give up," the other woman warned, barely sounded winded. "I don't want to kill you."

"One of us is going to die here and now," Chimehara promised, wiping her eyes clear with the back of her hand and adjusting her grip on her blade. "Because I won't stop."

Her foe sighed, dipping her head downward for an instant, eyes half-closed, before raising her chin again. "So be it." She settled into a fighting stance, the little knife held before her. "Do your worst," she commanded, her voice steady, eyes calm and cool.

Seeing this woman, who had taken her pupils from her, so relaxed, so collected, so unruffled—everything Chimehara usually was herself—was the last straw. All her anger, all her hatred, not just at this stranger but at everything about this city, this kingdom, this life, came boiling up in a single incoherent scream as Chimehara leaped, knife held in both hands, blade downward, descending upon her rival like a frenzied owl swooping down upon a mouse—

and the other woman spun to the side, evading the attack, even as her little kogotano glittered in an arc of its own, up and out like the path of the sun.

Chimehara crashed to the ground, her knife falling from her hands as they grasped for her throat instead. This time the cut was deeper and off to the side, a burning pain that choked her, leaving her struggling for balance. She clawed at it, her fingers covered in the blood that gushed from the wound, those extremities already starting to go numb.

A shadow fell across her, and she looked up, still gasping, to see the other woman standing there, a look of pity etched upon her pretty face. *Do not pity me!* Chimehara wanted to snarl, but no words emerged, only a wheeze of desperately needed air escaping from her lips and from the tear where her throat had been. The emperor was there as well, finally off his throne, and now other figures emerged, a man in simple clothes and then a warrior in green and another in black, all of them cast in shadow by the sun that had finally fled overhead, leaving the room to darken even as Chimehara's sight began to fade. She felt her strength leaving her, leaking from under her grasping fingers, soaking her robes and spreading out upon the floor, and slumped, no longer able to lift her head.

"It is over," someone said, and her vision swam too much for her to tell who it was. She tried to speak, to cry defiance, to threaten, to cajole, to seduce, but all of that had washed away along with so much else, and for an instant she wished she could have been someone different, something different, anything that might have led to a different fate than this one.

The last image that flashed to her mind was Kohori, smiling at her as she died. *I am sorry,* Chimehara thought. *You deserved better than me.*

Then there was nothing left in her, no more dreams, no more thoughts, no more breath. The room fell dark, and as the Saisai-hyu ended, so too did her life, there upon the throne room floor.

CHAPTER FORTY-THREE

After the Saisaihyu

Seikoku was having trouble staying focused.

This meeting was important, and she was grateful for it—and grateful to Noniki for arranging it, and the emperor for sanctioning it. Even so, she kept glancing around. They were in one of the smaller meeting rooms in the palace, a space she had not seen before but that was far less ostentatious than the throne room or even the Rojiri council chamber, with a less elaborate pattern in the tiles of the floor and simpler wall panels, carved jade flowers affixed to pale silk so that the petals and stems seemed almost to glow in the light of the lanterns that protruded from the corner beams and the larger light that hung down over this table in the center. The room was quiet, and pleasant, and regal without being overbearing—but she kept looking to the door expecting to see a tall, broad-shouldered woman with gray hair in a chonmage glancing in, the gold trim of her red armor setting it aflame.

She still could not believe Maniko Kohori was dead.

The stern Taikoro had been one of the first people Seikoku had met in Awaihinshi, during the attack by those strange bone creatures. Kohori had been directing guards and residents alike, placing people where they could best defend themselves and the city. She had co-opted Seikoku and the rest of her friends, but she had not minded. Far from it, they had all been eager to help, and happy to be given a place and a task, however temporary.

And now she was gone. Killed, they believed, by the same woman who had tried to kill Seikoku, the woman whose pupils had each attempted to kill her.

The woman she herself had killed instead.

After the Saisaihyu had ended, with all the former Rojiri's

warriors either dead, incapacitated, or in custody, they had gone searching, unsettled by something their leader had apparently said to Hibikitsu—right before she had been killed herself, also by that woman. Eventually one of the Honteno had recalled seeing her earlier that day, with a picnic box and a stated intent to surprise Kohori with lunch. They had checked the small, secluded garden where the two had rendezvoused, and there they had indeed found the guard commander.

She had been seated in a cross-legged position upon the sandy path between the palace wall and the garden proper, clad in only hosode and hakami, her armor and sword collected on a ledge nearby, hands on her knees, eyes closed as if meditating. At first, they had wondered if her heart had given out, or some other strange and sudden ailment had taken her, but then Noniki had closed his eyes, studying the scene somehow, and had declared that she had in fact been poisoned. The funeral was tomorrow, that being a more auspicious day for such a farewell, and so today the body lay in state in the throne room, a mark of the emperor's high regard for his former protector—and not far from where Kohori's killer had breathed her last.

A nudge to her side made Seikoku start, and she glanced up to see the others all studying her. None of them looked particularly angry, and a few even appeared sympathetic, but nonetheless she had asked for this meeting and now she was wasting their time. Concentrate on the here and now, and the future, she told herself sternly. Kohori would tell you the same—she would be furious if your grief over her death interfered with accomplishing this goal.

Accordingly, she cleared her throat. "Thank you all for agreeing to meet with us," she began, bowing her head as a mark of respect. "We have never wished to inconvenience or upset anyone, and it is our fondest hope that we may overcome our differences and all come to an understanding that will satisfy everyone."

One of the men, an older, portly gentleman with thick eyebrows and a small thatch of hair sprouting from his chin, cleared his throat. "That is a pretty speech, Miss," he declared, tapping bejeweled fingers upon the table. "But the fact remains that you and your friends have been selling wares and services within Atsani, and that is not permitted." Of course he would say that— Wakiza Yukane was the karo of the district and clearly considered it a personal affront that they should even be allowed to live within that level, let alone attempt to earn a living there!

"He is not wrong," a sturdy-looking woman a few seats away volunteered. "It is not right that you should be allowed to pursue jobs in that district. You are taking work away from others who have long since established their reputations and their connections, but who now lose out to you solely because you live nearby!" Her clothes were far less fine than Lord Wakiza's, and her squared hands and equally blocky face bore faint smudges of rice flour, informing Seikoku that this must be Hasebe Towa, the karo of Bejinuri. That district contained most of the city's craftsmen and artisans, which meant those were the people most likely to be hired by the nobles of Motohiri. Thus she also had a vested interest in this matter—and not in Seikoku's favor.

Seikoku glanced to her side, where Noniki sat quietly. He smiled and patted her arm but did not say anything, nor could she wholly blame him. She knew that he felt the same as she did, both about their friends and in general, but he had been right in what he'd told her that night—he was a Rojiri now and it would seem like nothing more than simple favoritism if he were to interfere, especially seeing as how the place in question was his own home.

She frowned and straightened, facing these district governors directly, not presumptuous but not intimidated either. "We understand that you are concerned about your residents' ability to make a living"—that was to Hasebe—"and you are concerned about propriety"—and that to Wakiza. "We have no desire to steal anyone's business, nor to trouble our neighbors. However, we must also work to survive and, more than that, to contribute, for we have no desire to be a burden upon this city or upon anyone." She held up her hand to stop the pair from interjecting. "Tell me, for I am still new to this city, is it in fact forbidden for business to be conducted within Atsani?"

Lord Wakiza sputtered a bit at that, causing his beard to bob about, but finally was forced to admit, "Not expressly, no."

She nodded and turned her attention to Hasebe. "And are any of your residents suddenly without any work due to our arrival?"

The other woman shook her head. "No. But they're not happy about it," she stated, scowling.

"That is understandable, and I am sorry for that, but surely they understand that if someone offers a better service, finer wares, better prices, more convenience, that they must match those factors somehow or stand to lose some customers? Even long-term ones?" She shook her head. "My friends are all honest craftsmen and artisans, hard-working and good at their various trades. They have no desire to cheat anyone, client or rival, nor will they be offended if someone offers a better deal than they do, or better wares. That is the nature of business, is it not?" Hasebe still grumbled, but there was little she could say to argue that.

Having settled that aspect, Seikoku shifted back to Lord Wakiza. "Have we disturbed any of the other residents of Atsani in any way, with loud noises or foul smells or blocking the roads?" she asked him.

"That is not the point—" he began, but again she held up a hand.

"I will take that as a no," she said. He did not contradict her, as she had known he could not, for their estate was large enough that any sounds or smells would never reach the people in the surrounding properties. "However, in the interest of being neighborly, we have undertaken certain other arrangements." She smiled. "A merchant has approached us, one Iwaki Matsu. Perhaps you know him?"

Hasebe and Lord Wakiza both shook their heads but the other woman at the table, a slender, older lady with heavy lines on her face but bright eyes, smiled. "Iwaki Matsu is a fine man and an upstanding member of our community," she stated, for she was the karo of Sakiriti. "His showroom is not large but his crafts are of the highest quality."

Seikoku dipped her chin to acknowledge this and thank the lady for her contribution. "Iwaki-san has offered to carry my friends' wares in his showroom," she explained. "They will continue to create them on our estate, of course, but they will no longer offer them for sale from there. Does that satisfy your need for propriety?" she asked, and when Lord Wakiza nodded grudgingly, she manufactured a smile. "Excellent. Then I hope everyone will be happy with this new arrangement?"

It was then that Noniki spoke. "There is one thing more," he stated, smiling at everyone, "and I am glad you will all be present to hear it. I have spoken to the emperor. He agrees that this is an unusual situation we find ourselves in, where an estate is now home to a small community instead of a single noble household, but that it may not be the last time we see such a change in state. Certain accommodations must be made, for an enclave does not function the same as a family and must therefore be treated differently. Accordingly"—he rose to his feet and produced a scroll from his sleeve, its edges sealed with the tsodami of the emperor himself—"I am very pleased to announce that Sorainasei is henceforth to be considered its own town in the same way that each level is its own region, and Seikoku will be its buhiyo."

He nodded toward Lord Wakiza, who had begun sputtering again. "Sorainasei is still within Atsani and will still obey its dictates and contribute to its shared expenses, such as repaving the roads or repairing the gates. Seikoku will meet with you regularly to discuss any problems or concerns on either side." He grinned at the other man. "This is akin to a promotion, Lord Wakiza, for you are the first karo in Awaihinshi to have a township within your province."

That clearly struck the nobleman, who stopped making strange noises and suddenly adopted a pose of great dignity. "I live to serve the empire," he declared, bowing his head, and then glanced up at Seikoku. "And I look forward to working together, madam."

"As do I," she managed to find it in her to say, accepting Noniki's hand as he pulled her to her feet and presented her with the scroll. "Thank you." Sensing that the meeting was at an end, the others rose and began to file out, several of them pausing to congratulate her on the way.

Only once they had gone did she turn and punch Noniki in the arm. "What was that?" she demanded. "Buhiyo? I never agreed to that!"

He rubbed his shoulder and tried putting on a pitiful face, but he was laughing as he answered. "No, which is why we didn't tell you!" Then he sobered. "Seriously, this makes sense. Sorainasei is more than just a handful of friends. We're a community. We've even just taken in our first new residents." He was referring to the brothers Ibaru and Iraku, who they were provisionally allowing to stay until it could be determined if they would fit into the little enclave permanently. "Whether anyone likes it or not, we're our own unique entity," he continued. "And now everyone will have to treat us as one."

"Then you should be its leader," she muttered, but she knew what he would say to that, and indeed, he was already shaking his head.

"I cannot be a Rojiri and a matekai *and* a mayor," he pointed out. "Besides, I am not there half the time. You are. Everyone looks up to you, everyone turns to you to make the decisions. You are the right person for this job."

She frowned, then cocked an eyebrow at him. "Everyone?" When he nodded, she tilted her head. "Even you? So that means you'll do what I say?"

He grinned and sketched a deep bow. "I am yours to command, madam buhiyo," he intoned, which made her laugh as well.

"I'll hold you to that," she warned, waiting until he'd straightened up before flinging her arms around his neck and kissing him soundly. "I already have some ideas."

Noniki's face flushed, but his eyes were bright and his smile brighter as he kissed her back. "I am all ears," he promised.

Seikoku thought even Kohori would have grinned at that.

CHAPTER FORTY-FOUR

ven now, staring down at Maniko Kohori's stiff and unmoving face, Hibikitsu found it difficult to believe she was dead. She had been a fixture in his life, first serving his father and then him, unchanging save for the graying of her hair and the tiny lines that had sprung up about her eyes and mouth, this tall, stern woman who had guarded them and theirs so fiercely, those sharp eyes alert to any danger, that mouth always ready to voice concerns or deliver warnings or even instructions about their safety.

Yet here she lay, decked out in her full armor, naked nihono clutched in her hands, eyes closed as if asleep—to open no more upon this world.

She looks peaceful, he thought as he rinsed his fingers in the basin and then took the packet of incense from his sleeve and deposited a pinch of its contents in the incense burner that sat upon a little table before the coffin and the stone tablet leaning against it, which bore her name and title. She had never looked that peaceful when she was alive.

He bowed and then rose and circled the coffin to ascend the dais and settle onto his throne as the priests took his place around Kohori and began their chants. He had wanted to sit among the other mourners, who were in rows facing him, but Master Eijiri and Kishin Narai had insisted that this would not be appropriate, or kind. "If you seat yourselves among the others present," they had argued, "everyone will be forced to behave differently, because their emperor is among them. With you in your customary place they can be themselves and mourn properly, without concern for any impropriety."

He had picked up on the underlying message they were subtly

conveying—"do not be selfish, think of others as well as yourself"—and had heeded it, even though that meant separating
himself from Noniki and Kagiri and the rest. This was not about
him, however. It was about Kohori. And she more than deserved
to be treated with every possible respect, and for those who had
cared about her to have the chance to grieve fully.

A few hours later, after the ceremony was done and everyone had
repaired to the larger of Aihiri's private gardens, Hibikitsu cleared
his throat. Immediately every conversation ceased, all eyes turning to him where he stood near the arched entrance.

"Maniko Kohori was perhaps the finest woman we have ever
known, and certainly the most dedicated," he began, raising his
voice so that it projected across the space, with its delicate walkways and neatly trimmed trees and shrubs and small decorative
urns and boulders. He would have liked to have held this in the
smaller garden where she had been found, but that would never
have been big enough to accommodate this many, for all her Honteno were here, along with his Rojiri, Shizumi and several of her
Honjofu, a few of the palace staff, and a handful of nobles and
other Kohori had interacted with regularly.

"There was never any question as to her loyalty or her integ-
rity," he continued, "and one had only to meet her eye to know at
once the correct course of action. Her death is a great blow to us
personally and to this kingdom, and she will be sorely missed." He
raised his glass, which held tsekuri from the palace's private stock,
and the rest of the assemblage followed suit. "To Maniko Kohori!"
The cheer, repeated from every throat, echoed about the gardens,
and Hibikitsu hoped it reached to the very heavens, and that Kohori, looking down, would hear and see just how many people had
truly loved her.

Later still, the priests returned and the head priest presented Hibikitsu with a handsome urn, its rough glaze reminiscent of a midnight sky in its shades of blue and black. Hibikitsu accepted this with a short bow and with great reverence, for it contained Kohori's bones. But they were not his to keep.

Glancing about, his eyes fell upon a woman standing nearby. Though not of Kohori's stature she was still of goodly height and solidly built, and looked competent and dangerous in her crimson armor, despite the sturdy cane upon which she leaned. She straightened upon his approach and saluted, gauntleted fist rapping against her armored chest.

"Taikoro Reizei," he addressed her, for so she was now, though her armor had yet to receive its golden edges. Yesterday he and his Rojiri had met with her and Itamon, Kohori's two lieutenants, both of whom had been clearly shaken by their superior's death but were professional enough to keep their grief contained and perform their duties. He had asked them a simple question, both at once, as he wished to see how they would react: "Which of you should we select to take Kohori's place?"

After a second, glancing at each other, the woman had taken a step forward. "It should be me, Your Majesty," she had stated boldly, even going so far as to meet his gaze. "Itamon is the better warrior and the better squad leader but I am the better organizer and commander. Besides which"—she had thumped her fist against her injured leg—"even once it is fully healed I may never be as fast or as agile as I was. That is a hindrance in combat but in no ways impedes my ability to give orders or to lead. Nor would it prevent me from laying down my life to protect you and yours."

Hibikitsu had turned to the other chuisu, the ever-loyal Itamon, who had nodded. "I agree with Reizei's assessment, sire," the man had stated, his broad face earnest. "She will make an excellent Taikoro, and I believe it is what Taikoro Maniko would have chosen."

That had settled the matter, and so it was to her that Hibikitsu handed the urn now. "These belong to you," he told her. "We expect that you will only draw upon them when you truly have need of her experience and wisdom to augment your own."

Reizei saluted. "Only in the direst of circumstances, sire," she promised, accepting the heavy container. "But their mere presence will help remind me of her and guide me to act as she might have done."

When Hibikitsu made to walk on, Reizei fell in at his side and a little behind him, in flanking position. Her cane beat a steady rhythm upon the small stones of the garden walk as he sought out his Rojiri, who were all gathered beneath a small pavilion, sipping tea and admiring the flowers and trees that filled the grounds. Shizumi was there as well, and Hibikitsu felt sure Kohori would have appreciated having all of them here together.

His attention went first to the little group's newest addition, a tall, thin woman with a long face and robes of blue and green who bowed deeply as he joined them. "Your Imperial Majesty," she declared, her voice deep and resonant.

"You do not need to bow and scrape every time you see me, you know," he told her with a small smile, and her eyebrows quirked in reply.

"I hope you will allow it at least a little while longer," she answered, and he laughed, feeling once again that he had made the right choice here. Yesterday he had met her for the first time and she had quickly abased herself on the throne room floor, an arm's length from where Kohori's body lay, as he and his Rojiri had looked on.

"Thank you for agreeing to see me, Your Imperial Majesty," she had intoned, her forehead pressed to the tiles. "I have come to beg your forgiveness."

He had frowned down at her. "Your kinsman raised arms against us, Heiayuki Futoba," he had reminded her sternly. "Even now, Ieuyuki Nagao languishes in a cell, awaiting his execution for treason. Many felt we should treat the rest of his house and kin in that selfsame manner."

"And you would be well within your rights to do so, sire," she had agreed, still face down, completely unmoving. "But nonetheless

I am here to beg for mercy on behalf of myself, my house, and its members."

"Rise," he had told her, and she had done so, but not quickly, not eagerly. She had taken her time, demonstrating that she stood only because he had commanded it. "State your case," he had told her when she was on her feet once more.

"Your Majesty," she had begun, "the Heiayuki were only a minor house, of no real distinction beyond our connection to the Ieuyuki. Most of our lands and holdings are well outside Awaihin-shi, and even I myself, though the head of my house, have not been here in many a year. We had no knowledge of Nagao's treachery, and no participation in his crimes."

"You say 'were'," he had noted, and she had nodded.

"We have divorced ourselves from the Ieuyuki, sire," she'd confirmed. "We are no longer linked to them in any way, for they have brought dishonor and shame upon themselves and all those associated with them." She had plucked at her kitoro, which he saw now was decorated with silvery birds, as long and slender as their owner—cranes, rather than the swallows that Heiayuki and Ieuyuki had shared. "Only by severing all connection can we hope to demonstrate our continued loyalty to you and to the empire."

Hibikitsu had considered her words. It was a bold move and a risky one, for by denouncing their kin they had forfeited any claim to the Ieuyuki's lands and titles. Lady Heiayuki had struck him as sincere, however, and he had felt that she genuinely disapproved of her former cousin's actions.

That assessment had only been cemented when Noniki had leaned in to say something to him privately. "I know her," the young Rojiri had whispered. "Or, rather, I have met her. In Atsani, a few days ago. She told me why the nobles there were so upset about Sorainasei. She seemed sympathetic to us over our troubles—and less concerned about propriety and tradition than those around us. It was also she who recommended the merchant Iwaki Matsu to Seikoku, as she had evidently dealt with him in the past."

"Interesting." He had also remembered what Shizumi had said a lifetime ago, before the Saisaihyu, about Lady Heiayuki—how she had come to beg forgiveness but also to see to the well-being of her remaining kin, and how she was highly regarded. Sitting there now, studying her as she waited patiently for his verdict, no hint of impatience or arrogance upon her face, he had made yet another of his quick decisions.

"We have chosen to grant you the mercy you seek," he had stated grandly, with a wink at Noniki. "Provided you are willing to serve us."

She had immediately dropped to her knees and from there to full prostration once more. "I live to serve, Your Majesty," she had insisted. "My life and all that I have is yours."

"Good. Then here is what you must do—" He had enjoyed watching her face as he had explained, and as she had slowly realized that, far from being punished, he was making her one of his imperial advisors instead.

And now they were six: Noniki and Kagiri, born of common stock but now the land's only wizard and its greatest warrior; Master Eijiri and Kishin Narai, merchants, both wealthy men and clever, particularly with words; and finally Fujitai Takami and Heiayuki Futoba, both nobles but young and open-minded. Together with Misataki Shizumi and now Reizei, and the recently made buhiyo Seikoku, this was Hibikitsu's inner circle. These were the people who would help him reshape the empire.

Indeed, they had already begun. "I feel that, despite what occurred, the Saisaihyu itself was a success," he told them now, eschewing the royal "we" since they were alone, the other mourners far enough away to afford them some privacy. "After the first few days, people learned to manage without the need for aishone."

The others all nodded. "By the end, most seemed almost to accept it," Noniki agreed. "Though I think we might wish to wait a bit before having another."

But Hibikitsu shook his head. "We will not wait at all," he replied, then laughed. "At least, not entirely." He paused before continuing, for even among such people as this he was hesitant to state what came next. "We will have Saisaihyu for a single day each sihu," he declared. "On Dayabei. One day when people are not only encouraged not to use aishone but actively discouraged, even prohibited, from doing so. Over time, everyone will become accustomed to this." He grinned. "And then, once we are sure, we will increase that to twice each sihu. Then eventually to three days, and so on."

Everyone considered this. "Wise," Master Eijiri finally decided. "It will ease everyone into not relying upon aishone, and by casting it as a holiday, a relief from the stress of work, this will be seen as a boon rather than a curse." He bowed. "Very clever, sire."

Hibikitsu waved off the compliment, but inside he was beaming. This was it, he was sure of it. This was how he would wean his people off the Relicant Touch. It might take some time—years or even decades—but eventually they would no longer need aishone, would no longer rely upon it. People would develop their own skills and talents instead, learned themselves instead of being handed down—learned anew, and thus giving birth to new ideas in turn.

This, he was certain, was the beginning.

He only wished Kohori had been here to see it. But he was sure, wherever she might be now, that she would have approved.

EPILOGUE

A short distance away, back in the larger, more open part of the gardens, a heavyset man in the garb of a palace chef sighed happily. "There, you see?" Yamana Muiada stated contentedly, popping the last bite of ujiro into his mouth and chewing with obvious delight. "Everything is perfect, everyone is happy. This is why you should come work here!"

On the other side of the table that had been set out to display and offer various delicacies, drinks and, at this end, sweets, the server, who was dressed in somewhat plainer garb, smiled and shook his head. "You hired me to provide desserts for this event," Hajime reminded the heavier man, "and I am grateful as always for your patronage. And yes, you are right, it is beautiful," he added, gazing about them, at the lovely, carefully tended greenery, and the clean walls of the palace behind, the gilding of its roof beams and supports glittering in the sunlight beneath the glossy expanse of its roof. "But I am still content with my shop and my current customers, though I thank you for the kind offer."

"Suit yourself," Muiada declared with a heavy sigh. "But you know if you ever change your mind you have only to say the word!" He bowed to the sweets-maker, reached across to carefully pluck another square of ujiri from the tray with already sticky fingers, and, with his prize safely in hand, wandered away, greeting some of the other palace staff as he walked.

Behind him, the man known as Hajime continued to smile pleasantly to everyone around him, and to take in the sights as only a visitor might do, one suitably awed by its grandeur and majesty.

Yet, behind that sorcerous mask, Dai Yi's sharp eyes saw a

good deal more than just elegance and wealth and power. They also picked out the Honjofu and Honteno standing alert at every entrance, and their fellows mingling among the other mourners, their faces sad but their armor as imposing as ever and their hands either grasping their yanoi or not far from their nihono. Hajime noted the archers stationed at the corners of the roof, umi in hand, quivers at their feet, ready to fire down upon the crowd at the slightest hint of trouble.

And he saw how, even as the emperor stood and spoke and laughed with a handful of others beneath the pavilion, three of those same people—the tall man in green armor, the woman in black, and the woman in red—were constantly glancing about in turn, their eyes roving everywhere, taking in everything. More than once he felt those same gazes light upon him and was careful to maintain his own façade of awe and humility, as befit a lowly dessert-maker serving in Aihiri for the first time.

The three of them were in constant motion as well. Not in the sense of dancing about or waving their arms or leaping to and fro, but each of them kept shifting their footing, adjusting their stance, turning their bodies. They were providing a constant shield between the emperor in their midst and the garden's other occupants, Dai Yi saw at once. They were protecting their ruler without his even being aware of it.

Yes, those three were dangerous, he decided, grudgingly admiring their poise and the fluid way in which they moved. As was he, of course, but even he would not want to risk pitting himself against three such foes. One he could best, perhaps two, but all three? No, between them and the other guards he would be dead long before he went after the emperor, if he were foolish enough to attempt that here and now.

Which he was not. He was now doubly glad he had chosen to hold off, rather than rushing to attack during the Saisaihyu. Yes, he could have used the cover of the attempted coup to sneak in, but that attack had failed, in part because the imperial guards had caught on quickly and been able to respond with the necessary force and skill. He would not have wanted to be caught in all that.

Instead, he had watched and waited. Now he had a better idea of how Aihiri's defenses worked. He had seen where and how the guards gathered, how they responded to a threat—and where there were holes he could exploit. Plus, he had now been admitted here into the compound as Hajime, which meant the guards had already been introduced to him and would not be surprised or startled or suspicious when he visited again. Especially since he could count on Yamana Muiada to invite him in, provided he arrived with sweets in hand.

And if he needed to be able to move about more freely once he was inside—well, that would not be difficult to manage, either. In his own particular fashion.

No, he had made the correct choice in waiting. His time was still to come, of that he had no doubt. But when it did, he would have planned carefully, allowing for all possibilities, all variables, all dangers.

Unlike Zhen Shu, he would not fail. Dai Yi smiled at the thought, dipping his head as a noble couple paused to select a matching pair of kabingo, his pleasant demeanor to the richly dressed man and woman giving away none of the icy resolve within.

The Rimbakan emperor would die by his hand, he vowed. It was only a matter of time.

END OF BOOK FOUR

GLOSSARY

Adai: a kind of soup broth, made from seaweed, dried fish flakes, mushrooms, and water

Ahaiinko: a formal stamp of office used to sign official documents

Aiashe: "foot bone," a foot soldier in Rimbaku's army, typically garbed in maikiro, hanketo, suneoto, and jingaso and armed with yanoi and chokoto

Aikaye: "sea bone," a sailor-warrior in Rimbaku's navy

Aio-akeo: a riverboat that runs the channel between Tabichi and Iwikaru

Aishone: relic bones

Aisho Hasume: Bone Collectors, a group of Buddhist-like traveling priests who wear the skulls and bones of their revered teachers dangling from their belts.

Aitachi: The Relicant Touch, the ability to absorb ancestral memories, skills, and knowledge by touching or consuming objects or people from the past

Akatai: family or household demons; malevolent ancestral spirits

Aragei: chicken that has been chopped into chunks and fried

Atorido: a traditional hanging lantern with four or six sides

Atuma-yio: sweet potato

Awaihinshi: The City of Polished Light, the marble capital of Rimbaku. Divided into six tiers (one for each level of the soul), with a shanty town/slum (Suranmui) at the bottom outside the walls and the emperor's palace at the top. Each tier has an outer wall of a different shade of marble, growing lighter in shade witch each height, from black to white. The tiers are:
    One: Aihiri, the Imperial compound at the very top. Walls of purest white marble.

Two: Atsani, where the Daijin and other important nobles live—and home to Sorainasei, the first "town" in Awaihinshi. Walls of palest yellow.

Three: Motohiri, where the most influential merchants and the minor nobles live. Walls of peach.

Four: Sakiriti, mid- to lesser merchants and the most important artisans. Walls of the hue of cherry blossoms (a pale rose).

Five: Bejinuri. Other artisans and craftsmen. Walls of pale violet (red wisteria).

Six: Mazihini, laborers and other menials. The walls surrounding this level are pale blue like water, and the outer walls of the city as a whole.

Bakiro: a bag, typically a large bag used for carrying one's personal items and equipment

Banezhan: a cylindrical ring worn on the thumb when using a bow, most often made of bone, ivory, horn, or jade.

Bannin: guards, watchmen

Baraken: a wooden practice sword, typically made of either teak or bamboo

Bezenkai: a southern province

Birabiro: a town in Korito, closest to the Fyushan-Rimbakan border

Botetsu: a little village in Yunigiri

Buhiyo: a mayor, responsible for a town or small city

Burahone: the Bone Blind. These women's aitachi is so strong they are constantly overwhelmed by memories and knowledge, drawing it from the very elements around them.

Chahito: the pommel or endcap of a sword

Chasai: symbolic baton, typically of lacquered wood with metal caps at both ends and a tassel at one.

Chayaburi: a small, fast sailboat

Chinbiro: a town in Korito, near Birabiro

Chituju: a house steward

Chohu: a prosperous merchant house specializing in gemstones

Chokoto: a straight-edged sword with a ring pommel

Chonmage: a hair bun, particularly favored by warriors

Chosinichi: A "reservoir," someone who can hold absorbed skills for a long time

Chunsin-inori: a full feast, served in three courses, each on its own tray

Cuioburi: the smallest class of military boat, most often used for patrols and search missions

Darakada: "body thief," a sorcerer whose magic allows him to steal another's face and form

Dayabei: the seventh and final day of a sihu, often a rest day

Deo: a breastplate or cuirass, part of a suit of armor

Dobuichi: "animal-touched," those who use their aitachi on animal bones instead of human ones

Dojo Kuge: aristocratic bureaucrats

Doh Bridge: a wide bridge spanning the Zinyang River and connecting Obanari to Hochiro

Edishu River: a small river running from the Tonawa west to the ocean. Awaihinshi sits beside it.

Essa: a doctor.

Esuge: the Rimbakan cedar, the most commonly used wood in the land

Eioha: a form of dumpling

Eikono: a formal outer robe with a round collar, wide sleeves, a long tail, and sewn sides

Enwara: a small town in Bezenkai, south of Ginzai

Eto-riantzu: a large wheeled cart with sliding front doors

Ferume: an inkbrush, used for writing

Fumisoni: a style of kisoni, the most elaborate and formal, with long, wide sleeves

Furotingawa: "floating tower", a legendary tower, long since in ruins, at the southern edge of Rimbaku, near the mouth of a river

Furukotai: the largest town in Korito, home to the regional governor

Fyushu: a rival nation to Rimbaku's north, constantly testing the borders. Symbol: a black gauntlet clenched in a fist.

Ganabo: a massive two-handed war club, usually spiked or studded

Gensaiba: "Living blades," legendary warriors of mythic ability

Ginzai: the nearest large town to the brothers' home

Goji: a folding stool most often used by men in full armor

Gotaiburi: a large, multi-masted boat designed to carry troops

Guisuke bitte: a chest for holding one's armor

Guisuke kai: a stylized stand for displaying armor, usually set atop a guisuke bitte

Haidoto: thigh guards, part of a suit of armor

Hakami: close-fitting pants, often worn under armor

Hakara Ikibanichi: the Brothers of Many Spirits, a monastic order

Hanketo: armored gauntlets

Hantien: a short, padded winter coat

Happoa Kappua: "The Foamy Cup." A tavern in Ginzai

Hakichuekai: a small, brightly colored bird, known for its trilling and its sociability

Heioki: fried octopus balls

Higeibara: the red spider lily, the official crest of Rimbaku

Higinasi: a nation bordering Rimbaku to the southwest. Symbol: a stylized blue wave

Himsu: a town in Hochiro

Hiromura: a small village in Bezenkai

Honjofu: "Bone warrior," Rimbaku's elite military unit. Clad all in black armor.

Honteno: "Emperor's bones," the Rimbaku Imperial Guard. Clad all in red armor.

Horohaba: a lost city of Ritakhou, known as the "City of Beasts" for its renowned menagerie

Hosode: an undershirt, usually plain and unbleached and typically of silk.

Hozaiburi: a large, heavy warship.

Iematsu: the red pine tree, often used for beams and posts

Ikibanichari: Castle of Many Spirits, the mountain monastery of the Hakara Ikibanichi

Iniro: a small, segmented box worn at the belt to hold small items, often beautifully carved and detailed

Irogaso: a circular bamboo hat

Irohito: a small town strategically located at the intersection of the Tonawa and Edishu rivers, guarding the way to Awaihinshi

Ishtaya: a tailor or seamstress

Itoyako: the lily of the valley, known for its soft, drooping petals that shade from white to pink

Ittei: a blunt iron rod with a wrapped handle and a hooked tine just above that, used by guards when they were not allowed to carry swords

Jagimato: a town in Saruto, between the Wagata and Edishu rivers

Jigekugi: lesser bureaucrats, the lowest rank of nobility

Jingaso: a conical iron helm, worn by the aiashe

Jogoturi: "Lords of the Street," a gang in Ginzai

Jubanichi: The "perfect touch"—someone who absorbs quickly and holds for a long time

Kaemusei: "the Silent Change" or "The Silent," a magical being of limitless hunger

Kanashi: a hair stick

Kaoni: a hip- or mid-thigh-length open coat with long, wide sleeves, worn over a kitoro

Karo: a regional governor, who reports to the Emperor

Karute: a helmet, usually with a menatu attached in front and one or more modato above

Kazure: iron plates hanging from the front and back of the deo to protect the pelvis and upper leg

Kenroichi: A solid touch, someone who can absorb decently and hold it decently

Kibango: small sweet dumplings made from rice flour

Kindichi: bosses or kings

Kisoni: A loose robe, wider and looser than a kitoro, that can be worn as either an undergarment or an outer layer.

Kitoro: a silk outer garment, like a wide-sleeved robe, usually decorated.

Koshitsu: a graverobber

Kosshiki: "the Bone Spirit," sword of the Relicant Emperor

Kogotano: a small utility knife, often found in a small channel carved out of a sword scabbard, or in a writing set

Kotone: baby bird

Kune mato: a merchant's safe, usually made of metal or thick wood and with several locks.

Magojifu: a small town in Bezenkai, between Ginzai and the Rumiri river.

Maikiro: a war vest of lacquered plates on a cotton backing, secured by cotton straps, worn by aiashe. Smaller plates hang from the front and sides to protect the groin and thighs.

Mamusha: a large, deadly snake, very aggressive

Matoyan: a small hunting village up in the mountains between Rimbaku and Yatamoro

Matekai: a wizard or wizards.

Megaita: a green tea made with roasted brown rice

Menatu: a warrior's face mask, made of metal and hooked onto or tied to a karute

Modato: a crest affixed to the top of a karute

Mosi: an inkstick, made of soot and animal glue, ground down and mixed with water to create ink

Mukanichi: An "untouched," someone who can't really absorb at all, the lowest of all people

Muraito: A larger town or small city not far above Ginzai, on the southern edge of a mid-sized lake

Nahiya: a townhouse, usually two or three stories tall, with separate apartments on each floor

Naritaba: a pole weapon, a wooden or metal shaft with a curved single-edge blade at the end. The blades were forged in the same way as nihono. Often used by mounted warriors, and by women warriors.

Nafti: a fruit, round and juicy, with mottled green and gold skin and crisp white flesh.

Nigasi: a dry, pressed sweet made of sugar and rice flour.

Nihono: a long sword with a curved, single-edged blade, carried by nobles and elite warriors in Rimbaku

Nizukai: a mythic water dragon, daughter of the sea god Satumasu, "king of all waters"

Nodaki: a "field sword," a longer, heavier nihono typically used against cavalry

Okube: a traditional sash-style belt worn around the waist, particularly with a kitoro

Onokura: a small village in Miniri, near the south end of the river that separates Nariyari and Bezenkai

Otainui: housekeeper or household manager

Otomi: a small fishing village on the shores of the Wagata

Pokanu: a type of bird, tall and ostentatious, with bright and luxurious tail feathers

Ponmei: loose cotton pants with a drawstring tie and tapered ankles.

Quisuin: a poisonous snake

Raeteru: the common tree frog

Rajo: purple yams

Rakawa: a small village in Bezenkai

Riantzu: a traditional portable storage chest, usually made with no nails, screws, or adhesive

Rimbaku: "land made barren from cursed magic," the land after the Schism

Ritakhou: "land rich with blessed magic," the land before the Schism

Rojiri: counselors to the emperor

Rumiri River: the wide river that runs north-south through Miniri, connecting the Tonawa to Rimbaku's southern coastline. It is the dividing line between Bezenkai and Nariyari.

Saisaihyu: a ten-day period of purification and contemplation. During this time, everyone is expected to not allow any outside influence—including the use of aishone.

Sashiko: a style of patching clothing, often in a pattern

Sehiro: a steaming basket, usually woven out of bamboo

Senkuniki: ancestral spirits—typically akatai are considered the darker, more malevolent ancestral spirits, while senkuniki are those more inclined toward benevolence

Senkousa: a Bone Reader. These women have strong aitachi and can actually "read" aishone, telling what memories and knowledge and skills each bones possesses.

Senoha-a: a plant, whose name means "Mother of Thousands." Often seen in gardens and homes but highly poisonous, particularly the flowers.

Shakomi: a town in Bezenkai, a little north of Ginzai

Shatage: a shirt, generally thicker than a hosode and dyed or lightly embroidered or both.

Shugiri daimyo: grand nobles, closest to the emperor in status and power

Shugodiri: lesser nobles

Sihu: week

Sokuichi: A "crude touch" or "rough touch," someone who doesn't absorb easily and needs a lot of material to absorb anything

Sorhu: a wide scarf or shawl, either silk (for milder weather) or wool (for cooler weather)

Subayaki: a species of flower, also called the common camellia, related to the tea plant and to the tsodami but less vibrant in color. Its seeds are pressed to produce Subayaki oil, which can be used for skin care and hair care.

Suneoto: armored shin guards

Suponichi: A "sponge," someone who absorbs quickly

Suzeri: an inkstone, used like a small mortar to grind mosi so that it could be mixed with water to create ink

Suzeri kabo: "inkstone box" or writing box, which held the implements and utensils needed for writing.

Taikamage: a vertical hair bun, clean and elegant, with the hair piled up on top of the head and secured by a front comb and, if necessary, several kanashi

Takaneburi: a long, narrow, flat-bottomed boat mostly used on rivers to ferry freight.

Takotsu Hakara: Home of Brotherhood, the mountain monastery of the Hakara Ikibanichi

Tanakia: a wild animal, essentially a racoon dog, rumored to be able to shape-change to human form

Tanu: a modular set of trunks and cabinets, usually arranged in a stepped pattern.

Tawasiri: the Tower of Ghosts, an ancient tower at the southeast tip of Rimbaku, long since abandoned and believed to be haunted. Originally the meeting place of the matekai of Ritakhou.

Tayomi: a traditional flooring made from compressed rice straws tightly bound together and covered with woven straw

Tehuya: the guard on a nihono, roughly disc-shaped

Tienbao: a rice paddy, typically one tien in size (approximately 3200 square feet)

Tokimichi: A "flutter touch," someone who can't hold the absorbed skills for long

Tonawa River: a major river that branches off from the Zinyang and runs south along the eastern edge of Saruto before turning southeast and then east and separating Hochiro above from Bezenkai and Nariyari below.

Torito: rough hemp work trousers with a drawstring tie and tapered ankles, often paired with a hantien

Tsao: a boat hook

Tsekuri: rice wine

Tsodami: the red camellia, the royal flower

Tsukifuko: the Moon of Lawlessness, a month during which no rules or laws apply

Tsurogo: a double-edged nihono

Tukaiono: pickled vegetables and tubers, such as radish

Ujiro: A favorite dessert in Awaihinshi, a steamed cake made from rice, water, and sugar, done in a variety of flavors.

Umi: a long bow, made of laminated wood, bamboo, and leather and typically taller than a grown man, with the upper half twice as long as the lower.

Uridon: a thick rice noodle, often used in soup

Urigani: the art of folding paper into shapes, particularly animals

Utume: the art of packaging, particularly by wrapping an object in carefully chosen layers of paper

Uzumoya: A covered pavilion.

Wagata River: a tributary of the Tonawa that splits off to the west as the Tonawa continues north past Awaihinshi. The Wagata forms the southern border of Saruto.

Wara: a sturdy straw bag traditionally used to hold rice. A full wara provides enough rice to feed two people for one year.

Watamato: a small town in northern Bezenkai, not far below the Wagata River.

Yanoi: straight-bladed spear.

Yanokai: Rimbakan cypress, very durable and water-resistant

Yatamoro: the kingdom neighboring Rimbaku to the east, across the mountains. Symbol: a winged serpent reared back, ready to strike. Ruled by a High Council.

Yori-toki: a dagger with a thick blade made for armor-piercing. Often worn in conjunction with a nihono.

Yoto: the small river that runs through Ginzai

Yudishu: a small town in Nariyari, headquarters of the Kindichi

Yue Judei: "Good Times," a zaihaya in Bejinuri, in Awaihinshi

Zaihaya: a tavern or pub, a casual place where people can go to drink together

Zinyang River: the "Central River," the large river that runs east-west across Rimbaku right through the center of Chibiri, separating Hochiro and Saruto to the south from Obanari and Yunigiri to the north.

Rimbaku is divided into four regions: Kitini (north), (Chibiri) central, Miniri (south), and (Shitimi) island

Within each region are two or more provinces. They are:

Kitini:

- Tabichi (northwest region, bordering Fyushu above and the ocean to the west)
- Korito (northeast region, bordering Fyushu above and Yatamaro to the east)

Chibiri:

- Yunigiri (northwest, bordering the ocean)
- Obanari (northeast, bordering Yatamaro to the east)
- Hochiro (southern band, bordering Yatamaro to the east)
- Saruto (the capital region, with the ocean on one side and the southern band on the other)

Miniri:

- Bezenkai (southwest, bordering the ocean)
- Nariyari (southeast, bordering Higinasi to the west)

Shitimi:

- Iwikaru (the northern island)
- Tatsuma (the southern island)

Rimbaku is roughly 1200 miles wide by 2000 miles long, or 2,400,000 square miles (somewhere between China and India in size).

Military groupings, smallest to largest:

Bantao -> Squad (4-10)

Shotao -> Platoon or troop (2-4 squads, 16-40)

Chotao -> Company (2-4 platoons, 60-160)

Dantao -> Battalion (4-6 companies, 300-900)

Reitao -> Regiment (2-4 battalions, 600-2000)

Tyodao -> Brigade (3-6 battalions, 1000-3000)

Sudao -> Division (3 or more brigades or regiments, 3k-6k)

Gaodao -> Corps (2 or more divisions, 25-50k)

Gyunao -> Army (2 or more corps, 100k-150k)

Gyunshadao -> Army Group (2 or more armies)

Chukogao -> Regional Theater (the entire military force in a region)

Sanseidao -> Front (the entire military force in a war)

Military ranks:

Sotaisho: commander-in-chief, usually the Emperor himself

[Karo: military governor]

Dogenriku: Lord General, the field marshal (in charge of tactics, fills in for the Emperor on the battlefield if he is not present)

Taisho: general

Issa: colonel

Chusa: lieutenant colonel

Shosa: major

Taisu: captain

Chuisu: lieutenant

Shosu: junior lieutenant

Gunso: Sergeant

Gocho: Corporal

Naval ranks:
    Dogenkaishu: Lord Admiral
    Kagono: admiral
    Kagusho: vice-admiral
    Daiso: captain
    Kumigashi: commander
    Kogashiri: lieutenant commander
    Chudai: lieutenant

Special units:
    Taikoro: Lord Commander, in charge of an entire elite
        force (like the Honjofu or the Honteno)
    Chuisu: lieutenant, can command a chotao
    Gunso: sergeant, can command a shotao
    Gocho: corporal, can command a bantao

ABOUT THE AUTHOR

AARON ROSENBERG is the best-selling, award-winning author of over 50 novels, including the Twin Cities Cryptids urban fantasy/cozy series, the DuckBob SF comedy series, the Relicant Chronicles epic fantasy series, the Areyat Islands fantasy pirate mystery series, the upcoming BEO Reports urban fantasy series, and, with David Niall Wilson, the O.C.L.T. occult thriller series. His tie-in work contains novels for *Star Trek*, *Warhammer*, *World of WarCraft*, *Stargate: Atlantis*, *Shadowrun*, *Mutants & Masterminds*, and *Eureka* and short stories for *The X-Files*, World of Darkness, *Crusader Kings II*, *Deadlands*, *Master of Orion*, and *Europa Universalis IV*. He has written children's books (including the original series STEM Squad and Pete and Penny's Pizza Puzzles, the award-winning *Bandslam: The Junior Novel* and the #1 best-selling *42: The Jackie Robinson Story*), educational books, and roleplaying games (including the original games *Asylum*, *Spookshow*, and *Chosen*; work for White Wolf, Wizards of the Coast, Fantasy Flight, Pinnacle, and many others; the Origins Award-winning *Gamemastering Secrets*; and the Gold ENnie-winning *Lure of the Lich Lord*). He is a founding member of Crazy 8 Press. Aaron lives in New York with his family. You can follow him online at gryphonrose.com, on Facebook at facebook.com/gryphonrose, on BSky at @gryphonrose.bsky.social, on Instagram at the_gryphonrose, and on X (formerly known as Twitter) @gryphonrose.

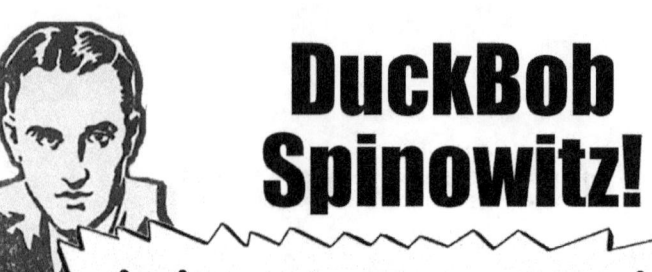

If Jane Austen wrote about pirates, this would be that book!

Isabella Parsons is the well-mannered daughter of a baron in Regency England.

Cannon Belle Pearcy is a feared pirate captain raiding the German Sea.

They are one and the same.

But when a handsome Navy commander arrives on the scene, intent upon quelling the recent pirate threat—and wooing the loveliest lady in the region—Bella's two worlds start to collide!

Other problems quickly ensue, including a second Navy ship, an intriguing other suitor, and a deadly threat from her combined past.

Now Bella faces dangers both on land and at sea, in each of her identities. She finds herself battling to keep either from destroying the other, or the people she holds dear. All while struggling with a threat she never expected: true love.

The Adventures of

CANNON BELLE

Aaron Rosenberg

A thrilling new historic romance, full of adventure and intrigue, from the author of the Areyat Isles pirate-fantasy-mystery series and the Twin Cities Cryptids urban fantasy series!

PIRACY, MYSTERY, & ADVENTURE

awaits a pair of...brothers?

Sundra is a prince running for his life.
Ruhi is a young woman disguised
in order to seek her freedom.
When they are captured by pirates,
they claim to be brothers.
Now the pair has to navigate cruel masters,
mysterious murders, missing mages,
vicious feuds, and violent storms.
But at least they have each other.